C000064646

Pretty Thin

By

Stephen Burrows

'Made In Birmingham' Book II

First Published 2019

By

Bostin Books

This edition 2020

This is a work of historical fiction. Story names, characters, businesses, places, events and incidents are either the product of the author's imagination or used in a fictitious manner. Any resemblance to actual persons, living or dead, or actual events is purely coincidental. I have endeavoured to research and verify all facts relating to David Bowie, 'The Spiders From Mars' and other real persons associated with him. If I have made any mistakes I will gladly rectify upon notification.
In particular, 'Rick' is entirely fictional.

To David Jones.
Thank you, here's hoping that wherever you are isn't boring.

Cover painting: 'Worshipping 'Ziggy Stardust' by kind permission of John Kapalin. **www.deviantart.com/gagambo**

Books by Stephen Burrows.

(With Michael Layton)

Fiction:
'Black Over Bill's Mother's' 'Made In Birmingham' I
'Keep Right On' 'Made In Birmingham' III
'The Touch Of Innocence' 'Made In Birmingham' IV

Non-fiction:
'Top Secret Worcestershire'. (Published by Brewin Books)
'The Noble Cause'
'Tara-A-Bit, Our Kid', a little book of slang used in Birmingham.
'One In For D&D', a little book of Police slang.
'It's a Blag'. Police tricks and funny stories
'Walsall's Front Line Volume One'
'Walsall's Front Line Volume Two'
'Reporting For Duty'. West Midlands Police 1974 – 1999.

Table of Contents

Part One: The Rise

Part Two: The Fall

Part One

The Rise

Chapter One

'Where Are We Now?'
November - December 2015

Alice:
Music is a time capsule. A record, a whole album, even a snatch of melody, intrudes without warning. The brain, the senses, react, Pavlovian, uncontrollable. Memories, smells, even the tastes of the past manifest, overwhelming, provoking reverie.

The music has been in my mind constantly recently, coming unbidden, summoning the ghosts of my youth, the heady days of the early Seventies – and my first, best, and only, true love.

***

I am walking Genie in a London park. I suspect that I have moved here, to this alien city, because of him, my lost love. To be near him once again, after all this time, but the revelation only comes to me now - maybe that is the reason for the music in my head.

Perhaps this is the first time since those long ago days that I have been strong enough to really think about him, consider what happened, and my part in it, my guilt. Or is it the first time that my life has been empty enough for him to pour back into the vacuum? It seems to me now that I have tried to fill the void he left with whatever came along, including a husband.

Genie is a Staffie, always smiling, as they do, and despite being the true and only love of my life now, is not the reason for me being here. Everyone asks why I gave him a girl's name, until I explain the spelling; but I don't tell why I chose it. He got a new name when I re-homed him, and he seems to like it, so that's that.

At the start, I didn't really like the strange man who became a superstar, but he became entwined in my life during those mad eighteen months, and despite everything, his music and his story are the only links to Danny that I have left. And Danny loved him.

—

A lifetime has nearly run its course, and there have been other loves, lusts, infatuations. One I married, then divorced, a tale of disappointment. I was searching for that peak again, that purity I found in the beginning, with Danny, and failed, as always. There are no children, probably a good thing, but now I sense old age lurking, just out of view, its hand reaching out to touch me. I have started to fear loneliness, and a child might have saved me from that at least. But that is a selfish thought, and my selfishness and guilt have stalked me for all of my adult life.

It has been empty, my life, without meaning, and I still don't know whether my 'one true love' was the 'real thing', or in my head. What is 'love' anyway? And we were so young.

The air is cold, and a sudden gust of chill wind breaks into my thoughts as I walk. I can see my breath, billowing out like a smoker's exhalation. Christmas is a few weeks away and the shops have been crammed with the usual festive rubbish for what seems like weeks already. I hate it. The false jollity, the pressure to be happy, to be with a family. No wonder that so many people give up at Christmas, there's no escape, only the ultimate opt-out, but I'll never do that.

Genie isn't bothered by the cold, and as we reach the park I let him off the lead and he puts his nose to the ground, looking for places that need marking with his scent. I am gazing into the distance, without actually seeing anything, lost in another thought. He barks, shaking me from my reverie, and he's off, having spotted a Labrador playing with a ball.

An old man is throwing the ball, using one of those cups on a stick to launch it miles. I hurry across the grass after Genie as he bounds away, his tail straight out and wagging wildly. Some people are frightened of Staffies, some dogs take an instant dislike to them, so I like to be close at hand whenever there is an encounter.

***

The dogs dash around madly. The other dog is friendly and wants to play. I arrive huffing and puffing a little after the uphill climb, revealing my age and the lack of interest I've had in taking care of myself in recent years. Mental note: New Year Resolution. Less baking, comfort eating, and drinking, and more dog walking.

The man is watching them play. He is very still and says nothing, so I think he's annoyed about Genie.

"I'm so sorry, he'll be after the ball."

He turns towards me. I'm not sure he's quite as old as I thought, maybe late sixties. Not easy to judge. A wooly hat crowns a mass of long grey hair, and it's difficult to see his face through a substantial white beard

I immediately think that he could do a stint as Santa in the local shopping centre if he wanted some cash The abundance of hair echoes the face that peers from every shop window at this time of year, even down to the rosy –hued cheeks, which I put down to the brisk Northerly wind.

I take in the rest of him, and change my mind. He is tall, but my impression is of thinness, gauntness even, not Santa - like after all. The true shape of his body is obscured by an expensive-looking three-quarter length waxed coat with the suspicion of several layers beneath. I wonder what he would look like clean-shaven and without the cloaking clothing, then admonish myself – 'Alice, haven't you had enough of men to last a lifetime'. I suppress the thought and reconsider him.

Overall, he has the air of a distinguished older man, despite the uncared for appearance. Some men are lucky that way, and their deterioration is offset by a nobleness of bearing and appearance. Through the hair I glimpse good bone structure, and his eyes are nice, with plenty of laugh lines. The fact that he has a dog is reassuring of course, as it appears to be well treated and behaved.

"That's OK", he says, "It's good for them to have a run around and play."

He's a Londoner from the accent, perhaps that rare beast, a genuine Cockney. Polite dog-walker type conversation ensues, the weather, dog antics and similar fluff. Then, at the moment when the conversation falters and we are poised to go our separate ways, just

—

passers-by after all, he gives it a fresh spin. A moment of fate that passes me by, as they all have.

"Are you local, or new in the big city?" He asks, "I haven't seen you before and I'm here nearly every morning, health permitting."

" Sort of. I live in London, but a few miles away, so probably not local in London terms," I reply, conscious of the Birmingham accent that has never taken its leave "I fancied a long walk today, saw the park and thought he could have a run off the lead".

Is he trying to chat me up? I smile inside. At our ages, it all seems a little futile, although I admire the unquenchable human spirit it represents, if it is the case. When I was young I could never conceive of old people loving, but now I'm one of them I know the allure never fades. Until death we do part.

"That's a shame, they seem to be getting on rather well, it's always better for him to exercise with other dogs, I can't keep up these days." He indicates the pair, now engaged in a marathon sniffing session. He has a nice smile, I decide. Then I scold myself, I'm imagining any attraction, deluding myself. What could he see in a slightly overweight, middle - aged refugee, bearing the scars of a bad marriage and worse love life? But he continues chatting. He is good at it, and easy to speak to.

Is there an interest there, from me? I mentally kick myself for falling into the old routine. Stupid. Stupid. Haven't you had enough of love or sex or lust, or whatever it is, yet? My eyes dart from head to toe and back, making another appraisal. I confirm that he is tall, a couple of inches over six-foot I guess, late sixties, early seventies perhaps. Not really too old for me. Age gaps matter less and less as we near the end, but at sixteen, two years is an abyss.

I wonder what he sees, thinks? I know I was beautiful once, but would probably be described as 'overblown' now. I'm carrying a few too many pounds but to a man of his age, I am probably a prospect. How arrogant am I? How sure of my looks, which are fading? And what good have those looks ever done me?

But I can't stop the persistent little voice inside asking whether I would be interested, so soon after the disaster of Alan? I reproach myself. I had firmly resolved to give up on men, on sex, and yet here I am, like a young girl again, flattering myself about a man's interest – an interest I'm no doubt imagining. He's probably married anyway, and I've already played the mistress part, and second fiddle to a rock star. I'm not doing it again.

I've completed my assessment now, a lone woman in a park meeting a stranger. He seems pleasant enough, and I sense some buried frailty. He's older, definitely seventies. He doesn't offer a threat, probably just lonely. I reproach myself, he is no doubt just being polite, and here I am as usual, looking for hidden agendas.

I feel the need to offer him something for his efforts. "Perhaps I'll come by again, when the mood takes me, sometimes I need to think, and a long walk helps."

"Yes indeed, concentrates the mind, purges it of the complexities of modern life, although everyone seems to have their head stuck in a screen these days and they miss the obvious." He indicates the park with its trees and paths.

I laugh. " I stopped doing social media after my divorce, got fed up with both the pity and the nastiness online." 'Why have I just told him that?'.

He reaches into his pocket and produces an iPhone – it looks like one of the latest models, a surprise, given his comment. He picks up on my look. "It stays in my pocket when I'm out, unless it rings, especially when in interesting company," (he is flirting I think), "but I have to confess to being a silver surfer. I love the internet, so much knowledge and fun right there, at your fingertips, so much opportunity to learn and enjoy, don't you think?"

"I guess so". I hesitate, I can sense that something more is coming. Do I want this?

He proffers a hand, "The name's Robert, I don't like being called Bob by the way." He waits expectantly.

I take the hand and we shake. His grip is stronger than I expected, perhaps not quite so frail, then. I don't know why I do it, but the next thing I say is a lie. "Mine's Tina."

* * *

Brownian Motion. I remember that from school, a survivor from a distant physics lesson embedded forever in a nook of my brain. The random collision of particles.

We travel through life, bouncing against each other as we go. Some collisions are slight, having little effect, others, even minor ones, change our direction, our lives, forever.

That day in the park, a chance meeting, my untruth, all trivial and meaningless, and yet it preys on my mind for some reason. I feel guilty, lying to a harmless and friendly old man. And if he was being more than friendly, so what? I am hardly in a position to pick and choose. And, I tell myself, be honest, you've always liked the company of men, so why pretend otherwise? Started young after all, trying to build the perfect love, and how did that work out?

Why is it nagging away at me like this unless there is a flickering of interest on my part? Life is pretty boring, a slow and lonely slide into old age and memories, so why not make an opportunity? What's to lose?

Several days pass whilst mundanity crowds my time. My new life takes shape. I bury myself in arranging the new flat. It is small, and in a less than fashionable part of the capital, all that my share of the broken marriage can afford, even though Alan built a successful business. London prices are in another world. I don't even really know why I'm here. It's going to be a mistake. What do I expect to find, to feel? It was all so long ago, and another me.

I remember 'doing' the sights with Danny, how thrilled I was by the history, the glamour of the capital city. He was bored stiff, but he put up with it because he loved me. Am I trying to capture his essence preserved amongst these immutable buildings?

I start a new job. At least I've got a skill that still counts in the modern world. I was always 'arty' as my mom used to say. Drawing and painting as a teenager became graphic design in the

---

11

digital age and now I prostitute my talents, such as they are, to advertising on the internet. It seems that the whole world buys and sells on the net now, so I'll always have employment of sorts. I have enough work to get by, from a number of agencies who sub-contract to me, and I can do it all from wherever I call home, so long as I have a fast connection. Is Broadband the only reason I have not retreated from the cities into a hermit existence in some rural backwater?

Looking back, I can clearly trace my long descent into this solitary existence. And now, although I'm in a teeming metropolis, I still live in a bubble, just Genie and I.

I resolve to walk him more, the temptation to remain in seclusion is great, but both of us could do with the exercise, maybe to the park. Lying to the old man about my name is disturbing and probably a touch paranoid. I could put that right.

One morning, I wake filled with determination to change my life. I sort out the step-counting app on my phone and set myself a target of ten thousand a day. I doubt I will do this, but it presents a challenge that I need, otherwise I'll just drift. The younger Alice, the one full of hope and ambition, drives me. That Alice must not end up alone in front of the TV. I mustn't let her down.

Perhaps I will go to that park. I'll probably never see him again, but this time I'll try and be normal with any other human beings that I come across. I lay in bed, wondering whether the whole step target thing is about seeing the man again, fitness, or a flight from isolation? I decide that it doesn't matter either way, and sleep finally arrives.

***

It is December 15th when he asks me to go for a coffee with him. I say, 'maybe'. I'm sixteen again, agonising about a relationship. Do I want this or not?

I write it in my diary with an exclamation mark. A landmark event, another person – male even, actually wants to spend time with me, voluntarily. I had thought those days were past.

I have kept a diary for most of my life. I have a drawer full of them, although my thoughts have been recorded on a laptop for years now. I began long ago, after my first genuine attempt with the pills. The doctors saw the scars of self-harm on my arms and referred me for counselling. Thank God for the National Health!

Molly, the psychiatrist, started me on writing things down, and it helped, so I continued after she declared me much improved. In rehab from suicide - as I like to think of it. Writing the thoughts down somehow captures and orders them, stops them spinning around in my head, creating turmoil and sleepless nights.

I have been expecting Robert to ask me. Somewhere deep in my brain is a part that wanted it to happen, not the rational part, the bit linked to my battered heart. I must be a secret optimist, secret even from myself., I have been to the park every day since my resolution, despite the fact that the New Year hasn't yet arrived. And of course, we meet there. I like to think that he goes at the same time for a similar reason, an unspoken appointment in an unmentioned relationship. How bizarre at our ages!

As the days pass, we have built upon that initial chat, layer upon layer, as we share moments, and the words begin to hesitantly dive beneath surface pleasantries and the weather.

I suspect that Robert is also holding secrets, a whole lifetime that is hidden from me – and that he is as yet unsure and untrusting of me. Are we both damaged beyond repair? This attracts me, although I'm not at all sure it is a sexual attraction. I am uncertain whether he sees me that way. The little signs are missing, the signs that women spot.

There has been no physical contact, but there are hints of mutual experiences - rejection and loneliness amongst them. It is a shaky platform to build upon, but a start of sorts nevertheless.

I'm going to meet him and see what happens. After all, given my track record, what could possibly be worse than the bookends of my love life; the teenage heartbreak and the failed marriage with its recriminations and bile? And I like a mystery.

***

David:

In mid–December 2015, publicity for a new album, his 25th, begins to appear. Producer Tony Visconti heralds it as something new, a contrast to 'The Next Day', which deliberately referenced the singer's past. There is speculation as to the meaning behind the title and it is noted that it is the first studio album not to feature its creator's image. One theory is that 'Blackstar' relates to the rise of Isis, but this is quickly dismissed by a spokesperson. No explanation is offered and Bowie seems to be keeping himself away from the publicity.

***

I sit with the ever-faithful Genie, waiting for Robert at a roadside table, sheltered by screens and awnings and warmed by patio heaters. It occurs to me that this is probably my last 'first date', and the smell of coffee reminds me of the place I had my actual, 'first date'. My mind wanders back, passing across the years to a night that since the therapy, I've put in a little mental compartment with a securely padlocked door.

I was fifteen, and my spending money came from a Saturday job at Chelsea Girl in Birmingham City Centre. My girlfriends and I regularly graced the coffee bar at the Fox Hollies Youth Club with our presence. It was better than hanging around outside the outdoor asking adults to buy us cider, or shivering in a bus shelter.

The Youth Club took place in a church hall, an ideal location for teenage debauchery. There was a coffee bar, no skinny lattes in those days, just a spoonful of instant, but with proper cups and saucers from the church hall stock. There was a pool table and table tennis, and the latest music boomed out non-stop – the main attraction. The big room doubled up as a regular disco, a place for first fumblings in the dark, rendered into stop–go motion by the flashing lights.

I met him there, at the Christmas disco. Nobody danced to the Christmas Number One that year, 'Ernie' by Benny Hill, but music was awakening from its post-Beatles and Sixties doldrums, the

*flag of 'Glam-Rock' borne by a glitter-dappled Marc Bolan. There
was Rod with 'Maggie May', and local boys Slade, skinheads from
Wolverhampton, who always looked slightly uncomfortable in their
make-up, but had recently been at Number One for weeks with their
first hit single, 'Coz I Luv You'.*

*He wasn't a dancer. He was one of the boys who stood
around the edge. You could sense their desire, but stronger was the
fear - of being made to look foolish if rejected. The walk across to a
group of girls with the chance of a very public, usually brutal, and
humiliating rejection, must have been daunting unless drunk or
drugged, and too much of an ordeal for many. Which was a pity, as
the nicest boys were often those without the bravado, but the rules
were the rules, and boys asked first back then.*

*I had seen him at the youth club a number of times before,
and once from the top deck of the bus, wearing his black blazer with
the red badge, so I knew he was still at school. The interesting thing
about him was that although his appearance was striking, he acted
as if he did not know, or truly believe it. He would hang around
tentatively in the shadows, no awareness of his impact on the few
others who took the time to look closely. I looked closely.*

*When I say striking, he was beautiful, not handsome. I
remember thinking that before I knew him, and that he surely must
have known, and hated it, played it down, obscured and diverted
attention from it. Because embracing his beauty would have been
suicidal in those days, a fifteen-year old boy at an all-boys school.*

*He seemed to go out of his way to hide his looks, sporting
nondescript and frankly unfashionable clothes, adopting a
downward turned head, partly obscured by medium length, straight,
lank, mouse-coloured hair that had never seen a style. But when
those curtains of hair parted, people looked twice. He had the face of
a Pre-Raphaelite siren, sculpted in long, flat panes, a full mouth and
sharp nose, surmounted by deep-set eyes that flashed blue.*

*These days he would have been gracing an advert for men's
after shave, or appearing in a Sunday supplement photograph lying,
tanned, by a blue sea. But such opportunities for beautiful boys did*

not exist in the grey world of 1970's England, let alone in Birmingham. It was a time of strikes and naked prejudice, laced with nostalgic longing for the brightness of the Sixties, but soured with cynicism by Vietnam and the loss of hippy innocence. It was a hard time, for old and young alike. It was the music that brought the sunlight in for us kids. That is how I remember it, anyway.

A car horn blares, jolting me from my reverie. As usual I have retreated into the past, and Danny.

My attention returns to the present, and a coffee bar in a London square. The day is dry, but with the promise of sleet or snow in a flat steel sky. The bare branches of the Plane trees wave and rustle in the breeze. The outside tables look out onto the park and are dog-friendly, and suddenly here is Robert, in his long coat, full of apologies for being late, his Labrador, Charlie, straining on the lead, searching for food beneath the tables.

He buys while I hold the dogs, and we sit and make small talk. Then a meaningful silence falls. It is time to crack the ice on the surface that we have been skating around upon and sample the deeper waters below. I let him start because he asked me to come. I find that silence is usually filled, and I have become quite skilled in creating it at the right moment.

"Tina, I asked you here because I like you, I like talking to you, in fact you are pretty much the only person that I really talk to in London. I'm trying not to sound pathetic, just being honest. I'm old and worn and at the wrong end of life and I haven't got time to dance around. I suppose I have a good life - better than most, but it's empty of other people. And I've found that I look forward to my walk in the park, to our chats. I don't really know you, and you certainly don't know me, and we may not like what we find, but I'd like to try and be proper friends, no agendas, no strings attached, no expectations."

He falls silent and waits. I realise that this is a man who also knows the power of silence.

It is such an adult, matter-of-fact proposition. Why have I agreed to come here if not to take things further? But now that

16

moment has arrived I'm unsure, and a frisson of panic, a desire to flee, sweeps through me. I fight it down, That is the Alice of the past, and here is the chance of a fresh start. But I am no ingénue either, and will not be rushed. Without answering I open my bag and proffer a ten pound note,

"Go and get two more coffees and I'll think about it."

He looks me in the eye, sees something there, and without protesting about who is paying, takes the money and disappears into the café.

Why does this innocuous proposition seem significant, such that I need to buy time? In reality nothing much hinges upon my decision. But I know how small moments change lives.

I weigh the pros and cons, the main one being that I'm not sure that I want to be in any sort of relationship with a man again; they have only ever bought me heartache. And yet, and yet, perhaps this is a last chance, the last bus headed into a sunset of companionship rather than solitude. And I do find him attractive, or to be more precise, I find his mind and manner attractive. And he's not bad looking, now the facial hair has gone, the long hair styled, revealing a strong-boned face, clean of the mottling of age bar a few wrinkles. I enjoy talking to him, and I enjoy the feeling that I am not irrelevant, that another human being has some sort of interest in me. Even if it's just friendship he's after, who knows what that might become, and I can dictate the pace, or run away.

He returns, sits, and waits in silence, fussing the dogs.

"The answer is yes but with some conditions."

He smiles. "Conditions? I'm intrigued."

"Nothing too difficult, it's just that I'm still pretty bruised by life, men and my ex-husband in particular." I see Robert's expression change.

"No, nothing like that, he never touched me, in fact he pretty much ignored me. I'm just wearied by it all, my expectations are pretty low, and I thought I'd permanently retired from the relationship game. You might be the last hope – or the final disappointment."

He smiles. It's a nice smile, reaching his eyes. "No pressure then."

"I just want to take things slowly, step by step, and be able to call a halt if I don't feel comfortable."

He sits back, then laughs. "Well that suits me just fine. I'm just asking for some company, and it sounds as if that might suit you too." He leans forward and suddenly he has taken my hand in his. I am surprised but do not pull back. He is earnest now, confiding.

"Tina, I'm a very lonely man, the tide of my life has almost gone by and I feel just about washed up at its far shore, and so alone. Our meetings in the park, sad though it sounds now I say it out loud, have become an oasis in my day to which I look forward. It has surprised me, if I can be honest. If we can extend them, on any basis, that will make a huge difference to me."

I am not sure how I feel. Am I disappointed? Perhaps a little – doesn't he like me in THAT way? But why should he? Haven't I got an over-inflated view of my own attractiveness based on a past that is now long gone, faded like a summer bloom scorched by the frost.

Am I relieved that there is no pressure, no rush? – Yes.

"Then we have a deal, no strings, no expectations, just see how it goes." I say. The feeling of guilt returns, invoked by his simple friendship.

"And if we are being honest and open, I have a confession to make. I told you a lie, because I wasn't sure of you, in the park, that first day. My name's not Tina, it's Alice."

***

It begins well and gets better. There is no pressure. He is a very private man and there are whole sections of his life that are closed to me, but that is fine. We are not lovers, although an easy familiarity has emerged. I wonder whether doors will unlock for both of us as trust builds. I am so wary of that word, so fragile, so scarred. This is truly a last chance, probably for both of us. Two lonely planets in the vastness of existence, our orbits meeting once in a lifetime.

He is clearly well off. He eventually, almost shyly, reveals that he has another house, his 'main' house, in Dorset, somewhere around Lyme Regis, a place where I used to go on holiday with my parents as a child. I tell him that I haven't been since then.

"Then you must come and rediscover your childhood haunts and stay," he says when I tell him. "But not yet, after Christmas. I usually go there in the New Year to refresh myself after London."

He dismissively refers to the London house as just a base for business. I don't ask why he needs to be here, what he does, and he doesn't volunteer any information. This is how we are together, both holding secrets, and revealing things a snippet at a time, These are the unwritten rules.

We walk the dogs, meet at cafes. He recommends a trusted dog-sitter and walker, (a London essential apparently), and pays for her to look after them whilst we go for a meal, and to the theatre. I find to my surprise that I am having fun for the first time in ages.

Christmas comes and goes. I don't see him, as he has 'commitments', which I suspect are family duties of some kind. I tell him that I have some personal things to deal with, which is another lie, and I spend the holiday season with Genie, walking and watching television. We agree not to do presents and cards.

I wonder what Robert is doing, then tell myself that he has no obligation to me, and that is the way I wanted it. Companionship is enough for now, and Robert has shown no sign of wishing to change that.

On Boxing Day, he calls me, wishes me Happy Christmas and asks if I am doing anything on New Year's Eve, which is a laugh. "Going to bed at ten as usual."

"Not this year. We're are going to go out and party like it's the end of the world." He laughs. "Actually, I've arranged a dog-sitter for both of the hounds at my place, I've booked a table at a nice Italian, and I'd like you to share the New Year with me, a little thanks for your company. Afterwards I'll pay for a taxi, or you can stay, no funny business, scout's honour. I've got a very nice guest room. Forgive my presumption in booking it all, and say yes."

I say yes. I can't help but feel pleased – and intrigued. This is the first time he has invited me to his flat, which I see as a major step forward and perhaps the harbinger of a closer relationship. I've already decided that I will stay. Something might happen, but I will also get a chance to sneak a look into his world. I'm hoping I'll find out more about the real Robert, and what better way than seeing where and how he lives.

Perhaps we'll share all our secrets then.

Chapter Two

'The Wild Eyed Boy From Freecloud'
Early 1972

Danny:

A birthday on New Year's Day is the absolute pits. The big highs of Christmas are already stale memories. Everyone is exhausted, fed up with present buying and the 'Christmas Spirit'. Another celebration for a mere birthday is a downright inconvenience.

My best tactic seems to be to ignore the lack of promise and hope that lies ahead in the stark light of a new year, with winter months still to come, and stay in the sack.

As seems usual for my 'special' day, 1972 dawns grey, cold and uncompromising. A total downer. The weather matches my mood. Surely fifteen should feel better than this?

I am still in bed and it's Ten O Clock. Not much point in getting up yet. It's fucking freezing. The tip of my nose stings with the cold and I can see 'Jack Frost' on the inside of the windows, no thaw as yet to wet the curling drip strips on the window ledge. No sounds from elsewhere in the house, both still asleep no doubt, after a late night and an excuse to get pissed that they grasped with enthusiasm. That means no electric fires switched on yet.

I pull the sheets up over my head and my exhalations at least warm my face. I stare into the white nothingness of the sheet and my mind wanders.

I should have been happy today. Instead I'm ashamed of myself. A gutless fucking wimp!

My life is a bucket of dung stirred with a stick of cowardice. I allow myself be bullied and coerced, made to conform, when all I feel is rebellion, to shake things up and escape this mind-numbing boredom.

Bullied by my father, who hates me for not being the rough, tough, man-to-be that he expected. My mother complicit in the bullying by doing nothing. Using me to hide behind.

Bullied at school by fat Phil Lowe and his mates.

Bullied by life. What happened to the freedom, hope and revolution of the Sixties? Those days have already faded away into a misty, golden-hued past, filled with Hippies and Beatles, ''Free Love and dope.

My world feels hard and unyielding, sprung back into its old rigidity. There is a re-assertion of older people's authority, the establishment is in charge and doing things 'the old way'. The country is divided, by prejudice and violence, and filled with conflict. The Unions are against the Government, Skinheads are attacking immigrants; there is injustice and intolerance everywhere.

Boring, boring, and scary. Birmingham is grey and lifeless, and the only things the adults are interested in are strikes, trade unions and their battles with Ted Heath. Big trouble with the miners is brewing - and that will spell more misery for everyone.

Here I am - wanting to be different, but not knowing what that really means, and not brave enough to face the consequences.

Relegated to the margins at school, along with the other faceless mediocre. Average academically, useless at sport, no good at making things with my hands; unremarkable. What is my purpose? I have no fucking idea.

But none of this is the reason for my especial unhappiness on this, my landmark day.

Not school, or home, or the grey world of Birmingham. No. It is sex, the female sex specifically, and the lack of it, that occupies my mind. Shagging is the top subject at school, the focus of all minds. The merits of various girls, pickup techniques and venues are endlessly dissected. There is plenty of boasting and bullshitting from which I try to filter the truth.

My conclusion is that, out of ninety boys in my year, at most half a dozen have gone all the way, followed by about half who have actually had some sort of physical contact with a girl. The remainder are a mixture of the shy, ugly, lying and inept - and I suppose the queers who keep quiet for fear of a good kicking and a life of ridicule.

I am numbered amongst the sad half of this little world, and I'm kicking myself because blew the chance to join the winners. Which is why I am now lying in bed on my birthday, depressed, when I should be ecstatic.

The long-awaited chance came. It was on a plate. I, (sort of), grasped it, then I let the moment pass. I let her walk away without asking to see her again.

Which just about sums up my first fifteen years. What's worse is that older people keep telling me that I'm having the best days of my life right now. If that's true, I want a reset and another go at it.

No, that's crap, blaming everyone but myself. If I found an ounce of courage and determination with girls I could change this.

Be optimistic. I've seen her at the Forum before. She must be local. She'll be there again, hopefully this weekend. There may still be a chance, unless she thinks I'm either a wanker, which let's face it, is likely, or that I don't fancy her, which would be a tragedy, because I do.

Today starts a new year. Fifteen. An important age – nearly grown up. I vow to find her again, and, if I'm granted a second chance, this time I'll grow a pair.

***

David:

On the 17th of December 1971, David Bowie releases his new album, 'Hunky Dory', to minimal acclaim and almost total disinterest. He is unknown to all but a minority of enthusiasts, most of whom are invisible to British society, and if glimpsed, are dismissed as hippies, queers and 'weirdos'.

A band is in place, with Mick Ronson on guitar, Trevor Bolder on bass and 'Woody' Woodmansey on drums. As yet they have no name. Rick Wakeman is drafted in to play keyboards.

Hunky Dory is a brilliant album, but the quality of the songs makes no impact on the record buying public, or the charts, even though 'Changes' is chosen as DJ Tony Blackburn's 'Record of The Week'.

The album cover hints at what is to come. Bowie takes a set of Marlene Dietrich portraits to the cover shoot and dictates the image he wants –an 'old school' Hollywood star - a female one.

The resultant cover photo depicts an androgynous Bowie, striking a pose and sporting long, blonde, 'film star' hair, sexually ambiguous. It is rumoured that the record company has to be persuaded to use it for fear that shops such as W.H.Smith will not display it.

'Hunky Dory' and 'Changes' both fail to chart. Bowie has only had one big hit, 'Space Oddity'. Since then he has remained on the margins, failing to capitalise on his initial breakthrough. He hasn't performed live for many months and seems to be caught in limbo between his many interests; performance, art, theatre, music, mime, books.

'Hunky Dory' seems to be a backward step after the heavier experimentation of 'The Man Who Sold The World'. The songs are more conventionally structured for mass appeal. Bowie is out of contract when he starts recording the album, and has a new manager, Tony Defries, but is quickly signed up by RCA when they hear the tapes.

Bowie has a new plan. He has another album in waiting, and this one is the 'real' Bowie expressing himself. He has observed the 'rock business', the hype that breeds success, and has invented a rock star, a persona he can inhabit, hide within, whilst embarking on the ride to the top.

He can flout convention, safe within his new shell. He will show Bolan what 'glam' really means, but as a vehicle for art instead of artifice. He senses that he has the key to success within his grasp, but as he works on his own 'Frankenstein monster', he has no conception of the personal price that will be exacted by his creation.

***

Alice:

I see Danny again from a distance. I am on the number 50 bus, coming home from town on a bleak January Saturday afternoon. He is walking along Kings Heath High Street, on his own. Head down as usual, oblivious to two girls doing a double take as he passes.

***

I haven't been to the Fox Hollies Forum since we danced just before Christmas. I'm still annoyed with him about it, and I've a nasty little worm of doubt as to whether he fancies me, or is it just terminal shyness?

The sight of him brings it all back. It should have been perfect. I relive it. I'm sat next to him at the coffee bar. I can sense that he's conscious of my presence. In the other room the Christmas disco is in full flow. 'American Pie' is playing. It's not my kind of music, but you can't escape it at the moment.

I've been watching him for weeks, trying to catch his eye without much success, whilst fending off unwanted attentions from the brasher, more confident, boys. When I look in the mirror I know I am pretty, confirmed by growing attention from boys. I suspect that there are some discussions or challenges amongst them as to who could get me to go out with them – or more. But I find them boring and predictable, so I turn them all down.

They're beginning to look at me in another way now, putting my disinterest in their charms to my being perhaps into girls? It could never be their fault could it? That would be truly exotic for a Kings Heath girl; the only lesbians I have ever heard of are in dirty magazines that I overhear the boys talking about, although I wouldn't be surprised if some of the leathery old women teachers at school aren't into it.

I'm not a lesbian.. I'm just fascinated by Danny. Have been for months. He is so different, fragile looking, with a pale beauty. So quiet and withdrawn, moody and brooding. I suppose that I've got a crush on him really. I think about him all the time.

Anyway, there I am, sat at the coffee bar next to him. It is nearly the end of the night. Don Maclean finally finishes, and the slow songs start. The siren tones of 'Got To Be There' by Michael Jackson waft from the other room. It's a sign that time is running out for tonight. Here is his moment. I'm right here, and a slow record playing. I wait for him to ask, but he looks sideways at me from beneath those blonde locks and I can read the indecision in his wonderful eyes. Up to me then. I smile, lean towards him and ask him to dance.

He brushes his hair away from his forehead, smiles, and I'm lost.

"I'm no good at it, just shuffle around really." He says.

"Doesn't matter, but if we don't shift, the record will be over when we get there and we'll look like a right pair of tits."

He hesitates even now, so I pull him from the stool and lead him towards the disco. As we pick our way between the chairs and tables and through the door I feel eyes on us, and smile as I imagine a lot of jaws dropping. It is much louder in here, darker, with strobe lights and the odd puff of dry ice from the DJ deck set up in the corner.

The first challenge is getting him to take hold of me, he doesn't know where to put his hands, so I have to do that for him as well, placing them in the small of my back. I feel a thrill as we touch and can smell patchouli oil. All the boys douse themselves in it, I try not to imagine what they want to hide, but I like the smell. It probably means that he shops at Oasis Market in town, which at least is trendy.

He is honest- he's a crap dancer. We shuffle awkwardly around in a tight circle. He is as rigid as a 'Tip-Top' straight out the freezer. After about thirty seconds the song ends, precipitating an awkward moment. There are a few couples dancing and I utter a quiet prayer that the DJ plays one more slow one. I fill the silence,

"I'm Alice."

"Danny."

Not the most interesting or romantic exchange I admit, but it fills a vital gap. The next song starts and luckily it's the slow and smoochy 'Top Twenty' hit, 'Let's Stay Together' by Al Green. We resume our shuffling. It's too loud to talk, and I spend the next three minutes wondering what's going to happen next.

What happens next is that the disco ends, the lights come on, stark and unforgiving, and any chance of privacy and a spot of romance evaporates.

I will him to do or say something. I've done it all so far and I'm looking for some sign that he likes me, wants to take it further. Around us, people are starting to leave and I know my friends will be coming to find me, joining up for the bus ride home, when I will no doubt be interrogated as to recent events, which won't take long at this rate. I have a temper, and suddenly it is there and I decide that he has to make the next move, so I just look at him.

He looks back at me, we are still entangled and the obvious thing to do would be to try and kiss me. But he removes his hands from me and takes a step back. The potential of the moment evaporates, unfulfilled.

He's back in his shell, muttering, "Thanks for the dance, sorry, told you I was no good."

And then he is turning away and suddenly here are Jenny and Lesley and the gulf between Danny and I snaps back to its pre-dance size and he is gone.

***

Danny:

Sunday. A nothing day. Shops shut, everything shut. Weather is crap again, cold and drizzling. The miners go on strike at midnight.

Nine days into the year and she didn't turn up at the club this week so my master plan is rat shit. School is bad. We've only been back a few days but it's been non-stop from Lowe and his cronies, plus a lot of the others keep looking at me as if I've let them all down.

It started as soon as I went back into the coffee bar after the disco finished. I stood, rooted to the spot, mind a blank, trying to think of a way to engage, and watched her walk into the night with her mates. As soon as she was out of sight I was surrounded.

Questions were fired at me, answers demanded. I had none, but was saved by the youth club workers throwing us out and closing up. I slipped away in the usual melee outside the doors, and legged it before anyone noticed. But I knew what was coming.

Term started three days after my birthday. Dreading it, and I wasn't disappointed. First break time I was pounced upon by Lowe and his mates, with all the usual hangers-on listening in the background.

What chat up line did I use?

What did she say?

Did I cop a feel, if so where?

What was she like to kiss?

When am I seeing her again?

Most of these questions were conveyed in tones of disbelief tinged with jealousy, but as I stumbled for answers the piss taking began.

The conclusion of the interrogation was that I was a total wanker who didn't deserve a girlfriend and probably couldn't get it up if I had one. I had to agree.

Worse if possible, was the gentle disappointment displayed by my few 'almost friends', who had clearly hoped that one of their loser company could put one over on the class shaggers by pulling a bird they couldn't.

Now I'm nine days further into my misery, and it's become the most important thing in my life to stop waiting for her to magically appear, and start doing something for myself. Track her down and put my cowardice to the sword.

Monday, and I start asking around. It's an all-boys school; female lives are clouded in mystery; plus, no-one is exactly falling over to help me steal the girl of their wet dreams, but by four o clock I have a clue. She wears a green school uniform and has been seen around Kings Heath and Billesley. That can only mean one place, Swanshurst Girls School, in Brook Lane, opposite the Billesley pub. A hot bed of talent that hosts end of term school discos, legendary amongst those who have the confidence to play the field.

I brood alone in my room that evening, but awake full of determination and with a plan. Wednesday afternoons is swimming at Moseley Road baths. The teacher, 'Greasy' Morgan, so called because his hair looks like he's emptied an oil can over it, and smells as if it's old chip-shop oil at that, is not only dozy, but disinterested. He never takes a register and it's always a doddle to go missing. That means I'm free at two.

Wednesday dawns a rare bright day, the first real sunshine of the year. I hope it's an auspicious sign. At lunchtime I bolt down my corn beef sandwiches and Penguin bar and sneak out across the playing fields and through the woods that border them. Nobody sees me and that's the way I want it. No awkward questions, no pressure to report back if I fail.

Mom is momentarily startled by my unlooked-for appearance at home, but swallows my explanation of forgetting my swimming stuff. She is busy cooking, leaving me free to have a quick spruce and change out of uniform into some better gear. I wait until I can hear pans clanking then dash down the stairs and out of the door, yelling goodbye before she can emerge and interrogate me further.

I wait impatiently at the bus stop as crucial minutes tick by. Eventually the blue and yellow Number 11 'Outer Circle' bus lumbers into view, and by three-thirty I'm on the corner opposite the main Swanshurst school entrance, hoping it's the right school and exit.

I try to merge with the gaggle of mothers collecting younger girls, but I stick out like a spot on a bum. The car park of the Billesley pub begins to fill up and the usual chaos picks up momentum.

Suddenly a torrent of green-clad girls begins to pour out onto the road. So many, and they make an absolute racket, screeching and giggling. I duck back into the sparse cover offered by a nearby tree trunk and attempt to keep my nerve. Her mass of blonde hair should stand out, although there are an uncomfortably large number of light hair colours on display.

I'm just beginning to panic, my resolve dissolving, expecting at any moment to be confronted as some sort of pervert, when I see her. Almost the last out, straggling along, happy-go-lucky, with a couple of friends, deep in conversation. The group splits up and she begins to walk away from me towards Kings Heath, now with only a slim, dark-haired girl for company, one I recognise from the youth club.

I follow at a discreet distance, expecting at any moment that some busybody has reported a suspicious person hanging around, and that a cop car will pull up and ask me what I'm up to.

I don't believe in any sort of God, but I'm praying that they will split up, and that she isn't going to get on a bus before I can catch up. Yes! They do, with the dark girl going up Institute Road, whilst Alice carries on down Billesley Lane.

I speed up, and the gap begins to close. By the time she crosses and goes up Clarence Road, I am fifty paces behind her. That's when she stops and turns around, stopping me dead in my tracks.

"Thought I'd punish you a bit for the other night, make you work for it. I saw you skulking behind that tree when I came out of school," she says, but with a smile playing around the corners of her eyes. "You can come closer you know, I won't bite."

I'm taken aback for a moment, then I gather my courage and close the distance between us. I decide that honesty is the best way forward – at least it gives me something to say, and right at this moment everything I meant to tell her has fled from my brain.

"I was a bit of a tosser wasn't I? Been kicking myself ever since, because you're gorgeous and I fancy you like mad. I've had nothing but stick at school because of it."

Instead of the expected smile her face becomes stony. " But what makes you think I fancy you, 'Mr. I Play Hard to Get'? Maybe I just wanted a dance and to keep the other wankers away.

I am instantly rendered speechless – I hadn't thought of that. This wasn't in the plan. I search for a response and I have a feeling that my mouth is doing a goldfish impersonation. This must have worked because she laughs and the stern face disappears instantly.

"Oh dear, you look so sad, I can see that I'm going to have my work cut out with you. Go on then, say something else nice to me and I might be nice back."

I take a huge dive with both feet. Shit or bust. If it's bust I'll just run for it. "Will you go out with me?"

"Yeah, but where are we going to go – not the bloody Forum with everyone gawping?"

Elation fills me, and with it a tiny spurt of confidence. For what seems the first time in my life I have actually made something happen myself

"You ever been to the 'Top Rank' in town? The Tuesday night disco?"

"No. Isn't that an adult's club?"

"Yeah, but on Tuesdays they do an under 16's disco. I've only been once, got dragged along by a mate one night, it's ok, they play some good stuff. We could go there if you wanted?"

"Ok, but that's nearly a week away."

Perhaps she is really interested. Emboldened, I have an idea. " Why don't we go up town on Saturday together? I could meet you here and catch the 50 in with you?"

Our first date. A street corner, a bus stop; wandering around the Bull Ring and Pallasades Shopping Centres where it's warm. Not exactly flowers and dinner at a posh restaurant. I'd thought about the Kingsway Cinema, but decided the back row better wait until I'm certain this is really happening, because it seems like a dream.

But we are together and alone, and no one we know sees us. I worry that there will be long silences where I desperately search for something to say, but it isn't like that at all. Alice is interesting, a chatterbox and seems to know about stuff that I like too, like books and music. And art. She tells me about her drawing and painting, her hopes to go to Art College

She is beautiful and fashionable. Don't know what she sees in me. I'm just 'Mr. Average', ordinary, a non-entity.

It seems natural to take hold of her hand and she doesn't just keep her hand in mine, she pulls closer and interlocks her arm with mine. A shiver goes through me. I can feel her body close to mine, smell her perfume, her hair shampoo.

The rest of the day passes in a daze although I remember laughing a lot, a café, and shops, shops, shops.

She comes from a family that encourages her to explore things, intellectual or otherwise, she seems to know lots more about the world than me, but I've had no reason to, no 'push' from my lot. Quite the opposite.

She describes her parents as 'old Hippies'. Her Dad, John, is a Philosophy lecturer at Birmingham University and her mom's a teacher. She sounds posh with a name like Eleanor. I'm already worried that I'll disappoint. Mom and Dad are a long way from posh.

They live in one of the big houses on Cambridge Road. I envy her freedom and her parents, can't help but compare her life to mine. Mine loses.

Then it's all over and we are walking back down the hill in the rain towards her house. We are huddled under her umbrella. I decide that rain is good, I am in a strange land called happy. I feel different. She has sown a seed of self-belief, and a dawning realisation that my life can be different if I make it happen.

Before we reach her house I stop. She turns and looks at me. "This has been the best day of my life," I say, and kiss her. It is the 15th of January. Our first kiss.

***

Alice:

I spot him straight away when I come out of school. My heart leaps, he could only be there for one reason – me. I make him work for it though, and have a moment or two of quiet satisfaction when I see him hesitating on the street corner. But I can't keep it going. Another failure might damage and destroy him, he would shuffle off in confusion, and that would be that. Forever. And I don't want that.

He needs me to shatter that shell he puts around himself, release the true Danny.

The day in town goes better than I expect, and I can see him growing in confidence, but his true self seems buried. His family isn't like mine. His dad works for the council as a foreman and sounds a bit of a bruiser and his mom doesn't seem to be much of a presence in his life. I don't think there's much encouragement to do anything but be a typical man like his dad, but anyone with half a brain could see that he will never be like that. He is too sensitive. Our first kiss is good, especially as I don't think it is ever going to happen, despite me trying to engineer the opportunity all day. Thank God for the rain – and my collapsible umbrella. I think it's a big step for him to take, that kiss. I think a line has been crossed.

The 'Top Rank'. I've told mom and dad that I'm at Lesley's, then going to Jenny's. I feel guilty about lying because they trust me and won't check. They will probably be ok once they meet Danny, but I'm not about to risk a, 'no you can't go.' That would be a disaster. Who knows what Danny might think or do if I cancel?

It is my first time in a proper nightclub, and I'm with the boy I want. I love it all, the dance floor, the lights, the DJ, the music; and the way they announce, 'the Shandy Bar is now open,' followed by a stampede up to the balcony bar where everyone can pretend to be adults. I love being part of it - the other kids, sporting the latest fashions, flares, platform heels, tank tops and cheesecloth shirts. This belongs to me, my generation. We are the future.

We talk, we dance, we kiss again. Already he seems different, less shy and stooped. He is actually quite tall and I can see some of the other girls looking., But he's with me, and I'm filled with laughter, energy and love. I know that this is it.

***

Danny:

It's been a month now and she's changed my life. She encourages me to be myself, do what I really want, dress how I like. Now I've seen what her life is like I know what I'm missing, and I've begun to stand up for myself at home and school.

33

Dad has noticed, and we've clashed a few times over music volume, clothes and going out. I think he is secretly pleased that his son is finally showing some balls – although it's always on his terms and I can foresee trouble if I push it. I'll have to be careful, don't want any more bruises. Luckily he's pre-occupied with work, the unions, the battle with the Government. We've got the candles out now. Power cuts every day as the power stations run out of coal.

Mom, as usual, just carries on, doesn't get involved between me and him. He rules. She is such a doormat. Perhaps that's where I get it from.

School is different. I kept the fact of Alice and I quiet for a while, but we got seen together and it went around school like wildfire. Another interrogation, but this time I stood up to Lowe, let it be known I'm going out with her, but refused to answer more questions. I'm beginning to suspect he gets his kicks from other people's love life. This time there was a silent respect from the hangers-on, and I sense a reappraisal of me is going on. I'm no longer on the margins, I've got a proper girlfriend who's a cracker and that means they have to think differently about me. I notice that I'm taller than Lowe now, a surprise that I file away for future reference.

There is a world full of stuff out there for me, and I'm going to grab it.

***

David:

Bowie is drawn to the style of Japan, especially the costumes of 'Kabuki' theatre where men play both the male and female parts. He wants to do music in a different way, make it theatrical, a performance, and the androgyny of 'Kabuki' resonates with him. Also significant in 'Kabuki' is that a change of costume denotes a change of character, and David Jones / Bowie is about to inhabit a new character.

He discovers a Japanese clothes designer who uses the styles of traditional 'Kabuki' and 'No' theatre, Kansai Yamamoto, and buys one of his designs, a jump suit imprinted with woodland animals – it is cut-price, no one else wants it.

One day, reading a magazine, he sees a photograph of a Japanese model wearing an outfit designed by Yamamoto. She has bright red spiky hair. Bowie takes the picture to his local hair salon, the Evelyn Paget Salon in Beckenham, and asks for his long hair to be cut and styled to match the picture. A young stylist, Suzy Fussey, takes on the task and does a good job. She will become Bowie's hairstylist on tour and marry his guitarist, but that lies in the future.

Bowie loves his new 'butch' haircut, and subsequently dyes it bright red to match the picture of the model, using Schwarzkopf 'Red Hot Red' hair dye. The 'Bowie cut' is born.

Bowie is planning his assault on the music world. He has been trying things out, mime, theatre, musicals, 'arts labs', folk music, rock. He intends to merge these elements into something new. He is married now, to Angie, a wild and ambitious woman, and they have a son, Zowie. They live a hedonistic life in a rambling Victorian mansion in Beckenham called Haddon Hall, frequenting the local clubs, including the gay scene in the 'Sombrero'. Bowie is fascinated by gay styles.

He has an 'open marriage' and is regularly to be found in bed with his wife and various pick-ups from the previous night's debauchery, both male or female.

Mick Ronson is dossing on a second hand mattress on the landing and they are creating music in the basement. Something is about to happen.

On 22nd January he gives an interview to 'Melody Maker'. What he says makes headlines, and shocks, as is the intention. Something is about to happen. In the dark and dimness of the miner's strike and the power cuts, a light is guttering weakly into life.

Chapter Three

'Changes'
Spring 1972

Danny:

What has she has done?

When I look back to that New Year morning I don't recognize the kid lying in bed. How can I have been such a loser? I'm changing fast. She is the catalyst, but I understand now that the base material must be there to get a reaction, and it's becoming a chain reaction.

To begin with it was all because of Alice, her feelings for me, her wish to be with me. She is so pretty, so nice, and all my mates- and the others I don't consider mates, are aching with jealousy.

It was a huge shock when she first came on to me, an injection of self- confidence. I'm different now. It's taken time, but instead of hiding away on the margins I'm a mover and shaker. I've got the best-looking girlfriend in my year, and nobody can take that away from me, no matter what happens.

It feels really natural to be together. I don't feel the need to fill the silences with inane chatter. It must mean that we're comfortable in each other's company, and don't need to force conversation for the sake of it. We fit, simple as that.

We've moved on from shopping centres too. She looks older and can pass for eighteen. She charms the pants off the doormen, I'm sure they'd like to reciprocate, but it gets us into all sorts of places. I think being with her makes me look older too, although Alice tells me that it's me that's changed.

The absolute best recently was getting into the Kingsway to see the 'X' rated, 'A Clockwork Orange'. Alice had read the book and was talking about the meaning of it all, how it showed that we all need freedom to make our own choices – for good or bad, but all I could see was how cool it all was. The outfits, Malcolm McDowell in make- up, the 'ultra-violence', and that rape scene – ashamed to say it gave me a hard on, but I hid it.

I felt ten feet tall when I walked out. Us teenagers are strong and getting stronger. We are going to change things for the better, free ourselves to be, and do, what we want. It's there for the taking, we just need some self-belief, actually do something, grab what we want.

I went home after the film wanting to give Dad a good slapping but thought better of it once I'd cooled down a bit. He'd beat the crap out of me. I think I'm getting on his wick all the time now that I'm beginning to stand up for myself - and the feeling is mutual. Wish I could leave but it's just not possible. He scares me though.

***

Alice.

I'm in heaven. A dream, but I know I'm awake. I'm so much in love with him, and I've released him from his self-imposed prison – he says so himself. The girls are green with envy. They overlooked him, thought I was mad for chasing him, but they didn't really 'see' him, see what was hidden. And now, he has blossomed, his beauty there for all to see, standing tall and straight, and growing in confidence every day. I just hope it doesn't change him, because it's the thoughtful, quiet and shy Danny that first attracted me. He was all mine at first, but now I have to share some of him, some of the time.

It started slowly, just teenagers together, feeling our way forward. I've always looked a bit older, and I think the way Mom and Dad treat me has made me older inside too, I seem to like more adult things and know stuff, and I think that shows on the outside. Once we teamed up and Danny started to come out of his shell, the world began to open up.

We started getting into pubs and other forbidden things, including that film Clockwork Orange which is for over 18's only, but only us kids want to see it. I've read the book, and found it interesting, but to me the film was disappointing. Bit of a parody, glorying violence and seeming more concerned with being shocking, fashionable, and 'cool, rather' than telling the moral of story. I found the rape scene difficult to watch with Danny, made worse by the fact that he was riveted to every moment.

But we are great together, we are truly becoming soul mates. We still go to the 'Top Rank', but we are moving on, they seem so young in there. Now it's the 'Locarno', 16 to 18's night, which has a much older crowd. Great place, even the resident band, Red Sun, are ok. I also love 'The Bull' in Moseley, mainly for its strange crowd of all ages and types, including a hippy bloke who never wears shoes. A couple of drinks there, then on to Cannon Hill Arts Centre for the Friday disco, which focuses on progressive rock and is totally psychedelic. You can really chill out in the darkness with the cool light show. I love music, and mom and dad have a great collection going back years, so I've got loads of records and they encourage me to try different stuff.

There is dope about, especially at The Bull and the Arts Centre. We have both tried it, and got the giggles, but I didn't like smoking the Rizla roll ups with a piece of rolled up fag packet instead of a filter - too strong. In fact, I don't like smoking at all, I can take it or leave it.

Danny seems to like it though, the dope and the smoking. He's started using those Menthol cigarettes, which are just about OK. I only have them to keep him company. I don't need anything other than him to make me happy, I'm just about bursting as it is, but I suppose boys want to look manly and experiment. I'll not be taking anything else though, and I'll try to encourage Danny to deff it too.

***

David Jones:

On the 29th January 1972, a new rock star begins a tour that will last for eighteen months and change both music and attitudes. The difference with this star is that he appears, fully formed, from nowhere, and is a total fabrication.

The first appearance of 'Ziggy Stardust' is at a warm-up show at Friars Borough Hall in Aylesbury. The controversial 'Melody Maker' interview Bowie gives a week earlier generates huge media interest, but that does not initially translate into success.

'Ziggy' has spiky, orange hair and wears a bomber jacket, with the addition of a large codpiece, as worn by the delinquent gang in 'A Clockwork Orange', stuffed into rolled up trousers that in turn reveal red plastic boxer style boots. A doppelganger for David Jones, allowing him to 'act' the part of rock star. It is a natural progression. He has always been interested in theatre, and performance art, and now starts to experiment with his newly forged 'star' trying to turn rock into an artistic medium.

The character of 'Ziggy' is a construct of two real people known by Jones and captured in his magpie-like mind for future use. The first is a crazy thrash Country and Western performer – 'The Legendary Stardust Cowboy', not a star, but possessed of a strange alien persona and obsession with science fiction and space.

The second is the 1960's 'French Elvis', Vince Taylor, a colourful cult figure renowned for massive drugs and drink binges and accompanying mental health problems. A rock tragedy in the making.

The band backing 'Ziggy' at the Aylesbury warm-up do not as yet have a name. On drums is Mick 'Woody' Woodmansey, on base Trevor Bolder, and on lead guitar and support vocals, Mick Ronson. Lads from Hull who have had to be persuaded to wear their brightly coloured jumpsuits, Ronson in gold, Woodmansey pink, and Bolder blue - modelled upon the 'droogs' in, 'A Clockwork Orange', which Bowie has recently seen in London. However, once the boys discover that girls go mad for them when they are in 'glam' getups, their attitude quickly changes, and they become enthusiastic wearers of the outfits – and a little make up. 'Ziggy' himself is modestly billed as the 'Most Beautiful Person in the World'.

The band appear on stage to Walter Carlos' 'Clockwork Orange' theme. They play well together and by the time the song 'Rock' n Roll Suicide' closes the show, the audience is in uproar.

The gig costs the Friars Club a £110 fee for a night that redefines music performance for the rest of the Seventies. Rock theatre has arrived.

***

Danny:

'Three Day Week', what a miserable fuck-up that was. Dad was even more of a pain in the arse than usual, stuck at home and moaning non-stop about Ted Heath. Thank God it's all over and he's out all day again. Sitting in candlelight, no TV, no record player, and Mom suggesting we play Monopoly!

At least I've got Alice. They've met her and it went ok. But now that's done I'm keeping her away from them. Tell the truth I'm ashamed of them and there's something about the way Dad is with her that makes me uncomfortable.

Her parents are a lot cooler than mine, a lot more forgiving, and actively encourage Alice to experiment and experience things. That's probably why she seems older than me and knows more.

I want to get out of my house so badly, but Alice says to hang in there and focus on a long-term target, get my 'O-Levels' and see about 'A Levels' and University, but I'm not sure. She doesn't know the half of it. I'm not sure I'll ever tell her.

We go into pubs now, especially The Bull in Moseley. It's on the corner, opposite some ancient public piss-holes and seems to be stuck in a time warp, full of hippies and weirdos. You can smell the dope from the street before you go in. I don't think they're much bothered about age so long as you spend money.

We've got a bit of cash between us as we've both got jobs. She's at Chelsea Girl up town, and I'm stacking shelves at Kwik Save in Kings Heath on Thursday evenings and Saturday mornings. I think she's got the better deal.

The supermarket is a bit mind-numbing and there's always an odd smell - of decaying cardboard I think, but some of the older women there are fun, and a couple are definitely flirting, Of course I'm faithful to Alice, but it's a boost to my confidence and it does no harm if I encourage them a bit.

There's a good lad there too, called Derek, a full-timer who left school at sixteen; bit of a character, full of bullshit and chat and he seems to like me, so I'm learning from him about being the life and soul and putting myself forward. We often see him up town, and his trademark is to have a white handkerchief trailing from his back pocket. I asked him why and he just said 'why not'.

I've bought one of those 'Bullworkers' and been using it regularly, much to Dad's amusement. He says I couldn't knock the froth off a pint, but actually I'm getting stronger, and I've put on about half a stone since I've been using it. Love is good for me.

***

David Jones.

On 26th February, 'Ziggy Stardust' and his band, now christened, 'The Spiders From Mars', play the Mayfair suite at the Belfry night-club in Sutton Coldfield. This performance passes almost completely unnoticed by the local press and population.

At 7.30pm, on the 17th of March, He makes his debut at Birmingham Town Hall: Sixty New Pence for a seat in the stalls. The traditional building with its colonnaded portico and balcony is an old-fashioned contrast to the show it hosts. The hall is only half-full and the audience is enraptured rather than boisterous, intensely focusing on the performance and submerging themselves in its spell. Bowie is filled with energy, a gaudy firework exploding against the Victorian backdrop of the Town Hall interior.

New Musical Express photographer, Mick Rock, is at the concert on behalf of the magazine, and introduces himself backstage to Bowie before the show. The pair instantly hit it off and share a train journey afterwards. As a result, Rock becomes the main photographer for 'Ziggy Stardust'. He captures his first image of 'Ziggy' at the Birmingham concert.

***

Danny:

Sex is on my mind. It's always on my mind but I'm not sure how to broach the subject.

On Sunday, spring is in the air and the Daffodils are out. We get the bus to Cannon Hill Park. Whilst avoiding the Canada Geese shit, and taking swigs of Cider we've got from the 'outdoor', she gets all intense.

" Danny, can I ask you something?"

"Course, anything."

"We've been going out for ages now. Do you think we get on well?"

"Really well, I don't want to be with anyone else."

"Do you think we'll stay together for a long time?"

"Don't see why not, you've changed my life for the better."

We sit on a bench and contemplate the lake for a while in silence. She breaks it with a big announcement.

"I love you Danny, I have since I first saw you creeping around in the shadows. Do you feel the same?"

"Course I do, you're beautiful and funny and clever and we get on great."

Another hesitation, then she whispers,

" Are you holding back from doing it - or don't you want to?"

"You bet I want to, but I didn't want to rush things, upset you and fall out. Didn't want you to think that was all I'm after"

The right thing to say. She smiles and puts her head on my shoulder.

" I was thinking that I'd be your first – I would wouldn't I? And you'd be mine. But I need to be sure that you feel the same about me as I do about you?"

"Yes, you would," I admit, clearly not to her surprise.

For the first time I see her look shy.

"I'm not doing it just anywhere. And you need to get something first don't you, because I'm not on the pill. And you need to get cracking because Mom and Dad are going to some big dinner at the university this Friday night and the house will be empty all evening."

So that was how it happened. Luckily the toilets in The Bull have machines that haven't been screwed for the money, so that was sorted easily and without embarrassment. I worried for the next few days that I'd do it wrong or something, but I had a pretty good idea from reading the dirty magazines like Forum and Penthouse that some of the lads used to get hold of and pass around.

The 'Reader's Wives' letters are the best. Ordinary housewives, bored with their husbands but experienced, often went through it step by step in great detail in their letters. I often wonder though, if there are so many rampant housewives about, how come nobody at school has ever to my knowledge come across one and been seduced? Perhaps the milkmen, window cleaners and plumbers get them all? Perhaps it's just fake?

I needn't have worried though. Alice's parents are totally modern and had several 'little chats' with her about the birds and the bees, hence her insistence on using a 'johnny'.

I managed to get a bottle of cider and a packet of Consulate. Alice got some snacks and we cuddled down on the sofa and watched the TV for a bit. Then we kissed, she led me up to her room and we did it. Don't think she came though; girls often don't do they? Didn't take long and I'm not sure it's everything it's cracked up to be, but at least the deed is done. I'm a man.

***

Alice:

I suppose the biggest event of the past few months has been losing my virginity – at least it's supposed to be a big deal. In the end it was a definite anti-climax – in every sense, although at least that's out of the way now and we are not only in love, but lovers. It will get better.

It had to be with Danny. He didn't really need to tell me he loved me, I would have done it anyway, but it was fun getting him to say it. It might even be true.

***

Danny:

Between getting off with Alice, getting laid, Derek and his antics at Kwik Save, and some of my own doing, I feel able to take a long look at myself and measure up against that awful New Year's morning in bed. Progress, but more work required.

I see a difference in the mirror. I am growing up, putting on some size, and with Alice badgering me to stand up straight and stick my chest out I realise that I'm not only getting tall for my age, but I don't look like such a scrawny wimp any more. Dad's a big bloke, so why not?

Because of my progress with the 'Bullworker' in my bedroom, I feel able to join the weight-training club at school without being ridiculed. Once a week a few of us chuck ancient weights about in a tiny room just off the stage in the school hall, and we are allowed to use them after school too. I'm surprised how quickly my strength goes up. I don't start popping muscles out all over the place, I think I'm always going to be thin, but I'm filling out nicely. The best part of doing weights is the kudos though. Once word gets around I earn more respect, and my journey from the 'Outer Limits' is nearly complete. There is one last hurdle to be negotiated.

Phil Lowe hates me being the centre of attention. He tries to put me down, but he doesn't have the backing like he used to have. I can tell that a number of his old cronies are doing a re-assessment of the pecking order. Some of them have even taken to talking to me.

It all reaches a head one dinner hour. It's warm and I'm dossing on the far side of the playing field, chatting about the usual stuff, girls, music, drinking, and going out.

Lowe made an absolute prat of himself this morning in maths, and the teacher, who couples his impatience with a devastating razor wit, gave Lowe the full benefit of his opinion in front of the whole class, whilst emphasising each acidic observation as to Lowe's future chances in life with a tap of the board rubber on the tosser's head - until his hair went totally white with the chalk dust.

I found the whole thing hilarious, having suffered at Fat Phil's hands for years, and without realising it, led the class in laughter and ridicule. When the bell went Lowe shot me a murderous glance and I left expecting trouble, hence situating myself at the far side of the playing field.

Someone looking forward to some spectator sport must have told him where I am, because after about ten minutes I see him marching across the rugby pitch towards me, clearly fuelled by a combination of anger, humiliation and a desire to take me down a few notches and put me back in my proper place. Behind him straggle about twenty kids, a combination of Phil's mates, those who sit firmly in the middle, and the purely curious, glad of anything that provides entertainment.

I stand up and we face off, a ring of spectators around us.

It is going to end up in a fight whatever I say, and a devil gets into me. I'm flooded with adrenalin brought on by fear, but fermenting within it a newborn emotion – a reckless 'shit or bust' sensation, tinged with a pent-up anger brought on by years of being the victim. But it is my father's angry face that I see.

"What do you want Chalky?" I say with a big smile, feeling the impact of each word as it rolls out of my mouth. There is a ripple of nervous, disbelieving laughter amongst the gawkers.

Lowe goes berserk, launching himself at me, arms flailing. He catches me a good one on the side of the head, setting it ringing, and we both go down in a bundle, with a ring of spectators shouting, 'scrap, scrap' and drinking in every precious moment. 'I was there' they will say, and re-live the story for others.

It is my first fight, and against an experienced opponent. But Lowe isn't Dad, not in the same league.

To begin with it goes badly. Lowe ends up astride me and punches me twice in the face. I can feel blood running. Then he hesitates, probably thinking it's all over, that I will give in, and he can spend some time having some 'sport', ridiculing me to the onlookers from that position.

Something happens though. I don't see him, but Dad. As he turns slightly to address someone in the crowd I push up with both arms and drive the top of my head into his face. It isn't a clean blow but it clearly hurts and the surprise makes him lose his balance. I spin him off me and will myself to get up. I am quicker, he is a fat bastard after all, and I get a really good kick into his face, sending him sprawling and uttering a strange, shocked cry, never heard from him before at school.

I stand over him and as he gets to his knees I'm sure I can see tears, that's when I know I have him. As he tries to get up I punch him in the face, putting all my weight behind the blow. The 'Bullworker' and weights must have an added effect because he flies backwards and ends up on his back. He looks like a beached hippo and I wonder why I had ever put up with his nonsense. I can see hatred smouldering under the tears, but he is finished. Then a teacher breaks through the circle surrounding us and it is all over bar the recriminations and detentions.

As I am led away I see the faces. Shock and amazement. I know that never again will they take the piss.

***

Alice:

Something new. He arrives proudly displaying a black eye, a trophy from a fight with some kid at school. I am shocked when I open the door and I can see Dad checking him out from the corner of his eye, reassessing.

The bruise intrudes shockingly into Danny's beauty. It drags him down to earth, makes him look like just another boy. I don't like that. He isn't some scrapping, arrogant, bullying kid, he's my Danny and I want to keep him how he was. Then I think that it's me that's messing with his head, I don't really know what I'm doing, what I've set in motion. I've no control. Might he grow away from me?

I reassure myself, we are so close, he relies on me for everything, says that I 'woke him up', so I can influence this. It's just a one-off - I hope.

***

David:

On 16th June 1972, Bowie's new album, 'The Rise and Fall of Ziggy Stardust and The Spiders From Mars' is released. His management company, Mainman, hype the record as if Bowie is already a star, but he isn't, certainly not of the status of Bolan. They claim that 'Hunky Dory' is a hit in America, but it has only reached a high of number 185 in the charts there.

Initial reviews are mixed, with many critics expecting another dense and philosophical offering in the style of Hunky Dory. They miss the point. 'Ziggy Stardust' is about a ready-made rock star, his rise and collapse. There is plenty of space for the listener to adapt the rather vague story to their own lives and likes. The subtext is that Bowie is making a comment about the falsity of rock music. He is using the trappings of the rock star to become one, but also to undermine the illusion, whilst at the same time, selling himself. It is an album about a fake rock star by an aspiring rock star.

Whilst very loose in narrative structure, there are several themes that fuse into the 'Ziggy' character, and the stage performances that evolve as the tour progresses. The rock star as an alien visitor, a star child, a fictional 'God', worshipped by followers who later destroy him.

It is not a concept album; the final song list being compiled from a large stock of previously written songs that Bowie has stored away. RCA, the record company, insist upon a lead single, and at the last minute, a song called 'Starman', recorded in February, and released in April as a single, is included.

'Starman' is about a visitation from space by an entity that gives youth hope, and leads them to salvation. A new type of deity. The song is loosely based on 'Somewhere Over The Rainbow' from 'The Wizard Of Oz' with a 'boogie' section that references the style of 'T Rex', and especially the playout style of their recent Number One, 'Hot Love'.

When the album is released, 'Starman' has failed to chart for some seven weeks. 'Ziggy' the 'rock star' has been on tour for nearly five months. The smallish venues attract enthusiastic but small crowds, with many venues half-filled.

The stardom project and success of the album have reached a critical moment - and there is a real risk that it could all peter out to nothing.

*

The day after release, photographer Mick Rock attends a 'Ziggy' concert at Oxford Town Hall. Before the gig begins, Bowie warns Rock to be ready to capture something new on stage. During the concert, 'Ziggy' falls to his knees in front of the guitar-playing Ronson, who is bearing his usual expression of sexual ecstasy as he coaxes the solo from the guitar. The singer grabs Ronson's buttocks and simulates fellatio whilst playing the guitar strings with his teeth, in the style of Jimi Hendrix.

Rock captures the moment in all its homoerotic glory, and the resultant published image, a full page in New Musical Express on July 15th, smashes into the consciousness of the 'normal' world. The shock it causes is intense, enticing to some, drawing vitriol from others. Two men, covered in make-up and feminine clothing, one with spiky carrot coloured hair, the other long blonde flowing locks, entwined in an apparent homosexual 'blowjob'. It is a calculated move, propelling Bowie into notoriety instantly. Controversy and publicity is very good for the rock business, and the interest in, and awareness of, David Bowie surges.

***

Alice:

> *Things have settled down again since the day of the black eye. Danny explained that he had put a stop to a bully by standing up for himself and I can't object to that, can I? From the very start I've been encouraging him to be more confident; it is a big thing to overturn years of being put down, by facing off the tormentor.*

> *There are changes. He seems older and more self-assured. It's very subtle, most wouldn't notice, but we are so close and together such a lot. It's what I wanted, for him to come out of his shell, and it's working. Just need to steady things down a bit. I'm not*

48

sure how fragile the foundation is; I don't want it all to crash and burn, undoing all my good work, leaving me with a wreck back in his shell. It is a dilemma, this tension between too much and too little confidence.

I've met his parents. Not like mine at all. His Dad looks a bit of a bruiser, rough and coarse. Works at the council on the building. There is an undercurrent of anger and violence. Danny's Mom is a mouse of a woman. She hardly says a word and almost jumps when her husband makes one of his pronouncements. I bet the tea has to be on the table on time.

I find it difficult to believe that this man produced my quiet boy. Perhaps he didn't and she had it off with the postman or something - got her own back while he was at work. What a laugh that would be? I'm going to pretend to myself that it's true, otherwise her life would be too horrible to contemplate.

I try to talk to Danny about it but he shuts down, changes the subject. This is at the core of him, the thing he has to deal with. He talks about leaving, but I've poured cold water on it. He's fifteen, he's doing ok at school and mustn't sacrifice his chance to be something, go to university, find an escape that way. A couple of years to put up with it. Such a short time, but an eternity at our age. It's the rest of his life at stake though. I'm definitely going to university, can't wait. We can go together.

*

I don't know what Danny's been doing for the past few years in his little bubble, but it certainly isn't listening to proper music. I've got a stereo deck in the bedroom, which I thought might be a problem, but once Danny met Mom and Dad it was ok. I think because he was quiet and polite they liked him, although I did overhear Dad describe him once as 'nice enough but a bit saft', which I think means Dad thinks he's no threat. So, they are OK with us going up to the bedroom, although they do find reasons to 'pop in' at regular intervals. Still they are cool about me being with him. I'm so lucky to have my parents and not his.

I'm more into serious music than pop, stuff like 'Yes', although I do like some of the new 'glam' stuff and 'T Rex' especially. They come from quite a hippy, fantasy background. Danny and I recently went to see them at the Odeon in New Street. It was 75p for a front stalls seat and we got right to the stage, I could almost touch them. There was so much screaming that you couldn't really hear the music, spoilt it for me.. It was Danny's first live gig and he seemed really caught up in it, couldn't stop talking about it afterwards.

Summer's finally here. It's the long holiday soon, six weeks of freedom. Then it's 'O Levels' and we'll both need to knuckle down. Got to make the most of our time until then.

Chapter Four

'Starman'

July 1972

Danny.

It begins with an episode of 'Top Of The Pops'. I watch avidly every Thursday evening, much to the amusement of the Lord of the house, who spends the whole of the programme making snide comments from behind the Birmingham Evening Mail.

Mom reads her book and avoids making eye contact with the screen, as if she is frightened of allowing a slice of real life into her brain. I am allowed to watch it on sufferance, but it is a rubbing point every week.

On the whole, I hate the gimmicky 'pop' stuff on 'Top Of The Pops', the ridiculous DJ's and their unfunny attempts at humour, old blokes trying to be hip. None of them are my generation, they don't represent us, they just have their snouts in the trough, making money and enjoying being at the centre of the attention of the young girls.

I watch because there is usually the odd gem of a live, (or often badly mimed), performance by someone I like. I've just started exploring, thanks to Alice, and this slice of the music scene is the only one I get to watch on the TV. It's the only time in my otherwise mundane week that I glimpse another, seemingly happier and more colourful world.

It is Thursday 6th July. I think that my world has already changed as much as it can, because of Alice, but that belief is about to be shattered, and my feet set upon a new course.

***

I am sat in the living room with Mom, the lovely but useless Betty Rogers, and Dad, the much less lovely George – apparently widely known as 'Gorgeous George' – for his looks rather than what lies beneath. I hate everything about him and try hard to believe that he isn't my Dad.

I hate him for his boring, selfish, blokeish ways. I hate him because he makes my life a misery. But most of all I hate him for what he has done to me, to Mom. And the fact that she so meekly puts up with it, uses me to divert his attention, makes me despise her too.

He is violent, always has been, as far back as I can remember. He hasn't even got the excuse of being a drunk, because he doesn't touch a drop, I suspect gave it up because he was afraid of going too far.

He is prone to massive rage, directed at just about anyone, politicians, workmates, people on the TV, immigrants, Irish, you name it, he has an opinion and a grudge. The anger bubbling under the surface can erupt at the slightest provocation. He can't take it out on those people, so he uses the next best thing, Mom, and me, but usually me.

From an early age I've dreamt of defending myself, her, but there is no hope, he's big, nasty, and handy with his fists. I tried once, a couple of years ago, and he punched me in the stomach then gave me a clout round the ear that knocked me to the floor. Mom just stood there.

He's got a reputation. No one messes with George. I suppose some kids would be proud of having a hard knock as a Dad, but I'm ashamed of him - and me for doing nothing about it. I guess that in my own way I'm as guilty as Mom, hiding within myself and hoping it all goes away.

But now I'm getting bigger and stronger, he's getting older, and one day I'll do it, I promise.

***

This evening he is ensconced in his usual position, king of all he surveys, flopped in his favourite chair nearest the TV, digesting the news in the local rag, whilst occasionally farting and scratching his balls.

Mom is knitting, and the click of needles is no less aggravating. She seems to be in a trance - about par for the course. She was cowed into submission long before I arrived on the scene.

Then it is time, and that twat Tony Blackburn is on the screen, making his useless jokes and flashing his cheesy smile at all the young girls, dirty bastard. Bet he gets plenty.

It starts as usual with the chart countdown and the crowd dancing, and it's 'Join Together' by The Who playing over the top – which is OK. Number One isn't though. 'Puppy Love' by Donny, 'scream, scream', Osmond. His smile is even cheesier than Blackburn's. It's all so nice and wholesome, where's the edge, the danger, something new? Certainly not the next act, Lulu, with some forgettable new drivel, thought she'd retired in the Sixties.

It gets better with 'Silver Machine' by Hawkwind, although that gets a bit monotonous after a while, and out of the corner of eye I can see the old man getting edgy – about to make some pronouncement. He seems to think better of it and subsides back into the chair, muttering, 'wankers', and shaking the paper straight.

Then a bolt of lightning strikes. A blurred shot of a blue acoustic guitar with a hand strumming. Singing starts, a strange looking face fills the screen. I'm upright in the chair, something new here.

He has an unearthly look, reminds me of the descriptions of the elves in 'Lord of The Rings'. A thin, pale, sculpted face, with high cheekbones, all crowned with a riot of orange hair, cut short at the sides but spiky on top. It looks like a girl's hairstyle. He is beautiful.

For a moment I doubt that it is a 'he'. On balance I think yes, but it's not certain, the features seem to be genderless. And then I notice the eyes, weird, alien almost, the black centres different sizes. They reflect the lights differently. It's a small difference but it jars, abnormal.

I am sat forward in the chair, holding my breath. I cast a surreptitious glance and see that Mom has stopped knitting and is staring at the screen. The absence of clicking needles registers with Dad and he lowers the paper. I see his face. The astonished expression makes me instantly love the guy on the screen. I think that the bastard is going to jump up and change the channel, but the spell is cast and he remains in his chair, the newspaper flat on his lap.

In the meantime, the camera pans out, revealing what Bowie is wearing, for it is he, playing 'Starman', which has just entered the 'Top Thirty'. I've heard it a couple of times on the radio but it hasn't really registered. I've never taken much notice of Bowie, he's been in the background, blotted out by the big 'Glam' stars such as Bolan, Slade, and Glitter.

Bowie's thin body is sporting a patterned jumpsuit. It is alien too. His neck is bare, but the crew neck of the jumpsuit is done up to the top. It screams out 'queer', it is fascinating and shocking, I've never seen anything like it.

Whilst I'm still taking it all in, conscious that the old bastard is getting fidgety again, the camera pulls back to reveal the rest of the group. The drummer is wearing some sort of pink romper suit in satin. He looks bent too, with bouffed up hair, a smooth, hairless face, which looks like it's been powdered, a hint of makeup on his eyelids. The suit he is wearing reminds me of the 'Droog' gang in 'Clockwork Orange'.

As the song gets to a sound like Morse Code, and the chorus, the camera goes to blurred lights then back to Bowie, on a slight side angle, his head filling the screen as he sings.

In the background is the guitarist. Long blonde locks framing another powdered and hairless face, he is adorned with a yellow satin jump suit. In close up he has laughter playing around his eyes, and I think that he's finding this all very amusing.

The chair to my right erupts, "Fuckin Pooftas, shouldn't be allowed on the telly, they need a good fuckin kicking if you ask me, that'd sort em out." Mom nods in agreement but remains transfixed by the screen, needles stilled.

I think that he is about to leap up and switch the channel to ATV but he doesn't – I think he's really shocked, maybe a bit intrigued. It's a good job, because if he had have done, I'd have missed it, the moment that changed my life.

The guitarist approaches Bowie and the single microphone, and straight away their heads get *very* close as he joins in with the chorus. He is looking at Bowie's face - into his eyes like a lover, and it seems as if they could almost be about to kiss.

"Fuckin stroll on, they're gonna have a snog, total benders, look at them," my commentator intones. I think he's beginning to enjoy this, yet another excuse to have a moan.

Then Bowie puts his left arm around the guitarist's shoulder and waves a very limp wrist as they cuddle up whilst singing. They both smile broadly. They know what they are doing, and saying, with their bodies.

For the first time we see the other guitarist. He's got ridiculous sideburns and somehow doesn't quite fit with the others. He looks like a bloke made up – more traditional 'Glam Rock' than queer. In fact, he looks a bit embarrassed and smirks at the camera.

As the chorus finishes, Bowie and the guitarist part company for the instrumental section; although the guitarist momentarily sinks to his knees then gets back up quickly; the idea comes into my head that he was getting into position to give Bowie a 'blowjob' but thought better of it. On 'Top Of The Pops' – sensational!

Then it happens. It's the second verse and Bowie's face fills the screen. He looks directly into the camera as he sings the line about phoning someone and picking on you. He is talking directly to me. The tip of his pointing finger is held just below his right eye so I can't help but look into that window into his soul. We connect.

It's a call to arms, to a new and exciting world, fresh, 'other', and alien. I know in an instant that I must be part of it, I need to be in that world, not this one. Just that one short glimpse has me hooked.

With a twirl of the finger and a smile, the performance moves on. The ending is really bizarre. As the final chorus is sung, my eye is drawn to a crowd member, a kid wearing a red shirt and grey tank top with a faraway look in his eyes, dancing – really badly. He is trying so hard to be hip in his moment of fame, but he looks so outdated and ordinary compared to what is unfolding right in front of him. A sparrow next to a peacock.

Bowie's arm raises, obscuring the youth's face, and the blonde guitarist steps into another cuddle. Suddenly the dancing youth appears behind and between them both, his face perfectly framed between the two performers. The youth smiles, then he turns sideways looking at the girl dancing next to him, as if he wants it known that he is dancing with her rather than these two made-up blokes.

I think that the kid is watching himself on a monitor screen, and has realised that he is being broadcast to the nation, perfectly framed between the erotically charged male cuddle in front of him. He's probably thinking about what school's going to be like tomorrow and is trying to assert his manliness by cosying up to the girl next to him.

Dad thinks it's funny, guffawing loudly, "look at that twat, doesn't know where to put himself, he looks a dozy bastard, a right piece of piss, but even he knows what's going on and is trying to get out of the way. Shouldn't be allowed, corrupting young minds it is."

Bowie is hamming it up now, close to the guitarist, looking directly into his face, again like lovers about to kiss. The kid in the tank top reappears and the camera pulls out sideways, putting him out of sight. The 'lovers' part as this happens, then the guitarist deliberately steps back into close quarters. It must be deliberate, they only have one mike to share, but they surely could have had two. As the song ends, Bowie is serenading the guitarist, singing directly at him, like Romeo and Juliet. The camera cuts to the lights, goes out of focus, and bar a spot of happy clapping from the crowd, it's over.

There is silence in our living room, Mom and Dad are staring at the screen, seemingly bewitched.

Before my eyes their world has been rocked, and Bowie has done it. In three minutes, he has fucked with my parent's minds and I love him for it.

"Fuckin hell, what a bunch of fairies. How can the Beeb put that load of crap on?"

I know better than to enter into an argument, but the condemnation just reinforces my determination. If he hates it so much it must be GREAT. The knitting needles clack again and next up is 'The Sweet' singing 'Little Willy'. The rest of the programme is all downhill, with a really wank playout list, Glitter, Donny and Cassidy – vomit time.

***

At school, last night is top of the gossip pops. Opinions are divided. The school of thought amongst the 'Fat Phil' brigade is that Bowie and his band are 'right faggots', others are clearly excited, but are cowed into silence by the implications of 'queerness' for liking it – the kiss of death in a boy's school.

I keep my own counsel. Overnight I have resolved a new course for my life, they can all kiss my arse. I do what I want now, I'm someone they look up to since I sorted out Lowe.

Saturday can't come quickly enough, and early doors I get myself round to Alice's, having emptied the old piggy bank of my Kwik Save earnings. I am bubbling with excitement, babbling on about Bowie while she stands in the hallway, looking slightly askew at me.

"Blimey Danny, I've never seen you this excited about anything."

I sense a warning, and tone it down a bit.

Then it's off up town, and straight to the record shop, emerging with 'The Rise and Fall of Ziggy Stardust' clutched in my greasy donnies.

There he is on the cover, wearing the jumpsuit, looking so, so – outside of things - that's the only way to describe it. Has he come from outer space to lead us all to a better place? I could easily believe it. It's almost impossible to believe he's human, having a childhood in some English suburbia with old- fashioned normal parents. He surely must have arrived fully formed, a gaudy creature from another world.

On the back cover he's posing in a phone box, bare chest on show, the suit unzipped to the waist, giving it the queerest 'come on' I've ever seen. It's all so fascinating, so different.

We cut short our trip because I can't wait to play it. All the way home on the bus I've got the inner sleeve out, devouring the lyrics, then its straight up to Alice's room where we lay on the bed listening to it for the first time. I will never forget this moment, my beautiful girl, head on my chest, and the wonderful music.

***

Alice:

I don't know what to think, whether to be pleased or upset. Danny appeared at my door beside himself with excitement – I've never seen him so animated, and over what? David Bowie, that's what. Everyone's talking about it of course. A lot hated it, or were simply left cold, but others can talk of nothing else, as if they had seen some big secret revealed, and it seems that Danny is one of them.

I saw 'Top Of The Pops' of course, and yes it did make an impact and was something new, but I thought it was all a bit staged and theatrical. Apart from Bowie, the band all looked a bit embarrassed poncing about like that on the TV, although I have to admit that he does have something very special. Difficult to encapsulate it in words, he is eerily beautiful and seems to be neither male nor female, just some creature from elsewhere, not human. 'Starman' is about an alien 'God' who has come to lead kids to a better place, and Bowie is playing on this, although it leaves me a bit cold. Can't deny that he has something unique though.

I'd already heard of him, I remember 'Space Oddity' and actually bought and liked 'Hunky Dory', but had stopped playing it, hadn't thought to let Danny hear it. Nice songs, but they didn't really match the person exploding onto the screen last Thursday.

Danny has gone for him in a big way. I feel a bit jealous. He's never seemed that excited with me, even when we have it off, even the first time. I bet he doesn't go on endlessly to his mates about how wonderful I am either.

On the other hand, Danny is truly alive now, and I can claim credit for that. It's what I wanted isn't it? I just wonder yet again what I've released and whether it's beyond my control. I'm just going to have to ride out this storm.

'Ziggy Stardust' is pretty good, but it doesn't connect with me like it does with Danny. He's obsessed, trying to work out hidden meanings in the songs. He's learnt every word, and can, and does, recite chunks like poetry. He's even done extra evenings at work so he can buy more records. I've given him my 'Hunky Dory'; at least he might think of me when he plays it. I've signed the sleeve, with plenty of hearts of course

I know what's coming next, we'll be off to see 'Ziggy Stardust' somewhere. Still, it'll be fun, I'll be with Danny, and something exciting is happening.

***

Danny:

I spend the next few weeks devouring everything Bowie. I've got plenty of catching up to do. I play 'Ziggy' over and over again until I know every note, every inflection of his voice, every word. I pore over the cover, seeking its hidden secrets, and find none, unless the sign 'K West' is code for 'quest', but a quest for what, it's all so obscure. The less I understand, the more I want to find out.

Alice has given me her copy of 'Hunky Dory', and I've bought another LP, 'Space Oddity'. They are so different to 'Ziggy' and each other, but both great.

I can't understand where Bowie has been, why I've never heard of him before. It must be an adult plot to keep him away from us teenagers in case he corrupts us. They made a big mistake letting him on 'Top Of The Pops', and he made the most of it.

I want to be corrupted, yes please, anything instead of my life to date. Anything that's for me, for teenagers, about us - anything that upsets Dad. I'll grab it with both hands and worry about corruption later. Corruption looks like fun from where I am.

I'm not neglecting Alice. I see her all the time, and she seems to like Bowie too, so it's something to share rather than something to come between us. I can tell that she's not as bonkers about him as I am, but I think she will be, once we see him in the flesh.

That's the aim now. He's on tour and I can't believe I missed him at the Town Hall just a few months ago – and according to a review I read it was half full so I could have got in easily.

There's a rumour that he's playing in London soon, so I'm buying Sounds, NME and Melody Maker, and scouring them for ticket news. London and Bowie, what an adventure that would be. And sod whether my parents will try and stop me going - because they won't.

***

Alice:

Bowie, Bowie, Bowie, that's all I hear these days. Sometimes I think I'm second–best. But Danny is chasing a mirage and will never get closer than the front stalls of some concert hall. Bowie will be gone, fired into the heavens of stardom like some fantastically coloured rocket, never to return to earth, into the company of mere mortals like Danny and I.

And when that happens I'll still be here to fill the vacuum he leaves, and take back the place usurped by 'King Ziggy'.

First I am going on a journey, and I have to admit that I'm excited. We are going to see him, got stalls tickets, Danny queued all morning outside the record shop in Birmingham .It's in London and I'll be with Danny when he's in the presence of his hero for the first time. Plus, we'll have time to see some sights, I'm as excited about that. Always wanted to see London, all the history. I've cleared it with Mom and Dad, they approve of a bit of adventure. They've even bought our train tickets and given us money for taxis. I'm so lucky to have them. Poor Danny has had an awful fall out with his Dad, nearly came to blows, but nothing is going to stop him going, especially that horrible man.

***

David:

The day after the 'Top Of The Pops' broadcast, Bowie is preparing for a big concert at the Royal Festival Hall in London.

———

Stage One of the UK tour is drawing to a close. From modest beginnings it is reaching a crescendo. There is great excitement, as it is hoped that Lou Reed will appear at the Festival Hall and perform alongside Bowie.

The concert is a charity function in aid of 'Friends Of The Earth', compered by Kenny Everett, who introduces Bowie as 'the next biggest thing to God'. Lou Reed does make an appearance, and he and Bowie sing 'White Light, White Heat', 'Sweet Jane' and 'Waiting For The Man', together. But it is Bowie who leaves the stage triumphant.

The reviews are gushing. Melody Maker declares that Bowie has 'made it', and is now a 1972 'pop giant'. Record Mirror predicts that Bowie is destined to become the most important pop musician on either side of The Atlantic.

The following weekend, the first UK leg of the 'Ziggy Stardust' tour draws to a close at the place it started, The Friars Club in Aylesbury. Bowie receives a bloody nose in the crush of fans afterwards as he makes his way to his pink Rolls Royce. He has arrived, and has USA in his sights.

But at the moment of success, a small but significant change sets a minor, but disturbing, undercurrent running. The backing band are now called 'The Spiders', as in the 'Spiders From Mars', 'Ziggy Stardust's' backing band. David Bowie is shown as 'Ziggy' on promotional material. The line between the tragic but totally fake rock character and the real-life artist is already becoming blurred.

Bowie himself begins to 'be 'Ziggy Stardust' in real life, and the human being, David Jones, is submerged.

Chapter Five

'Ziggy Stardust'
August 1972

Danny:

I don't believe in God, but if I did, he would be 'Ziggy Stardust'. Being a fan is special. It's like being part of a religion, a cult I suppose.

You have to be brave to be a proper Bowie fan.

The more I see, hear and read, the more of Bowie I want. I am becoming obsessed, I know, but set against this year's dreariness of strikes, power cuts and my dad's antics, Bowie is a beacon, pointing to an escape to a much better place. I search out, soak up, every mention, every TV appearance. Bowie is becoming the centre of my world, and I'm feeling a bit guilty, shouldn't that be Alice? But she seems ok, and she's coming to see him with me.

You have to be brave to be a proper Bowie fan, and that's because it hasn't taken very long for the matter of his 'queerness' to surface. I had deliberately ignored the 'in your face' limp-wristed queening about, labelling it as a publicity stunt, and taking that stance when defending him. And defend him I have had to do, and myself, for bearing his standard at school. The consensus there is that he's as bent as a nine bob note, and so is anyone who likes him, which makes things kind of difficult for a fifteen-year-old in a boy's school.

Some of my hard-earned respect is trickling away, and of course 'Fat Phil' Lowe is taking every opportunity to cast doubts upon me. He's spotted a chink in my armour. He is circumspect alright, after his bloody nose, but all the same, there is a drip, drip of comments, and I know it's having an effect. He'll never forgive me for what I did, and I know I need to watch my back – which is a statement that he would find amusing in the circumstances.

I am tempted to go a step further, start changing my looks as a sign of my loyalty to Bowie, but at the moment the thought of what that would mean at home and school is holding me back. Which makes me feel like a coward again and I thought that I'd got past that by thumping Lowe.

I have to confess that a big part of the appeal is the androgyny, (a word I'd never heard before Bowie – which shows how he is already expanding my horizons). It's a 'V sign', to my dad and all of his generation, the prison wardens of my dull world.

I'm missing one album, it's becoming rare already and I just can't find it anywhere, but the pictures I've seen of him, in a 'man's dress' and sporting long, blonde, 'film star' hair, on the front of 'The Man Who Sold The World' LP, are gloriously shocking. I ignore the critical opinions, the sniping as to whether it is a genuine gesture of sexual ambivalence, or one-upmanship on Marc Bolan in the make-up and glitter stakes.

My room is plastered with images, some bought from the poster shop in the reliably trendy Oasis Market, others saved from magazines and music papers.

Bowie stares down at me when I'm in my room, which is most of the time. The posters are both alluring and disturbing. I'm pretty sure that I like girls, after all I've been with Alice for months, and I think I love her, but Bowie is strangely attractive to me, and exciting. The unusually delicate features, feminine to the eye, are in jarring contrast to the bulging crotch revealed by the skimpy, tight Japanese costumes that he wears. Sometimes I think about what's in there.

At night I lie in bed, reflecting as I always do on the day, tomorrow, and life in general, and sometimes a little voice in my head is nagging away, asking what it would be like to be with a man that way? I can't make it go away.

***

The defence of my hero's sexuality is profoundly shattered when I discover an old article, an interview published in Melody Maker in

January this year. As usual it is my nemesis at school who brings it to my attention, using it as ammunition in his latest skirmish.

I am outside one break time, smoking a Consulate behind the cricket pavilion, and Lowe is doing his usual routine - going on and on to his crowd of cronies about Bowie being 'a queer', and loudly asserting that I must be too, because I'm a 'pretty boy'.

It's beginning to get to me. Combined with those sneaky little thoughts in bed at night, I'm beginning to wonder. Does he see something in me? Do others? No, I decide that he is just being, as usual, a nasty thick twat.

Anyway, here I am yet again defending David's honour, when he says,

"Call yourself a fan, don't you know, he's a fucking bender, it's been in Melody Maker, him confessing he likes a bit of cock."

I laugh it off, ask him to produce the evidence, and he can't, but the taunt sticks in my mind. Phil isn't clever enough to make something like that up.

***

Saturday afternoon a couple of weeks later, and I'm doing my usual drift around town with Alice.

I spot a pile of back copies of Melody Maker for sale in a corner of Reddington's Rare Records. I ruffle through the stack, see a photo of Bowie on the front of the January issue; if it's got Bowie in it I buy it. A few New Pence later and I've secured my prize.

***

Alice:

I can't put my finger on it, but there is something not quite right between us. It's a feeling that's been growing since he has been so fixated on Bowie. It's so minor that I tell myself that I'm imagining it, and we seem as happy together as ever, see each other as often, but there's a change.

***

Danny:

I kiss Alice goodbye at the bus stop then hurry home. I go straight to my room for some privacy. Dad isn't happy about the posters and my adoration of a 'poofta', so it's best to avoid any more confrontations.

There is definitely trouble brewing, but the more it riles him, the more I want to pursue it, and I'm afraid I make no secret of the fact – just to wind him up. I wonder why it's so important to me, when I can foresee how this will end?

The headline of the piece is 'Oh You Pretty Thing'. I devour the article, reading and re-reading every word, searching for the truth of what David himself said, unscrambling the words, seeking meaning, my heart sinking at first, then coming to terms with what I read.

The photos are of David looking beautiful, in one of his 'Ziggy' outfits, one posed to reveal a totally smooth and definitely 'unmanly' chest, the other with his head coyly cupped in a very limp-wristed hand, hair blow-dried to perfection. The pictures scream 'queer'.

My stout championing at school crumbles as I read. They are *his* words. If David believes these things, then as a true fan there is nothing for it but to embrace them. And then I am happy, isn't this why I love him? He is extraordinary, strange, brave, challenging and rebellious.

The article confirms that the two most pig-ignorant people in my life, Phil and Dad, are right, although the question of 'bisexual' versus 'queer' I put aside for further consideration. To be fair, up until now, I haven't had to think much about 'queers', or types of 'queerness'; it's a new and forbidden world to me, one that isn't allowed in my house. And that gives it an allure.

There it is, in black and white, David says that he is gay and *always has been*, even when he was David Jones. But I know that he married Angie and has a son, Zowie. How can that be? More food for thought.

I read on. It seems that he is a 'queer' idol, and lots of them flocked to a recent gig featured in the article, where he brandished a large velvet hat in a very camp manner. All of this has passed me by, or more truthfully, I have tried my best to ignore it, so I don't have to deal with its attraction to me, and what that means.

What a mystery he is! Both male and female – so beautiful, a bright star in the greyness, alien, colourful - and the music and lyrics are like nothing I have heard before. He dominates my thoughts, disturbing, not in a nasty way, but fascinating and intriguing. Bowie is a secret in himself, he allows nobody to get close. It's hard to see the line between 'Ziggy Stardust', David Bowie, and David Jones. I'm not sure that matters much anyway.

***

Alice:

I go up town as usual with Danny. It's a lovely sunny day, and all the kids are dressed to the nines in the latest fashions, tottering around on platform shoes and boots, flares flapping in the breeze. It is a bit of a tradition on Saturdays to go and meet friends, do a bit of shopping and show off how fashionable you are by strutting around town giving it large.

Today starts the same as usual, but ends on a strange note. The old paper he brandishes – Melody Maker I think, has got Bowie's picture on the front, why else would he buy it? He must have flicked through it because I notice an immediate impact, he suddenly can't wait to get home and read the bloody thing. What can be so important about an old article? And he doesn't show it to me, which is odd – in fact he's downright shifty about it, and dismisses my questions with a shrug.

At the time I barely notice what he has bought as I'm focused upon leafing through the racks of records. You miss the important stuff because it seems so trivial at the time.

So off he goes, treasure in hand, and straight away when he calls round later and we go to The Bull there's an undercurrent. I'm very switched on to his moods. I guess I'm a bit more sensitive about his other 'love' than I should be, I'm watching for anything different. And this is different.

He is odd tonight, reserved and quiet. We sit in an alcove in the pub, he's got a Brown and Mild and I'm stirring my Babycham with the cherry on the stick when I broach the subject.

"What's wrong?" I ask

"Nothing," he replies. He never says that. It's dismissive. I don't like it.

" Have I done something?"

"Course not." He gives me a hug, which reassures me a little.

"You seem quiet tonight, thoughtful"

"No, I'm ok, just something at home, nothing to worry about."

I sense a lie, and test the water.

"Was your Melody Maker article good?"

There is a reaction, fleeting, and I can't quite work out what emotion is registering before it vanishes.

"Yeah, fine, just stuff about Bowie you know."

"What stuff?"

"Just the usual, music, clothes, usual bollocks."

"You seemed very keen to get home and read it though?"

This time I see irritation.

"Give it a rest, what's this, the Spanish bloody Inquisition. It was just an article." He takes a large swig of beer and changes the subject.

I'm shocked. It's hardly a blazing row, but it's the first time we have ever had anything close to a cross word. The first time he's ever been secretive with me. I decide to let it rest. No doubt it will surface in time. I start prattling on about some TV programme and the moment passes, but won't be forgotten. I just hope it's nothing.

***

Danny:

I'm so excited. 'Ziggy Stardust'! Today, I'm actually going to see him in the flesh. I've been counting down for weeks since I got the tickets. It's the first night of the next stage of his UK tour, at the Rainbow Theatre in London. He's got Roxy Music as support

———

act. It's rumoured in the music press that he's planning something special – and I'll be there to see it happen.

I'm so glad that Alice will be there at the moment when I see him for the first time. We will get near the front as we've got stalls tickets.

***

David:

Bowie spends several days rehearsing for his sell-out concerts at the Rainbow. He has new ideas for the show – revolutionary ideas. He has seen the rock theatre of 'Alice Cooper' and wants to outdo it. His friend, the mime artist Lindsay Kemp, is drafted in to help design and choreograph the new, improved, 'Ziggy Stardust Show'.

***

Danny:

I'm actually going to London! I'm awake at first light and the dawn chorus is loud through the window, not a sound that I'm used to hearing. I'm not tired though, in fact I feel full of energy. I'm truly alive, first Alice, now Bowie. What a year! A year of awakening.

We get the bus into town and walk to New Street. For once the grey concrete monster that is the train station doesn't depress me, today it's the gateway to another world. Alice is excited too, chattering away about sights she wants to see. She's got sandwiches, Penguin bars, crisps and pop, all courtesy of her mom. What a contrast to mine. They were still in bed when I left, not a word of goodbye, and no snacks made with love. It suits me, I think that this is the first step towards leaving them behind. They tried to stop me, then sulked when I made it plain that whatever they said, I was going. Yesterday evening there was cold disapproval, couldn't find it in themselves to say a word to me. He's been very strange about this trip. It's almost as if he can't decide whether it's a sign that I'm turning into something he can approve of, or the beginning of an expected decline. I suspect that his indecision is the reason I'm going without suffering any more ructions. Mom won't dare say anything until she knows what he thinks.

I went out for a walk before I exploded, didn't want to give him any excuse to ground me. It wasn't the time to provoke him into a decision.

I could have gone around to Alice's but I had some time alone thinking to do. I wandered and wondered, what does life have in store for me?

It's late morning by the time we arrive at Euston, which is about as welcoming as New Street. Alice has a plan, has worked out routes on the Underground. I fight down an ungrateful flicker of anger at being organised, and acquiesce to her tourist schedule.

We trudge across Parliament Square, visit Westminster Abbey and continue past Downing Street. The sights leave me cold. They are just buildings. Parts of a world that I don't belong in. They are dead, and the people in them are as dead to me as the bodies interred in the Abbey. They mean nothing to me, to my life.

But Alice is enthralled, giving me the benefit of a running historical commentary, which she has obviously spent time researching. I humour her.

By the time we have taken in St Paul's and its vertigo-inducing dome I have had enough. I sit down on the steps of the Cathedral and stretch my tired legs out. It is mid-afternoon and the day is fast disappearing into a whirl of boring edifices and their lifeless contents.

"That's it. I can't take another historical sight."

I catch surprise and something else – hurt, disappointment, in her face, then it's gone and her smile lights up.

"I was hoping to take in the National and the Tate, but I think I've cocked up on the planning, taken a lot longer than I thought."

That decided me. "No art galleries, I'll die for sure. There's nothing to stop us coming back another time."

There is a silence. I can almost hear her thoughts churning. Then she gives in.

"What do want to do then?"

I check my watch. "It starts at 7.30, so we've got a few hours left, minus the time to get there. I need something to eat and drink, but more than that I want to try and find the bits of London that are alive. This can't be all there is, it's supposed to be the centre of the bloody fashion and music world. A wacky idea strikes me.

"I know, we'll go and try to find where the cover for 'Ziggy' was shot. It's called Heddon Street, near to Carnaby Street, even if we don't find it, it's got to be livelier than here."

I have absolutely no idea where it is, but I must sound convincing. She rummages in her pockets and produces a dog-eared A-Z of London.

"Here, this is Dad's, it's a bit old but it'll be on here somewhere."

Off we go on a more fitting quest for the day - walking in Bowie's footsteps! Suddenly my legs have energy again and it is Alice dragging behind.

***

Alice:

The day of the concert begins perfectly. Danny looks great in flares, cheesecloth and Wrangler bomber jacket. He's remembered not to wear those platform boots and has got his monkey boots on. He says they are a hangover from a flirtation with skinhead and suedehead fashion; crombies, two-tone trousers and Brutus check shirts. Thankfully, the boots are the only survivors, and he can at least walk a long way in them.

I've got on my flares with the patterned inserts, comfortable cowboy boots with Cuban Heels, a white blouse with a huge collar, a tank top jumper and a pink satin jacket that I got last week from Chelsea Girl.

Recently, all he's talked about is seeing 'Ziggy', but we'll have about hours to kill before then, so I've made plans to fill our time seeing as much of London as we can. Danny's shown no interest at all, which has irritated me a bit. He seems preoccupied, his life full of Bowie. Will there be any space left for me?

We slip into our normal, relaxed and comfortable relationship, as we journey down to London. We must look the picture of young love, full of excitement and chatter, hugs and kisses.

This lasts until the afternoon. I can sense that he's losing interest, dragging his heels and grunting when I tell him all the stuff I've found out. It annoys me because I'm loving it; the grandeur, the sights I've only ever seen on the TV or in film;, the feeling of being able to touch history. He's done nothing to help me plan the day, so he shouldn't sulk if it doesn't suit him.

When he flops down on the steps of St Paul's I ponder my choices – have a blazing row in the middle of London that could prove terminal to our relationship by pitting me against Bowie, or go along with him. There's no choice really, I love him and I need to manage this. I'm sure we will come through it. Everyone goes through their ups and downs.

We trek to Soho via Carnaby Street, and I have to admit that it's an exciting and vibrant place; shops full of the latest fashions; pubs and clubs; crowds of the hippest people; it feels like the centre of the world.

The worst bit is the one that excites Danny most. We finally track down Heddon Street after going around in circles, and what's there? Nothing.

Danny makes me take his photo under the 'K West' sign, and in the phone box at the end of the street, the one used on the LP cover, but it feels embarrassing to me. I don't understand how someone with a brain like Danny can be so excited about following around someone he's never met? Where does it end?

I dutifully put up with the nonsense, but it doesn't fill me with good feelings about what is going to happen later on when he's actually in the presence of 'Mr. Wonderful'.

***

Danny:

Job done. Alice was golden, following me around until we found the place and even taking pictures of me posing like Bowie. What a great afternoon! London got under my skin this afternoon.

———

It's alive and, having had a taste, I want more. I'm already hating the thought of going back to home and school life. I'm getting past that shit.

We get something to eat in a coffee house in Soho and soak up the atmosphere, then it's finally time.

As soon as we get on the Tube to Finsbury Park I start to see the 'Ziggy' fans. There are blokes wearing make-up. I'm beginning to feel as if I'm not properly dressed, not a true fan. Something else to think about, although I'm not underestimating what the effect of taking such a step would be, at home and at school. Especially at home, that wouldn't just be words.

We emerge from the station. A short walk and I see the Rainbow. It's on a corner, a white, blocky building with green inset decorative panels that even I recognise as art–deco. Once a cinema, I remember now that it was reopened as a rock venue last year and 'The Who' did the first concert here.

As we approach and join the queues to get in I see the signs for 'Ziggy' and a thrill runs through me. It's actually going to happen, he's going to be here, might already be inside, and I'm going to see him. He really exists. I'm in a daze, holding Alice's hand.

While we wait, I check out the people around us. The concert is sold out and there's a feeling of excitement, a buzz in the air. There are shrieks and shouts, groups of people singing snatches of Bowie songs, a constant hubbub of chatter and laughter. We are all here together, Bowie fans. It is a wonderful feeling to belong.

Then I catch a sight of him, the spiky haircut, a glimpse of a heavily made up profile and I start to get excited. I'm about to shout out but realise that he wouldn't be wandering around in the crowds on his own.

The figure turns around and with a thrill I realise that it's a fan made up as 'Ziggy', with the haircut, and everything. The image is only spoilt by the face, it's a jowly kid with none of the beauty of Bowie, in fact he's ugly. But to have the courage to do that, the devotion to Bowie to appear like that in public, impresses me, makes me question my own level of commitment.

***

Alice:

Danny is staring at the kid with the hair and the make-up. At first I almost laugh out loud because it's just some fat kid, looking stupid. But I see the impact on Danny.

The doors open and people shuffle forward, waving their tickets. As we enter the glitzy auditorium there are people handing out souvenir programmes with the 'Ziggy Stardust' LP cover in miniature on the front and back cover. I'm impressed – it's a nice touch to give something like that away. I open it and the inside is yellow with black writing. The heading is 'David Bowie at the Rainbow' leading into a line drawing of Bowie, guitar slung across his chest, arms and legs outstretched. Drawings of a radiating star, a rainbow, and the word 'Ziggy' adorn the space between his legs. There are other line drawings of the drummer, the guitarist, a woman in a long flowing dress, and a little bald man. The rest of the leaflet lists:

THE SPIDERS
Mick Ronson
Woody Woodmansey
Trevor Bolder
THE ASTRONETTES
Annie Stainer   Ian Oliver
Barbara Ellla   Carling Patton
Guest appearance of Lindsay Kemp

It's a clever gesture, and if the show to come is as slick, it will be something special. Danny is so taken with the leaflet that he hands his to me and goes around twice to get more.

We reach the stalls. We are early and at Danny's insistence we push towards the front, reaching a halt about twenty feet from the stage. It is all standing, and I resign myself to a lengthy wait in the crush.

The excitement builds steadily as the Rainbow fills up, and by the time the support acts come on, the place is hot and heaving. I've never heard of Lloyd Watson but he does a good acoustic set.

'Roxy Music' are really good. I think I like them more than Bowie, but I daren't say that to Danny – sacrilege! They sound really different and the synthesizer played by that strange 'Eno' bloke gives it another dimension. Not sure about the lead singer, he might be a bit false with his flat singing, his smooth act, but it does all add to the newness. Must get their LP.

Waiting for the main man, and Danny is fixated on the empty stage. There are chants of, 'We want 'Ziggy', and the tension builds.

***

Danny:

I have no words. I wait in the darkness. I have a queasy feeling in my stomach, almost a feeling of panic. What if he's a disappointment?

I hear music, music that I recognise. The theme from 'Clockwork Orange'. An organ plays some of Beethoven's Ninth from the same film. A guitar strums, and clouds of dry ice billow across the stage, the spotlights come on, and there he is. Hair blazing in the lights, a halo framing a china-white face. He's wearing a silver jump suit, which is gaping down to his navel, and silver boots.

He is singing "Lady Stardust', and an image of Marc Bolan appears on the screen behind him. He's taking the piss out of Bolan and I love it.

He stands in the spotlight, legs apart, hips gently swaying, a faint smile playing across his lips. He is beautiful. I feel overwhelmed with love for him.

Three dancers, 'The Astronettes' are wearing fishnet body stockings and David Bowie masks. They are doing some sort of mime whilst dancing, led by a heavily made up man. 'The Spiders From Mars' are in their sparkly 'Droog' jump suits. It's overwhelming.

The stage is covered in multiple levels of scaffolding, like a circus, with sawdust and ladders at either end, the screen off-centre to the left. The lights are amazing.

It's straight into 'Hang Onto Yourself' and everyone goes crazy, jumping around, bumping and jostling. Girls are screaming, looking like they are going to faint.

It's the anthem next, 'Ziggy Stardust', a magical moment, I'm almost within touching distance, surely this show is going to go down in history. It beats everything I've ever seen in my life before.

'Life on Mars' with everyone swaying and singing along, holding lighters in the air, then one I don't know very well, off 'Man Who Sold The World'. A dark and atmospheric number called 'The Supermen'.

The dancers are cavorting, the lights flashing, the band playing their hearts out, his voice really strong. Into 'Changes', and then Bowie dashes off stage whilst 'Woody' drums the opening beat of 'Five Years' for what seems like forever. Heavy breathing through a mike, and Bowie is up high on the scaffolding, a fresh costume on, he must have dashed up the ladders after changing.

He's wearing the 'woodland animal' Japanese jumpsuit, bare legs shapely, and shining in the lights. It's skimpy, and tight. He may as well be naked, and even from the stalls his physical presence, his sexuality can be felt.

He's so talented. He does an amazing mime routine. He seems to be feeling his way along an invisible wall with the palms of his hands. Suddenly he finds a narrow gap, pushes his fingers through with a huge amount of effort, and pushes the wall apart, like a lift door opening. Just when he seems about to get through, the invisible wall snaps shut again with him still on the other side of it.

After a rendition of 'Space Oddity', during which Bowie and Ronson make us all laugh, trying to do a spectacularly bad vocal improvisation of the synthesizer launch sequence in 'Space Oddity', it's 'Andy Warhol'. Then he speaks to us.

He tells us that the next song is 'My Death' by Jacques Brel, not the usual one he sings by him, 'Port of Amsterdam'. It's a very quiet, sombre number and we all stand in enraptured homage while he performs it.

The show goes on, and on. When he sings 'Starman', the lead mime appears on the scaffolding as 'The Starman', wearing a wig and a pair of wings, smoking a fag and leering at us. During the song Bowie breaks into 'Somewhere Over The Rainbow', which fits the chorus exactly.

'Queen Bitch', then 'Suffragette City' and we all go crazy, thrashing about like lunatics. It finishes with two songs by Lou Reed then it's all over bar the encore.

He stands at the front of the stage, smiling and exhausted. I'm so close that I can track the beads of sweat running down his face and legs, and see that the outfit is wringing wet. It's been going on for hours. He's exhausted and so are we. The performance of a lifetime. No false moves, nothing to indicate a human being is inside the outfit, behind the make-up; he seems divine.

Then he's speaking again, thanking the band, the dancers, the mime bloke who's called Lindsay Kemp, and is clearly as bent as they come, and us, he thanks us. It is a moment of communion. I'm sure he is looking right at me when he says it. We are alive to him, we are in his presence, we worship him, and he knows.

He introduces the encore as a 'number by 'Ziggy' – he is 'Ziggy Stardust' . It's 'Moonage Daydream', then it's all over and they are gone. There is a brief moment of darkness, the lights come up and the magic spell is broken.

Emptiness. I am happy and sad at the same time. I've seen him at last, but he's gone, leaving a vacuum that cannot be filled by anyone else. I need another fix already. The world is mundane and grey. I snatch a glance at Alice, squeeze her hand, but she is grey too.

Chapter Six

'Moonage Daydream'
August – September 1972

Danny:

Early on Sunday afternoon I wake and lie in bed re-living and digesting the previous day. It already seems unreal. Did I really go to London and was I within twenty feet of him? He will be playing there again tonight. Then he will be gone, to another crowd waiting to worship him.

That's how I feel - how I felt at the concert. I was *worshipping* 'Ziggy' last night, and that feeling, that belonging, meant everything. I must be true to him now.

He is a God to me, a Rock God, but more than that. He's better than the boring old Christian God of my parents, well my mom at least. That's all rubbish, spouted to keep people under control - stop them from really living.

That God has his Commandments and they just stop you doing what you really want to do, make you conform. I don't want to do that anymore. Plus, that God is cruel and uncaring, letting good people, even innocent kids, die, get hurt. Look at Biafra, all those kids dying, stick arms and legs, pot bellies and ribs sticking out, what type of God lets that go on?

My God is real, tangible. Now I've seen him, I know there is something more than human about him, something 'outside'. He cares about teenagers, wants us to enjoy ourselves, tells us we matter. He shows us new possibilities, new worlds there for the taking, and the fact that he shocks the older generation proves that he is the way to go. They are scared of him. They think that he is going to tear apart their stupid rules and I'm going to be part of that.

London too! Not the old buildings and history, can't see why Alice gets so excited about that. Once you've seen 'Big Ben', that's it, just a big clock. It doesn't add anything to life, doesn't change things for the better. In fact, those buildings, that history, is our repression. It's the underside of London that calls out to me. Soho; the cafes, pubs and clubs; the buzz of the place; the people, carefree and modern. That's what 'Ziggy' is all about, freedom.

Nothing seems to matter, other than being free to do what I want. I need to decide what that is. I can't think straight at the moment. But it can't happen here, living at home.

The bedroom door bursts open, crashing against the wall and bouncing back, smashing into my daydream. My reality.

"Get your arse out of bed, you lazy cunt."

He strips the covers from me, hurling them across the floor. He knows I am vulnerable at this moment. Just awake, unclothed. He looms over me and his fists are clenched. I can smell beer. He must have been to the pub. Something has happened to cause that, and it scares me.

"If you want to go dossing around with your queer friends till all hours you have to pay the price, so fucking get up."

He pulls me off the bed by an arm, wrenching my shoulder, and I land flat on my back, winded. I haven't seen him like this for years. He is capable of anything at this moment. I can't fight him, not now.

I curl up into a ball, an instinctive protective move. I am six again and he is the monster, worse than any under the bed. I can see Mom stood just inside the bedroom door. I send her a look of appeal but there's no reaction. There will be no help from her, never has been. He kicks me twice in the back then he grabs my throat and his face is inches from mine, the beery fumes filling my nose.

"You'd better fucking shape up. I'm warning you, no son of mine is going to act like a fucking poofta so think on. I'm gonna make a man of you. That starts with you getting out of your fucking pit at a decent time and doing something useful. I'm not having this, so think on." He slaps my face hard then he stands back. He regards me, curled up naked on the floor, with a look of sneering disdain.

"You're a fucking disgrace. No son of mine." He turns to Mom.

"What are you fucking gawping at woman? Get the fuck downstairs and sort the tea out or you'll get some too."

He turns back to me, must glimpse the hatred in my eyes. "Yeah, you'd like to wouldn't you? But you'll never be big or hard enough. And you'll never even try – you haven't got the balls for it." He gives me a parting dig with his foot and then he is gone, crashing down the stairs and yelling at Mom.

I lay there, filled with shame and loathing, for him, for myself, for my weakness. Perhaps this is a test. Achieving anything requires sacrifice. If I needed motivation to get a grip on life and find a way out of this prison, I've got it now. Should feel guilty about leaving Mom with him? She's never done anything to help me. I don't care what happens to her now. Although I do hate him enough to do something before I go. Would he see that as a good or bad thing? He'd probably be pleased in his warped mind, having a son that stood up to him.

Bowie is the gateway to a better place. He is pointing the way.

I'll have a couple of bruises from today, nothing more than I've had before. I pass the test. I'm on my own now, it's up to me. I'm not going to bow to that bastard anymore. Just need to decide what to do, when and how. I'm fifteen, at school and I've got a little job stacking shelves – hardly the basis for a new life. But I'm getting out, all I need to do is find a way.

And I've got Alice.

***

David:

The Rainbow gigs are a triumph. The reviews are gushing. They all agree. He is beautiful. He has great legs. The show is something new, 'rock - theatre'. The songs are fantastic, as is his voice. Undecided members of the audience are converted. He has arrived.

For Bowie, the plan is working, but he is fast 'becoming' 'Ziggy Stardust'. He eats his breakfast as 'Ziggy', dresses as 'Ziggy', talks as 'Ziggy'. David Jones is gone. He confesses that he can't remember what that person was like now. He has created a monster, that has made him the real star that 'Ziggy' is a parody of. One review asks 'What next?' It predicts the usual slide into drugs and sexual excess, or perhaps another 'Rock 'n' Roll Suicide'?

The first support act at the Rainbow, Lloyd Watson, blues singer and guitarist, goes on to work with 'Roxy Music' as a session musician and later takes part in a 'Roxy' offshoot band. He reveals that his guitar was stolen from the dressing room at The Rainbow and Bowie leant him his own acoustic instrument for the performance.

'Roxy Music' make their own debut on 'Top Of The Pops' with 'Virginia Plain'. There is some suggestion of bad feeling between them and the Bowie management at The Rainbow due to the latter's rigid control of promotional material and photography. But they too have made it, the stardust spreads.

***

Alice:

I awake exhausted. The train home was so slow, stopping at every tiny station. I managed to phone home from Euston, but Mom was still up waiting for me when I got home. No recriminations, no telling off, she was just worried, and then interested, pumping me for information over a cup of tea in the small hours of the morning. My parents are so great, I wonder how Danny's were about him being so late? I can guess.

The next evening, I review the previous day with mixed emotions. Exciting, new, interesting. The show was fantastic. I am glad I was there with Danny, in his moment of pure joy, seeing his hero. He was so happy.

But there is shadow. I have a feeling that he has moved a step further away from me. We should be closer after sharing the day. It started so well, but in the end I know that for Danny, Bowie blew away everything else, including being with me.

He was tired on the way home, we both were, dozing on the train, but he hardly said a word. I expected him to be full of chatter and excitement, but he was thoughtful, brooding.

I don't know what else I can do, other than carry on being there for him. I'm worried. I don't know what's going to happen next, but I know something is.

Danny's, life on the margins is coming to an end. Partly my fault, and I still think awakening him was the right thing to have done, but I never bargained for a pop star getting into his head, and then between us. That's how I feel, there is another person in this relationship, and I think he is winning. How can I compete with that? I find myself crying a little and I don't know why.

***

Danny:

At school I am once more the centre of attention, having to tell the story of my big adventure on Saturday several times. Going to London with a pretty girl, seeing Bowie in the flesh, I can see the envy in their eyes.

I am now *the* Bowie fan at school, but it's not enough. I need to show more outward loyalty. There is an obvious way to do that, but it will cause uproar.

I mull it over for a few days. On Thursday evening I run it past Derek while we stack shelves. He looks at me, and I think for a moment that I've upset him somehow, but I'm totally wrong.

"If you think it's the right thing to do, and you can take the hassle, then do it. Don't know if I'd have the guts, but I admire you for being true to yourself mate."

Filled with purpose, the next day when we go out, I finally summon up the resolve to speak to Alice about it. I don't know why I've been hesitant discussing it with her, she's my soul-mate after all. Perhaps I can sense that she isn't as keen as I am on Bowie, that he's a potential problem between us I persuade myself that I'm being daft.

I tell her about my Dad beating me up, and about my idea. She is appalled about what he did, and hugs me as I'm talking, but about the other thing she seems lukewarm.

"Do you think I'll look stupid or something?" I say.

It takes her a second too long to answer. " No, it's not that. I'm just worried."

I don't expect that answer at all. "Worried, what about?" I feel another one of those moments of truth looming, this year's been jam-packed with them so far.

She hesitates. "Well for one thing, I think you're going to open up a world of hurt, especially at home, but also at school. What will the teachers think, and how about your mates?"

"Stuff the teachers, and my friends, such as they are, know. I've got you and that's all that matters. Anyway, I think they'll see it as fashion, rebellion, nothing more. Some of them look to me to set a lead now."

She looks doubtful. "And have you got me?"

"What do you mean?"

"Well, you seem different, a bit distant." I see tears in her eyes. "Don't you love me anymore?"

The words come easily. "Course I do, why would you say that?'

She takes a gulp of Rum and Black. "Well, it seemed like you were fed up with me in London, and then all you could talk about was David bloody Bowie."

She *is* jealous of him. I try to pretend that it's laughable, but I can't. There are two important people in my life now, and I want nothing to do with choosing between them. I'm actually a bit resentful. Why is she picking at this sore and pushing me into a place I don't want to be? I honestly don't know what I really think.

I need to buy time. I definitely don't want to split with her, hurt her, but so much has happened, I'm confused and uncertain.

"I was just excited at seeing him, you know how much I like him."

"More than me." It is a statement, not a question.

82

"No, just a different type of like."

"If I didn't know better I'd almost think you fancied him."

That touches a nerve. This is getting too deep, too fast and I can't cope with it right now. The truth is that I haven't a clue what I really think, I'm just following a compulsion that I seem unable to resist. I laugh it off. It sounds unconvincing, hollow to my ears, but it's the best I can do.

"Don't be daft. I want to be with you don't I? Here I am and I'm asking your advice."

I can see that she's unconvinced, see the cogs turning, but she pulls back from probing further, a decision for which, at this moment, I truly love her. She is just so good, perhaps too good for me.

"Ok, but you'd better have a good think before you do it. It's not school that worries me so much, it's your Dad, he'll go crazy won't he? "

I admire her skill at getting straight to my vulnerability.

" Probably, but I'm not a kid any longer. I need to start standing up to him. He can't do much more to me than he's already done. And if he does, then I'll leave."

"But how can you do that? Where would you go, what would you do for money, what about your exams?"

Bang, bang, bang she hits the bullseye every time. I have no answers.

"I'll think of something, or something will turn up." I say weakly. Then I say something stupid. "Perhaps I'll just kill him when he's asleep."

Her lips thin, I know what that means. I desperately try and recover the position.

"I'm joking. Look I'll just do the hair, that's not a big deal, he'll probably be OK, he's always telling me to get it chopped off. The other I can do at yours when we go out then get rid before I go home. But without you I can't, because I don't know what I'm doing with it. Will you help me?"

There is silence and I can see her agonizing over her response. I feel pretty shitty and selfish putting her in this position but I need to do this thing. Eventually she sighs.

"I don't really want to Danny, but I will, for you."

I give her a hug and we snog a bit. The tense moment passes and we resume our normal chatter. Triumph and guilt swirl about within me, but in the end I don't care. I want this and that's that.

***

Alice:

On Friday night I get a good look into the abyss that would be a break up with Danny. We are sat in the back room at The Horseshoes on the Stratford Road after a Number Eleven bus journey to Hall Green. It's a new find, another pub we can get into without any trouble. It's always packed in the back lounge and it's easy to remain out of sight from the bar.

The instant that we sit down I know that he has something on his mind. At least he asks for my opinion, that's something I suppose.

I'm not really surprised about the subject matter - I expected a reaction to him seeing the person I'm beginning to think of as his true love, for the first time. He is besotted. I tell myself that it's just hero worship, but the little voice inside nags away. This is past a joke.

I consider digging my heels in, but pull back from taking the plunge. Any resolve I had evaporates when he tells me about getting a beating off his dad. It's understandable that he would react to his upbringing with total rebellion against that man. And along comes David Bowie, who embodies everything his Dad hates. I can see the attraction.

I can also see emotions and confusion boiling around. It isn't the moment for confrontation. I'm frightened that I might win the argument, and lose him at the same time. I'm scared of what might happen to him if he continues down this path. He might need me. When he talks about leaving home, killing his Dad, I see a different Danny. I start to wonder where I fit in.

This is all getting so difficult. I can't see a clear path through the complexities. I'm fifteen, I don't have the knowledge of life. I thought that it was supposed to be boy meets girl, they fall in love, and that happy ever after was possible, but that seems to only be in fairytales.

How do you factor in a shy boy finding himself, an obsession with someone who's not even there, and a family life I can't even begin to comprehend?

I feel trapped. I love him and I don't want to lose him, but I don't want to let him walk all over me either. I'm beginning to think that I don't really know him at all. The worst would be if he's like his Dad, and it's beginning to surface now he's got more confidence. I don't understand what's going on in his head. And I've got nobody to talk to about it. I can't even begin to put my fears into words. My friends would be no help. They are still into 'Jackie' magazine love stories. I want to speak to Mom, but would she understand, would it lead to disapproval of him and an end to the relationship? I can't think straight. In the end I avoid the argument. He did say he loves me still, and I'll have to be content with that – for now.

I say I'll help him, despite my misgivings. I tell him that I'm worried about the reactions he will get, especially at home, which is true, but way down in the depths of my fear is something I'm not ready to contemplate.

There is one amusing thing in all this, which demonstrates that he still has no real idea about himself. He asks me if I think he'll look stupid. But he won't, he'll look wonderful, and that gives me a feeling of impending doom.

***

Danny:

I manage to get some extra evening shifts and put the money away ready. I've started making some plans but to do anything I need money.

I've got some wild ideas about leaving home, perhaps go to London, but more lucid moments tell me what a hopeless dream it is,

I can never afford that. I think about asking Alice to come with me, with two incomes we might be able to do something, but sanity prevails - she isn't going to do it, her life, in contrast to mine, is nearly perfect, her future mapped out.

Why would she want to throw all that away? She says that she loves me, and I think that she truly believes that she does, but it would be unfair to use that love to force her to choose between a hand to mouth life with me, or her assured future here. I can't take on any more guilt.

London proved that we are different, she found no thrill in Soho and living on the edge, but I'm finding it increasingly difficult to resist that siren call. I do the extra shifts, and hide the cash. Money can buy freedom, so I may as well save some. At least that way I can feel that I'm doing something, making a start.

The week seems to drag, as if my old life is clinging doggedly onto me. I read in Melody Maker that Bowie is going to America on tour soon. America may as well be the Moon. I panic, I need another fix, to see him again before he goes. But this time it'll be me the others in the crowd will be looking at.

The last show before America is at the 'Top Rank' in Hanley, near Stoke, on September 7th, after that he's gone until nearly Christmas. I must be there, and it's close enough to Birmingham. I get two tickets after queuing outside the record shop in town again. Had to get there really early to guarantee getting tickets- something worth getting up off my lazy arse for, Dad?

Alice refuses to go because it's on a Thursday and I can't persuade her to wag it off school. I've already gone further than she ever will in rebelling, and I started really late. I ask Derek, and he says yes - even offers to pay me for the ticket. He is really pleased and excited to be going.

I meet Alice on the big day and we go into town as usual. There's a frosty atmosphere, and I know it's because of Bowie. I've got an appointment at two o clock and I've been really careful to choose the right place, even rang them up to check they could do it properly.

Alice announces that she's going shopping while I have it done. Then it's the moment of truth and I'm sat in the chair. It's a young guy called Luke doing me, very pleasant and chatty. When I show him the picture out of Melody Maker he laughs and says that he's wanted to do one of these for weeks but that I'm the first. He says he's glad it's me because I've got the right type and length of hair and it'll suit my face. He asks me if I want it dyed red too, but I've thought about that and say 'no'; that would be too much too soon, and I'd promised Alice that I wouldn't push my luck.

As Luke works away I watch every cut in the mirror. A new me gradually emerges from the mass of long, lank locks. My hair isn't lifeless anymore, it springs and spikes, drinking in energy from the scissors.

He is chattering away, pausing every now and then to admire his work. He is a Bowie fan too, but I it dawns on me that it's not just the music he likes. He turns the conversation in a different direction, asking me what I think about Bowie's self-confessed bisexuality. He is looking into my eyes in the mirror, assessing my response.

My response comes from the heart. Something about Luke encourages me to say that I admire Bowie's courage, don't see his sexual choices as a problem, quite the contrary. He asks me if I find Bowie attractive. I've never been able to talk about what is going on in my head to Alice, and it feels like a release to confess to him my unresolved thoughts, my confusion and uncertainty.

As we speak, his touch becomes gentler, and a sensuality permeates his strokes of my hair. Suddenly he is standing very near whilst he cuts, the front of his body close, then touching my side. It's lucky that I've got the barber's cover over me as I can't prevent myself getting hard. Bloody Hell! I can't control my own body now, what is happening to me?

"Perhaps you're bi too," he whispers.

It's in my body's reaction to his touch. Perhaps I am. I say nothing, but I don't pull away. I sample the moment, the feeling.

He laughs. "But you're not sure yet. That's ok, it can be a difficult time, being young, experimenting, confused. Went through the same thing myself a few years ago. I'm settled in my mind now – I know what I like." He caresses my hair again.

He stands back to check out the finished article and I can't help but notice the bulge in his jeans. "Well hello gorgeous," he says. "You are going to cause a stir."

I look at the image in the mirror and I'm stunned. It is another person. The 'Bowie Cut' frames a face, hitherto hidden, that I don't recognise. It looks good, not a parody like the fat kid outside the Rainbow. I'm probably deceiving myself, but it seems I am beautiful too, and I look a lot like him now.

Out of the corner of my eye I can see the street outside through the window. I can see Alice approaching.

"Here comes my girlfriend."

He turns and looks, "She's very pretty. Lucky old you."

I stand and pay him. As he gives me my change he presses a piece of paper into my hand.

"That's my phone number, I've got a flat in Harborne. If you ever need a chat to help work things out, give me a call. We could meet for a drink or something. No pressure at all, just talk if you want to, everything at your pace."

A final whisper as she enters the shop. "What's your name, just in case you call, so I know it's you."

I tell him.

Chapter Seven

'Star'
September 1972

Alice:

At least he doesn't get it dyed red. He is really strange again when I get back to the hair stylists, almost furtive and guilty. I put it down to him not wanting to be seen in a woman's salon. Once we get outside he's pleased as punch.

My worst fears are realised, it looks brilliant. His hair is just like Bowie's, straight and spiky, and his beautiful face is now on full display. The stylist, who is clearly a complete poofta, can't take his eyes off Danny, but Danny doesn't notice.

He even looks a bit like Bowie, the same high cheekbones and long thin face, but Danny has fuller lips, a more snub nose and no wonky eye. Every girl is going to notice him now, and every queer is going to fancy his chances. Danny doesn't know what's coming, and I haven't a clue how he's going to react. Just a few weeks ago I would have trusted him completely, but this new Danny? Not sure.

And I've promised to help him with his make up too. I need my head examining.

***

David:

Bowie's challenge to straight-laced British society continues. On the 1st of September the single, 'John I'm Only Dancing', is released. It is about a bisexual man telling his male lover that he is just dancing with a girl and has no sexual intent. Bowie calls it a 'bisexual anthem'. The BBC doesn't seem to catch on and plays it anyway. The single spends ten weeks in the 'Top Forty', peaking at number 12.

On 2nd and 3rd of September, Bowie plays two sell-out concerts at Manchester's brand new 'Hardrock' venue. Stardom, in Britain at least, has well and truly arrived. A thousand ticketless fans are turned away. The show features a revolving stage and 'quadrophonic' sound. Lindsay Kemp and his dance troupe have been quietly dropped after the Rainbow concerts, as manager Tony Defries feels they detract from the stage presence and impact of his star.

The September concerts are shortened affairs, lasting an hour, the dates hurriedly added in order to capitalise upon the wave of success generated by the Rainbow concerts, and to provide a warm up for America.

Bowie's management company, 'Mainman', controlled by Defries, sets up shop at 240 East 58th Street in New York in preparation for the USA Tour.

This is the biggest challenge he has ever faced. Can his creation 'Ziggy Stardust' succeed in the United States, graveyard of many an aspiring British rock star? He has Britain in thrall, but how will the God-fearing American 'bible belt' react to his camp persona?

Mainman have a tactic for the tour. They will fund and promote Bowie and his entourage as if he is already a fully-fledged international rock star. The best hotels, flash cars, no expense spared, including food, drink and drugs. The promotion of an instant 'star' was the foundation of success in Britain and they hope that the same ploy will work again.

It will cost a fortune, and Bowie is unaware that he will be footing the bill from the tour profits. He thinks that the money is coming from RCA records. It is a seed of future discord, and begins to germinate from the moment of his arrival by transatlantic ship in New York on 22nd September. But Bowie's attention is elsewhere. He is overwhelmed by the avalanche of sights and experiences that surround him from the moment he alights onto the dock in Manhattan.

He is only the second British act to arrive in America as a headliner, the first was 'The Beatles', but Bowie has had little exposure in the USA. It is a huge and expensive gamble. Bowie has to perform at his best. The pressure is on.

***

Danny:

When I return home from the stylists, Dad is fixated on the Olympics. He is sport-mad anyway, but seems to have taken an extra interest in the gymnasts, especially that Olga Korbut. Worrying; but there are no young girls in this house and I keep Alice away from him - and here. It's another change, for the worse, and he's definitely started drinking again. It will get out of control, and that makes me think that I'm running out of time before a bad situation cracks off.

I still haven't got a scoobie how to escape from here. The invisible ties holding me down seem tighter than ever. It goes around and around in my mind like a chant, nowhere to go, not enough money to pay for anything, no chance of a job. London calls but how could that ever happen? And then there is Alice. Why am I beginning to think of her as part of the problem – a tie? She is so perfect and has done so much for me.

When, the next morning Dad eventually takes some notice of me, it goes as I hoped. He is late for work - which is good, but I can see a hint of bleariness in his eyes which is bad, drinking late last night then. I can smell it on him, stale. He takes a long hard look and I can see him assessing what my new look means, but he doesn't really know the context or what it could stand for.

"Got your fucking hair cut at last I see - good. Looks a bit poncy, but at least you can tell you're not a girl now."

"Just got fed up with it long, too much hassle."

" Yeah well, perhaps you're finally growing up, perhaps not, we'll see, won't we? But I'm keeping an eye on you."

Mom just toes the line and makes no comment.

Mental note to make sure I get all the make-up off before I go home, every time.

School is both bad and good. Opinions are split almost evenly, but it is the quiet ones that tend to be supportive and admiring and the loudmouths who take the piss, led of course by Lowe.

He hasn't dared as yet to confront me face to face, but I know what he's saying behind my back. I'm a *'homo'*, a *'bum bandit'*. I can feel it's gaining currency, acceptance. Lowe is beginning to claw back some of his supporters whilst my hard-won power base is starting to ebb away – not to him in the main, but to some neutral 'wait and see what Danny does next', stance. It is all entertainment after all.

The incident with Luke has caused real self-doubt. I can't get him out of my mind. They might be right about me. I deflect the issue and buy time by acting tough at school, exactly the opposite of the way I think a queer would behave.

I'm ashamed though, where is my resolve? I have shown weakness and opted for an easy life. They want a leader, a rebel, so I start behaving like one. I cheek the teachers, smoke at break time, start pushing my luck with what I wear at school, become disruptive.

It is easy to do, quite addictive, and works. Lowe retreats into the shadows, his sneaky whisperings nullified. Being a leader at a boy's school means being tough and macho, and everybody knows that I'm with Alice, which blows away any doubts about my masculinity. I don't think the concept of bisexuality has penetrated the consciousness of kids at school. They have enough trouble grappling with the mystery of girls and how to get their leg over. If any do have other thoughts, they keep them well hidden.

As fast as I am learning to enjoy playing the rebel, my interest in studying is waning and the teachers are beginning to pick up on what is going on. I guess they've seen it all before, some kid stretching his wings. I think that I may be the topic of discussion in the staff room. There may be more hassle from that direction soon. They are bound to try and crack down on me at some stage.

When I go out with Alice it is still good, about the only time I feel alive, and really me. I also get on with her mom especially well. Her Dad is often out at university functions and tutorials when I'm there, so she sees the most of me. She is everything my own mother isn't, and it is almost unbearable, what might have been. She is so supportive of teenagers being themselves, standing on their own two feet, living their own lives, forming their own views and culture. She talks about the Sixties and the power of the young to change the world.

She helps with the makeup too! Alice does it, but I feel her heart isn't really in it. Not that it matters, I'm learning fast, eyeliner, lip gloss, eyeshadow and foundation - soon I'll be able to do it without any help. So far I've only worn it a couple of times on a Friday and Saturday night when we went out together, but it feels really good, and I know it looks good from the stares I get, from both boys and girls. Nine months on from nobody looking at me, now everybody is. I wonder what would happen if I didn't have Alice with me?

The pain is the half an hour getting it all off afterwards which means either going back to Alice's early or a walk home late at night after the last bus, and getting home even later. Which doesn't go down well at all.

***

Danny:

Just a few days to go. I can't wait, but there's been upset. Alice was distant last weekend, we argued again. She doesn't like me wagging school, seeing Bowie again, or going with Derek.

It's as if she thinks she owns me and can control me. I've got enough of that at home, thanks very much, I don't need it from someone who's supposed to be on my side. A lot of what she says makes sense, and is difficult to argue against, which makes me angrier. Sometimes it seems she thinks I owe her somehow, although she's never actually said that.

In her cosy little family, everything is nice and easy, and safe. There's no conflict, she has no wish, or need, to get out. Her life is progressing along its well-defined route. She has no real idea what my life is like; she thinks she does; and I can't help feeling resentment at her lovely existence; her attempts at interfering in mine.

Something is building. I'm unhappy and unsure about so many things. I'm resolved that I'm going to see Bowie before he leaves for America, nothing is going to stop me. And I'm going in full 'Ziggy'.

Thursday 7th September finally arrives. The Olympics have turned bad, terrorists have killed Israelis and even Mark Spitz's seven golds can't put the glitter back. What a shit world.

Derek and I have it all planned out. His parents both work all day so I go out in my school uniform as usual, taking a rucksack stuffed with all the things I need. We meet back at his house once it's empty of parents. We both worked last night instead of tonight so that's sorted. He bought the bus tickets at the weekend.

Derek phones up my school and puts on an older voice. It's the secretary who answers and she doesn't know who it is. It's a right laugh, I have to stop myself giggling out loud as he gives it large about me having the shits. This evening, both sets of parents think we are at each other's for tea, then at work, then going to the pub afterwards. That gives us until about eleven tonight. Dad didn't care, mom muttered about being late on a school night, but sometimes there are advantages to being ignored most of the time. I think they are well on the way towards wiping their hands of me – which suits me just fine.

On with the glad-rags and make-up. Platform boots, Levi's that I spent an hour soaking in the bath, shrinking them tight, then cut the bottoms off so they sit high up on the boots, like Bowie's. A white embroidered shirt and my new black satin bomber jacket. It was put together from various posters and photos so that the get-up is a bit like the video for 'John I'm Only Dancing' that I saw on 'Top Of The Pops' this week.

We get to Stoke in mid-afternoon, and this time there's no poncing around old buildings. We find a café for a bite then an off-licence and get a bottle of cider. There's a park and we spend an hour drinking, smoking and generally enjoying life and freedom. Derek is good company as usual. He hasn't made any efforts to dress up, just normal jeans, monkey boots and a denim jacket, and no make-up, so we look a right odd couple, one peacock and one sparrow.

We get to the Top Rank in Hanley early, a good job as the queue we join is soon around the corner and out of sight. When we first walk along it I can see people pointing at me and a few do a double-take like I did with that kid in London. Feels good. We are pretty near the front of the line, which is all part of the plan. I want to get to the front, want Bowie to see me.

Once the doors open we rush through and fight our way forward. I can nearly touch the stage. Derek and I link arms and hold our ground as the melee subsides and our position is staked.

These concerts are going to be short, about an hour. They are extras that David has put on to thank his fans before leaving for America. It's a pity they aren't longer, but it's actually made the whole evening feasible for me.

No more time for thinking, the familiar Clockwork Orange music powers up and there's 'Ziggy', powering into 'Hang Onto Yourself', and we are all going crazy again.

Time passes in a flash, with a major highlight for me near the end. As the familiar strains of 'Rock 'n' Roll Suicide' mark the final song of the evening, Bowie comes to the front of the stage. He is right there, looming above, me and as always he is touching hands in line with the song lyrics and he touches mine! But that's not all, before the hand-touching part of the song I see him look directly at me. He smiles, then points and tells me that I'm a 'Rock and Roll Suicide'. I can't believe it. I've actually registered with him and he's shown approval. Everything is worth this.

It's all over and the lights come up. The crowd begins to shuffle away and the magic evaporates. I look at my watch. It's still early. I haven't had enough yet and the buzz from my moment of communion generates an idea.

"Hey Derek, we've got loads of time, let's go around the back and see if we can get an autograph."

He looks momentarily unsure, then nods. He's older and always seems so sure, but I'm wilder. We hang back so that we are almost the last one's out, then wait a few more minutes until the crowds begin to dissipate.

The Stage Door is easy to find. There's about a hundred kids outside, and it's shut. Derek looks at me and shrugs,

"Looks like a waste of time to me."

"Let's give it a while, have a fag, he's gotta come out sometime."

After about half an hour, the doors remain firmly shut and implacable. Some of the crowd starts to drift away. Apart from Derek, we are the die-hards, sporting various degrees of 'Ziggy' appearance, although a surreptitious scan makes me think that I'm looking the best. Derek is getting fed up, slouched against the wall, picking his nose.

"They could be bloody hours yet Danny, come on, lets leg it and get the bus."

I'm like a fisherman waiting for a bite, I know it's going to happen, that door is going to open, they can't stay in there all night. When will I get another chance like this? Who knows what will happen in the U.S? If he cracks it then he'll be gone, perhaps forever, and I'll never get so close again.

"You go mate. I'll be ok, I want to hang it out for another hour. No point you staying here bored to tears. It's great you've been here with me but let's face it, I would have come on me own."

He looks doubtful. "Shouldn't just leave a mate, it's not right."

"Don't be daft, what's going to happen? I'll walk back to the bus terminal with some of this lot and then I'll be home in a jiffy, not far behind you."

He demurs for form's sake, but I can sense he wants to go and is trying to salve his conscience. A bit more persuading and I'm watching him disappear into the distance. My vigil resumes.

I start to have my doubts, but then I hear the bar on the door rattling and one side opens. Those remaining go to high alert. A couple of heavy-looking security men stand outside the door, inside, shadowy figures, peering out at the supplicants lit by the streetlights.

A man appears, but it's not *him*, just some bloke in full denim sporting a long ponytail. He has a 'Jason King' moustache and wicked sideburns. He's having a right good gander at us. He makes an announcement and everyone stops talking.

"I see real fans." He shouts. "Right, we've got posters and a souvenir programme for you all. But no scrumming, line up nice and orderly." He's got a strong Cockney accent, and that, together with his appearance from the coveted inner sanctum, bestows glamour upon him.

Another bouncer appears with an armful of the promised goodies and we dutifully queue up to receive them. As we do so the man inspects us closely. Once we have all filed past he speaks again.

"Ok kids, we're having a bit of a knees-up inside, as it's last night of the tour. David ain't gonna be out until really late so you may as well save yourselves hours in the cold and fuck off to your pits."

There is consternation and muttering, but people begin to move away, mollified by the gifts. As they do so the man points to some of us. "You six, you're inside for an hour if you want to join the party." With a surge of excitement, I realise that I'm included in the invite! A few of the departing fans hear this and start to plead, but the security men usher them away.

We are escorted inside, four girls and two boys, all young, all pretty. The girls are together and are having a fit of the vapors. They are totally star-struck and look like they're up for anything.

"Listen up, a few rules. No screaming, no mobbing David, in fact leave him alone unless he speaks to you. Any monkey business and you'll be out on your ears."

We are led down a corridor, and into the bar area. It is small, dark, rowdy and packed. There's music blaring out from a hi-fi stack system somewhere behind the bar. The heaving throng must be roadies, stagehands, sound engineers, assorted hangers-on and management. I can't see anyone that I recognise. A posse of men descends on the girls and they all disappear into the darkness. That's the last I see of them.

Me and the other kid are left with ponytail man. "Come on you two, let's get a drink, there's something special on tap tonight."

He leads us through the crowd. I catch sight of Mick Ronson and Trevor Bolder, no mistaking those sideburns, sat in an alcove with a couple of women. They are in jeans and T-shirts and look just like ordinary blokes at the pub. I'm straining my eyes peering into the crowd. I can't see *him* anywhere.

We reach the bar. "Give these beautiful boys a couple of 'Ziggy' cocktails, and I'll have a pint." He turns to us, shouting.

"It's a special drink, made just for tonight's party to celebrate the end of the tour." We are handed two glasses of bright green liquid. I take a gulp and the spirit hits me, burning my throat. I stifle a cough. I don't want to embarrass myself by looking like some young kid who has never had a drink before. I turn to my companion.

"Alright mate, I'm Danny, can't believe this, can you?"

He holds out his hand and we shake. "Bernie. Fucking right, it's like a dream. Trouble is I can't stay long, if I miss the bus home to Stafford I'm right in the shit. I was only expecting to get an autograph."

He is a good-looking kid, blonde and square jawed. He's got the Bowie cut too, but with a sneaky feeling of superiority I see that he's wearing no make-up. He seems to read my mind.

"You look fucking A1. Where d'ya learn to put that stuff on?"

"Would you believe, from my girlfriend and her mom."

"Cool, well they taught you well. I'd look like a fucking clown if I tried. Anyway, I ain't got the guts to walk around in public with it on."

I realise that ponytail is stood close, listening. He is laughing too.

"I'm Rick, a vital part of this circus. I sort stuff out, all sorts of stuff. I chose you two myself, bit of a reward for you trying so hard in your looks, and waiting it out. Especially you. Danny is it? I bet you're the closest I've ever seen to a 'Ziggy' lookalike all tour. You've got the face for it, very delicate."

I take a closer look at him. He's quite old, could be thirty, maybe a bit younger. He's tall and he looks fit, not big, but like he uses the gym. He's ditched his Levi jacket somewhere and his jeans and white T-shirt are tight fitting and show a V-shaped torso and broad shoulders. His arm muscles are defined and I can see the vein in his bicep clearly. His hair is very blonde and I wonder if he dyes it. I can see a tattoo peeking out from under the cap sleeve of his shirt, it looks like 'OK' but I can't see it all.

"Is David really here?" I ask, prepared for disappointment.

"Sure, I think he's still in the dressing room with Angie, having a fag and a drink. He's always totally knackered after a show but he'll be out later I bet, he won't miss the last night party and a 'Ziggy' cocktail to drink."

Bernie interjects, "Sorry, I'm really grateful for being let in, but I got to go in about twenty minutes. I was only hoping to get an autograph."

Rick pulls a sad face. "That's too bad, you sure, you'll probably miss him, he's a bit of a night-owl?"

Bernie is resolute, although he does accept another cocktail, as do I. My head is beginning to buzz.

Rick seems like a really nice bloke. He tells us to wait by the bar and returns with two photos of Bowie. "There you go Bernie, and one for you Danny, there's your autograph, it's genuine, not just printed on."

Another treasure. This man is the doorway to magical things and I am very keen to be his friend!

Once Rick realises that Bernie is really going to leave, he shifts his attention back to me. Bernie is a fool; this will never ever happen again in his life. I don't care about consequences back in the grey world, In for a penny, in for a pound.

Rick questions me about my devotion to Bowie, asks what concerts I've been to, admires the make-up once again, and the drinks are all gone and he's getting some more. Bernie refuses, and Rick summons one of the bouncers to show him out.

"Let's go and sit down somewhere, I've been on my dancers all fucking day."

We fight our way through the throng to find a seat. Rick seems very popular, a number of those we pass exchange a greeting or a high-five. I've never actually seen anyone do that except in films, a silly little thing, but it impresses me.

We reach a shadowy alcove. There are two others sat in it, and Rick shoos them to move over. I'm squeezed between him and an older kid, older than me anyway. He looks a bit worse for wear and is having trouble keeping his eyes open. The other bloke is much older, older even than Rick, and I can't help but notice that he's got one arm around the lad's shoulder and the other is under the table and moving like he's stroking his leg or something.

"Danny, meet Mal, one of the sound wizards, and this disreputable looking thing," he tousles the kid's hair, "Is Mickey, who works for me."

Mal is as camp as they come, and makes a frank appraisal of me. "My, my, aren't you a pretty boy? Where do you find them Rick?"

Rick laughs, "wind it in you old queen, he's with me so you stick with Mickey. Now then, who wants a smoke? Got some good blow here. Danny, you up for it?"

I nod enthusiastically. I'm living the rock and roll life, if only for an evening, and loving it. This is what it's all about. So what if Mal's queer, what did I expect in David's world?

Rick produces a Rizla pack, and with practiced expertise crafts a five-skin roll up. It's passed around and I take a few tokes. It's good stuff and it isn't long before we are all giggling and laughing.

Suddenly I see movement out of the corner of my eye, a parting of the crowd, and there he is, still wearing his 'Ziggy' face, the woodland animal jumpsuit, and boots. A space is made at a table near the bar and as he makes his way towards it, chatting and laughing as he goes, he catches sight of us, and, I can't believe it, comes over. He is smaller than I thought, dwarfed by most around him, but his aura blows everyone else away. He simply radiates. I'm lost in him.

He speaks to me, the voice I know so well, slightly camp, slightly London, almost posh. "Hey, saw you at the front, you've done a fantastic job with the make-up, who did that, your mom?"

I blurt out something about my girlfriend and he laughs, then he moves on, leaving us in the shadows. He sits at a table prepared for him, hidden by the crowd surrounding him.

I'm drunk, star-struck, high, all of them at once. Rick is laughing, Mickey is slumped forward on the table, while Mal carries on furtling about below. Can you get used to rubbing shoulders with a God?

"Danny, Danny, come back to earth." Rick brushes my hair and I think of Luke, but I don't experience the same instant attraction. I start to pull away, but remember that this man has made my wildest dream come true. My gratitude surely extends to letting him get a bit more familiar. His arm rests around my shoulder and strokes the top of my arm.

He asks me about my girlfriend and I tell him all about Alice, then there's another drink and I'm unburdening myself, blabbing to him about how confused I am about everything, and about what it's like at home and how I feel trapped. He's got his hand on my thigh and it's creeping up and in and he leans really close.

His voice is kind. "Do you want to try something different then? You are beautiful. I can teach you a few things."

He picks up my hand and moves it towards his crotch. I don't know if it's the drink, the dope, or the unreality of the moment, but it's all too much. I stand up in confusion and knock over a cocktail. It runs across the table and over Mal, who stands up, swearing. I clamber over Rick, who looks surprised, and in a mindless drunken panic I run towards the way out. I hear laughter and think it's David laughing at me, but when I glance across he's gone, the table is empty.

I can't find the way out. A bouncer grabs hold of me and shouts, "cool it". Then Rick is there, his voice soothing, calming. He's apologising, saying something about not meaning to frighten me.

They take me into a corner and Rick goes and gets my coat and the posters and stuff. By the time he returns I've calmed down a bit and I'm feeling embarrassed at looking like some stupid kid. He sends the security man back to his position.

"I'm sorry Danny, misread the signals; you're so beautiful I just couldn't resist taking a chance, but I got it wrong. Will you forgive me?"

I'm churning inside and unsure, but it's time to put on a brave face. A tiny sliver of gratification wriggles into my head too, after all it's good to be fancied, and told that you're good-looking, no matter who by.

"It's ok. Too much to drink and smoke and it all got a bit on top of me. You must think I'm just a stupid kid."

"Not at all. My fault completely. I bet you've never seen anything like this before." He indicates the party behind with an expansive wave of the hand."

"No, but I should have expected it. After all, I love David because he's different and outrageous and he's into men and women and I just feel so stupid. I'm just not sure how I feel or even should feel."

Rick gives me a friendly and comforting smile. "That's no problem." He holds out a hand. "Still friends eh." I nod and shake it and everything is ok again. I check my watch and it's nearly ten.

"Shit, I'm going to miss the last bus home if I don't go now, and I'll have to run all the way to get it as well."

" No, you won't, I'll get Phil over there to run you to the bus station." He calls the security man back.

He reaches into his pocket. "This is a present for you. Get some more records, make-up, clothes or whatever, it's a sorry from me for upsetting you." He presses a note into my hand and I stick it into my pocket without looking at it. He carries on,

"I've written my phone number on the back of the autograph photo, I know you won't ditch that, so you'll always have me with you. David's away now until Christmas, but when he's back you phone me and I'll get you some tickets, bring your girl if you want. And if you need to talk, need any help, just give me a bell. Who knows, you could even come to London, bet you'd like that wouldn't you?"

I nod. I know exactly what he is offering, but need time to process it. He ruffles my hair. "Good, now off you trot, but I expect a call. I like you Danny, you've got something about you, something special. Don't forget me."

'As if I could', I think.

Halfway home, half asleep, on the coach to Digbeth, it seems so unreal. I actually met *him* and he spoke to me. I feel as if stardust has rubbed off on me, I'll never be the same again. Life can never be the same again. I remember the money and extract the note from my pocket. It is folded up. I spread it out. It's a fifty-pound note. I've never seen one before in my life and I bet my Dad hasn't either.

Chapter Eight

'Unwashed and Somewhat Slightly Dazed'
Autumn 1972

Danny:

It takes a few weeks to even begin to settle down after *that night*.

I don't get home until after midnight. I'm sober enough by then to remember to get rid of the make-up, and lucky that I get into the bathroom and get that done before mom meekly pokes her head around their bedroom door as I head across the landing. I can hear him snoring like a buzz saw behind her. She asks if I'm ok, and for a brief moment I think that she might actually care. But then she spoils it all by motioning for me to be quiet with a nod and grimace towards her room. All she is bothered about is the trouble I could cause for her if I wake the bastard up.

The next few days are a shock. Back to real life with a vengeance. A school kid again. Under the cosh at home. Doing the usual stuff with Alice. Rules, rules and more rules, it's doing my head in. My brain feels dislocated.

As the days pass, the party at the 'Top Rank' fades into a blurry and gold-tinged glimpse of heaven that I file away in a secret room in my mind. When I'm alone I take the memory out and polish it, inspecting it from every angle.

My school friends, such as they are, the hangers-on and weak-minded alike, are incredulous at my story of meeting Bowie. I leave out some of the finer detail of course, which somewhat weakens the tale as no one can comprehend why I would have been invited to such a party in the first place.

They don't believe me, think I'm making it up to bolster my image; but I don't care anymore, and some admire my capacity to bullshit.

I've moved on, and their little opinions mean nothing. I realise now that they never did, even when I was alone with myself, before Alice. She did free me, but I never needed other people, and I still don't.

Only Derek believes me about Bowie, I'm not even sure Alice really does, she says nothing and thins her lips whenever I mention that night, or anything to do with him.

I am totally detached from my day-to-day life, going through the motions, waiting for something to happen. But it never will unless I do something about it. My mind goes over and over the options, but I come back every time to just one. I skirt around it, unwilling to face the implications. I must seem like I'm in a daze or on drugs. I barely interact with others and live inside my head, in a world where Bowie knows me.

As the days become weeks, school and home get worse and worse. I have begun to get sloppy with my secrets, because I resent having to hide my true self, and my level of caring what anyone thinks is plummeting fast. Inevitably, and I suspect I was sort of hoping it would happen, one Sunday morning the old man clocks some eyeliner that I haven't removed properly.

I am ready for a stack-up but he is both sober and hungover, and I just get a bollocking and grounding for a week before he takes himself off out to top up on the booze. An eruption is coming though, it could be either one of us, because I am feeling less and less inclined to give way and put up with his shit.

His slide back into the booze is accelerating. I don't know why. He's having some sort of private crisis but I have no feelings for him other than hate, so I don't bother asking what's going on. He's been like a stung grizzly the last few weeks, not helped by 'that posh wanker Ted Heath', as he calls him, putting a freeze on wages prices and rents. He hates the Tories, in fact he seems to hate everybody. I'm beginning to see that that includes himself, perhaps that's why he drinks. I don't care.

The thought of speaking with Mom never crosses my mind. I have no relationship with her - in fact I despise her for her weakness, her use of me as a shield, almost as much as I do him.

Whatever the reason, by the time the mornings get colder and the first frosts sting my nose on the way to school, he's started going to the pub after work again, turning up half-pissed, and treating my Mom like a skivvy. I avoid him as much as possible but it can't last much longer. I'm spending more and more time out of the house, some of it with Alice, some with Derek, and plenty with my own thoughts.

I'm hauled in by the Deputy Head, 'Snot' Williams, and read the riot act. I've had detention three times in a week for different reasons, smoking, fucking about and being disruptive in class, and not doing my homework. As he bawls at me I retreat into my head and concentrate on the dewdrop hanging from his nose, the reason for his nickname. Fuck him, fuck them all. I don't want to be part of their stupid school, with its stupid rules. Something has to happen soon or I think I'll go mad.

The glimpse into the other world has totally fucked me up. All the things that I can't get out of my mind, the things that I want, that intrigue me, lie there.

***

Alice:

I don't know what to think. Is he going crazy? He comes back with a story of meeting Bowie but it all rings hollow and untrue. Why does he feel the need to concoct this crap? When I start probing he just clams up, so once again I have to humour him and pretend to believe it. Even if it's true I don't like it, whatever has gone on, and is going on in his head, it's unsettling him. He is searching for something else, something more, something I don't give him, and that hurts, makes me feel inadequate. It's eating away at our whole relationship.

I get upset, then it's as if nothing's happened and off we go, back out on the pub, club and the Saturday up town circuit. One minute we are love's young dream, then he goes all quiet and it's as if I'm not there. It's bloody selfish. There's never a conversation about what I might want, it's all about him and his problems. It's just assumed that I'm ok, everything in the garden's rosy - and it's not, Danny, it's not, it's you that's making me unhappy.

He's getting wilder and wilder. He seems to be addicted to causing outrage everywhere he goes, and I end up on the receiving end of his anger and resentment when other people react. I'm afraid that he's careering faster and faster towards something very bad.

I can't see how this is going to end, but in my heart I know it won't be good. No happy ending for Alice and Danny.

Sometimes I cry in bed when I think of the Danny I knew those few months ago. He has been replaced with a stranger. I'm terrified that I'm losing him, but I still love him, I really do.

***

David:

A new and thrilling chapter begins.

He departs Britain on the QE2 on September 10th, arriving in New York on the 17th, fear of flying leading him to choose a sea crossing. The tour is initially only intended for eight dates, but is later extended by another eight weeks. Bowie is relatively unknown in America prior to his arrival, but the tactic chosen by the management company, Mainman, and record company, RCA, of portraying him as a 'superstar' act from the UK, first since The Beatles, begins to make an impact upon the consciousness of the USA population, particularly on the East Coast.

The first concert, held on 22nd September, at The Music Hall in Cleveland, is crucial, and there is high pressure on Bowie to deliver a peak performance. He is on top form. The concert is a triumph and results in a ten-minute standing ovation.

The following day, Bowie begins to write the songs that will eventually become the 'Aladdin Sane' album. They are inspired by the stream of images he soaks up from the windows of his chartered Greyhound bus as he tours.

On 28th September, the most important concert of this first visit to the USA occurs when the 'Ziggy Stardust' roadshow rolls up at Carnegie Hall, New York. Bowie is still a relative unknown in America, and none of his LP's or Singles have as yet charted. Before him lies the ultimate test. Success in New York equals success in America.

RCA and Mainman pump maximum spin and hype into the concert preparations and publicity, distributing hundreds of tickets to journalists, celebrities, even using the cast of Andy Warhol's play, 'Pork', to give tickets away to members of the New York 'counter-culture'.

The concert is advertised as 'Fall In Love With David Bowie'. It is a sell-out, with the touts charging $50 for $6 tickets outside the venue, although, so many tickets are given away that doubt remains as to whether the audience is, in the final analysis, manufactured.

The 'giveaway' ploy is a success, and the concert becomes a hip 'social event' attended by many of New York's 'movers and shakers', including Andy Warhol, Truman Capote, Anthony Perkins, Alan Bates, a member of the Kennedy family, and the 'New York Dolls'.

The concert itself features the standard 'Ziggy' set, Bowie's red hair shining in the stage lights, sporting only two costumes, multi-coloured, and gold and black chequered, jumpsuits.

Bowie is not only extremely nervous, but full of flu, and fears that his voice will break down at this critical moment in his career. He has to subdue his normal stage antics due to low energy levels, but he gets through the ordeal and few people notice. The Mick Ronson 'fellatio' scene is performed as usual, a core concert moment, required to ensure that the 'outrage' of 'Ziggy' is exported.

Whilst the concert itself is a great success, several other significant events take place on its margins.

Bowie conducts interviews for 'Rolling Stone' and 'Newsweek' magazines. He also signs a new contract with Mainman, in the mistaken belief that he is being given partnership in the company. This misunderstanding will eventually contribute to the rupturing of his relationship with Mainman.

An old friend also turns up, hailing from, of all places, Columbia. He is a classmate from Bromley Technical High School who has, in the intervening years, implausibly become a dealer in Cocaine. The introduction of Cocaine into Bowie's drugs use is a growing cancer, first steps on a downward spiral, at the very moment of triumph. The erstwhile classmate is immortalised in 'Panic In Detroit', as the one looking like 'Che Guevara'.

***

Danny:

I just can't get that party out of my mind. Another world, another life, fading into history, beginning to take on a dreamlike essence. I fear it has ruined me forever.

Life is going downhill fast, at school and at home. At night I stare at the signed photo of my hero, framed and on my bedside table. That phone number is burning through from the back. An invitation. 'Just call me', it says.

I know what he's after, and what he is offering in exchange. But to go to London, gain entry to a world that I can never experience otherwise, freedom! The allure grows as the mundanity of Birmingham is scoured into my brain by every little frustration, every shackle that school and Dad try to put on me.

And then there's Alice. We see each other as often as ever, have a good time, have it off, but it is getting to be routine. And the sex, well it's fine, but it's beginning to feel more like a duty, something I have to do to prove my love, than real desire. Is that the same with all relationships, staleness, fading excitement, or is it my other imaginings, the secret ones, that are making me dissatisfied?

I'm full of guilt when I'm with her. Guilt because I'm keeping those secrets. She makes it worse by being so lovely, tries to help in her own way, but she can never understand how I'm feeling. A nasty little feeling I can't get rid of is growing inside me. She is so comfortable, it's so easy for her, with her great parents, her mapped-out future. I'm jealous, even resent it, but is her 'normal' life what I want? Or is it excitement, to be in Bowie's world, even if people do think it's full of freaks; all that Alice can offer is envelopment, suffocation, a boring life, now and in the future.

But the other, darker secret threatens us more, and that secret is wound up in Rick, that night, and any escape to London I might fantasise about.

The big question. Am I bisexual, or even queer? The truth is, I don't know. Who can help me decide? I see men and other kids looking at me. Some are aggressive, some take the piss, but the glance of some contains desire and the unspoken question.

I blank it all out, because I don't know what to feel. I don't know what to do. Confusion. I suppose that, just like with girls, there are some you fancy and some you don't, and that seems to be the case with boys, as some repel me, some interest me, some provoke no reaction at all.

I wrestle with the concept, applying it to the only two times in my life when I've flirted with a man. My reaction that night, when Rick started touching me. I felt no desire, only an instinctive repulsion. Filled with panic, I fled. Yet if it had been David I wouldn't have run, because the reality is that I'm enormously attracted to him, have been since I first saw him that night on 'Top Of The Pops'. Say it plain, I fancy him. So why run from Rick? And if I do keep running from him, that ends any notion of going to London and being part of that world, because I'm trapped here and will never be able to afford to go, to escape.

And Luke? I compare them, my reaction. Perhaps it was the difference in situation, perhaps it was the age difference. I haven't been able to get Luke out of my mind either, and his number is still in the bedside table drawer.

***

David:

Across the Atlantic, Bowie continues his tour, oblivious of burgeoning money issues. On 6th October, he records 'The Jean Genie', the riff of which is created in a jamming session on the Greyhound bus, and based on a 'Yardbirds' song. It is catchy, and an obvious single.

The tour has its lows too, concerts in St Louis and Kansas City are not well attended. Eventually the party reaches Los Angeles, staying at the ostentatious, and expensive, Beverly Hills Hotel. Money flows out like it is on an endless tap, and they hit the clubs, especially the 'E Club' on 'Sunset Strip', which later becomes famous for rock and film star decadence and glamour. Bowie thinks RCA and Mainman are paying, but in reality all the tour costs are being drawn from his record sales profits.

***

Danny:

Hair grows. By late October I badly need it done again. I've been putting it off, but I wake one morning with clarity of mind. I need some resolution so I can stop treading water and move my life forward.

In a mood of reckless determination, I phone up the salon and ask to book Luke. This time I don't ask Alice to go with me. I don't know whether she wonders why, I don't really care, she doesn't own me. I've got enough people telling me what I should and shouldn't do.

Luke remembers me straight away, greeting me with a cheery, 'hello beautiful' as soon as I walk in. I am relaxed and chatty, telling him about my night with Bowie, as he snips and caresses my hair. I slyly observe him in the mirror, trying not to be obvious.

Luke is good looking, square-jawed, but with really feminine eyes, long lashes, a tint of green in the corneas and obviously manicured eyebrows. He is clean-shaven, his hair is lush, dark and curly, and falls to his shoulders, a bit like Roger Daltrey from 'The Who'. He is slim and boyish in the body and looks younger than his age, which must be close to mid-twenties. I fancy him. A sense of relief washes over me. I don't know why.

For a few more minutes I watch as the 'Bowie cut' reappears, then he stands back.

"It looks really good again, but it needs a finishing touch, I should have asked before I started, do you want it coloured?"

I am already calculating and planning, and this is a step that needs to wait, until after a bigger one.

"Maybe next time, I'm not sure I can cope with anymore hassle at the moment."

He smiles, then pulls a sad face, "Ok, but what's upsetting you, my little 'Ziggy'?"

I find courage from somewhere.

"I think my head is going to explode, there's so much whirling around inside it. I need to sort something really important out, and I think you can help, if the offer you made last time still stands, remember?"

He moves close and whispers in my ear, "Of course it does." There is a suggestion of a caress of his lips on my face and once again I am aroused.

"Perhaps a drink somewhere so we can talk, somewhere out of town?" I whisper, conscious of the other customers and staff.

"Yes, that's a good idea. I promised it would be at your speed, and whatever happens will be your call, my dear."

I'm seeing Alice as usual over the weekend and I need my head totally clear of her for this, so we arrange to meet next week.

***

Alice:

He is all attention and cuddles, as if he has switched it back on again, after a few weeks of growing coolness. It's a lovely weekend. He's had his hair done again but things seem to have settled down. He seems to be back with it, so perhaps we will get back to normal now. No mention of Bowie, how much he hates his life, of escape to some fantasy showbiz world that he will never see. As we part on Sunday night I'm filled with love and hope. Perhaps he is growing up a bit, coming to terms with the value of what he has. Maybe my Danny is back.

***

Danny:

I've made a real effort with Alice. We had a great weekend, just like old times. I'm struggling to live with myself. What a two-faced bastard, she was so happy, and here I am using her to conduct an experiment in relationships.

Tuesday comes around quickly. I haven't stopped thinking about it since the haircut. Luke picks me up at the Maypole island as planned, and heads off up the Alcester Road. We land at a country pub hidden up the lanes at Inkberrow.

It's an old-fashioned place with alcoves and red velour seats, dark wood tables and a bored barmaid sat on a stool reading a book. She barely looks up as Luke orders and I make for a seat in a dark corner. The place is nearly empty, just two old farmer types sat at the bar, and a couple alternating between munching crisps and eating each other's faces. interspersed with giggling. Everyone wrapped in their own little worlds, oblivious of our presence.

In unspoken agreement we sit next to each other on a padded bench, backs to the wall, facing the room. We can see everyone coming in or out. We make some small talk, fill in a few details about each other then he asks me to tell him about it. I take a deep breath and start to talk.

It floods out, everything I've been unable to say to anyone else, ever. He listens quietly, and eventually the flood dries to a trickle, stops. I'm surprised to find I have tears in my eyes. He leans towards me and wipes a stray tear from my cheek. I keep Rick to myself. I'm not about to divulge that to anyone.

"You poor darling, keeping all this inside, no wonder you're unhappy."

"There's no one to tell, nobody would understand, but I'm hoping you do."

He takes hold of my hand under the table, I don't resist. It is comforting. Then he starts to talk about himself. His loneliness as a teenager as his body matured. The growing realisation that he liked boys not girls. The secrecy, the fear of ridicule, exile, and worse. His first experience with another boy, leading to months of guilt and feelings of being dirty and abnormal. Hiding it from his parents and friends. His gravitation towards hairdressing, which he loved, and a life where 'his type' was accepted. Leaving home, getting a flat in Harborne, living his own life, leaving his childhood and teenage years behind. Drawing a line on the past and starting again. Happy now, alone, bar a few fleeting relationships, but alone with his true self, no longer a fraud. I envy him.

So much of what he says resonates. I hang on every word, fascinated. He stops.

"But it's not quite the same for you is it? I never fancied girls."

" Alice is lovely, but I don't know whether I just fell into that because it was the 'done' thing. It was, is, good for me. I was shy and she brought me out into the real world. I feel guilty because she loves me and I'm cheating on her in my mind and I thought I loved her but now..." I trail off, uncertain.

"Now you need to know, so you can make a decision, because if she is so nice, then she doesn't deserve betrayal." He finishes my thought process for me. I nod, nothing left to say.

"Of course I can help, you know I fancy you. But you are a risk, because you are young, and I'm older. You must be my secret, and I yours, if we carry on."

Who would I tell anyway? Secrets suit me just fine.

It doesn't happen that night, or that week. Luke insists that we see each other a few more times. In some ways he is quaintly old-fashioned and wants to build a relationship. I steal away, always in the week, and we go to remote pubs or visit places like Stratford and Warwick.

I am enjoying it. It is exciting, different. I like him, he makes such a fuss of me, and he makes me laugh. We become closer, conscious of being discovered, and progress to kissing and cuddling, then stroking. I experience no repulsion, quite the opposite.

He asks me if I feel ready and I am. In my fifteenth year I lose my virginity for a second time. Not many people can say that.

***

David:

By the end of October, the spending is completely out of control. Mainman are nearly out of money. Bowie's travelling group has grown to nearly fifty, including the inevitable 'hangers on', 'groupies' and purveyors of drugs. Manager Defries persuades RCA to advance more cash, once again set against record sales, and the party goes on, unabated, with Bowie still ignorant of the fact that he is actually paying for everything. Angie and son Zowie return home, amidst rumours of arguments, jealousy and resentment.

A concert at Santa Monica Civic Auditorium on 20th October is recorded live and broadcast on the radio, resulting in further beneficial national exposure and a sell-out the following night, but the two San Francisco concerts are not well attended, making a loss, and leading to the cancellation of poorly selling November dates at Houston and Dallas. Bowie has still not conquered the Southern States.

At home, 'Space Oddity' and 'The Man Who Sold The World' are reissued with new sleeves and inserts.

In early December, recording sessions for the new album 'Aladdin Sane', begin in New York, featuring Mike Garson and his innovative 'jazz style' piano playing.

***

Danny:

Christmas crap is once again in the shops, festive tunes abound. Another year-end is approaching fast, and I reflect upon the past, whilst sneaking a glimpse towards the New Year. A significant moment is approaching. Life is very complicated. I'm juggling Alice and Luke, sliding into a dark abyss at home and school, and Bowie is coming home soon. A decision about Rick and London won't wait much longer.

Adverts begin to appear in the music press for a Bowie homecoming concert tour, billed 'Bowie's Back', starting at the Rainbow at Christmas. I've just got to be there. I avidly watch the music papers for news but I'm one of thousands of fans now, and tickets for the Christmas Eve concert are like rocking horse shit. It's three weeks away and I'm desperate. Alice has no interest whatsoever in going,.

My desire is further fuelled by the release of a fantastic new single called 'Jean Genie', with a pounding guitar riff that turns over and over in my mind when I'm trying to get to sleep.

My days are an endless repetition of nothingness and I'm caring less and less about the waves I make. There's one particularly bad day at school where I actually walk out of class because I'm bored stiff, while a supply teacher watches with a slack jaw. The other kids can't believe it, my reputation receives a short-lived boost before settling into a consensus that I'm going barmy. I get hauled up before the Head, detention for a week, and a final warning.

They phone my Mom and ask to see her. She knows better than to tell the old man about it, so she goes alone after he's gone out to work. I sit next to her, radiating complete disinterest, which is the truth, and which completely pisses off the Headmaster. He leaves both of us in no doubt that the next time I step out of line will mean suspension, or worse.

When I leave school that evening, to my dismay and mortification, she is waiting at the gate. I try to ignore her but she insists on walking home with me, much to the amusement of Lowe who not only spots us, but follows, making loud comments about 'mommy's boys' and 'bum bandits'.

I wait for him to get closer, then turn and chase him. He isn't quick and I apply a boot to his arse propelling him into a hedge. As he rebounds I punch him in his fat gut, causing a whoosh of air to escape his mouth. That shuts him up and I just walk back to my shocked Mom, and we both walk off in silence. Lowe doesn't try to follow. He knows that I'm capable of anything at the moment. He's just a fat coward. He can't do anything to hurt me anymore.

After a few moments I hear snuffling at my side. For a moment I feel sorry for her, but then my heart hardens.

"Stop that bloody crying, for God's sake."

She gulps a couple of times and stifles the tears.

"What's happened to you Danny? I don't recognise you anymore."

"What do you care? You've never done anything for me, never protected me, never spoken up for me, never shown any love for me."

She starts crying again.

116

"For fuck's sake shut up. Why have you come here, look what you've made me do." I indicate the distant figure of Lowe who is watching us, his face filled with a mixture of fear and loathing. He turns and shambles off.

"I needed to speak to you before your Dad gets home, and I wasn't sure you'd be straight back, you never seem to be at home these days."

"That's because there's nothing there for me, I want to be with you both as little as possible."

"But you've got your room, food, clothes, you've never wanted for anything."

I look at her in disbelief.

"I can't believe you said that. Shows how little you understand. Him I hate, but you, you've let me down. All my life, every time, you took his side, did nothing, kept quiet, looked after yourself, let me take it off him. What kind of mother does that? It was bearable when he had the drinking under control, but he's boozing and it's started up again. But it's different this time, I'm older. I don't have to put up with his shit, your shit, school shit." It floods out of me, I'm enjoying it, relishing her wincing at each accusation I spit out at her.

"Please Danny, you don't know what it was like for me. Before you…it was terrible." She trails off into tears again.

"Yeah' I bet it was. We can agree on one thing – he's a bastard, but you hid behind me, used me to divert his attention. Don't expect me to ever forgive you for that. You made the choice to marry him, but I didn't have any choices, father, mother, and if I had, I wouldn't have chosen either of you."

"You need to understand..." She begins.

"No, I don't. I don't need to do anything anymore. It's you that needs to understand. I don't care what happens, about him, or you, about school, about living in this shithole. He's finished it for me, and you've let him."

The shock has stopped the crying at least. She is suddenly colder, the face I know so well.

"Well if that's how you feel, you wait and see what happens if you get suspended or expelled….or if he finds out your dirty little secret."

This time I stop dead. How could she know anything?

"I don't know what you're talking about."

"Yes, you do. It's unnatural, the make-up, the hairdo, and …."

She knows, I can see it in her eyes. She knows, but how? I play for time, brain racing. I hadn't expected this. I'm not ready.

"And what? Loads of boys wear make-up and have long hair, it's called fashion."

She is still cool, and iterates her words slowly and deliberately, as if they are unclean and she can't bear for them to travel from her throat to mouth.

"You like boys, in that dirty horrible way, just like that creature you adore. We had a note, pushed through the door. Luckily I saw it on the mat and hid it from him, so I did save you, and you do owe me."

I say nothing. I have no words for how I feel at this moment. Everything is crashing down around me and I've nowhere to go. And, it's so obvious that my own mother is going to try and blackmail me.

"It's a lie, show me this note."

She fumbles in her handbag and hands it to me. It's scrawled in a childlike hand, but the content is devastating.

'Your son is a queer. He's in love with a hairdresser called Luke from the place he has his hair done and they shag each other at his flat in Harborne, dirty bum bandits.'

There is a grainy, poor quality photograph, but my hair stands out proud, it's clearly me, and I'm kissing Luke. I remember that kiss. We took a risk and stayed in Harborne. The only time we touched in public that day was that snatched embrace in Grove Park.

I try to attack, but she's having none of it.

"So what, it's my choice, my life, I don't care."

She is frigid, icy, I realise that she is terrified, trying to save herself – as usual.

"It's not though, is it? You're not sixteen, not legal. Your boyfriend could go to jail for this. And what would Alice say?"

She has won, for the moment. I need time to think, plan.

"What do you want me to do?"

"You'll knuckle down at school and stop causing trouble. You'll tell this Luke to go away, far away, or I'll be going to the police. You'll be nice to Alice and go back to being a normal kid. Or I'll tell everyone. Starting with her."

I'm trapped again, another chain, a thicker one. She lets me keep the note and photograph, to get rid of it and to show Luke, but I don't get rid, I want to work out who wrote it.

*

I debate whether to tell Luke, but in the end decide against it. I need time to try and sort my head out, so the plan, such as it is, is to wind my neck in on the run up to Christmas and start making some decisions in the meantime. I'm confident that Mom won't let the cat out of the bag if I steer an even course and don't wind the old man up. Let's face it, that's all she's bothered about, and now she knows I'm queer I doubt she gives a toss about me.

So, on I go, juggling Luke and Alice, trying to decide between them, wondering if I actually have to, thinking about Rick and London. I am the model student, it's only a couple of weeks until the end of term and I'm sure I can grit that out. But in the meantime, I have detective work to do, and some big decisions to make.

Chapter Nine

'Hang On To Yourself'
Christmas 1972

Alice:

    I used to love Christmas, but this year I'm afraid of it. The gaiety seems forced and false to me, and there is a falseness between us too. On the surface things carry on as normal; but it isn't like it used to be when we only had eyes for each other. There is something lacking, a depth of feeling that went unsaid, because it was almost tangible. We 'do things', but Danny doesn't seem to 'feel things'.

    He seems distracted, somewhere else in his mind, or people-watching, rather than paying attention to me. Maybe we have been going out for so long now that our relationship has changed, matured, like a married couple, but it doesn't feel that that. It's not like mom and dad, or even what Danny's parents are like. They are 'together' - even if it's an unhappy togetherness. There are secret places in his head, I can't access, and I'm not sure where Danny has filed me. It feels as if I'm not everything to him anymore. That hurts, because I still love him as much as ever.

    There is a voice in my head that nags away, suggesting that he has found another girl. I smother it, excuse him by trying to understand what he is going through, at home and in his head, believing that he is just trying to find a way forward, to find himself.

    The Christmas songs, the shop decorations, the adverts, provide a backdrop of love and happiness, when all I am feeling is growing despair and powerlessness. Christmas feels like a deadline, which will expose the truth between us, and I don't want to find out what it is. Then it will be New Year, a time for new beginnings, and I fear what 1973 might bring.

    I get really upset when I suggest that we go to The Forum Christmas Party and he looks at me as if I have gone crazy.

"Why would we go back there? We've outgrown that, it's for kids."

"You really don't know why?"

"Not a clue," he snaps brusquely.

I swallow a lump in my throat. "Because it's where we met, it's a year ago next week, our anniversary. That doesn't matter to you any more does it? You haven't given it a thought. In fact, it feels like thinking about me doesn't feature much anymore in your life. Your hero comes first. It's like you're screwing him behind my back. I don't want to go and see him ever again, you can go on your own. Hope you enjoy it, and your own company."

I get up to leave, trying to cover tears. He's shocked, and all over me. Once more I allow myself to be persuaded, placated. How many more times can I give in? I caught a glimpse of something cross his face; something I said hit deep. He promises we will go to The Forum, but he doesn't say anything about giving up seeing Bowie a week later, although he hasn't got a ticket, and it's a sell-out, so that would be an easy sacrifice.

***

David:

On 13th December, Bowie boards the RHMS 'Ellinis' for the week-long crossing. His first American adventure is over. The next album is taking shape, as is a new character, 'Aladdin Sane'. Back home, the adoring fans keenly await the return of their hero.

***

Danny:

I'm such a shit. Two-timing Alice with Luke. If it was another girl it would be unforgivable, but with a man...

I like both of them. Alice can get a bit heavy sometimes and I sometimes feel that she's trying to cage me, but she is so lovely, both in looks and personality. Do I love her? What is love anyway? Not what my Mom and Dad have got, that's for sure. Sometimes I wonder if they were like Alice and I, when they first met, that scares me.

Alice is no fool. Every time I see her, I'm on tenterhooks because I think she knows something is going on, and will ask me direct. I'm a bad liar. That comment about screwing Bowie was far too close to the truth for comfort.

She is far too good for me. The deceit is eating away at my insides as if I've swallowed acid. I don't like to think of myself as a bad person, but I must be. Can I bear to lose her, and what if I lose Luke too, now our secret is out, and exposure hangs by a thread? Do I love him too?

He's fun. There's a thrill to our secret relationship, we both agreed it *is* just fun, nothing more. And the sex is good.

The days are rolling by. So far I have kept the plates spinning at school, home and in my relationships, although sometimes it seems that my brain is going to burst. I keep my head down and promise myself that I will make some decisions after term ends, ready for the New Year. Something inside whispers, 'coward', and it's the truth. I'm making excuses so I don't have to face up to the decisions I don't want to make.

The days and nights continue, the sun comes up in the morning. I go through the motions, but the pressure to make one significant decision soon is growing. It's not Alice, Luke, school or home that is forcing me into a corner, it's Bowie. He started all this, showed me a different kind of life. I just can't get a ticket for the Rainbow concerts whatever I do, and the prospect of missing him is not an option. I love him too, it seems.

My resolve to wait finally cracks. I carefully remove the 'Ziggy' photo from its frame. I've got a pocketful of shrapnel for the phone, but spend all day at school gnawing away at the well-chewed bone of whether I should make this call or not.

By four o clock, when the bell rings, and everyone rushes about collecting bags and books, I'm still undecided. I walk down the school drive as usual, for the same bus journey as every other day, to the same load of shit at home, and I'm filled with resolve. I get off the bus two stops early and before I know it I'm in a phone box in a side street, away from eyes and ears.

I lift the receiver, feeling nervous and stupid. My hand is actually shaking as I dial the number, body filled with conflicting emotions. Will he remember me? Will he even answer? He's probably moved on by now, there will be loads of other kids for him. That would be a decision made for me. The pips sound and I push in some coins. The phone rings a few times and I'm about to lose my nerve when a Cockney voice answers with just a, "Hello".

Straight away I know it's not Rick and once again I nearly hang up, but something inside me thinks 'fuck it, grow a pair' so I ask for Rick. There is a short silence then the voice asks who I am. I tell him and stammer an explanation about meeting Rick and him asking me to phone. This seems to satisfy the voice, which orders me to wait, and there is silence. Another chance to back away, but I am steel inside now, nothing ventured, nothing gained.

His voice fills my head. "Rick here. Who is this?"

"Danny, we met after the Hanley concert …and I ran out on you, don't suppose you remember."

He laughs, and immediately the tension is gone and everything's ok. "Course I do, little 'Ziggy'. How you keeping Danny?"

We progress through some pleasantries, then his voice becomes more businesslike. "So, why are you calling me after all this time? As if I can't guess, given that he arrived back yesterday."

"You said to call if I needed anything." I hesitate, unsure, but he fills the space.

"And now you want something I can get, don't worry, spit it out."

"I need to see him and wondered if you could get tickets for the Rainbow…"

He laughs again. "Thought so. It's sold out of course, the Christmas Eve one. That's the one to go to, another big party afterwards."

That's it then, I've left it too late and he's moved on, trying to let me down gently. "Ok, sorry to bother you, thought it was worth a try."

"Whoa, not so fast, I didn't say no, did I? As it happens I can get a ticket, but it's not easy, so I can only get one, and I'd want a favour in return. Would you be ok to come alone?"

Here it comes, but I'm in a different place to last time. He continues before I can answer.

"I'd want you to come to the party afterwards as well, as my guest. I promise I won't make you run away this time."

The die was already cast when I stayed on the line, so I agree.

"Will your parents be ok with you coming down alone, being out late?"

"Yeah, I'll tell them I'm staying at my friend's."

He laughs again, he is making this a lot easier than I expected.

"Probably a good idea, it'll be a late one and there won't be much transport in the early hours of Christmas Day. You won't get turfed out into the cold, so don't worry. The party might go on all night, but there are always places to crash out. You might need to square it with Mom and Dad that you'll be away at Christmas though."

"That'll be ok, they aren't bothered." A lie, and the truth. I know there'll be consequences but at this moment I don't care. Who'd refuse a chance to be with Bowie, and at Christmas?

If I'm not going to be a coward about everything in my life, I've got to do this thing. I can see what's on offer, and what the cost is. Until I know, I can't make my choices. Making the phone call has made me feel better about myself because I've done something for myself, the first step on a path that will end in decisions.

" Ok, good. I've got to go now Danny, busy, busy. Perhaps I'll tell you about it at Christmas, there might be something to interest you. I'm always looking for a bit of help, and I took to you right away, despite you running off. Go to the Rainbow on the day, to the box office, and a ticket will be waiting in your name. I'll find you after the concert. Wait inside till the crowd has cleared. Be sure to wear all that 'Ziggy' stuff, it looks good on you. Tell you what, go and buy something cool to wear and I'll give you the money back when I see you. Any problems on the day, phone me, someone will be on this line who can get hold of me, but I'll leave details with the ticket as well."

The phone goes dead before I can reply.

That's it then. Now to face the future, and the consequences.

***

Alice:

Happy Christmas Alice! School has finished for both of us, and, as we walk past that stupid 'King Kong' statue in Manzoni Gardens, he suddenly announces that he's bloody well going to London on Christmas Eve for the Bowie concert, and might not see me until Boxing Day. He won't say how he got a ticket, where he's staying, or who he'll be with.

I snap. Tell him not to bother; that I'll let him know sometime if I want to see him, and that he can keep his Christmas present, if he's actually bothered to get me anything.

I regret it straight away, because this time, instead of the usual apologies he says, "if that's how you feel, let me know what you want to do," and off he goes without a backwards glance.

I've let him off the hook, absolved him of making his own decision and telling me what's going on. I stand in Manzoni, by 'King Kong', crying, then realize the absurdity of the scene, and go home.

Some Christmas this is turning out to be. Our first one together, and we are apart, maybe forever. I spend most of the following week in my room, inconsolable, despite the efforts of Mom and Dad. It's not just the hurt, the lack of feeling for me that he shows, putting me second to a pop star; or the suspicion there's someone else. I'm not sure about any of that. The truth is, I'm really worried about him, what's driving him along this path, and where will he end up? Why do I feel so responsible, or even care?

***

Danny:

So that's it then. Finished. Can't say I blame her. I feel relief, and guilt at my relief. It's solved a problem, bought me some space and time, without me having to do anything. Spineless or what? I think I may still love her, but the intensity she needs is too much for me at the moment, and, if I am bisexual, how can I carry on misleading her? What sort of relationship can we have? Despite what's happened, I can't stop my thoughts turning to London and what it may hold for me.

I put it her to the back of my mind. Time to concentrate on Bowie and Rick. Maybe things will become clearer.

It's teatime on day before Christmas Eve before I steel myself to broach the subject at home. It doesn't go well. Dad is in a bad mood because he has been to the pub for a 'festive' drink, which turned from 'a couple' into 'a few' and he's feeling the benefit. I can't leave it any longer, so while Mom is busying herself dishing up tea I casually mention that I'm spending Christmas at Derek's, because we are going to see Bowie in London.

For a moment I think I might get away with it as it seems to hardly register. He is half-cut and dozy, but Mom unexpectedly throws in her six-penny worth.

She stops what she's doing and slams down the spoon she is using to dole out lumps of mashed potato. The sound wakes the old bastard from his reverie with a start, and he instinctively looks for someone to take it out on.

Mom says, "No, I forbid it, you should be at home at Christmas, with your family."

In a weirdly comic moment, both of us look at her in disbelief, Dad's jaw actually drops open. Mom has never forbidden anything. I didn't even know she knew the word. Perhaps, she is changing too. I might be something to do with that. Trouble is, she's picked the wrong moment.

I start to reply, but Dad decides it's time to wade in with his usual level of tact and diplomacy, and clouts me across the head, knocking me onto the floor, along with various items of cutlery. My head is ringing as I lie there, hating him. I glance across, and she doesn't look so confident now. Her face registers a mix of emotions, fear, shock, hate, and perhaps regret?

"*I* fucking forbid it, never mind her, you're not going to see that poof, you're not going anywhere until you grow up and start taking some responsibility," he barks. "If you wanna live in my house you stick to my rules."

I say nothing. No need, I understand all too well. This moment has been coming for a long time. Phoning Rick was the first step in a chain of events that is now beginning to unfold, and I'm being carried along, towards a decision. Is that weakness on my part? Am I seeking justification for the decision I ultimately make? I lie there on the floor, feeling pathetic, ashamed of my cowardice.

Eventually, I stop fantasising about killing him; get back up onto my chair, after meekly collecting the scattered knives, forks and sauce bottles. Not the time for confrontation.

Nothing more is said. In a bizarre parody of domestic normality, Mom continues as if nothing has happened, and we eat in silence, following which I go to my room to contemplate my accelerating journey towards an unknown destination.

Raised words from below, he is shouting at her, then the front door slams. I look out and see him shambling off along the street, no doubt to top up on the booze and have a good moan to his mates, whilst bragging about how he, 'doesn't stand any nonsense' at home. Do his friends know the reality, would they care?

He's barely out of sight when she comes into my room. It's the new Mom again, crawled out of her shell now he's gone. Her voice is trembling, full of what I guess is a mixture of emotion and newly discovered anger.

"I told you didn't I? Warned you not to rock the boat. But you can't stop yourself can you? I bet you're making your little plans right now, another rebellion, but you better think on about what the result will be. I warned you what I'd do, and you better believe me."

She waits for a reaction, but I'm so tired of it all that I can't even be bothered to react. She takes the silence as acquiescence and ploughs on.

"I'm just about at the end of my tether, it's enough coping with his drinking and temper, I can't have you making it worse. You'll do as I say, be a good little boy, because that's what you are, just a little boy, with your petty issues; selfish, that's what you are. You don't care what happens to anyone else as long as you get to do what you want."

The sheer enormity of her blaming her own failures on me renders me speechless. There is no answering this level of blindness, it's in my own hands now. I've got to weigh up the consequences, which are fast becoming very clear, and make my own decisions.

"You be here for Christmas, play the loving son, keep him happy, or you know what I'll do." She doesn't wait for a reply and slams the bedroom door behind her.

I consider carefully. I'm strangely calm. I've crossed a line and there's no going back. Everything falls into a logical order: I'm going to London and that's that. I'll handle the repercussions on myself, but others mustn't get hurt. I know what I must do.

Within minutes I'm out of the door, calling a cheery, "goodbye, I'm popping out." Let her mull over the meaning of that, it might give me some time.

Luke is at home when I get there. As soon as he sees me he knows trouble and ushers me inside. We embrace, and sit close together on his sofa bed. I haven't got time to mess around.

'We've got to finish, this has got to be the last time we see each other."

He is taken aback, but quickly recovers.

"What's happened?"
I explain, haltingly, and with some tears.

"You see, we have to finish, you have to go away or something, I'm going to London and she'll tell Dad about us, and maybe the Police. Not sure about the cops, but I know for sure that my Dad will kill you, he's capable of anything."

There is no alternative. I'm steel. All these people and their lives hanging on my decisions, Alice, Luke, Mom. It's not fair. They are all using me. Alice, trying to create her perfect boyfriend, Luke

---

taking the opportunity to gratify himself, and my wonderful mother, using me as a punchbag to divert Dad's anger from herself. I need my own space, to find my own path.

The penny is dropping with Luke. He thought he was in control, but now my decision is what matters. I'm sorry for him, but he went into this eyes open, and I'm going to London, whatever the cost.

I wondered how he would take it, hoped he would understand, but in the end he's like all the others. He starts getting angry.

"So, I've got to uproot my life or risk going to prison, because you've got a juvenile fantasy about being a pop groupie? You need to grow up Danny."

"That's unfair. You know how old I am, I made no secret of it. You've helped me Luke, but don't tell me that you didn't get your rocks off doing it, because I know you did."

That shuts him up.

"I am growing up, trying to find out what sort of life I want. You, Alice, my parents, none of you own me, and none of you are going to. You think I owe you something? You're wrong. You, of all people, know what I've been putting up with at home, and I'm not taking it any more. Today was the last time he's going to punch me and get away with it, the last time Mom uses me. I'm going to London, going to see what's on offer, going to find out what other types of life there are, instead of this shit, so you better get used to the idea fast."

He starts pleading, and I see him for what he is. Now, at the end, I'm the one in control, it feels good.

I get up to leave and fire off a parting shot.

"I didn't want it to end like this, you've been good for me, I'll always remember you with fondness, but its run its course. I need to get a hold of my life, and to do that I need freedom. No more emotional chains. Goodbye Luke, I hope you find something good in life, but my advice is to leave Brum while you can, and disappear. Maybe it'll be a new start for you too, I hope so. Goodbye."

As I walk back to the bus stop I should feel sad, and sorry, but my steps are lighter, a weight has been lifted, and this time I've done it myself instead of just letting things happen to me. It feels good.

Mom looks at me quizzically when I arrive home, but I just continue with the happy face and go to my room, the perfect son.

***

I barely sleep, lie there listening to the rain drumming on the window.

I'm sixteen, and busily burning every bridge I have, not knowing where I'm going, or what's going to happen. Putting my trust in a man I've met once, who wants to screw me, possibly in more ways than one, and I'm doing my level best to put myself into his clutches.

It's been an emotional day, what with the family scene and finishing with Luke, I've been surfing my emotions, but that has to stop or I'll end up in a worse mess. There's no way that I'm missing Bowie, but I'll compromise, try to get home on Christmas Day, and I'll leave a note for Mom. Just for her. She can wrestle with her conscience, and the implications of her actions, after all, she started it.

Finally, my mind stops whirling, and I sleep.

***

Christmas Eve begins with a piece of luck. I hear Mom clattering about early, no doubt starting on the preparations for a 'family' Christmas. I sense an opportunity and I'm right, he's comatose. I heard him crash in through the front door well after midnight, no doubt after a skin full, and with him dead to the world and no work today, I've got Mom to myself. Still high on the feeling of being in control from the night before, I decide to ditch the note idea. It's a gamble, but there are no secrets now, so nothing to lose. And I know Mom better than anybody else.

She looks at me with a mixture of anger and fear, but does her usual thing, pushes the emotions down, preferring to skate along on the surface of normality, her protective shield.

"Breakfast?" She asks with a false cheeriness.

As she busies herself I take a deep breath and begin.

"Mom, I want to talk to you while he's asleep, so I don't get another clout round the head. Is that ok?"

She carries on, not even looking. This sort of thing makes her uncomfortable.

"Depends what you want to say."

"Well, I've tried really hard since our big conversation outside school, haven't caused any trouble for you – until yesterday, have I?"

"I suppose not."

"I want you to know that I've finished with Luke, it's over for good. And I think I've lost Alice too."

I can almost hear her brain processing this information. We both know it means that most of her hold over me has just evaporated. I press on.

"I really want to go and see Bowie, got a ticket and everything. The reason I said about not being home for Christmas is because there's no trains tonight and on Christmas Day, and I wanted you to know where I was and not worry. Derek's got a mate in London with a flat and we're going to crash there." A small lie.

She is silent, buttering toast.

" Well, that's some good news, about him I mean, not Alice, I like her. A nice, proper, girl, she is.

It upset me so much that you didn't want to be here for Christmas. I knew what your Dad would be like." She knows her position has weakened, I know that she isn't a strong person. I twist the knife.

"Look, Mom, neither of us want him mad, want him cracking off like last night, I don't need the bruises, and I can't believe you like me being the punchbag on your behalf".

That starts her crying. I'm getting good at this, and I confess to satisfaction at a little payback.

"I'm being up front with you about going. I am going, and I'll do my best to be back on Christmas Day. It's up to you how you want to play it. If you make a fuss, carry out your threat to tell him, tell the police, tell everyone, then we both know what will happen. I'll be gone for good, probably via the Q.E Hospital, and there'll be no going back. If you tell him that we've had a chat, I'm being responsible, can be trusted, calm him down, then we can carry on when I get back. I'm in your hands totally, if you want to press the destruct button, you can, but you can only do it once."

That hits home. I'm banking on my hard-won knowledge of her. She's hidden from every confrontation, until last night, and I'm betting that was the fear of me going and not coming back. When she answers I know I've won.

"You promise me you'll be safe, stick with Derek, and none of that 'funny business'…"

"Mom, Derek's not like that, he'd run a mile."

"And you'll do your best to get back for Christmas dinner, I'll do it later, your Dad will go to the pub anyway and sleep all afternoon – won't take much encouragement."

"I promise I'll try, but it's up to the trains, and I bet there'll be strikes or something, there always is at Christmas."

"Ok, but I want you to talk to me from now on, no more surprises, I just can't cope with it anymore. I don't know where it's all going to end."

She is still my mom, and she looks so small and defeated that I give her a hug, and just for a few seconds it's like it should have been. Then I remember what it's really like.

"Thanks, I've got to go and get ready now, I think it's best if I'm gone when he gets up, then he can't do anything to stop me.. Tell him to go to the pub with his mates, he'll forget all about it by teatime, and he might pass out and leave you in peace."

I stuff toast into my mouth and I'm gone before she can change her mind. I wonder if she's going to get a slap, but then again, she deserves it. I don't hang about putting on make-up and clothes. That would be pushing my luck. I stuff a few things into a rucksack and I'm away.

I spend the train journey gnawing at my fingers, a bag of nerves. Will there be a ticket, where will I end up tonight, what will it be like when I get home, and, will Bowie be worth it? I've risked everything for this.

I go straight to the box office at the Hammersmith Odeon, remembering every minute of my last visit, thinking of Alice, whose ghost is everywhere, I catch a faint echo of her laugh, see her smile, feel her touch, smell her perfume.

The woman behind the counter looks at me sternly. When I say a ticket has been left for me, I expect her to burst out laughing, but she asks my name and then ruffles through numerous envelopes in a drawer, eventually producing one and pushing it under the screen with a triumphant flourish.

I open it slowly, not knowing what to expect. A ticket, front stalls, and a note from Rick.

'Hi Danny, hopefully you've arrived and are looking forward to the concert! I've got something very special to tell you about the party afterwards and I can't wait to see your face. Hope you've got your best 'Ziggy' stuff on because you're gonna need it! If you are early enough there are directions to my place on the attached note, and the phone number in case you've lost it. You can crash out tonight, (well tomorrow morning!), at mine, and you can get changed etc. It's gonna be a great night! Rick.'

I know what sort of a night Rick is after. I'm excited about this 'party'. Rick can put me into places no other fan can get, so this must be something special.

An hour, and a couple of false turns later, I'm tentatively rapping a heavy brass door knocker. It's a cold but dry afternoon, one of those still, steel-coloured days with a pale winter sun just giving some warmth. The house is in a quiet square with a small grassed area in the middle. Railings are topped with gold spikes here, and there is a rich looking woman in a big fur coat walking a pampered poodle. The smell of money is everywhere.

Rick's house is in a terrace and has a bright red door. My knock is answered by Mickey, the lad I met at Hanley. He is a bit more with it than then, but I still catch a slight slurring in his voice and wonder whether he's already used something today. Rick is out doing some 'business'. Inside, the house is huge. It goes back miles and has four floors. The furnishings are cool and modern. I can't help but be impressed. I know nothing about houses, but this one shouts 'cash'. There are real paintings hanging up, those swirly abstract ones, and ones with blocks of colour.

Mickey shows me to the top floor, an attic room. He indicates the double bed,

"You can crash here. Bathroom's one floor down. I'll be in the kitchen at the back on the ground floor if you fancy a drink. There's plenty of time for a chat and I'll tell you what the plan is. His tone conveys that this is more of a requirement than an invitation.

"Sure, I'll be down in ten."

For the second time – the first was when he answered the door, he gives me a strange look. I can't decide if it's curiosity, anger, or whether he's laughing quietly at me. I mentally shrug my shoulders. I'll find out soon enough. He shuffles out of the room. I ask myself why I'm doing this.

The kitchen, is huge, bigger than our whole ground floor at home, with its own dining area, and two white bucket seats hanging from the ceiling in a corner. Mickey indicates I am to sit, and I slowly revolve while he cracks the tops off two bottles of Coke.

"Bit too early for the hard stuff," he says as he hands me a bottle and sits in the seat opposite, assessing me. He produces fags and offers me one.

I take him in properly for the first time, having only seen him slumped and sloshed, in the shadows.

I put him as early twenties, with spiky dark hair like Rod Stewart's. He is tall, over six feet I guess, and thin, but his arms have muscles, well defined under a thin layer of skin, devoid of any fat. He has a face like a ferret, with sunken cheeks and defined cheekbones, a nose like a blade and a thin moustache that he would look better without. When he smiles I see crooked teeth, but the whole ensemble produces an unlikely charm. His smile is genuine, reaching his brown eyes. I wonder if he is queer.

He quizzes me on my reasons for coming, seems satisfied when I tell him about my love for Bowie, and my home life. As I talk about Dad he nods, and I know he has been there too.

"Last thing I remember seeing of you was your arse as you ran away from Rick, got cold feet did you?"

I am taken unawares by the sudden change of conversation. Mickey is leaning forward, waiting for a reply.

"It was the first time a man had touched me that way and what with the party, Bowie there, the booze and everything, it just got too much. I was a bit of a prat wasn't I?"

He flashes a look of what? Amusement, pity, something else?

"I've been there mate. You had something to run back to, I didn't. You've still got something, are you sure you should be here?"

"That was then, I've done a lot of growing up since. I've tried a few things out. I don't know how much longer I can take the old man, his fucking rules, and worse. Mom is worse than useless, this is a chance to get out so here I am. I know what the price might be."

He takes a while to answer. "I hope you do."

Then it is time to get the make-up on and head to the Rainbow.

***

David:

The 'homecoming' Rainbow gig on 24th December 1972, kicks off a short UK tour. Bowie asks the audience to bring a toy to donate to Dr Barnardo's Children's Homes where his deceased father worked as a Public Relations officer, and they respond enthusiastically, filling a truck.

'Jean Genie' is in the Top Twenty, and the concert is a 3000 - strong immediate sell out. Bowie's currency in Britain is riding high, everyone wants a piece of 'Ziggy' – or is it Bowie they want? No-one, including Bowie, really knows anymore.

The audience is frenzied, the screaming of hysterical girls louder than ever.

Bowie is recovering from flu. He jokes with the audience that it might be caused by he and the boys putting too much in their mouths. What he is alluding to is not made clear.

There is a slick new concert set, beginning with 'Let's Spend The Night Together', including the UK debut of Mike Garson and his jazz-style piano. The performance is polished, the effect of playing constantly together, and much 'rockier', with no acoustic set, although 'Rock 'n' Roll Suicide' is still the finale and 'The Jean Genie' is the only new song featured.

The show finishes late, and, being Christmas Eve, even the Underground has stopped running. Many fans are left stranded, either having to walk home, pay for a taxi, or sleep rough, 'Bowie freaks' in full 'get-up' crash in doorways and on park benches.

The band are mobbed by fans outside the stage door, with one girl nearly sticking scissors into Ronson's eye whilst trying to cut off a lock of his hair. 'The Spiders' make it back to Yorkshire via limousine, in time for Christmas Day with their families. Bowie goes home to his flat at Haddon Hall.

His spectacular year has come to an end. Voted by Melody Maker as their 'mainman' of 1972, and 'Top Vocalist' in a poll. The 'Ziggy Stardust' album is deemed best album, selling 200,000 copies in the UK and US.

What next for Bowie? One critic muses that perhaps it is time for him to move on and retire 'Ziggy'.

Part Two

The Fall

Chapter Ten

'Blackstar'
New Year 2016

Alice:

    *I'm surprisingly excited about New Year's Eve. It's been a lonely Christmas, my first since parting with Alan, and it **has** been a total parting. We have gone our separate ways, exhausted with each other. There isn't enough feeling left for animosity, just emptiness. There are no ties, no need for further contact. Twenty - three years gone, without trace or regret – apart from regretting the waste of it all. I would trade the lot for another twelve months with Danny.*

    Perhaps, if we had stayed together, we might have gone the same way, gone stale too. The memories are old now, tinged with nostalgia, viewed through a golden haze. It's difficult to see it clearly; but I know that we were soul-mates, destined to be together for all time, until life got in the way.

    *One day we **will** be together again, I sense that strongly, especially when I hear 'Starman', 'Ziggy Stardust', or especially 'Changes', which feels like a song about us. He is out there, somewhere, and we will meet, and we will be young again. He'll remember me and love me still.*

    But for now, I've got something, with Robert, or nothing. And Christmas has underlined just how tough nothing can be.

    He sends a black cab round for Genie and I at 9pm. Normally at this time I would be contemplating bed and a book. Going out, staying out, seems a huge effort, outrageously wanton, but it is New Year's Eve, and tonight I plan to stay awake until after midnight!

    The cabbie is the sort who knows a little, and has an opinion about, everything, and never shuts up. I nod politely in what I hope are the right places, grateful for the background noise, which is enough to stop me dwelling on what I'm doing, the recklessness, or stupidity, of it.

We pull up in an area that was clearly once industrial, with large warehouse or factory type buildings, but no longer grim and grimy. No sons of toil have entered these doors for decades. They have been converted to house the new London gentry, with acres of tinted glass and large balconies, full of expensive greenery. The air of opulence makes me wonder whether the driver has got the wrong address.

The cabbie tells me that he's been paid, but pockets the tip adroitly. He hands me a slip of paper and indicates an imposing portico with a uniformed doorman.

The doorman, a retired soldier or policeman by his bearing and manner, looks at Genie and I slightly dubiously, but is instantly polite when I show him the address,

"Oh yes, Mr. Harper, the penthouse. Of course, top of the shop, best flat in the building. Very nice, and a very nice man if I may say so."

He is assessing me, trying to decide between gold-digger or prostitute. My age and looks must mitigate against the latter, but he is just being good at his job and indulging in professional curiosity, in case I commit some crime and he has to speak with the Police.

'Yes', I can imagine him saying, 'Didn't fit at all. Bit dowdy and plain, and too old to be a man like Mr. Harper's lady. I was suspicious straight away, I can tell you, never lose the nose for it do you?'

I'm probably doing him a disservice, because he is courteous and attentive, asking my name and insisting upon calling Robert via an inside intercom that I cannot hear, before I am allowed entry.

I wait on the doorstep until he returns, wreathed in smiles, picks up my case and shows me to the lift, pressing the top floor button as I enter. I guess that Robert is a handsome tipper, buying both the security and the extra service.

Robert is waiting when the doors open. I am instantly conscious of my old cocktail dress. His suit is exquisitely tailored and looks very expensive, as does his open-necked shirt. I am more than a little taken aback. No trace of the shabby and hirsute figure I first met. He is clean shaven, hair still fairly long, but recently layered and styled. I take in glinting gold rings, cuff links bearing some Greek style lettering and pleasantly understated aftershave. As he hugs and greets me. I can't help myself and blurt out in my Brummie accent,

"Bloody hell, you scrub up well, it's like suddenly finding James Bond coming out of disguise. I think I needed to put a bit more effort in, are we going somewhere that posh?"

He laughs, and assures me that I am gorgeous and will light up the restaurant. It's the right thing to say, but it slides out with the polish of a professional womaniser, and once again I wonder about his past, past women. I am glad I came. Already, I've started to see another Robert, but is this the real one, or have I just peeled off a layer or two?

He shows me into an entrance hall, then an open plan, loft-type, living area, with a fabulous flame effect central fire, plush furnishings and a panoramic view of an illuminated fairytale London that renders everything else into shadow. He notices my gaze,

"I left the blinds open for you, I never get tired of it, but Christmas nights are special, hides all the ugly parts."

"It's stunning." I am avidly drinking in the surroundings, scouring his home for clues. There is some expensive looking art on the walls. Twentieth century, a mix of abstract art and male and female nudes. One looks like a Lucien Freud. He is alert to my focus of attention.

"One of my little vices, I've been collecting art for years. Hopefully the nudes don't offend you, I am fascinated by different renditions of the human body, it can be so beautiful, or repellent."

He looks at me quizzically.

"No. not at all, I used to draw and paint when I was younger, and still do design stuff on the internet. I studied art actually." I walk close enough to see brushstrokes, and signatures.

"But that's…"

"Not a copy, an original. My Freud and Schiele, that one is a Dix, and that by Nolde. I've found a real affinity with Weimar decadent art, seems to tug at something in my heart, It's so real, so closely connected to its time and culture."

I become aware that my mouth is hanging open, and he laughs.

"But they must have cost a fortune."

"Worth quite a lot now I suspect, but I bought them a long time ago when I had too much disposable income and ran out of things to spend it on. They were relatively cheap then, unfashionable. It doesn't matter, I'm not selling them, and they'll go to an appreciative home after I die. I bought them for me, not for profit, in fact, don't you think that monetary value ruins art?"

We embark on a short conversation about the merits of art then he realises that I'm still holding my overnight bag.

"Not much of a host am I, showing off my paintings without making you feel at home? Let me take that, and follow me."

He shows me to my room, which is the most luxurious I have ever seen. There are even fresh flowers, a strange touch for a single man. I find myself hoping that there is a woman ' who does', and not another female in the background.

We have a gin and tonic, and during the general conversation I start to probe, carefully and gently, but he is clever, and diverts the conversation away from the past. The more he does it, the more curious I become.

Eventually, the effect of the gin combined with his evasions emboldens me, and I ask bluntly.

"Robert, just how bloody rich are you, and how did you get that way, self-made man or rich family?" Then I feel coarse and obvious, nakedly probing into something that's none of my business.

"Just interested, I've never met anyone truly loaded before, with genuine masterpieces on their walls. Doesn't matter to me if you're a millionaire or not." I take another gulp of gin and decide to slow down a bit.

"That's ok. I know you're not here for my money, because you didn't know I had any."

"Exactly, you looked like a tramp when I first met you."

" Yes, well, a combination of my dog walking clothes and..."
He stops.

"And what?"

"For the first time in my life I just got fed up with everything, it all seemed too much bother, so I stopped – bothering that is; stopped shaving or thinking about my appearance. It was quite nice in a way. I became invisible, until you arrived and took pity on me.

I was interested, wanted to get to know you better. You treated a shabby-looking old man like a human being. You didn't have to, but you did. I felt that I liked you, we made some sort of connection, and suddenly I felt like bothering again."

I'm a bit overwhelmed and confused by this sudden declaration, unsure what it means. After a silence he continues,

"To be honest, I don't know what would have happened if you hadn't turned up when you did. Charlie needs me, gives me unflinching love and loyalty, but no one else does. There is no one else.

One day I stood back from the mirror whilst shaving and thought, 'if you die today, no one will mourn you. The world will move on, and probably be better without you'. I realised that my life is empty, my success means nothing, that I didn't like myself very much at all..."

I'm shocked to see tears in his eyes and can't help myself from sitting next to him and giving him a hug. He doesn't respond, certainly not sexually, and it **would** *have been an opportunity if his soul-baring were a ploy to invite intimacy.*

We sit for a few moments, me with an arm around him, both of us staring into space, at the festive lights, the life of the capital below us. I feel as meaningless as he apparently does. All those millions down there, all those lives, mine is just one more insignificant little moment, a flash and gone. We have something in common, not a happy bond, but one with possibilities. I'm just about to push the conversation deeper when the door buzzer shatters the moment, evaporating it like sea mist on a sunny morning.

It's the dog sitter, a very attractive woman in her twenties called Penny who should have been out herself tonight, rather than me. Still, she seems happy enough, and I guess that she is being very well compensated for her lonely New Year. She makes a huge fuss of the dogs and Genie is straight onto her lap and cuddling in, so I know he will be ok.

"Right Penny, we'll be back by one, I promise, then it's your turn to go out with that man of yours." I notice the wedding ring, perhaps not a rival then. How much would I be bothered if she were?

***

David:

He is at his house in the Catskill Mountains, New York State. Christmas has been and gone. Every calendar date has taken on extra meaning. There will be no 'Happy New Years' this time. They may be said, but they will be shadowed. Because this will be his last one.

He is suffering from liver cancer, and has been undergoing treatment for the previous eighteen months. He has kept his condition secret, telling only a few very close friends, including Tony Visconti, who he met at the recording studio during the 'Blackstar' sessions, when he was completely bald from the chemotherapy.

There has been hope, a spell of remission in the middle of 2015, but in November the cancer not only returned, but has spread throughout his body, and that month, he is told it is terminal.

He has continued working throughout his illness, on a musical. 'Lazarus', a musical adaptation of 'The Man Who Fell To Earth'. Also, on what he now knows will be his final album, 'Blackstar', which he is crafting into a 'farewell' event. His last public appearance is at the premiere of 'Lazarus' in New York on December 7th, and he manages to keep his condition secret from the public. But after taking his bow, he sits, exhausted, backstage, and later he is escorted to his car by the Director, Ivo van Hove, who is left with the feeling that it is the last time he will see Bowie alive.

Everyone he works with who knows the truth admires his courage, and his devotion towards completing 'Blackstar', which is due for release on January 8th 2016, his 69th birthday. He is hanging onto life as the launch date approaches.

***

Alice:

We go to a really smart restaurant. Robert seems to be well known to them, so I know he isn't showing off, just taking me to a favorite place. I hope it means that he feels comfortable with me.

For a while the usual distractions of scanning the occupants of the neighbouring tables, the menus, ordering food and drinks, occupy our time, then we settle into waiting, and I remember that my earlier question wasn't answered. But the conversation has not regained the depth broken by the dog-sitter's arrival, and now, surrounded by New Year's Eve gaiety, Christmas decorations, balloons and streamers, it seems wrong to try to return to that moment.

We chat and the meal progresses, course-by-course, drink-by-drink. The sound level grows until the chimes of 'Big Ben' ring out over the sound system, streamers and balloons drop, and there is the usual false bonhomie that lasts about five minutes before everyone gets back to the London norm of either ignoring, or being rude and aggressive with each other.

As the last chimes sound, Robert stands, comes around the table, takes my hand and decorously encourages me from my seat, like a Southern Gentleman in 'Gone With The Wind'.

He draws me in to his body, whispers "Happy New Year – for both of us, I hope," and kisses me. I am ready to respond, but it is a chaste kiss, not prolonged, and he returns to his seat, summoning the waiter and ordering more champagne.

I reflect on the moment whilst observing him. Our first kiss. There have of course been plenty of other first kisses, but this one doesn't fit. There was a reserve, a reticence. Why?

Normally, the first brush of lips is a precursor to further pressure and an opening of mouths, which I would have accepted, but it did not happen. First kisses. I sip my champagne and watch others embracing and kissing. One I remember above all of course, the first kiss with Danny, my very first, the one that thrilled me to my core. I have never forgotten it, or that feeling, never recaptured it.

I observe Robert as he sits, composed, watching the mayhem surrounding us. What an enigma he is. Rich, good-looking, socially adept, clearly educated, nicely spoken, despite the London accent which wonder might be an affectation to fit in, and yet alone. No wife, no woman, no man even, on the scene, and no evidence of one, apart from those flowers in my room.

He must have blazed a trail of relationships and broken hearts; should have been 'society', in the paparazzi magazines, his every partner assessed. But here is, with me, tears in his eyes, secrets and pasts between us. It doesn't make sense.

We don't stay long. Robert is diligent in keeping his promise to Penny. "Trustworthy dog sitters are like gold dust, she also keeps me in order, put those flowers in your room, I wouldn't have thought of it. I try to pay her more, but she says she's doing her bit for the aged."

The same taxi driver picks us up, patter unrelenting. Robert plays the London game, chatting and debating. Two men from such different backgrounds conversing as equals. I'm pretty sure the cabbie has the best of it.

Soon, Penny is gone to enjoy her belated celebrations, and we are sat facing each other, London still ablaze with lights and sporadic firework displays, a living mural. The dogs are asleep, sharing Charlie's extra-large bed, reproaching us. I had thought to sit beside Robert, but I sense that physical proximity is not for this moment, and Robert makes no move to get closer.

I'm pretty drunk, and tired, but he seems   immune to alcohol, despite consuming his fair share of gin and champagne. In fact, he was supporting me up to the apartment and onto my current place of repose. If he wanted to sleep with me, I would, even if just to try and get closer to him, feel that someone still finds me attractive and wants to hold me. But there is no indication that he wants to do anything other than just be with me. I know that I will fall asleep soon.

I'm happy to accept the simple companionship of this man with no past. It is ok to be sat with someone, no need to force a conversation, with the bonus that he is good looking, rich and intelligent, an older woman's dream.

Throughout the meal, the drinks, the taxi driver's prattling, that unanswered question has remained in my head.

"You never told me how you got rich."

He looks at me for what seems like ages, then shrugs. "No big deal really. I didn't inherit it, I grew up on a Council estate in the East End, tough place, and it made me tough too. Never knew my father, my mother saw me as an encumbrance to enjoying herself, left me to fend for myself. A 'latchkey kid'.

I had to learn to stand up for myself, fight, or run, find the weaknesses of others and use them to survive. I was good at that, I was cleverer than the bullies, made contacts in the right places, got some protection. I learnt a lot about using people, buying them. I'm not proud of it.

I started in business, buying and selling, importing goods, then picking up property, both commercial and private rentals, I was good at it. Decisive, emotionless, ruthless. I made money, lots of it, and invested it in things that made even more money. There is always some luck in business, mine was buying a lot of poor quality London housing at a knockdown price, for rental, a fashion at the time, then I was sitting on an accidental goldmine after values rocketed.

I was driven, ambitious. I never wanted to go back to that Estate, live in a shitty little flat, scraping by. I made a lot of enemies and few friends – none of them close. Everything was 'business'. No time for proper relationships, and most people just wanted to use me too, or get hold of my money.

I resisted personal commitments,. It was who could do what, mutual back – scratching. I could never overcome the feeling that people had hidden agendas when they wanted to get close to me. I was always looking out for them, and often finding them too. That tends to kill off any chance of a true depth of feeling. I kept my distance, built a wall around myself and let nobody inside to hurt me.

One day I woke up rich, old, and totally alone bar a dog, with a solitary death to look forward to. I looked at my life and found it wanting. I don't like what I've done, but it is done and there is nothing I can do now to change that.

No one who knows me would believe that I've changed, they would all be looking for the angle. Sometimes I can't stop my old self emerging, and then I despise myself. And you turn up at the park, and here we are. That's it."

I don't know what say, so I say nothing. A short silence becomes longer. I know that my tongue will be thick and clumsy from the drink, my brain befuddled. I hadn't expected such an unburdening. In the end I opt for discretion.

"All I know Robert, is that since we've met you've been a total gentleman. Yes, a bit of a mystery, especially when you transform yourself like tonight. We've only known each other for a few weeks, but I don't see this 'dark half'. People our age all have a past, bear the scars of life, nobody gets through it unscathed. One day, when I'm sober and the time is right, I'll tell you the story of mine, and how I got my scars."

I hold my arms out so that he can see the silvery lines on my wrists. "Let's keep the past where it belongs, in the past, and enjoy today. I've had a great time tonight, you've bought some light back into my life. I'll accept that, with thanks. I don't know what to do about you either, so let's just take it day by day as we agreed."

He nods. "If I haven't frightened you off with my dark side, let's have a nightcap."

I wake with a start and realise that the alcohol and late hour have won. Robert is sat in silence, just looking at me.

"Sorry, how long have I been asleep?"

"Only twenty minutes. Don't apologise, I enjoyed seeing somebody sleep untroubled. Come on, it's time for bed." He winks, "And no funny business either, I'm a reformed character."

I don't wake until mid-morning, feeling that gravity has doubled during the night, my head throbbing, throat dry. There is a shaft of winter sunlight scything across the room from a gap in the curtains, and for a while I watch motes of dust dancing in the beam while I try to recapture the evening.

Some of it is hazy, but Robert's soul-baring is clear. My emotions are in a jumble, like some young girl stumbling through her first relationship, like that other Alice, with Danny. I haven't felt like this since then. But it is different, a different, more mature type of love, if that is what it is. Perhaps sex is naturally replaced by friendship and companionship, a sharing of life. Perhaps that is better.

Robert intrigues me. I don't know whether I want him as friend or lover, he doesn't seem to know either. He had every chance to screw me last night, and I would have, but he didn't. He might be gay, but my sense is that he is not, that instead he has buried his feelings and can't find his way back to them.

His past intrigues me too. What a life, what stories, what experiences, what effect it has had on him. His inner turmoil in coming to terms with it. I can't reconcile that Robert with the man I have known these few weeks, he must be exaggerating. In his loneliness he has brooded for too long, lost perspective. I know all about that, and what it can lead to.

My head clears a little and I make two decisions. One to get up, the second to be there for him, as a friend, whatever that entails, whilst we both work out what we want.

After a perfunctory toilet, I've gone long past trying to hide my age, and I really don't think he cares; he could buy beautiful women if he wanted them. I go in search of him.

The apartment is devoid of both Robert and dogs. The blinds are open and London, exhausted by its New Year's revels, spreads below me, eerily quiet on Bank Holiday, bathed in the weak glow of a winter sun hanging in a pale blue wash of a sky.

A note on the table.

'Thought I'd let you sleep that innocent sleep some more, so I've taken the dogs out. Coffee and breakfast in the kitchen. I've left some headache tablets out in case you need them! Help yourself. See you around noon. X'

I ponder that written kiss for a moment. Is it chaste, like the New Year one?

After coffee, food, and painkillers, I recover quickly. A glance at the kitchen clock tells me that I have about forty-five minutes before he returns.. In the end I give in to temptation, and, guiltily aware of every sound that might indicate his return, start exploring the apartment.

Apart from the huge, open-plan living area, and the kitchen with its breakfast bar and gleaming surfaces, there are just two bedrooms, both ensuite. I peer around Robert's door. All is tidy. The super king-size bed is made. There are no clothes 'processing' on chairs. I approach the bedside tables. A Bose sound system, a locked iPad, and that's it. No photographs. I had noticed the absence of photographs elsewhere in the penthouse. I open drawers. They are empty of personal belongings. The wardrobe is full of clothes, but no stored items. The bathroom has toiletries, a line of expensive aftershaves on a shelf, and that is it.

I return to the sofa with another coffee and take a look around me. There is nothing personal on display, nothing personal hidden away. If he has such things, and if he speaks the truth about his past, they must be at his house in Dorset, this is nothing more than a rich man's London base. I hear him returning.

We chatter idly, on a surface level, Robert almost shy and withdrawn. I wonder whether he regrets or is embarrassed by his revelations. He has business for the next couple of days, but promises to contact me soon. Is that a tactic to buy some time to think, a precursor to ending whatever it is we have between us? Is it fear of letting me inside that wall he has built?

By mid-afternoon I'm back in my drab little flat, dressed comfortably in leggings and a loose top. It seems like a fantastic fantasy, the Penthouse, the rich man with his mysterious past. I don't know whether I he will call..

But I know that I want him to.

Chapter 11

'The Man Who Sold The World'
Christmas Eve / Day 1972

Danny:

I stand blinking in the harsh lights. The enchantment is over, the magician has gone.

The auditorium is revealed in all its faded glory. It was better in the dark. I am better in the dark too. Now that Bowie is gone, my 'Ziggy Stardust' clothes and make up seem incongruous, as the real world snaps back into focus.

The crowd are filing out, high on the excitement of sharing communion with their hero. Girls with smeared eye shadow, boys, sweaty and boisterous, shouting and messing about. I am the only one not moving.

Within minutes I am alone in the first rows of the stalls and I can sense a nearby security guard's attention. *'Any minute now, I'll be out on my ear, if Rick doesn't hurry up'*. I feel stupid. What am I really doing here anyway? Doubts assail me, and I'm about to join the queue to leave when I hear my name being shouted.

There is a figure in the shadows at the side of the stage, and then the security guard approaches.

"Come on kid, move your arse unless you want to go with all the other punters."

I follow the man to the stage and up stairs at the side. For a brief moment I'm standing where Bowie sang 'Rock 'n' Roll Suicide to close the show. I scrutinize the spot, expecting to see some fading remnant of fairy dust, but it is just a stage floor.

Rick is waiting. He looks just the same, tall, rangy, with his hair in a ponytail like Francis Rossi in Status Quo - in fact he looks a bit like him. He wears no make-up and doesn't really fit with the rest of the Bowie circus. I wonder what he does.

I am nervous but full of anticipation, what's in store for me tonight?

"Hi Danny, you look great, let's go."

He is off at pace, through corridors and out of a rear door where a last few fans wait in hope.

"Sorry guys, David's long gone to have his Christmas, so you go and have yours."

He produces a few photographs from his jacket and hands them out and they drift away. A few look curiously at me; only three months ago, I was one of them. I have a foot inside, but don't know the full price as yet.

There is a big car with a driver, and the security guard, who has followed us, gets into the passenger seat. I remember now, Rick provides security for the UK tours. We get into the back, and I sink deep, taking in the smell of leather and cigarettes.

"Greg, 'Sombrero' please." Rick orders.

The traffic is surprisingly heavy, given the late hour, but it is Christmas, and this is London.

Rick assumes an easy familiarity with me, chatting away about Bowie, his forthcoming short January tour that begins in Scotland on the fifth, and then the return to the States in February. I can stand it no longer,

"Where are we going, you said it was something special?"

"Well, yeah, we're off to a Christmas Party."

I feel slightly disappointed. Have I gone through all this for just another party? Rick must see it on my face.

"Hey, cheer up, it's Bowie's party, and if you make yourself useful, who knows where it could end."

I've got a pretty good idea where it's going to end for Rick and I, but I'm already resolved to that. This is about seeing what's out there, what the opportunities might be in London, and what sort of launchpad Rick might provide.

"What sort of useful?"

"Can I trust you Danny, and know you're not gonna shoot your mouth off back home, even to that girl, or your mates?"

"She's not my girl anymore."

I can sense that he is not too upset at this revelation.

"That's a real shame. But you haven't answered my question, can you keep your mouth shut?"

"Yes, of course, I'm not stupid. Got nobody to tell anyway, especially at home, they'd freak out if they knew what I was up to."

"We can talk about what's going on back home in a minute. I just want to emphasise that if you aren't discreet, not only might there be police trouble, but I wouldn't be very happy."

His whole demeanour has changed from benevolent uncle to cold, no-nonsense businessman. At least he is being up front, and I suppose he is taking a risk with me. I know he is dodgy, too flash, too much cash, what was I expecting?

I try to sound grown up.

"I'll keep my mouth shut. I want things too. I want out of boredom, I want to be part of Bowie's world, and that means being here, with you. My eyes are wide open. I didn't just come because you got me a ticket to the show, I know there's strings attached, so let's get on with it. I've got some decisions to make when I get home, and I need what's on offer."

The car pulls into the kerb outside a club called 'Yours or Mine'. I notice a large Sombrero hat above the entrance, and realize the 'Sombrero' is a restaurant, with the nightclub beneath. The doors are open, but guarded by four solid-looking bouncers, prowling around a handwritten sign that declares,

'Private Party, Invites Only'.

People are filing in slowly, and what people! They light up the night with their beautiful clothes, hair and make-up. There are boys and girls, some where it's hard to say. Glittery tops, jumpsuits tucked into platform boots, boys in dresses, all the latest fashions. David's home ground, where he gets some of his ideas. It is magical.

"Here we are, we'll chat a bit more inside, then you can earn your keep if you want to. If not I'll get Greg here to run you to the station and we'll call it quits."

We alight, and the bouncers hold the crowd back to allow us entry. As we walk between them I feel special and important. One of the bouncers, a tough looking man with a weather-beaten, granite face sporting a large bent nose, nods and says,

"Evening Mr. Foster, have a good time, all's in order."

He replies, "Thanks Billy. This is Danny, he's with me and might join us, so keep an eye on him."

Billy looks at me long and hard. I don't think he's impressed. "I will Mr. Foster, I will." It sounds like a threat.

We don't go straight down into the club, instead diverting to a small office, I'm not quite sure if it's part of the restaurant or the club. A very large black bouncer with a towering Afro opens the door for us and acknowledges Rick, before closing it and resuming guard outside. I'm trapped and nervous.

Rick sits at the desk and points towards a seat.

"Manager's office, but he won't mind me using it. Now then, let's continue our chat. Tell me about what's going with you at home and what you think you want, and I'll see if I can help. Think of it as a bit of an interview."

The irritating little voice inside pipes up, asking if this is really what I want. I stifle it, and launch into a description of my home life, mom and dad, school, the feeling that I don't fit in anymore. I hesitate for a moment, then plunge into relationships, even my doubts about sexuality. He listens, nodding and smiling encouragement every so often, accompanied by pats on my legs. He seems to be in no hurry, and after about twenty minutes my stream of words dries to a trickle, and then stops.

He reaches into a drawer and produces a bottle of scotch and two glasses, pouring a slug into each.

"Here, I think you need this after that lot."

I've never drunk neat whisky. I take a large gulp and keep my face straight as the liquid burns its way down my throat and warms my stomach. The effect is almost instantaneous.

"Good. You sound like an ideal candidate for me. Of course, that's not why I picked you out of that crowd outside the stage door that night, you know that don't you?"

I nod. I know alright.

"But that can wait. First, to business. I supply the security to the Bowie roadshow. At least that's how it started, but he uses me for non-tour stuff like this as well. He's a London boy, like me, and I think he likes that. I had a bit of luck, was in the right place at the right time, before he got too famous. Also, I've got lots of friends, connections, who can get pretty much anything, and any service. Ok so far?"

I nod. I know where this is going, but want to hear it spelt out. I've never met a gangster, but it seems I'm sat right opposite one, drinking his whisky, and he fancies me rotten.

"I was running pub doors, but since Bowie I've got into other stuff, one-off shows, done some stuff for Bolan, 'Roxy', 'Glitter', and others. I started providing the transport - limos, cars vans, trucks. It all grew from there. I was there first, got it sewn up. I got more trusted, delivered what they asked for, that's why trust is so important. What do you think these arty-farty, rock people wanted from me on top of security and transport?"

I know what goes with 'Rock and Roll'.

"Sex and drugs?"

He laughs. "I provide protection from unwelcome eyes, including the law, so it's only natural that they asked me, especially as some knew that my door people have a little side enterprise, dealing."

Chilling to hear it spoken so matter-of-factly. This isn't a bit of shoplifting I'm dabbling with, it's proper criminal, and from the sound of it, serious stuff. After all, this is London. To be doing all this Rick must be a player. The whole evening so far has proved that. The access he has, the limo, the deference shown to him when we arrived. I've been minimising the obvious in my quest for freedom; there's no looking the other way now. No deluding myself. Being 'in' means joining it all, being bound by a new set of rules. Better than the ones at home? I don't know yet.

Rick carries on talking as I try to process the information.

"To begin with it was just dope. The hippies were still hanging in there, and that's what they were into. That was easy, as I employ a lot of West Indians. They are big, tough, frighten the troublemakers; grateful for the money - and the fact that I treat them the same as everyone else. They also have contacts I can't get into myself, wrong skin colour.

Once people knew I could be relied on to safely provide good gear, they started asking for other stuff, acid, pills. Not much smack at the moment, seems to be out of fashion and I don't like it, all those needles and overdoses, too messy. Lately it's been 'Coke', Bowie 'discovered' it in America, and they all want it now. It's made for them, helps with the parties, having a good time, having great sex apparently."

"Apparently?"

"Oh, I don't use myself, that would be bad for business. Booze and fags are enough for me, in fact..."

He proffers a cigarette and produces a gold lighter. The first inhalation, as always, send a rush to my head, adding to the effect of the whisky. Rick puts his expensive-looking cowboy boots up on the desk and leans back.

"Times have been good. They wanted girls - and boys next, a natural progression. There are always 'Toms' and 'Rent Boys' hanging around the clubs and pubs. My boys know lots of them. It's a piece of piss to provide them with security and punters in exchange for a cut. I've had a great couple of years, and I'm looking to grow.

I need good looking kids like yourself to front for me, if you're up for it. There would be more cash than you've ever seen, you'd be here, in the bright lights, in all the places where it's happening. I can even find you a place to live, but it's a deal I'm offering, and there are two sides to every deal."

He pauses, takes a long drag, and waits. I hesitate, unsure of what to say, uncertain of what I really want, how much I'm willing to risk to pay for it.

He fills the empty space hanging between us.

"Hey, not so glum. We're gonna have a great time tonight and at the same time you can see what you think. As long as you keep your trap shut there's no obligation to come back, I won't be chasing you, there's always others. I like you Danny, I see potential in you. You can go back to home and school and take a while, decide what you want. After that you tell me yes or no. What do you say?"

It's exactly why I came, so I say yes. He's taking a risk, and it's a fair offer.

He seems satisfied, stubs his fag out in the ashtray then puts his arm around me. "Good lad, that's made me a happy man, and when I'm happy everyone around me is."

We make our way back to the entrance, then down a sweeping staircase into the club itself. The DJ is set up under a flower–decorated archway. The club is basically square, with tables set around a tiny, under-lit dance floor that looks far too small for the room. The lighting is dim and it's difficult to make anything out, other than that the place is both heaving and rocking, the floor crammed shoulder to shoulder with shadowy bodies, in various stages of bodily contact from dancing to snogging.

As we make our way between tables, I notice that there are waiters. One comes close, offering us food, which looks like ham and a dollop of potato salad on a paper plate. He is so 'queer' it's almost a parody, voice and mannerisms completely over the top. Rick indicates his refusal and the waiter minces off, dispensing his bizarre offering elsewhere.

Rick shouts into my ear to overcome the pounding music. "They have to serve something to get the late night licence, that plate of shit gets around it."

Now I'm amongst them, the crowd are wonderfully strange. It is very intimate, all these bodies pressed close together in the gloom, lit by the dance floor lights and not much else. I see two boys dancing, closely entwined, some others holding hands, and then two locked in a passionate kiss at a nearby table. The darkness grants safety and security. This is a place at the very edge of acceptability, in fact it would be unacceptable to normal 'decent people' like my parents. I can imagine what Dad would want to do here, beat and crush, and he would enjoy it too. But I feel safe here. In fact, the only sense of menace inside the Sombrero is Rick and his men, but they are the protectors.

As we walk, my bottom gets pinched and I turn, startled, to be confronted by a vivacious woman sporting huge blonde hair that makes her look seven feet tall. Rick waves an admonishing finger. The woman shrugs, smiles, winks and sashays away with a pronounced roll to her arse. I realise it is a man under the thick make-up and gold lurex.

We arrive at a table set back under an arch, where the music is less overwhelming. It is empty, apart from the lone figure of Mickey, and a bouncer standing watch. Rick's table, held empty, awaiting his arrival.

Mickey stands as we arrive and I notice that Rick seats himself with his back to the wall and a clear view of the room. He motions for Mickey and I to sit. Mickey is looking at me intently, as if trying to read something on my face.

Rick leans towards me, so close that his hair brushes my face. "What do you think of this then Danny?"

I give an honest reaction. "It's unbelievable. I love it. But how does it stay open? I thought this sort of thing wouldn't be allowed."

"Perhaps not out in the sticks, or where you come from, but this is London. First lesson. This is a honeypot, it attracts all sorts to eat, and I'm not talking about ham salad either. Some are young and want to be free to be themselves. Many are artists, musicians – bohemians I think they would have been called once.

And then there are others. They are the most interesting to me. They come to consume the honey in secret, they can't get it anywhere else. A lot of them have something that is very useful, money, yes, but it's power and connections that are the most important.. We provide what they want, and those powerful people, they keep it safe. For themselves, because they are used to getting what they want.

And if they stop wanting to protect us, my people are all issued with cameras and might take the odd photograph. You have to be a member to get in here, and naturally the most important people give false names, but I've got a friend or two who are able, and glad, to help me find out who they really are. So, once I've got their name, what they do, and a few photos, their power and connections transfer to me. I rarely have to use them, but it's a nice little insurance policy. And that's why this wonderful little club is allowed to continue. Ah, here he is."

A buzz rises above the music, and then applause spreads through the crowd. I can see Bowie and Angie, surrounded by welcoming smiles and glad-hands as they pass. The music stops, and the DJ announces,

"Here he is, the man of the moment, with the lovely Angie. Merry Christmas and thanks for the party, David."

Bowie smiles and gives a theatrical bow, then continues his progress towards a table set almost opposite ours, but across the dance floor.. He is relaxed, amongst friends. There is no hysteria, this is his place, he is part of it, it part of him.

'John, I'm only Dancing' pounds through the speakers, and as I watch the crowd, listening to the lyrics anew, I see how the song, the club and Bowie link together. I think of all the thousands of fans who never get closer than a poster on the bedroom wall. I'm ready to do anything to be part of this.

Once the furore has died down, Rick slaps his hand on the table decisively. "Right, Danny, happy to give it a try?"

I nod enthusiastically, carried away by the moment, but not knowing what I'm agreeing to.

"Great, Mickey here will show you the ropes. Mickey, look after him and let me know how he does. Go and grab a drink at the bar and put it on my tab. I'll see you later, got a bit of business to do myself."

I follow Mickey to the bar and order a Bacardi and Coke and a packet of Consulate, which Mickey puts on Rick's tab.

"So, you made it here, you've had the chat and you still want to get involved? What's he said to you so far?"

I recap on the conversation in the car and office.

"He must like you, he was pretty cagey with me to start with. Mind you, he's nice while he's trying to get into your pants."

"What do you mean?"

"Just be careful, keep your wits about you. I'll look after you as much as I can, but you gotta watch my back too, that's the way it works. There's Rick, his heavies, and us boys and girls - and us kids need to stick together. We're the front, we're expendable, and we come and go. Except for me. I've been here forever. I was the first. This'll probably be our only chance to speak alone tonight. I know where you are in life, was there myself once. If you stay with him you need to know what you're doing and why."

"I'm not totally stupid, I know what he wants from me, and I'm ok with that."

" Yeah, he wants to screw you, he'll be wanting that, later, loves something new he does. And if you're ok with that, this time don't run away." He gives a little laugh, but it's more rueful than unpleasant. "But that's not the whole of it, not even the main bit of it."

He looks up, and I see the black bouncer with the Afro cutting a swathe through the separating crowd towards us.

"Here comes Rufus, he's ok, but he gets paid to do a job, and he does it well. Our protector, and Rick's spy, so keep your thoughts to yourself in front of him, other than chit – chat. No time to tell you anything more, just keep cool, and make sure you go back home after this to think things over. We'll talk some more if I get the chance, but that's unlikely."

He knocks back his drink, stubs his fag, I mimic the action.

"Hi, you two, introduce me to your new friend, Mickey."

"Hi Rufus, Danny meet Rufus."

My hand is enveloped and squeezed. The ritual test of strength, I decide competing is pointless. It is established that I would be at the mercy of such power. Rufus is well over six feet tall and nearly as wide.

"Welcome Danny. Let's get some work done."

He heads across the main room and up the stairs, with Mickey and I straggling behind.

We emerge into the crisp night, and I shiver, breath billowing into the air like steam, my thin clothes no protection. The street is quiet now, a few stragglers and the odd vehicle full of Christmas revellers passing by. Rufus enters the telephone kiosk on the corner whilst we wait nearby. He doesn't look like Bowie on the cover of 'Ziggy'. Soon after, headlamps turn the corner and stop.

Rufus is immediately alert. If he were a dog, his ears would be pricked up, nose in the air for scents. He seems satisfied, and we walk towards the car which is parked in a shadow outside the pools of light emitted by the streetlamps. A Ford Capri, with a black vinyl roof and flash wheels emerges from the gloom as we approach.

Rufus stops short, indicating to me to do the same, and Mickey speaks via the passenger window. I can't make out the occupants. Mickey returns and the Capri drives off.

"Special delivery," he jokes, adding, "second of the night, international trade at its best."

Rufus shepherds us back inside, all the time watchful, relaxing only when we are back down the staircase. We head for the toilets. Rufus enters first while we wait outside, four punters emerge soon after.

Once inside Rufus stations himself at the door. Mickey empties his pockets and lays an array of plastic bags and foil twists out across the sink top in front of the mirrors. He points to them in turn.

"Tonight's stock. You said earlier today that you've smoked some dope before, but let me introduce you to 'Coke', 'Uppers',

'Downers', and of course resin blocks and bush. We don't do 'Smack', at least not at the moment." He looks at me speculatively

"This is your last chance to walk away."

I shake my head; this die was cast a long time ago. A small moment, a big step.

He drills me in prices and that it's strictly cash up front. Then he gives me my share, telling me to put it in different pockets. Then he produces, and hands me, one of those glow-in-the-dark necklaces, that people wear at pop concerts.

"Put that on. It's the 'For Sale' sign. This is how it works. To start with you follow me, then you can have a go on your own. Rufus looks after us, any hassle and he will sort it, and I can assure you he will handle anything in here. If you feel something's wrong just put your hand up and start scratching your head and he'll be there. I doubt you'll need it – they are all cool in here, and nearly all bent, so physical violence isn't their thing.

Ground rules. You steal any money, you get a kicking. You steal any drugs, you get a kicking. It's all counted and logged. In the very unlikely event we get raided or you get arrested then it's down to you to take the medicine. It's your stuff, you are selling it for yourself, and nobody else is involved. If you grass it's much worse than a kicking. This is serious stuff and people don't mess about protecting themselves, so don't get tempted or greedy. Others have tried it on, and regretted it. You'll be well looked after if you do your bit, and well rewarded."

For a moment I think about walking. I could be out of here and on the train home. But this is where I want to be, this exciting world. The money isn't the appeal, although welcome. No, this is the first time, apart from Alice, that anyone has thought me worth bothering with, that I can be of use.

For the next hour I trail around after Mickey. We are far busier than the Italian waiters with their ham salads. To begin with, he does all the chat, then he lets me do some. I take to it, and enjoy it, including the numerous occasions I get a kiss or my bum patted by the punters. I remain alert, expecting at any minute that dark suited, heavy - footed police will crash down the stairs, but all I see is Rufus, a towering presence in the shadows, always watching.

On one circuit we get close to Bowie's encampment. I catch a glimpse of him deep in a conversation with a black girl. She has close-cropped hair, and they are clearly intimate, even with Angie sat nearby. There is much raucous laughter. The table is piled high with drinks and empty glasses A crowd of acolytes and hangers-on form a shield. Smoke lies thick in the air. One of them makes a purchase of dope and some packets of the white powder. We move on and I never see if the consignment is destined for the great man himself.

On another occasion we pass Rick, deep conversation with a rotund, balding man, whose polished pate is shining with perspiration, two bouncers watchful either side of him. The man looks foreign, and under pressure, suddenly producing a white handkerchief and mopping his brow. Rick looks up, sees me, smiles and nods briefly, and I can't stop a glow of satisfaction that such a man thinks enough of me to take the time to acknowledge me in the middle of an important meeting.

Mickey signals, and I follow him back to the toilets. Once again Rufus performs his magic trick and the occupants disappear, leaving us alone. Once again the goods, and this time, piles of notes and coins, are laid out. Mickey produces a notebook, logging sales and stock, then bags the money and hands it to Rufus who is stationed at the door. They have a conversation that I can't make out then Mickey returns.

"You've done well. The buyers like you, you're non – threatening and they think you're just another one of them, part of the scene. That's good for business. Rufus and I think you're ready to have a go solo. You stick with him, I'll be back with Rick when you've finished."

I pocket the remaining drugs and Mickey removes his glowing torc and scampers past Rufus. I eye the big man with some apprehension, but he breaks into a broad smile, winks and motions for me to follow him.

I had thought that I would be done quickly, but again we go up to the street, the phone call is made, and this time I approach the vehicle. I'm surprised that it's a middle aged white man behind the darkened windows, with a West Indian in the driver's seat.

"New boy eh?" He asks in a conspiratorial whisper. I wonder what he is doing involved in this, he looks so completely normal and straight. He rubs his fingers together in the universal hand motion for money and I hand him an envelope Rufus has equipped me with. The man opens it and, switching the interior light on, proceeds to count every banknote. He knows what the second half of the transaction comprises and hands me a plastic bag.

For the next hour I sell, sell, sell, then Rufus taps me on the shoulder. I look around and notice that the crowds are thinning. I have been so intent upon my task, enjoying the banter with people like myself, I haven't even noticed that Bowie and his entourage have slipped quietly away. I suspect that a back door was involved, no need for a grand exit after that imperious entrance.

I have very few packets left, and Rufus takes them, and the cash, from me in the shadow of a pillar and disappears. I am adrift for a moment, surrounded by glitter, style ,'otherness'. I'm approached by a handsome guy in his twenties, thin, with straight dark hair down to his shoulders and heavy framed glasses like Michael Caine wears, magnifying glitter sparkling around his eyes. He asks shyly whether I would like a dance; I think 'what the hell' and follow him to the dance floor as the first chords of, would you believe it, 'Rock 'n' Roll Suicide', strum out.

As we sway to the music, awkwardly rotating, I feel his hand on my backside, caressing, and allow him leave it there, sampling the moment. I'm in London, in the 'Sombrero', with Bowie. I'm being made love to by a beautiful man. I'm at the centre of things. The man leans in and kisses me, and I can feel myself becoming aroused.

Then a hand taps my shoulder and I see my dancing partner look up and then take a step back. Rufus is looming over us wagging an admonishing finger, an island on the tiny dance floor, the current of dancers washing around him. He waves the man away and my new friend fades into the current of people and is gone. Rufus gestures me to follow him back to Rick's alcove.

Rick is alone, with Mickey, who has resumed the slumped posture I first witnessed at Stoke, clearly under the influence of something. Rick smiles and indicates I should sit beside him.

"You naughty boy, going off and getting some action of your own." I don't see any humour in his eyes. I can't think of a suitable reply.

"So, up for a spot of action tonight, are you? Well stick with me, tonight is far from over. I've got something special lined up for you.

I sense the double-meaning lurking in the seemingly innocuous statement, but I'm too excited to care, what could be better than the evening so far?

Rick's voice changes to the efficient, businesslike one.

"Rufus and Mickey say that you did ok for a first-timer. The punters like you, you fit in and you don't frighten them like Rufus. Once you got into it you were chatting away like an old hand. What did you think?"

"I was shitting myself at first, but it was fine by the end."

"Good. We'll talk about what might happen next tomorrow."

Rick reaches into his jeans pocket and produces a huge roll of banknotes. He peels some off and hands then to me. "There you go, your first wages. It's a good screw, working for me, and there's a lot more where that came from if you want it. But that can wait. Next we enjoy ourselves, come on."

I look down. There are four £10 notes in my hand. More than Dad earns in a week, for about two hours work. *'I could earn enough to really break free'*, I think

Once again I trail across the rapidly emptying club, a few of the customers even wave at me. I'm sad to leave. I know that I'll want to come here again. It feels more like home than home does.

Greg drives us to a residential street. I can just about make out the dark, squatting bulk of a house, set back behind gates, windows illuminated. There is a square central tower silhouetted against the stars.

"Welcome to Haddon Hall, David's home, although not for much longer."

There is security at the iron gates, and they nod to Rick. Greg goes off in the car. As we approach the building I begin to hear party sounds, music, raised voices, laughter. The driveway bends round to the front door, which is at the top of a flight of steps. The entrance has 'Haddon Hall' in white letters emblazoned above it. I look up and the square tower seems to lean over me, blocking out stars. It has become a crisp and clear night and my breath rises towards the pointed roof of the tower. Not exactly what I expected. The place looks more like the set of a Hammer horror film, 'House Of Dracula' or something like that.

As we enter, sound assails us, breaking the gothic spell. There are people everywhere, lying or standing in groups along the corridors, shrouded in wraithlike mists of smoke. I smell both tobacco and dope. Music is booming out of an open doorway.

We traverse the corridor, stepping around some pretty zonked out people. It is a jarring juxtaposition; this relic of a house with its Victorian dark wood and crenellations, fading glory of another age; filled with the new, the future, the edge of convention and beyond. I had expected modernity, the latest Seventies decoration and furniture, but there is nothing like that. I see an imposing staircase, wide, with a threadbare carpet and carved wood banisters that lead up to what is almost a minstrel's gallery, overlooking the hallway. There are people draped over the rail and collapsed on the stairs. Someone has been sick at the bottom, a modern stain on the patina of history.

We enter the holy of holies. Bowies lives in a ground floor flat. The rooms are huge, with high ceilings full of plaster decoration. Even so, there is barely room to turn around, it is so full of people. The smoke is denser, more cloying in here. The furniture matches the house, dark wood, old, patterned fabrics. A bookcase is bursting and by the window stands a piano. Music is booming from a hi-fi in the corner.

Rick hustles me through to a kitchen where bottles of wine and spirits fill every surface, with a few 'bumper cans' of beer stacked on a table. There is spilt drink everywhere, sticky underfoot, filling the air with fumes. As at every party, the kitchen is also packed. I choose Vodka and Orange, and Rick fills a glass with a large measure. I notice that he just has Coca Cola himself. He offers me a fag and we begin contributing to the fug. In here the music is slightly quieter and he cups his hand over my ear,

" Some treat eh Danny? The ultimate for a Bowie fan."

I nod enthusiastically, I can't believe that I'm actually here. Just one train journey has taken me to a fantasy world.

"I'll take you for a tour in a minute, but before we do, a couple of rules. One. We don't do any business here, don't mention it at all. Anyone does then you refer them to me. If they've got stuff with them, that's their stash and their call if the place gets raided – which is unlikely but you never know when some zealot might decide to ruin everyone's Christmas. If you get offered some that's your call. There will be dope, pills and Coke floating around but I'd prefer you stuck to weed tonight as you're not used to too much other stuff. Don't want you spending the night in A & E with your stomach pumped do we? Two. We don't hassle Bowie or anyone else you might recognise. Tonight, you're my guest, not a fan, and if you start screaming like a hysterical girl, going hyper or saying stupid things then you'll get your arse kicked out. This is David's place, where he gets away from the fans. Got it?"

"Yep, I won't let you down, don't worry." I'm confident. This has a very different feel to a concert, the 'worshipping' part is missing.

I follow him back into the main room. I can see Bowie through the crowd, sat in a corner on a stool, holding court, the ever-present cigarette hanging from his mouth. He has removed the make-up and is wearing jeans and a loose white cheesecloth shirt. Without the 'Ziggy Stardust' 'face' and costume he looks young and slightly fragile, nervous even. His skin is so pale it looks like wax. There is no sign of the commanding stage presence, drinking in the adulation of the fans. What must it be like to put that personality on and off, how does he handle it, can he remember who he really is?

I notice Marc Bolan sat cross-legged on the floor. Two pioneers of glam-rock together. They chat, easy with each other. I see no rivalry there. Bowie notices us and waves us over.

"Welcome Doc, and your little friend."

Rick smiles and shakes his hand. Bowie looks at me again.

"I've seen you before somewhere haven't I? 'Little Ziggy', where was it?"

"After the Hanley concert, before you left for America."

"Got it, well, have fun, and watch this one." He indicates Rick who does one of his surface only laughs.

"Thanks, I'm sure Rick will look after me." I reply, to show Rick that I'm on his side in this, whatever this is.

"I'm sure he will." Bowie laughs, a nice unaffected, genuine laugh. "You've got the clothes, make-up and hair just about perfect, perhaps I could put you on stage and have a night off." He looks thoughtful. "But, you know, once I'm copied, I'm looking for something new, so watch this space, you might need something different by the summer."

"That's why I follow you." I blurt out. Rick intervenes by putting an arm around my shoulder and I realise that I'm getting close to 'fan' territory, but Bowie has turned his attention to a girl and my moment has passed.

As we leave the group I ask, "Doc?"

Rick laughs, this time genuinely, "Doctor Foster, my nickname, because I supply the medicine."

The next few hours pass in a blur. Rick takes me downstairs and shows me the recording studio in the basement, the back garden, which despite the cold, has its own complement of entwined couples in the shadows. I get given a few joints, but I'm not offered anything else, so there is no temptation to disobey Rick.

He knows pretty much everybody, or more accurately, they know him, mainly using his nickname. There is little real friendliness on show, and most keep their distance after the initial greeting, like he's a necessary evil. A few look at me with curiosity, some maybe with pity, perhaps at my Bowie 'fan costume', which ironically feels out of place here. We return to the kitchen for top-ups, and by the time I stumble down the steps, morning is just beginning to lighten the sky with a pale wash of light. I am pretty much out of it.

Rick has his arm around me and gives me a kiss on the steps. This time I don't resist. It's time to pay the bill, and anyway, he's not so bad really, not some dirty, smelly old bloke, I've had the best time of my life.

A pallid sun is rising as we arrive back at Rick's place. I'm as high as a kite with excitement, booze and weed. We've been snogging and feeling each other up in the back of the limo, with him telling me how lovely I am.

There is no question about what is going to happen next. Worth it though.

Chapter 12

'Life On Mars'
January 1973

Alice:

From the depths of despair to bliss! A rollercoaster
Christmas and New Year. I moped around for days after the big bust
up with Danny, Mom following me around, constantly asking
whether I was ok, and Dad making 'helpful' suggestions which I
didn't want to hear – especially that there were 'plenty more fish in
the sea for a good-looking girl like me'.

Being alone made me realise how much I want him. He is my
soulmate, I created him. At times I feel like Dr Frankenstein when
the monster turned on him. But, just like in that film, I don't believe
that Danny has evil in him, he's lost, unsure, hitting out when he gets
frustrated. The tension is buried deep within him. It's tearing him
apart. I know him better than anyone, but I can't solve it for him, it's
too complicated.

That house he lives in. He needs to escape, I can see that, but
he can't move out yet, he's too young. He needs to hang in there, just
a few more months, maybe a year, and we can make plans together.
But he can't wait and that's the tension between us.

Into that yearning to escape, to grow up fast, to be his own
person, have crept two things that I cannot control. David Bowie
and London. They are connected but not the same.

Bowie has filled Danny's mind, and ridiculously, seems a
competitor. That is the most worrying bit, and I know it's stupid,
Bowie is never going to appear and whisk Danny away from me. But
he is obsessed, and Bowie's influence is insidious, affecting how
Danny sees the world, what he wants, what he questions, taking him
away from me in mind, and mind motivates body.

This 'London thing', which I just don't understand, was, in
the beginning, all about Bowie and being part of that scene, but it's
more than that now, in fact that doesn't feel like what's going on

anymore. It's a battle for Danny's physical existence, a siren call to escape home, earn money, have fun, be at the 'centre of things', whatever that is. What can I offer against that?

But my joy is because there must be something, we are back together, my best Christmas present!

The day after Boxing Day, I am up in my room, lying on the bed feeling sorry for myself, when the doorbell rings. I hear my mom answer it and straight away I know it is him, sense it from my Mom's tone. I lie there, heart beating fast, wondering what to do. Mom makes him wait on the step. I can hear her coming up the stairs, each footfall pushing the moment of decision closer.

"It's Danny isn't it?". She looks momentarily surprised, then nods.

"If you don't want to see him, I'll send him away."

That makes up my mind, although there isn't really any doubt. I am already standing and can't help checking myself over in the mirror.

"I'll see him."

"Are you really sure you want to do this? He has made you so unhappy and hurt you so much I find it difficult to think kindly about him."

"I'm sure Mom. I've been unhappy because I've missed him, not because of anything he's done. He's going through a difficult time, he doesn't get the support at home that I get from you and Dad, in fact quite the opposite."

"It worries me that his problems will end up hurting you."

"I'm stronger than that Mom, you need to trust me."

"I do, but you're young to be dealing with this sort of thing."

"Mom, every song ever written is about love problems between young people, just add us to the list."

"Perhaps, but they aren't about my daughter. Remember that your Dad and I are there for you, whatever happens, and don't expect us to be quite as friendly as we were if you have him back. He's going to have to earn our trust."

We meet on the doorstep and for a moment we say nothing, just drink each other in. He looks vulnerable, a bit pale, and he's not all glammed up. No make-up at all. The Bowie cut is still there, but looks a bit limp and uncared for. He's wearing an Afghan coat I haven't seen before, and beneath it I can see loons with flowery inserts from the knee, a shirt with penny round collar and a tank top jumper with rainbow coloured bands. There are new shoes too, big platform boots banded in beige and brown. The extra height accentuates his thinness. I'm not sure I like the clothes. He looks anxious and uncertain. I break the silence.

"New clothes? Not your usual style. Turning Hippy?"

"Thought I'd have a bit of a change, see what it felt like to be fairly normal."

Something different here. Despite my resolve to be an icy fortress, I'm interested.

"What do you want Danny?"

He looks downwards, he seems to be searching for words. For a moment I wonder whether he's just come around to tell me it's properly finished, and that he's met someone else, but why would he bother to do that?

"I wanted to see you again. I've missed you. You're the only one I can really talk to."

"You'd better come in and talk then, it's freezing stood here."

We go into the front room and sit opposite each other, him on the settee and me on a chair. I imagine Mom listening at the door, but I know she won't, although she will demand a full debrief afterwards.

He starts, and straight away I know it's going to be ok, but make him work for it.

"I'm sorry for what happened."

"You really hurt me Danny. I thought that you didn't want me anymore; that you'd gone off me."

Silence. He is searching for words again. When he answers it is in short bursts, as if he is speaking each thought as it comes into his head.

"Never went off you. You're the only one who has been there for me. You never wanted anything back in return. Just me to love you. And I haven't done that very well. Don't know what it means really. Never had anyone love me. Not Dad, not Mom." *His eyes fill with tears and my heart breaks a little, but I hold firm. This is a moment of truth. The next few minutes could decide our future, if there is one.*

"I feel like everyone wants to use me for something. Dad as a punchbag, Mom as a shield, never had any close friends at school, people only seem to talk to me when they want something. In his own way Phil Lowe is the most honest, at least he hates me consistently and never pretends otherwise."

"And me, how have I used you?"

" You haven't, I realise that now. I was, well I am, so mixed up, confused. It felt like you were trying to turn me into some perfect boyfriend, what you wanted, not what I was; and that you were putting me in a box that only you could open. I don't think that now."

Guilt. It feels not so very far from the truth.

"Well, I might have been a bit demanding - a bit." *I concede.*

"No, I think you just want the best for us, there's nothing wrong with that."

I'm asking myself if that's really true, or do I want what's best for me, not us. More guilt.

"Well, let's move on from that, it's not the main thing, for me. I need to know something before we go any further. Have you got someone else Danny? Have you been two-timing me? That's how I feel, like you'd lost interest, like there is a new show in town. I can just about put up with you worshipping a pop star because he's never going to take you away from me, but another girl, here, that's different."

THE big question. I watch him closely. Would I know if he's lying? If he does, and I see, then it's over.

This time the reply is instant.

"There's no other girl."

Not quite good enough. "And was there? Is that why you've come back now, she's packed you in so you've come back to old faithful." I can see that hurts. Good, he deserves it.

"No way, you're the only girl in my life."

That's not quite the declaration I'm after, but I decide not to push it any further. I think he's telling the truth.

"So, what do you want to do now?"

He hesitates, and once again I wonder if he's being honest with me, but I don't think he's lying, surely I'd know.

"I want to give it another try. I don't want to lose you, I've missed you. I need you if I'm going to make a go of it here, because without you they'll drive me away, and if I go I don't know how it will end."

Hardly a declaration of undying love, but blokes only do that in films and books. The word 'love' never seems to actually pass a man's lips unless he's after something.

He is waiting for a reply, looking into my eyes like a chastised puppy. I should say no, but I love him and he looks so vulnerable, in fact he seems scared of something. Something inside, or someone? I don't know.

I pat the seat beside me, and he comes to me. Our bodies touch and the electricity is there again. We kiss and it's like the first time. We hug and I open my eyes as he pats my back. I wonder if I'm making the biggest mistake of my life.

***

Danny:

Christmas Day begins, not with the opening of presents, but with Rick having me. 'Peace and Love to All Men!' We sleep in his big bed until early afternoon and I am woken by his caresses. It isn't quite as easy without the booze inside me, and I have a wicked hangover, but it is no longer the first time, and he has kept his side of the bargain. It's no big deal. What does that say about me though? I suppress the thought.

Afterwards it's back to business. Over food and coffee, he outlines the deal. I can come and work for him, doing the drugs with Mickey, being his plaything whenever he wants, or stay at home.

He is brutally honest for a crook - ironic as most of the normal people I meet seem to be dishonest. Having him paw all over me is the downside. The sugar; living in London - he will even give me a flat he owns rent free, as part of my 'wages'; being inside the music and art scene; plenty of cash; being around Bowie, even going on the tours, although the next proper British one is not until May. The offer is not open-ended though, he gives me until the First of March to decide, because he says he wants me 'trained up' properly, well before Bowie's return from abroad. Pretty much everything I dare hope for if I want it, but do I?

It is time for me to go. Mickey appears while we talk. I don't know whether he was in the house or not, but he offers to show me to the station, claiming he needs some fresh air to clear his head. He looks absolutely shit, but Rick seems to think this is a good idea, and shoos us both out. On the doorstep he presses another Twenty Pound note into my hand and gives me a hug, then the door shuts and Mickey and I are alone on the step.

As we walk, Mickey begins to talk, haltingly at first, then becoming more confident.

"I heard what he said to you. It was like you was me, a few years ago. You seem like a good kid, and, after our little chat yesterday, I think I know what shit's going on. You've got a big decision to make. Before you get on that train home I want you to hear me out."

"Sure, Mickey, you know the score."

He offers a fag and I accept, savouring the first rush of dizziness.

"You need to be one hundred per cent sure you want to do this, in fact you want it to be your only option before you throw your lot in with him. It's too late for me to get out now, he owns me. Without him, I've got nowhere to live, no job, no gear, no money."

"But you seem to have a great time, you're in all the parties, meeting the famous.."

"Yeah, risking my freedom every day, trying not to get hooked. To a young kid like you it all seems too good to be true, I thought the same, but the shine wears off after a while and you start thinking about where you're going, and whether it's making you really happy. I've got no alternative. No family to fall back on. Never knew my Dad, Mum was a druggie so I got put into care. I won't go into that, it was bad, really bad. Rick wasn't the first by a long way, but at least I get plenty in return. He was my only way out – at a price.

He likes teenagers, so once he moves on, you've either got to cut the mustard in his business, be useful, earn him money, or you're out on your ear. He comes over all nice and friendly at first, but he can be a total cunt, and nasty with it. Believe me, I've seen what he is capable of.

What I'm saying is, you don't want to be relying on him unless there's nowhere else to go."

After this bout of soul-baring he goes back to his reticent self. Perhaps he's regretting that he's said so much. He seems paranoid, looking around to see if anyone is watching or listening. I try to probe a bit about what he does, but he just says.

"Only when and if you're in, otherwise I'd get my arse kicked and you'd be a loose cannon with knowledge that he might want to sort out to protect himself. Remember he took a risk with you at the club last night, his dick probably ruled his head. But I guarantee his brain will be back in control by now, he'll be having a little think about how much of a liability you could be. You keep your mouth shut and have a real good think about what I've said."

*

I manage to get a train home, spend the whole journey brooding on Mickey's words. I arrive in time for what passes for a family Christmas Dinner. Mom is pleased I've made it, and she must have had some influence, because the old man doesn't mention my absence. He's been to the pub and Mom has been feeding him booze all afternoon, so he is nearly comatose as he slobbers his way noisily through the turkey and promptly falls asleep on the sofa. She looks at me, and I look at her, silently acknowledging our new deal. I go to my room to think.

That's how I ended up on Alice's doorstep, doing the repentant sinner bit. By Boxing Day morning I've had a good sleep, and lie in bed putting the things I've learnt in some sort of order. I bet nobody at school has had a Christmas like mine!

Mickey's words strike deep. I decide there's nothing to lose by giving it another go here. I'm sixteen soon, time is beginning to tick away towards adulthood. Perhaps I *could* just knuckle down and make it to the point where I can be my own person, do my own thing, without having to sell myself, or part of myself, to anyone else. And if I'm honest, making a go of it has to include Alice, if I'm going to have any chance at all. There's a lot of 'if's' around; if she'll have me back; if the deal with Mom works; if Dad doesn't do something stupid; if I can hack school and swallow my lust for revenge; if I can put London and Bowie to the back of my mind. But by the time I walk downstairs I'm resolved to give it a good go.

***

David:

The mini-tour of the UK that begins on Christmas Eve is relentless. 1972 finishes with two concerts at the 'Hardrock' in Manchester. Thirteen -year old Steven Morrisey is in the audience, looking for something new, and finding inspiration. For Bowie, the reality of stardom is beginning to pall, the outrageous personality he has adopted is provoking a growing conflict with quiet, shy, David Jones, still submerged somewhere within the rock God, 'Ziggy Stardust'.

There is a triumphant rendering of 'The Jean Genie' on 'Top Of The Pops' early in the New Year. One friend, chosen to dance on the programme, observes that Bowie seems reluctant to do the live performance, almost shy, in contrast with his commanding and confident public image.

The tour moves to Scotland and the North of England, and his 26th birthday is spent performing a publicity stunt at RCA's record pressing plant in Washington, County Durham. A week later 'Ziggy', in full regalia, appears on the 'Russell Harty Show', where he is interrogated about his sexuality and beliefs. He looks and sounds increasingly bizarre, but is that real, or an 'in character' act. Perhaps even David Jones is beginning to be unable to tell the difference.

'Aladdin Sane' is nearly complete, the American tour is looming. The last one lost money, and Bowie is still unaware that it is his earnings that are paying. RCA, and Manager DeFries, agree a new tour structure, with an increased number of shows in fewer, larger venues, to cut costs. Mainman are to cover the expenses so DeFries slashes the tour entourage. Financial realities are beginning to surface. He even gets Bowie a cut price berth on the SS Canberra. Bowie leaves on his next Transatlantic crossing on the 25th January 1973.

***

Danny:

It's birthday time, and I've reached the magic age of sixteen. Not so magic. I'm legally free to make lots of decisions, but can't, because I'm living with fuck-face, with only one quick way out. If I hear, *'while you live under my roof you'll do as I say,'* one more time, I swear I'll…. no, don't go there, not now, not yet.

Reflecting, and realising what I've done in just twelve months. Where will I be when I'm seventeen. A year ago, I was mooning around over my cowardice with Alice, a scared little boy, frightened of my own shadow. I'd done nothing, knew nothing. And now, I count. Lost virginity – twice; met David Bowie – twice; tried dope and dealt drugs; beat the school bully; been part of the London scene, albeit for just one night. Been shagged by an older bloke I don't really like. Won with my mom, lost with my dad. Got the best girl around as my girlfriend, envied by all my mates, then lost her, then got her back again. No wonder I'm confused!

Soon, it's Alice's sixteenth too, and I make a huge fuss of her. I've got money, so I splash the cash, take her out for a meal and buy flowers, chocolates and take her clothes shopping. I buy her a fantastic leather coat. She looks at me really funny when I pay cash, so I tell her I've been working extra hours to save up for it. I'm not sure she really believes me, but there's no harm in a little white lie is there? And she loves the coat.

School. I feel about ten years older than my classmates. I've seen and done so much. It's hard to hide my boredom at their little triumphs with girls, their tiny adventures and rebellions. It's even harder not to blab about what I've done, but, although I'm bursting to tell, I remember Mickey's warning. Anyway, they wouldn't believe me, so what's the point?

It's difficult to be a schoolboy when I'm an adult in every other way. I resent, I resent, I resent. The teachers telling me what to do. Sitting in classes listening to stuff that means nothing to me, Algebra and Simultaneous Equations, Shakespeare and Physics, when are they going to be any use?

And Phil Lowe, now seemingly restored to prime bully position, the memory of my victory fading away. I never wanted to be top dog. I'm considered weird, a freak, a loner. They prefer a conventional bully. Lowe still gives me a wide berth, spending his time on restoring his network, bullying others. I suspect that he is truly frightened of me, instinctively knows that I'm capable of going way over the top, which is right, and something I bite down on every day when I see him. Getting suspended or expelled would be the first domino falling in a line that ends in the arms of Rick.

Home? I exist there, eat and sleep there. My body has presence there, but my mind is elsewhere. I don't feel a need to rebel, wind him up, confront him. There are bigger things to think about, I try to rise above it all.

Which makes it easier. Mom thinks she's got me where she wants me. I've toned down the clothes and make-up – having a good go at being 'normal', whatever that is. So, Dad has no excuse to go for me. He pretty much ignores me and I work hard to avoid him. Every day that passes is another step towards a different and better freedom than Rick can offer.

But it's not all 'Hunky Dory'. Dad is still wrestling with something eating away from inside. I have no sympathy, pity, or interest in what it is, but his drinking is worse since Christmas. He goes to the pub every evening, eats his tea and slumps in front of the TV. He is subdued, but I sense a fuse burning that could detonate a volcano, and that could bring everything crashing down.

Best of all is Alice, my rock and anchor. I don't know what I would do without her, doubt I could keep this 'normal' life going. I love her so much, and she loves me. We are perfect together, and everything is how it was in the beginning.

Except one thing. I am wracked with guilt for my lies and semi-untruths. I have this feeling that I will get found out, justice will be done, I will be punished. That, I could stand, but not the look of disappointment and hurt on Alice's face. I could never forgive myself.

My life teeters on a cliff edge, built on foundations that could crumble at any time. Me, Dad, Mom, school, Alice. And London is still there, beckoning.

Rick will need his answer in four weeks and I still don't have one.

Chapter Thirteen

'Aladdin Sane'
February 1973

Danny:

February, a hard month. Hard ice, frosty mornings, biting wind. Short days under heavy cloud with little sunshine to brighten the gloom. Everything grey. Not a month to be trying to live as a normal sixteen-year-old.

The world is harsh and unforgiving at this time of year. Everyone miserable, everyone on strike, or about to be. Trouble and anger everywhere. The Unions and the Government at loggerheads. On the streets, gangs of Skinheads, Suedeheads, Greasers and West Indians, looking scary.

Outside, walking, on the bus, in the pubs and clubs, shopping, it feels like there is a gauntlet to be run. I wonder how long the glittering people of 'The Sombrero' would last in my city, my reality. I have a vision of blood. bedraggled peacocks, tail feathers drooping and dirty.

Still, I am persevering with it. Nothing has changed to make living here any better, apart from Alice. But even she can't prevent me feeling that I'm tentatively stepping across a rickety bridge hung over an abyss, avoiding the gaps between planks. Rick's deadline is only two weeks away. There will be a finality then, no turning back, whatever I decide.

The memories of Christmas Eve are fading. So different to real life as to seem like fantasy. Time heals both body and mind by blurring the past, and already my memory of Mickey and Rick is no longer sharp. Strange to think that I was in his bed.

One day I went back to the hairdressers. I don't know what I thought I could do, but they told me that Luke had gone, moved away.

My fault – well sort of, I didn't write the note, but I can't get away from how I spoke to Luke that night, and the look on his face.

Worse, I couldn't prevent a feeling of relief sweeping through me when I found out that he had gone. No Luke, no chance meetings, no recriminations. No chance of Alice finding out. Luke is over.

I think I love her, whatever that means. I love what she has done for me, continues to do for me. Yes, sometimes I look at men, sometimes I fantasise about them, sometimes when I'm doing it with Alice. I make that enough. I keep saying to myself that it's a passing phase, an experiment, a teenage 'thing'. If I have Alice, then I can cope with everything else. And if I lose her again…

I've experienced so much, but I don't really know what true love is. Is it just use and abuse? Where are the hearts and flowers?

Luke accused me of using him. I accused Alice of using me – building her perfect boyfriend. Mom used me as a shield as far back as I can remember. Dad abused me. Rick did use me, but it was a transaction, so the most honest in a weird sort of way. I suppose, in the end, I've used Alice to help me get through it all as well.

I'm using my parents – their house and money. I'm in control, so no regrets, no guilt. I feel distant from my family, my childhood. When I'm home it's like I'm dislocated in time, in another dimension, a parallel world that I glide through without feeling anything. I live there. I eat there, because I have to. If I ever had love for my parents it has gone. I can't access it anymore. I am cold, a robot. They are nothing to me.

Mom seems to be content with this state of affairs. I hate her for that. What sort of mother puts herself, her safety, above her child? It's too late for her now. No going back.

Dad doesn't seem to care about anything anymore. I think he's really cracking up this time. I have no idea what's going on, but it serves him right. We live in separate worlds and rarely occupy the same physical space. We simply exist, a shell of a family. I wonder how many others are in the same boat? A fire burns beneath us, with only a thin veneer of keeping up appearances between us and the flames. Dad the volcano, waiting to erupt.

Alice's family life is a constant reminder of how it should be, what I should have had. I will never forgive them.

Rick's deadline is approaching fast. The crossroads of my life? As it closes on me it seems less and less important. I am drifting along and I will drift past the end of the month with no decision, which will be *the* decision. I will stay, conform, grow up a little, and have a life with Alice. I can see how that might be. Get a flat, share our lives, loving and laughing. It could be everything I've never had – I want it. More than I want Bowie's world I think. Not so much of a rebel.

Ridiculous. I'm proud of myself, of this non-achievement, doing nothing. The hardest thing I've ever done is not doing anything much.

***

Alice:

A new Danny in my life. The constant attempts to shock, the make-up and spiky hair, the head-turning outfits, have disappeared. I can't decide if they have gone completely, or are just submerged. In some ways I miss them. They made Danny who he was. Life is much quieter now, less exciting, but Danny is still beautiful, and he is mine.

I've made a big effort. I've stopped trying to make him into something he isn't - or doesn't want to be. I'm happy with what I've got. I've even got into Bowie. I like a lot of his stuff now, can see the appeal, especially to someone like Danny. We listen to the records together. I'm part of his adulation, instead of trying, and failing, to compete. It is a different kind of love. I can live with that.

Mom and Dad haven't accepted him. They keep their distance. They don't trust him. That hurts, but Mom is no fool. Does she see something I don't?

I avoid thinking about trust. We are good together. I can feel his love for me, and mine for him. It is pure and true and will be forever. We are making plans. A few more months, and 'O Levels' will be done. He is trying again at school, and if he does, he'll do ok.

We will have the summer to work out our future. By then I'm hoping Mom and Dad will be won round, and help us. Maybe Danny's parents too. They are my real worry. They are the fault line, lying deep in the foundations of 'us'. Their miserable life could ruin ours.

But every day that passes is another brick in the building of our future. Every night I look at the calendar on my bedroom wall and cross off a little step on the journey towards a life with Danny. Every morning that feels a bit closer.

***

David:

The first two weeks of February 1973 are taken up with tour rehearsals at the RCA Studio in New York. But there is plenty of time for clubbing, at 'Max's Kansas City Club' in the city, socialising and taking in the odd show. At Max's he sees a young Bruce Springsteen perform and buys 'Greetings from Asbury Park'.

On 7th February, Bowie attends a Motown party for Stevie Wonder at 'Genesis' discotheque, following Wonder's Carnegie Hall performance. Aretha Franklin and Gladys Knight perform an impromptu set, but Bowie's eyes are elsewhere.

A young backing singer. They are introduced and quickly become besotted with each other. Her name is Ava Cherry. She is unaware that her new lover is married, and is then shocked by the news - and by Angie's seeming acceptance of the relationship. The Bowie's have been conducting an 'open' marriage almost since meeting, including 'three in a bed' adventures. But how long can this arrangement last?

Bowie invites Ava to join the US tour at a later date. It is more than a passing fling.

Money continues to corrode relationships behind the scenes. Mike Garson, the jazz pianist responsible for much of the 'new' sound of the 'Aladdin Sane' album, inadvertently reveals that he is being paid £500 a week. 'The Spiders' are being paid £50.

The band members confront Defries prior to the Valentine's Day gig at 'Radio City', New York, demanding a rise and threatening to leave the forthcoming tour. Bowie gets involved and the accusations fly, leaving a bitter taste all round. 'The Spiders' realise that they are bound by contract to complete the tour and the show goes ahead, but the emotions aroused remain unresolved, begin to fester.

Defries secretly approaches Ronson, promising him a solo album if he stays; isolating Bolder and Woodmansey, and driving a wedge into the band.

Splinters in the world of 'Ziggy Stardust' start to appear, both in the real world, and in Bowie's mind. He begins to think about life after 'Ziggy', as the tour grinds its way across America and onwards, to Japan.

***

Danny:

I hear a regular bleep, bleep, bleep. It doesn't sound like my alarm. My mind tries to make sense of the noise. I open my eyes, it makes no difference, just darkness. Why is my alarm going off in the middle of the night? I'm confused. Is this a dream? I lie there and collect my thoughts.

Pain. I hurt. Was I on the lash last night? I seem to have the mother of all hangovers and I feel light-headed. Try to remember, grope around in the cupboards of my mind, they are empty.

I'm not dreaming. There are noises, alien sounds. A cough, breathing, the movement of other bodies.

My eyes are open now, and, as they grow accustomed to the darkness, variations of form begin to appear in monochrome. I turn my head. There is pain in my neck. Shapes in the gloom. Beds. I'm not at home. I look the other way and see a desk in the distance, lit by a cone of soft light. A figure in white sitting.

I try to sit up and the pain makes me give a little cry. The figure at the desk looks up, and hurries towards me. Curtains are drawn around my bed. Illumination. It is a nurse. I'm in hospital.

The nurse looms over me. She looks nice, with a jolly round face. About mom's age.

"Welcome back Danny, don't try to move too much. Doctor will want to come and see you in the morning to make an assessment."

I try to remember, and fail. I can't access anything earlier than waking up just now.

"Where am I?"

"Selly Oak Hospital sweetie."

I must have a completely blank look on my face, because she leans close over me. I smell strong perfume mixed with a faint trace of sweat. She looks into my eyes.

"Mmm, you still look a touch dazed. How do you feel?"

I try to work out an answer. Firstly, I have no idea how I am, and then the words don't seem to come out in the right order. I end up mumbling a jumble of sentences that don't seem to fit together.

"I think you're still a bit concussed bab. You've had a nasty fall and bumped your head. Just lie still and relax. I'll get you something for the pain and to help you sleep."

I get a flash of falling, but detail eludes me, dancing away into the recesses of my mind. I try to ask more questions, but my mouth won't obey. I take some pills and slip away.

The next time I wake there is spring sunshine turning the still drawn curtains a golden hue. I can hear sounds of busy life all around. My thoughts seem a little clearer and my hangover has gone, replaced by a headache.

I take a perfunctory inventory. I feel like I'm bruised all over, but by cautiously experimenting I find that I can raise each limb in turn. No plaster casts, so it seems nothing is broken. I try to sit up, but the headache intensifies, so I look around from a prone position.

I'm hooked up to some sort of monitor, the source of the bleeps. There is a drip in my arm. I'm wearing a hospital gown and my mouth is dry, with a faint chemical aftertaste. My throat is sore too. What has happened? Try as I might, recollection isn't there; just shadows dancing away into the distance as I grope for them.

I must doze off again, because the next time I wake, Mom is sat on a plastic chair by the side of the bed. The curtains are drawn back revealing a crowded ward. It must be visiting time, as nearly every bed has a seated attendant radiating various stages of boredom – and some, concern.

Mom stares vacantly into space. She becomes aware of my scrutiny and almost jumps as if scared. She takes hold of my hand. I'm too weak to pull it away, but I would like to.

"Danny, are you ok?"

" I don't know. I ache a lot and my head hurts like hell. I can't seem to remember what happened."

I wait for an answer but it seems a long time coming. In the end I get another question.

"What exactly do you remember?"

All I can think of at this moment is the bizarre situation I find myself in. What I need is answers but they don't seem to be hurrying themselves to appear.

"The nurse said I'd fallen and bumped my head. I can vaguely recall falling, but that's it."

I catch what looks like relief crossing her face, but it's gone so quickly I'm not sure.

"You fell down the stairs. Knocked yourself out. I've been worried to death."

I try to fit this piece of information into the puzzle of my last twenty four hours but it just hangs alone, twisting slowly in the vacuum in my mind.

"How long have I been here?"

"Since last night"

I'm worried. I can remember everything but yesterday.

"What day is it?"

"Monday, darling."

That word sounds false. I feel my skin crawl at its use. There's something wrong here, but I can't put my finger on it.

So yesterday was Sunday. What do I do on Sundays? Alice, I see Alice after Sunday dinner then we usually go out. I can remember yesterday morning. I was up in my room playing records. I try to inch forward in my mind. No good.

"I can't remember anything after the morning. What happened?"

She pauses just too long. There's definitely something not right. It's as if she is trying to decide what to say. That means he's involved.

"Well, we had dinner as usual, then you went out – to Alice's I think."

I interrupt, "Alice – does she know I'm in here?"

Too slow. She's holding back. "No, I didn't want to worry her, and anyway I don't know how to get in touch – you've never given us a number."

Too bloody right I haven't. The less opportunity for contact the better. I certainly don't want them chatting to her parents.

"That's ok, I'll phone her later, I'm guessing there's a payphone somewhere in here? How long am I going to be in here for?"

She looks relieved. I've let her off the hook somehow.

"I'll go get the nurse so she can explain."

She scuttles off and returns with a different nurse. This one's the other end of the spectrum. Thin and bony with a sharp nose like a beak. She doesn't look kind and reminds me of a chicken, complete with the jerky head movement due to her eyes darting about the ward constantly. She has clearly been briefed by Mom and intends to waste no time on me.

"Well young man, how are you feeling now?"

"I've got a headache and can't remember yesterday afternoon, or later."

She shines a light into my eyes.

"Some bumps and bruises, a knock on the head, bit of concussion, but I think you'll be fine. Doctor will come and see you now you're awake, and I expect he'll want you kept in at least another twenty-four hours for observation. Normal for a head injury. Perhaps you'll think before you drink too much next time. Your poor mom's been worried to death."

She has already dismissed me as just another drunken or drugged kid and bustles off to another patient demanding attention.

Mom is gathering herself to leave. I notice others doing the same, visiting time is ending. I'm about to make a last attempt to find out what has happened when I think better of it. My instincts are telling me that there are lies here, all I'll get from her are more lies. I'll bide my time and see if I can reach Alice, she won't lie to me.

"I'll bring you back some stuff for tonight, see you later," she says. I let her peck me on the cheek and describe what to get to read, she wouldn't have a clue. I also ask for my cassette recorder and some music tapes and headphones. It might keep me sane and block out the hubbub from the rest of the ward. This seems to satisfy her and off she troops, leaving me with my thoughts.

I know he's involved in this, and she's protecting him as usual.

***

Alice:

Danny wasn't there to meet me after school today. I spotted one of his classmates and he told me that Danny hadn't been at school all day. He didn't know why.

Everything has been going too well. I've been waiting for disaster to strike. Sometimes I've woken with butterflies in my stomach because we are too good to be true, too happy together. The world doesn't seem to want people to be too happy. It always sneaks up with something to ruin it all.

I go home. If he wants me he'll phone. If he doesn't, then I'll phone his house. I've got the number. Danny gave it to me, 'in case anything weird happens'. I didn't know what he meant, but this seems to fit.

At home I shout my usual, 'Hello', and go straight upstairs to change. I've got 'Hunky Dory' playing. The final notes of 'Life On Mars' are fading out when Mom appears and sticks a knife in my heart.

She doesn't know when she hands me a crumpled envelope. My name is scrawled on the front. It is sealed.

"This was pushed through the letterbox. Don't know when it came. It had gone under the shoe rack and I didn't spot it until you'd gone to school."

She waits. She has the 'sixth sense' that all good mothers have. For bad news. Is it a goodbye note? Has he gone? It doesn't add up, he was lovely yesterday. We had such a great time. There was nothing out of the ordinary – quite the contrary.

Inside is a folded piece of paper with a few lines of pencil scrawl. As I open it a photograph flutters to the floor, landing face down.

The writing is in block capitals, a child's writing. There is no punctuation.

'YOUR BOYFRIEND IS A BUM BOY HE HAS BEEN SUCKING COCKS FOR MONTHS ASK HIM ABOUT THE HOMO HAIRDRESSER THAT'S HIM IN THE PHOTO'

I stare at the note for what seems like ages, reading and re-reading it, trying to make it say something different, trying to rationalise it away – a trick, a vendetta, a lie, but I've gone cold because now things fit together.

I become aware of Mom and fold the note, but it's too late. She has read it too. She bends and picks up the photograph. All I can see is the white back. I really don't want to see the other side, because my heart is breaking.

She turns it round and holds it up. Danny, instantly recognisable, in full 'Bowie mode', in a clinch with a man, kissing him full on the lips. It must have been taken some months ago, judging by the weather and Danny's clothing.

I sink to the bed, crying. Mom sits beside me and I bury my face into her chest. She tries to comfort me.

"This has come from someone really nasty, and it may not be true – there might be an explanation." She tapers off into silence – probably trying to think of one.

I start shaking my head, and pull away.

"Yes, it's horrible and I can't imagine why someone would be so sick as to do this, but.." I start crying again.

After a few minutes and a good nose–blow, I sit up and wipe my eyes. Mom looks at me, she knows.

"But you think it might be true?"

I can't bring myself to say the words, I just nod.

"Why?"

It's such a little word, and such a big answer. Such a devastating blow to my belief in him.

"I ...I thought he'd got someone else – another girl. I was convinced actually. He was less attentive, less bothered, not really there. That's really why we split up before Christmas, I just had this feeling that things had changed, he didn't love me anymore. Then after Christmas, when he came around, I asked him straight out and he swore there was no other girl. I sensed something, but couldn't quite put my finger on it." I tail off as the implications of what I have just said strike home. Mom knows to say nothing. She can see I am working my way through.

"When he started with the Bowie thing, the make-up and all that stuff, I did sometimes wonder. I'm not stupid and I kept my eyes open, but all I saw was other girls looking at him, fancying him, so that took my attention. Oh my God, the hairdresser......"

I am thinking back to that first Bowie cut, when I left him in the salon. The good-looking hairdresser, 'bent as a nine-bob note'. I remember now how strange Danny had seemed that day. I had put it down to the haircut.

"You know someone who fits?"

"The man who cut Danny's hair .....let me look at that photo again....yes, that could be him, although the faces are hidden."

I can't stop another bout of tears. Mom holds me and proffers a tissue when the flood subsides. I blow my nose loudly.

"If it's true mom, it's not the liking men and women, although being two-timed with a man hurts. It's the lies and dishonesty. What he really thinks of me to be able to do that."

Mom, ever practical, is already looking forward. "Well, the only thing you can do is confront him. I'm sure you will know if he's

lying, it's not possible to explain away something like this. When are
you seeing him next?"

I look at the clock. Where has that hour gone? It's already
nearly six-o-clock.

"Tonight, he's coming around at about seven."

"You've got an hour to prepare then. I suggest you have a
think and write down what you want to say, what you want to cover.
Then you won't miss anything out."

I decline food, but she re-appears with a sandwich and cup of
tea and makes me consume them, assessing me all the time. She must
be satisfied, because she leaves me alone to brood, checking the
clock every five minutes.

But I'm not ok. I'm hollow inside. I keep reading the note,
looking at the photo, thinking and remembering. Little incidents,
strange moods, just not feeling right sometimes. Deep down, I know
there is truth here, and my pain is physical. I'm scared about what is
going to happen when he gets here.

Seven arrives and passes. By eight, I know he's not coming.
There's no phone call and that mean's he somehow knows what's
happened and doesn't want to see me. That's why he missed school
too. We are finished then, for good this time.

***

Danny:

After mom left I still felt woozy, spent a few hours slipping
in and out of sleep. I surface from my last doze, aware of crockery
and cutlery clanking. Vivid dreams, filled with dread and fear. It is
comforting to emerge into the bright lights and bustle of the ward.

The bruising and aches are worse, but the banging headache
has gone. For the first time since being in here I feel present.

I experiment with sitting up, and this time succeed without ill
effects. A nurse spots me and hurries over.

"Back with us then. How do you feel now?"

"A lot better, headache has gone."

She asks questions, including whether I'm hungry and I find I am famished. She takes my pulse, checks the bleeping machine by my side and nods, satisfied.

"I'll get you something to eat, Doctor will be doing his rounds soon. Hopefully you will have some good news by visiting time."

By eight-o-clock I'm fed, been told I've got to stay in until tomorrow and I've had another strange and stilted visit from Mom. It's cat and mouse, as if she is hiding something, but I still can't put the pieces together enough to challenge what she says. She is not anywhere near enough happy about me getting out tomorrow. She was hoping for another day's grace.

After she leaves, I suddenly remember about phoning Alice, but the nurse tells me that the only phone kiosk is in the entrance lobby, and there is no way I'm allowed to walk down there on her watch, so that's that. Anyway, I'm sure Alice will phone our house when I don't show up.

The next day, it's afternoon before I'm fully checked over and given the all clear to leave. Mom comes to get me. In the taxi home I tell her that I know why. I woke this morning, remembering. Remembering an argument, him drunk, him punching me, and then me falling. The details are still a bit hazy, but I'm sure they will come back.

She looks at me with those cow eyes and I feel nothing. The first thing she says doesn't help.

"Did you tell anyone at the hospital what happened?"

That's all she's bothered about; her precious life not being disturbed. I consider winding her up a bit, but can't be bothered, there are more important things to think about.

"Nah, I haven't. Police aren't about to swoop, although I can't think of a good reason not to." (Actually, holding it back is a better bargaining chip).

She looks relieved, then the bloody tears again. I'm sure she can turn them on and off when it suits her. I let her blub away without making any attempt to comfort her. I can see the taxi driver looking in his mirror. I bet he thinks I'm a right little bastard.

I decide to ignore her and look out of the window. It's the first time I've paid any attention to where we are going, and as the Rotunda floats past it's clear that home is not our destination.

"Hang on a minute....Shut the fuck up crying for God's sake. Where are we going?"

That just starts her off again and we are on the Aston Expressway before she answers.

"Your Nan's."

That makes sense, she lives in Erdington.

"Why?"

"Because it happened again, that's why. And this time I couldn't stop it. This time he's chucked you out. So, your Nan's was all I could think of. I think he might really hurt you if you go back at the moment."

I must look a bit blank.

"You said you remembered it all this morning. Not all, then."

"I remember a fight, not what it was about." I search my memory again; I can't think what I've done wrong.

"Mom, I haven't put a foot wrong for the best part of three months, what the fuck happened?"

Her speech comes in fits and starts, her voice catching at times.

"Another note, same as last time, and that photo. It must have been pushed through the letterbox yesterday afternoon. You was out, I was in the kitchen and didn't hear the flap go. He found it on the mat when he got back from the pub, pissed as usual. He went berserk when he read it."

She rolls up her sleeves and shows me the purple bruises. He's very good at dishing it out in a way that doesn't show, as I know only too well.

"He went back to the pub later and took the note with him. Said he showed all his friends. Said you're no son of his. Accused me of having an affair when he got back. Then you came in...."

It all comes back to me at once. The accusations, the argument, the punch. And now he's thrown me out. It's a fucking disaster of epic proportions.

We arrive at Nan's and Mom fumbles about in her handbag for change to pay. She pulls out a crumpled envelope and throws it at me.

"Have it. See what you've done. He tried to make me eat it, then threw it at me. It's apparently all my fault that you're a….," she searches for the right word, "pervert."

The taxi driver is goggling at us now. I think he would probably pay us so he could stay and listen, but we get out, and off he goes. Another story to tell to the punters.

Nan is on the step, ushering us in. She has one great quality - she hates my Dad. Must have caught onto him years ago. He never comes here. On the other hand, she's ancient, slightly barmy, and unlikely to provide me with much counselling or advice.

We have a ritual cup of stewed tea, some shallow conversation, during which I work out that Nan thinks I've had a row with Dad whilst trying to protect Mom from a drunken assault. I am therefore, 'golden bollocks'. I can feel Mom's eyes boring into me, willing me to keep quiet. That's easy, I doubt Nan knows what a queer is, and she'll definitely not have a clue what a Bowie is, so it's not worth expending breath on. She'll provide willing sanctuary while I work all this out, decide what to do.

Mom scarpers pretty quick, promising to return tomorrow, telling me that school thinks I've got the flu. Nan hasn't got a phone and I'm feeling pretty wacked, too woozy to walk up to the kiosk, so I decide to leave Alice until tomorrow evening, when I'll know exactly what the score is. She will probably have asked around and heard I've got the flu. If she phones home Mom will answer - she always does as he won't get off his arse, and she'll tell her the same. I just need a day. Tomorrow I can start to work this through.

I watch a bit of TV with Nan after fish fingers and chips, then I'm feeling tired so I go up. For a while I lie awake in the spare room, in a bed with a candlewick bedspread, looking at a picture of a stag on a Scottish hillside. It's a bloody long way from 'Rock 'n' Roll'.

I think I'm going crazy, how has this happened, what am I going to do? It makes my head hurt, as thoughts and options whirl round and round. Still, tomorrow I'll see Alice, and she will help me work it out. At least I've got her.

Chapter Fourteen

'All The Young Dudes'
Spring 1973

Danny:

I've read and re-read the note, but it doesn't get any better. It's the same author as before, the same childish scrawl. The same photo of me and Luke in the park. A moment of trying to be normal, frozen in time, is going to haunt me forever.

The next day I feel a lot better. I only have one thing on my mind – Alice. I can't wait until she finishes school, so I make the long bus journey via town and hang about by the fence until I see them all turn out at dinnertime in their green uniforms. The older ones stand out and I soon attract the attention of a group giggling and gossiping as they set off to the local shops to buy fags. After the obligatory teasing and flirting they tell me that she isn't in today. She never misses school. I have a bad feeling.

I walk to her house despite the aches and pains, brooding on what has happened. I remember it all. I wasn't drunk, he was, out of his head– and filled with wild anger. As I climbed the stairs he burst out of the bedroom, stark-bollock-naked, reeking of booze and sweat, and laid into me.

Taken by surprise, I had no chance. He battered me to the floor and when I got up and backed away, he knocked me down the stairs. I can remember every word he said. There is no going back now.

But the hatred I feel towards him – and there is plenty, is dwarfed by the enormity of her betrayal. I can remember seeing her, as I got up after the first beating, peering around the bedroom door, her face screwed up like a prune with fear. She did nothing, said nothing. Her first instinct was to protect him, to cover it up. She would have invented that cover story for the ambulance men, and later, the hospital. He must have gone straight back to bed, well satisfied with his work.

All done and dusted. Even if he changed his mind I wouldn't go back. They deserve each other. My little revenge will be to leave her there alone, let him dole out the punishment. That's one decision made.

It's mid-afternoon when I stand on her step again, where I stood those few weeks ago and pleaded for my love. It's all I've got left here now.

There is no reply for a long time, too long. I'm about to turn away when the door opens. She looks terrible, puffy face, wild hair and no make-up. She looks at me, starts crying. I know then.

"What's up, are you ill?" I ask forlornly.

In response she throws something at me. It flutters to the floor. An envelope. I recognise the writing. I don't need to pick it up. I can't think of anything to say so we stand there. I'm struck dumb whilst she weeps. Then she stops, drained, and raises her head.

"It's true isn't it?"

I don't even think of lying. There is nowhere left to go, no point. I just nod.

"I'm sorry."

Anger comes. Her words cut like blades because they are true. I *have* lied to her. I *have* betrayed her. I *have* used her. Nothing can excuse what I did, or what I did to cover it up. The possibility of a life together dissolves in the flow of invective. Eventually, I turn and walk away. I don't look back. I don't hear the door close; she must be watching every step I take away from her.

I wander around for what seems like hours. I remember going up and down Kings Heath High Street. She is everywhere, *we* are everywhere. In the shops, the Kingsway Cinema, waiting for buses, laughing and loving. Those two people are gone forever..

I catch the bus back to Nan's. I have nowhere else to go. Mom has been around with some more of my stuff, clothes mainly. She hasn't even waited for me, nor has she left a message.

The next morning, I phone Rick. The deadline is a day away. I haven't drifted past it after all.

***

Alice:

I watch him walk away - every step until he is out of sight. I empty of feelings as he walks, until there is only a void inside. Even on the doorstep, when he finally tells the truth, I still love him, feel sorry for him, pity him even. He looks absolutely terrible. Something has happened to his beautiful face, it is cut and bruised, and he limps as he leaves.

What am I supposed to do, or feel? He betrayed me. How can I ever trust or forgive him again? Where do I go from here?

***

Danny:

Nothing to lose. The next day I go home. I know Dad will be at work. She is there. There is nothing to talk about, although she prattles on about giving it time so she can 'work on him'. What a joke! She can't do anything, never could, never will. I don't bother discussing it. I go and pack what I want and get her to pay for a taxi. She thinks I'm moving it all to Nan's, which is true, except that it doesn't include me. There is nothing to stay here for.

It's not a hard choice, London versus Erdington – even if London does come with its own downside. I'm young, free, an exciting world lies before me, and I've been handed a golden entrance ticket. Fate has made the decision. I *have* drifted, just not in the direction I envisaged.

The next morning, I put on my uniform and go to school. The last day of school for me, end of term forever.

All morning I watch him, and he knows. At morning break I approach him in front of his sidekicks. I can see fear in his eyes. He can see something in mine that scares him. I don't know what I'm capable.

"I'll be wanting a word with you at dinner time you fat fuck." He tries to laugh but it doesn't happen, sticks in his throat. The others sense that this is more than schoolboy stuff. I look at them all. "And you lot can either be there, or keep out of the fucking way. This is between me and him."

As the dinner bell goes he scarpers but he isn't very quick. I catch up with him on the playing field. A gaggle of others trail behind, sensing drama.

Two of his mates catch up and stand either side of him. He draws some courage from them until I produce the carving knife and they back away. Lowe freezes, the tip of the knife just touching his neck.

"I matched up your writing the first time. Tried to ignore it and get on with my life, but that wasn't good enough for you was it? Couldn't leave it alone. Well there's nothing left for you to destroy."

He doesn't even try to deny it, starts gabbling that it was just a joke. The others goggle open mouthed, clueless and shocked.

I shut him up. "I've got nothing more to lose – even if I kill you, so I think that's what I'm going to do." One of the other kids runs off and I know that a teacher will be called.

He actually wets himself when I cut him with the kitchen knife, and it's only a tiny cut. He'll have worse when he gets past bum-fluff and starts shaving. I make him beg for his life on his knees. I'm not going to kill him, but he thinks I'm serious, collapses in a heap of blubber and sobs. He's just a spiteful little boy. Not worth the bother. But what damage he has caused.

I let the teachers take the knife off me. I'm supposed to wait in the Head's office for the Police, but when we are alone I just push him out of the way and leave. None of them try to stop me. I think I just got expelled.

*

Mickey is waiting for me at Euston. He looks rough, but he is a comforting sight of sorts, a familiar face in a strange land. I cleared out all my savings, packed a case and left without a goodbye to anyone. I could even be a wanted man, but I'm guessing that the law will have better things to do than bother about Lowe and his wet pants. Once they find out I'm gone, I'll be filed away and they can get on with catching some robbers and rapists.

Mickey looks me up and down.

"Last resort eh?"

"End of the line."

I tell him about it as we hop on and off tube trains. I'm completely lost, but he seems to know the Tube like the back of his hand. He likes the bit with the knife.

"Keep hold of that anger, know where to find it, you might need it one day."

We go to the East End, by the West Ham ground. It is rough, but Mickey is well-known, even the intimidating groups of West Indians acknowledge him.

"You seem to know a lot of people?"

He laughs. I like him when he laughs, his whole face lights up. I hope I can trust him, he's all I've got now.

"Well, you could call them business contacts. They know who I work for. This is his home ground. Nobody here wants to upset Rick, so they smarm up to me when they would probably like to stick me with a blade. As long as you don't rock the boat, if you pull your weight, you'll be ok. Just remember what I told you, never, ever cross him. Here we are then, home sweet home."

I had expected some filthy squat, but it's not too bad. A big terraced house with steps up to the front door. There is a row of doorbells. I've got the flat right at the top, almost in the roof. It's small – what you'd call a bedsit, and the furniture is old, but there's an electric fire and an ancient black and white TV that actually works, ex 'Radio Rentals' by the looks. There's a kitchen and the basics. For someone who has nothing, it's something.

"This is yours. Rick owns a lot of houses round here. They are all split into flats. You get this as part of your pay. Most of his tenants are kosha and pay rent though. He started buying these terraces up years ago when nobody wanted them. There's five of us in here. You, me, Pancho, Denise and Trudie. We all work for Rick in our different ways. He doesn't like mixing employees and tenants.

"I thought he liked boys, what do the girls do?"

"You need to wise up quick. Rick ain't a saint and he isn't just into pretty boys like you. The girls are for sale and Pancho looks after them - and others, in what he calls his 'stable' – and keeps them in line. We're never short of visitors here. They make a lot of money – for Rick. They are good girls, those two, but watch Pancho, he can be a nasty bastard. Very quick to get that flick-knife out and wave it about."

He leaves me to settle in. I'm still in shock. All my plans are dust and I'm shitting myself. I try to console myself that I might have decided to do this anyway; it was what I wanted, the excitement and action. But the thought of home and Alice, what I've lost forever, keeps creeping into my mind.

My life assumes a new routine. At first I'm teamed up with Mickey, 'for training'. Pubs and clubs, the little wraps of stuff, the piles of cash, the ever present 'minders', usually Rufus, who treats me well. Every so often I'm summoned to Rick's place, and his bed. It's not so bad. In fact, it's good. I'm here, where I dreamt of being, at the centre of things. Mixing with the 'in crowd', having a ball in the clubs. Every night is a night out.

I love the scene, the people, the glam and glitter. I fit in. People start to call me by name. I work hard. Rick approves and I get cash to spend. He's a really nice guy I think – I don't see any sign of what worries Mickey. I make some friends. A new sort of family envelopes me. Trudie and Denise are a laugh and flirt with me, despite them being much older.

Denise is tall and leggy with a liking for thigh-high leather boots. She has a great figure. She wears too much make-up and her long blonde hair shows dark roots. She is pretty, although her face is too round and full to be called beautiful. She seems sad underneath the bravado, and there are dark patches below her eyes that the make-up doesn't quite hide.

Trudie is a different kettle of fish. She is thin and flat-chested with a drawn, pinched face. She looks really hard. Her hair is cut short and dyed almost white. She dresses like a man. She has a wicked sense of humour though and an infectious, cackling laugh. She chain-smokes and has a leathery voice. She's 'in your face' and confident, always ready with a joke or a quick put down. I can tell that she is terrified of Pancho.

The pimp looks Mediterranean. Olive skin, brown eyes, a mop of dark curls. He is much older, probably forties. He sports a Jason King moustache and sideburns. He leaks aggression. Every conversation is a challenge. He's easily offended, quick to anger, to start screaming and shouting. He makes no secret of the flick-knife and knuckledusters he carries everywhere. He is dangerous. I think he's a coward, and because of that he's unpredictable and capable of anything.

One night there is a knock on my door. Denise is there. She has been crying and her smeared eyeliner makes her look like a panda. She asks if she can come in. We end up in bed. But there is no sex, we just hold each other. That is all we need right now. My new family, showing me more love than my real one ever did. It's been a good few weeks.

I miss Alice.

***

David:

Arrives at Yokohama to an ecstatic welcome, followed by a press conference at the Imperial Hotel, Tokyo. He is presented with nine new costumes by designer Kansai, a mix of traditional Japanese theatre and leading-edge fashion. They add exoticism and a further 'alien' touch.

The tour opens in Tokyo with Bowie putting on an extremely physical performance, resonant of Japanese theatre, because he is concerned about language differences. The fans are hysterical and the media gush praise.

Following a theatre visit with Angie, Bowie learns how to apply traditional 'kabuki' makeup – a skill he then incorporates into the new 'Aladdin Sane' image.

In the background, problems persist. On April 10th, Woodmansey and Bolder demand the promised, but as yet non-existent, pay increase from Defries. There is friction and Defries comments that the roadies are worth more to him. They storm out. Ronson has to persuade them to stay with the tour.

A bigger issue is brewing. RCA are refusing to underwrite the costs of a planned stadium tour in the USA later in the year, as record sales in The States are not matching projected costs.

Defries is fed up with the record company, and worried about the sums not adding up. Being 'Ziggy Stardust', even in the new guise of 'Aladdin Sane', is wearing thin for Bowie, with the line between the stage characters and David Jones blurring all the time. A secret decision is reached between Bowie and Defries. 'Ziggy' will be scrapped at the end of the forthcoming UK tour, but not just 'Ziggy', the whole act, including 'The Spiders From Mars'.

This will solve a number of problems at one stroke. The fractious Bolder and Woodmansey will, in effect, be sacked. Defries can extricate Bowie from a US tour that cannot be bankrolled, and precious time can be obtained, for planning, writing and negotiating. Bowie can follow his instinct to take a new path, rid himself of the alter-egos sucking his real identity away. He can be himself again.

Ronson will be kept on board. The promise of Mainman supporting him as a solo artist will be honoured. He is inducted into the secret plan.

On Friday 13th of April, the 'Aladdin Sane' album is released in the UK and enters the chart at number one. 'Ziggy' is reaching God-like status amongst his fans at home. David Jones is somewhere inside, wanting out.

On 24th April Bowie begins the long journey home, boarding the Trans-Siberian Express bound for Moscow.

***

Alice:

He's been gone a month. Nobody has heard from him; nobody knows where he is. I couldn't get his poor bruised and cut face out of my mind. I keep thinking about what happened, why it happened. There are things I don't know, don't understand. I still care. I begin to ask around. I hide it from Mom. She wouldn't understand.

Eventually, I pluck up the courage to phone his house, ready to put the phone down. She answers. When I tell her it's me, there is silence. I think she's angry, that I'll hear the disconnect, but then she says she's sorry. It's unexpected, as is the softness in her voice. Encouraged, I ask whether we can meet, and she agrees.

I recognise her the moment she walks into the café. She has his eyes and some of his looks. She would have been pretty once, but life has done her no favours. She looks old and worn. Her face is lined, her eyes are empty. Worry lines, not those borne of joy. I wave, she comes across and pecks me on the cheek. I didn't expect that either.

There are pleasantries, then silence. I decide to leave it to fester and see what happens. She fills it. Starts off by saying sorry. I think she's apologising for him, I'm about to say she doesn't need to do that when I realise that's not it at all.

"I've done terrible things," she says.

I keep quiet. I've learnt that works.

She talks, and talks, It's a torrent, an unburdening. The story of a life of fear, how that fear corroded the love for her child. There are no tears, I don't think she has any left. She finishes, a drained husk. For the first time I begin to understand Danny's world. Some of the hate ebbs away, and some of her guilt transfers to me. What was I doing, meddling around in his life, trying to mould him into something for me? I thought I was doing something good, but I was hopelessly out of my depth. Am I actually responsible? If I hadn't given him confidence, showed him what he could be, would seeing Bowie on Top Of The Pops have had the same impact?

"Tell me about what happened, how he got the bruises on his face." I finally ask.

After she has finished and I understand it all, she looks at me expectantly. I think she is seeking some words of comfort, some exoneration. Later, I think that perhaps I should have granted her some redemption, shown some sympathy, but I couldn't find it in me. She left looking broken and beaten.

She doesn't know where Danny is. Hasn't heard a word. He has vanished. I don't know what to do, where to go. I have a terrible feeling about this.

Danny:

The icing on the cake – Bowie is nearly home and we start in London at Earls Court in a couple of weeks. A new UK tour and I'm going on it with Rick! He is really pleased with me; says I've got a way with the punters. I've sold a lot of gear the past few weeks. I get asked to stay regularly and I can see that the others think I'm his favourite and a bit special because of that. Nice, considering how low I was a month ago. Fate, in the ugly form of that twat Lowe has finally done me a favour.

I love it here. My own place, the friendship of Mickey and the girls. Plenty of cash in my pocket. As much blow as I want. Entry to all the best places and the 'in crowd'. People like Rufus looking out for me. And now I'm going on tour with Bowie. It's a dream come true. I can put up with a lot for that. The nights with Rick, Pancho and his evil looks – he doesn't like me. If I ever fall out of favour I need to watch him. But I don't think I need to worry about that.

I haven't looked back. There's a bounce back in my step. My Birmingham life has ended. I don't care about what's happening at home – like they don't care about me, so I haven't sent any messages. If there's a trace of concern from Mom and Dad, which I doubt, I hope they are suffering for it. I really miss Alice, but that's over too. She would never have me back after what I've done, and I can't blame her. She'll find someone nice, and forget all about me. My way forward lies with Rick – my only way.

One night, I'm in the 'Sombrero' sorting out the merchandise, with Rufus on toilet door duty, when one of the wraps comes open, spilling some white dust on the worktop. I quickly close it back up, no one will know. I look at the powder for a good minute, then checking Rufus' attention is elsewhere I quickly scoop it into my palm and snort it, like I've seen others do. I check there's none on my nose and off I go to do my work. Whammo! It hits me a few minutes later, and I spend the next twenty minutes wandering around in a state of happiness and euphoria. Such a small amount, such a big high. It doesn't affect the selling, so nobody notices.

I've got a bit of a taste for it since then, but only tiny amounts, and it's all under control. It's easy to 'leak' a hit's worth every so often and nobody will ever notice.

After a couple of weeks, I realise I'm taking a stupid and unnecessary risk, stealing Rick's stuff, I'm walking round with a pocket full of wraps and I've got plenty of cash of my own. I can 'buy' a wrap dead easy using my own money and the books will balance.

I share it with Trudie and Denise. They get some bits and pieces off Pancho too – he sees it as keeping them sweet and under control. But there are no strings attached for them as far as I'm concerned. They've both been good friends to me since I got here and if it helps them to get through the days and nights, that's fine. I get the odd favour back, but it's mainly about having someone there to talk to, who you aren't frightened of, and doesn't want something from you. The girls are sworn to secrecy about me using. I daren't tell Mickey, he would look at me with those old eyes of his, and slowly shake his head.

*

If things were going well before – now they're brilliant. Bowie's back, and I'm right there with him. The UK tour starts at Earls Court, Rick providing security and transport as usual, and I'm helping with those little extras that every rock star and their followers need.

I watch the first show from the side of the stage – how good is that! From school to stardust in six weeks. And what an experience – a bloody riot in fact.

The hall is too big, and the sound just isn't right. Most of the crowd – and there are lots of them, can't see or hear anything.

As soon as David and the band come on there is an almighty surge and crush as people try to fight their way to the front – or to get a view at all. The stage isn't raised - what a crap decision by whoever had designed the place. I can see actual fights going on.

Of course, this upsets David, and he walks off stage. There is total confusion and I think, 'that's it, there's gonna be a riot', but guess who sorts it? Rick. He stands in the middle of the stage, telling them to calm down, move back, sort themselves out. In the end David says he won't come back on if they don't quieten up, and an uneasy order prevails. This just about holds until the end, despite some drunks stripping off and pissing on the seats. 'Jean Genie' seems to do the trick.

The concert itself has a very different feel, with lots of new stuff from 'Aladdin Sane' and some medleys. By the end, and 'Rock 'n' Roll Suicide', the crowd are as one, clapping along, and everything is alright. David saved the day I think, but he didn't look happy afterwards.

He is so beautiful. He wore some of the old costumes, but a new white kimono was stunning. His makeup looks superb, a huge gold circle on his forehead. I fall in love with him all over again.

Rick was the hero of the moment, which made him happy, and when Rick is happy, we all are. The drinks and cash flow, and everyone has a great time. I always watch him though, remembering what Mickey told me. Rick never uses, never seems drunk, always in control, observing, assessing.

I've kept my little bit of 'Coke' sniffing really low key, so he doesn't notice. I'll keep it that way. But why shouldn't I have some? Everyone is on it now, including David. It's the latest fashion, that's the world I live in.

The tour heads off to Scotland. Mickey has been left behind to oversee the operation in the clubs and pubs. A couple of new boys have appeared ,and I think Rick has asked him to keep an eye on their 'training'. They are both West Indians, I get the impression that Rick has had them to work for him as a favour to someone.

Wherever we go, there are meetings in back alleys, pubs and car parks. I'm trusted to do it now, but Rufus is my shadow, together with Glen, a cockney with a face chiseled out of granite. All these hard men scare the shit out of me, but they're on my side.

I take the envelopes of cash and return with the stuff. At first I am terrified. I wouldn't last a second with these people on my own. I've seen guns and blades and people who look like they would use them without a thought. But I'm part of the business now, part of the money-making machine, and I'm no threat. I think that's why Rick uses me. The other thing is, they all know who I work for, and Rick seems to be not only well connected, but respected. I suppose that so long as the cash flows, everything is 'Hunky Dory', to coin a well-known phrase.

After doing the buying, I go back to the usual routine of selling. There are a number of places the stock is hidden, and I carry only small amounts. The buyers are pretty regular. Some of the band, roadies and hangers-on don't use, but they all have some way of getting off their heads. There's loads of cash around, so they get what they want. It's just the way it is.

I get a hotel room of my own in each place, which I use when Rick doesn't want me for himself. I get to watch all the shows from side stage, go to all the parties. David knows my name and often makes passing comments. He is really nice, with a great smile. Everyone loves him. Except Rick. For Rick he is a cash machine and opener of doors. For Rick it is business.

At the end of May we are back at Hanley, where it all started for me, barely six months ago. I can't believe it's such a short time ago. I'm no longer a schoolboy. I'm my own person. This is the best thing that's ever happened to me.

***

David:

The last ever party at Haddon Hall is held to celebrate the return from Moscow. The old house is so well-known now that it is routinely besieged by fans, and normal life has become virtually impossible. Bowie and Angie move out – renting Diana Rigg's London flat.

The disaster of the concert at Earl's Court on May 12th results in the final venue for the UK tour being moved from there to the Hammersmith Odeon. There is a lot of criticism in the music press concerning the poor sound and visuals at Earls Court, the result of the venue being unprepared for rock concerts, and the sound system being totally inadequate for the vast arena with its very poor acoustics.

The tour begins in earnest, with wild scenes of hysteria including a whole row of seats being ripped out in Glasgow. 'Ziggy' / 'Aladdin Sane' is the hottest rock property in Britain.

***

Alice:

The 'Birmingham Evening Mail' is a regular in our house.. He reads it then leaves it for mom and me. When I was younger I used to look at the kid's stuff, like the 'Chipper Club', but now I scan it for local news and what's on at the pictures and clubs, although there's nothing really in it for teenagers and definitely no music news.

Murder seems to be the favourite for a good screaming headline, so I don't really pay much attention at first. The paper is lying folded on the settee arm, the headline shouting in inch-high letters,

'Man stabbed to death; woman held!'

I have my tea, sit watching TV. I absent-mindedly unfold the paper, paying it less than half of my attention. I do a double-take. There on the front page is a picture of Danny's Mom.

The story continues on Page Three. The details are sketchy, but there are two certainties – Danny's dad has been stabbed and is dead, and his mom's been arrested.

Chapter Fifteen

'Time'
May / June 1973

Danny:

Being on tour is really draining. I understand why rock stars get fed up and do such outrageous things. An endless round of packing and unpacking, hotel rooms that look exactly the same; dreary journeys through grey landscapes viewed through grimy windows. Only the parties and the shows bring colour and life. David looks tired. He's definitely lost weight. His face is pinched and his cheekbones are sticking out more. Sometimes when he slaps on the face paint he looks like some old 'prossy' with too much make-up.

But the shows are fantastic. Once he's on stage he takes on new life. He is energised, in command, he is 'Aladdin Sane', the hottest star in Britain, and I've got a ringside seat. My nomadic life is a rollercoaster of highs and lows and I'm not getting much sleep!

I've got the 'job' nailed now and I'm well in with Rick and the boys. Plenty of cash in my pocket and a regular supply of stuff to keep me sharp. Who needs to sleep anyway!

***

Alice:

I can't stop thinking about it. Danny doesn't know a thing. God knows what it will do to him on top of everything else that's happened. What he did to me was terrible, but it seems a bit insignificant alongside murder and imprisonment.

I'm really confused about my feelings for him. One minute I hate him, the next I can't stop thinking about him and the times we had together. I miss him terribly in truth. There's a big hole in my life and I haven't a clue how to fill it. I look at other boys, I've had a few try to chat me up but I just can't get interested, it's as if there's a wall between me, and them, life. My friends have dragged me out to clubs, there have been some slow dances, but as we wheel round and round, their arms around me, I'm somewhere else, his face floats before me. The slow songs leave me cold, and Eddie Holman strikes to the heart.

I wake up feeling decisive. If nothing else, I owe it to Danny as a friend to try and find him and let him know the news. Maybe an excuse for me to see him again, for other reasons. I don't know how I'll react; it just seems the right thing to do.

I scour the Evening Mail every day, but the murder has faded from the news. The next thing will be all the gory details at trial time, but that could be ages away. The only thing I can think of is to go to the Police station in Kings Heath. I don't tell Mom and Dad.

I sneak off early from school, it's nearly end of term now and no-one's bothered much now that 'O' Levels are over and done with. We are just going through the motions, teachers and pupils, until the blessed release of the summer holidays. For some, the end of school altogether, for me, decisions about Sixth Form. I'm staying on to do 'A' Levels I think, now there's no Danny, but what once seemed the natural progression, 'A' Levels and University, seems colourless and unappealing, the extension of a childhood that I've moved on from.

Kings Heath police station, between the library and the railway station, with an old desk Sergeant looking at me with faint amusement tinged with a suspicion that I'm playing him up.

"So, you're involved in murder are you?"

"No, I've told you, not involved as such, but I know them, used to go out with the son and know something about how things were. It might help explain what happened."

I'd thought of this as a way of trying to get some interest.

He sighs. He's tried to fob me off a couple of times but he can see I'm not going away,

"Take a seat young lady, I'll make a phone call."

The next day I've got a whole morning of free periods, so I go in and register, then disappear. One bus ride later and I'm sat opposite an old fat detective who reeks of tobacco and stale booze. I suppose it's the best I'm going to get.

He lights a fag and offers me one. He looks surprised when I decline.

"Ok darling, tell me about it."

I go through the whole saga, it seems a bit shallow and pathetic now I'm saying it out loud.

"So, let's get this straight. You're telling me that she was acting in some sort of self-defence?"

"Well –."

"But you weren't there when any of this happened, and it's come to you via your ex-boyfriend who has now done a bunk and can't be found: or it was said to you by the person we've got banged up, the murderer?"

It does sound a bit thin when he says it like that.

"But I thought it might help her if you could tell the judge about him?"

He leans back and laughs.

"Let me tell you something missy. She took a big carving knife and stuck it in him several times, then she cut his throat. Does that sound reasonable because of a few 'domestics', or an act of self-defence?"

"But that's not how it was. It was more than arguments ....."

"Well, she hasn't tried to excuse what she did. I interviewed her, and she seemed bloody proud of it to me. There'll be a guilty plea and life to follow, I'm telling you. You're wasting your time, and mine. Unless you know where the lad is? We ought to tell him about it, and he needs to be read the riot act himself for threatening some school kid with a knife – although it's only the school that's complained, so we aren't too bothered."

I shake my head.

"Sorry, I don't know where he is other than that he went to London."

I can tell he thinks I'm lying.

"Well, I think that's about it, isn't it, thanks for coming. I should forget about them if I was you. You seem like a decent girl, shouldn't be getting involved with scum like that."

213

There's no point in saying anything else. His mind is made up. I make a last attempt.

"What will happen to her?"

"She's on remand at Holloway. With a guilty plea she'll be done and dusted quickly. She'll probably go back there for the rest of her life; she won't be troubling you again."

"Where's Holloway, Could I see her?"

"It's in London." He laughs again. It's an unpleasant laugh, tinged with cynicism and insincerity. "Close to her son at least – if that's where he is. And no, you can't see her. My advice is to forget it. I bet your Mom and Dad wouldn't like to know you're here trying to get involved in this bad business."

It is a threat, there's no point staying.

***

Danny:

It was all going so well. Of all the places to come unstuck, bloody Worcester. I suppose we stick out like a sore thumb. Bowie fans all dressed and made-up, besieging the hotel where we are all staying. 'Weirdos' parading about frightening the locals. Boys wearing make-up. We are about as welcome as a fart in a crowded lift. Should've guessed that the dead hand of the establishment in the form of Worcester's finest might have something special planned for us - or least Rick should have planned better. He seems to have relaxed, got more up himself, since sorting out the crowd at Earls Court. He knows he's well in with the main man, I think he's taken his eye off the ball a bit.

The Worcester gentry and yokels are probably shitting themselves that we are going to corrupt their sons and daughters. 'Sex, Drugs and Rock 'n' Roll', and all that. Children turning queer, drugs everywhere. Flash London set in town. Something must be done!

We check into a hotel made of concrete blocks opposite the cathedral, then I walk through town to the railway station and hang about outside. As usual, Rufus is shadowing me. One of the regular London couriers appears and I do the usual passing of packages, around the corner in some bushes. He's straight off back into the station. Now I'm holding the baby, so to speak, which is the norm. I set off back to the hotel with the stuff in a rucksack, confident that my guardian angel will be around if needed.

When I get back into the shopping centre some bloke bumps into me, and before I know it I'm bundled into a side street and a doorway. There's two of them. It's a robbery, but they've picked the wrong one this time. I'm expecting the dark destroyer to emerge and sort them out and can see him approaching out of the corner of my eye, when one of my attackers shoves my arm up my back and shouts 'Police' in my face. They turn me round, strip the rucksack off my back, none too gently, and cuff me. Rufus saunters past and off around the corner. He must have heard.

"Keep your mouth shut, arsehole, you're nicked."

"What for…?"

One of them gives me a dig in the guts, winding me.

"You know, and I said shut the fuck up. Right, off for a little walk around the corner. Any funny business and we'll make sure you've resisted arrest – get my drift."

Within minutes I've been strip-searched, and given another smack round the head. They open the package in front of me, emptying the wraps on the desk.

"You're right in the shit son. Let's bang you up for a bit so you can have a think about things. Got some big nob CID wanker from the city coming over to see you specially."

I'm hauled unceremoniously to a cell. I've been in a daze, but the sound of the heavy door banging shut, and the hatch being slammed up, wakes me up sharpish and I'm left with my thoughts. I'm used to that. I can hear Mickey's words drumming over and over in my head, 'If you get caught you're on your own'.

After what seems like days, but is probably a few hours, I hear the sound of keys, and, as the door opens, the source of the noise is revealed as a fat cop with the most bored and disinterested look on his face that I have ever seen. He can't even be bothered to speak, just motions me out of the cell and points down the corridor.

He opens a door, pushes me through it, then turns and leaves, slamming the door behind him. He must hear the comment, but he doesn't return.

"Carrot-crunching wanker. Park your bum over there bab." There is one other person in the room, and from the accent he's a Brummie. He doesn't look like a cop. What he does look like is mightily pissed off. I sit opposite him and he fixes me with a stare for what seems like ages, until I look down.

"There ya go. Show a bit of respect. Don't go thinking you can do the uppity kid thing with me son. I ain't got the time nor the patience. The less time I spend out here in this god-forsaken shithole the better. Now pin your ears back, keep ya mouth shut and I'll tell ya how it is, which ain't good for you. Comprendez?"

I nod. He sits back and puts his feet on the table between us.

" Just a boy underneath all that crap ya wearing ain't ya, although you look like a right poofta. Well son, you've gone and got yourself in a bit of bother, and it ain't just a bit actually. You're in with a bad crowd and they're from London, which makes it twice as bad cos I can't stand fucking Cockneys at the best of times, and even less when they think they can come up here lording it about on my patch. We had word you'd be here with that poncey fucker Bowie, and someone called in a favour from me, someone I owed – or else I wouldn't be spending me precious out here in the sticks on a piece of piss like you. With me so far? Just nod. Good." He takes his feet off the table and leans forward, grabbing hold of my clothes and pulling me forward. I can feel his spit hitting my face as he continues.

"This is how it is. You're stuck in the middle of a lot of nasty bastards with enough fucking 'Coke' and other shit on you to get ten years. Can you imagine that? They'll love you in nick, pretty thing like you. Oh yes, they'll ream your arsehole out good and proper. Fucking you will be like waving a stick in the Albert Hall by the time you get out. But there's another way. And I've been asked to explain the facts of life to ya, Brummie to Brummie, so to speak. Pity you left home, I reckon you'd have been better off in Brum with me, but you've made your bed, what future you've got is down there now by the looks, at least for a while. I don't think Mommy and Daddy are going to get you out of this one are they?"

He has a strange look on his face. I say, "No, they don't care, that's why I left."

He seems to be about to say something, then thinks better of it and resumes the diatribe.

"Right, it's like this. You're gonna get out in the morning with no charges. Don't get excited - you'll be meeting my London mate DS Fisher in Birmingham in a couple of weeks when you answer bail, which is what you'll be on. That doesn't mean the charges are dropped, it means they're hanging over your head while you have a nice long think.

I'll give you a pretend charge sheet for 'Possession With Intent To Supply' to show your boss, with Birmingham Magistrates Court plastered all over it, and the same date as your bail. Means you won't get your head kicked in or worse, which is what'll happen if you walk out of here without a charge. You'll get a much longer bail period on that day if you play the game. What you gotta think about in the meantime is helping us out. That means carrying on as usual while you're on bail and telling us what's happening. We call it being a 'Sarbut' up here, but you'll be a 'Met' snout. They'll look after you and you'll even get some cash on top, plus there might be other favours in the future. The 'Met' will spin the bail for six months while you gather the evidence and if it all comes out right, you turn 'Queen's' and get off with a slapped wrist. And if you come back home to Brum in the future we can have a profitable little relationship. That's your only hope kid, so get ya fucking head on straight and take ya chance. Truth is, no-one's interested in a useless piece of shit like you. There are bigger fish to fry and you're the bait. So that's the deal."

He suddenly slaps me hard across the face snapping my head to one side. "That's for a bit of credibility and a reminder that we ain't messing about, this is no game. It's play ball with us or ten years plus. Now say thank you, Mr. Docker, and we can both fuck off."

***

'The night 'spaceship Bowie' landed'

5th June 1973. Worcester News. Reporter - Mike Pryce
'All the he-men', 'she-men' and 'in-between' men descended on
Worcester last night to see their hero David Bowie. He landed at
Worcester Gaumont from his planet far away, as part of his latest
'Ziggy Stardust' and 'Aladdin Sane' tour. I've covered loads of rock
concerts at the Gaumont, from Jimi Hendrix to 'The Seekers' by way
of Cliff Richard and 'The Faces', but never has there been an
audience like Bowie's. It's as if a box has been opened and all these
weirdly dressed people climbed out. Where are they all in the
daytime? Do they dress like that working the lathes at Heenan's or is
it their dark secret?

Bowie is the strangest dressed rock star I've ever met,
outside of pantomime. I've never met a man wearing so much
female make-up and sporting such strange clothes, but he is
disturbingly beautiful for a man. It's a look his fans try to replicate,
with mixed success, and the queue outside the Gaumont seemed to
comprise of travellers from a charabanc spaceship from Planet Zog.

Musically, it was a great night though. With the aid of the
excellent Mick Ronson and the rest of 'The Spiders From Mars',
Bowie powered his way through his back catalogue from 'Space
Oddity' to 'Ziggy Stardust'. There was also a rendition of 'All The
Young Dudes', which he wrote for Herefordshire group 'Mott The
Hoople', plus new songs from the recently released 'Aladdin Sane'
album.

Bowie, or is it 'Ziggy'? It's difficult to see a difference these
days, performed throughout with huge energy, Bowie puts on a
show, not a rock concert, with numerous costume changes. He
jumped on the speakers, performed an 'exotic' strobe-lit solo with
Ronson, and even climbed up the ornate embellishments of the
Gaumont walls.

He finished with Chuck Berry's 'Around and Around', and
then he was gone, leaving us with ears ringing from the volume,
back to whatever planet he comes from.'*

(*Constructed from excerpts from the original review and used with the kind permission of Mike Pryce)

***

Alice:

*I tried and failed, but I just can't get Danny out of my mind. God knows what he's doing, but he **should** know about his parents. What will happen once he does? I must confess I selfishly want it to be me that tells him. I want to see him again, and I have fantasies about him falling into my arms for comfort, and us starting up again. Me as his rock as he rebuilds himself, us together, forever. Because that's where I am in my head right now. There's nobody else for me. It's got to be him; I know it deep in my soul. It's fated to be. I forgive him. But I can't find him.*

Then, one evening, I get a lucky break. I am reading, in my favourite chair. Dad has his head buried in the 'Evening Mail'. The TV is on in the background. The 'Nationwide' news programme. It's a comforting babble, and then the words 'David Bowie' intrude and I look up.

It's a piece on Bowie, bit of a 'shock-horror, whatever next' type of thing, to frighten the parents and cause them to shake their heads. The commentary is all like that, full of a sense of disbelief laden with sarcastic irony at the shocking doings of Danny's hero, although it does end with Bowie admitting that he's an actor, which I could always see.

'Ziggy Stardust', 'Aladdin Sane', they aren't really him at all, just a stage thing. I could never get Danny to see it. In the interview that's part of the Nationwide piece, Bowie even refers to 'David Bowie' in third person, as if it isn't him at all, as if there's somebody else, another layer below that character, even.

The thing starts with Bowie in his dressing room, putting on the make-up, loads of blusher and a big gold circle on his forehead. Once the construction is complete, it looks like a mask, with the real person looking out through the eyeholes. He puts on a white Kimono outfit, drawing more sarcastic comments about rock stars in short dresses. The commentary refers to him as a 'freak'. I think Bowie loves to provoke this sort of coverage, it adds to the hype and makes him the figurehead of rebellion.

The film comes from Bournemouth and Brighton performances. There are hysterical girls, one weeping because she's missed him going into the venue, another crowing because she actually 'kissed his hand'. They are about the same age as me but they seem so pathetic.

They worship him like a God. But it's not him really is it? It's all an act, and they can't see it. The reporter is gently poking fun at them for their 'faith'. He can see it, but they don't, and camp outside his hotel room door, neglected but hopeful of entry later. One says she'd do anything to get inside and I believe her. She looks about fourteen. The whole commentary is about stupid and immature teenage girls' adoration, there's nothing said about boys fancying him, that would be a step too far for the BBC, although there is a passing mention of Bowie enjoying 'intimacy' with men, which surprises me.

Then the film cuts to corridors behind the stage as Bowie is about to go on. 'Time' plays, and I wait for the line about 'wanking', but it fades out just before the word. I think Bowie looks faintly embarrassed. There are loads of people milling about, and as the camera sweeps up and down the corridor, I see Danny.

It's definitely him, all made up and dressed to kill. I'd know him anywhere, and helpfully the camera lingers an extra moment to milk the full effect. Now the tales of meeting Bowie and going to the party come back to me. I didn't believe them, but what if it was all true? What if he's doing something on the tour? What if.?

I watch, fixated, hoping for another glimpse, but there is none.

Right at the end there is a quick interview with the man himself. He even refers to himself as an actor playing a part when he goes on stage. I wonder how long 'Ziggy' will last, whether he's getting fed up with all the making up, then it ends. No more Danny, but I've seen enough.

I scramble out of my chair and run upstairs. I grab my pile of old 'Melody Makers' and after a few minutes I find what I'm looking for. Tour dates. Yes, Bournemouth was on May 25th so only last week.

Damn! Worcester Gaumont was yesterday, then they're off up North again. I scan further down the list and give a quick prayer of thanks, he's at Birmingham Town Hall, two days, two shows a day, on June 21st and 22nd.

The next day I'm straight on the phone to the booking office, and I manage to get a ticket for the early show on the 22nd. That's a Friday, and with exams over I can spend all day up town if needs be. I'll find him if he's there. I'll just have to fit in with the rest of the hysterical girls.

***

Danny:

They keep me in for two nights to make it look realistic. Worcester looks very ordinary as I trudge back to the hotel in the early morning. No 'freaks', just a grey mass of people going to work. My room has been paid up until today and there's a message waiting for me. I briefly wonder how Rick knows when I'm getting out, but guess it's easy enough to pretend to be a relative or something and put in a phone call. They are in Sheffield now, at the Hallam Tower hotel. There is money for a train ticket in the envelope.

Mickey is waiting for me at Sheffield.

"Welcome back, Rick wants to see you – now."

He is searching my face, trying to gauge my reaction, but I have had plenty of time to rehearse.

"I bet he does. He doesn't need to worry though. I remembered what you said."

He looks puzzled, "what?"

"That if I got caught I was on my own."

He looks at me strangely. There is pity there, and I think he almost says something but pulls back at the last minute.

"Good lad, that's the ticket. He'll look after you if you keep your gob shut. But you're gonna get a right grilling now, so get ready."

"I am."

We walk across town to a restaurant, no limousine this time. It is lunchtime, but the place is empty. There is a heavy on the door, and I notice that the sign is turned to closed as I go in. "One of Rick's mate's places." Mickey informs me as we approach.

Rick is waiting at a table in an alcove, out of sight of the windows. He points to a seat. Rufus joins us, but stands by my side. He doesn't feel like my guardian angel today.

Rick looks at me, hard. For a moment I wonder what he can read on my face, in my eyes, and I nearly crumble, but I find I'm tougher inside than I thought, and I bluff it out, meeting his gaze.

"So, tell me all about it."

"Well, Rufus here saw what happened."

"Cut the fucking crap. I'm not stupid. That was no random search and arrest, they'd been watching hadn't they?"

I know this is coming and I've had plenty of time to prepare. I haven't decided yet whether I'm going to play ball with the law or take my punishment, but I need some thinking time, at least until my bail date.

"Yeah. Some fucking yokel big nob detective said they'd been told by the Chief to sort out a few of the Bowie crowd, said some of his Freemason mates must have put the pressure on. They'd set up undercover cops to watch what we were all doing. I think they must have followed me from the hotel to the station, saw me get something that made them suspicious, and turned me over. Their lucky day, my unlucky one."

"What about Rufus here?"

"They never mentioned him. You know how we work it, He's never close when we pick up on strange territory, we never speak, or show we know each other."

"Mmm. And the courier?"

"They wanted to know all about him. I think they lost him. He scuttled back into the station pretty quick, perhaps he just jumped on the first train there – or did a bunk somehow."

"And what did you say about him?"

"Told them I'd bought from him before in London, met him in a pub, but had no idea who he was. They didn't believe me, but I stuck to that, even when they gave me a few slaps." I indicate the red weal donated by Docker.

"I saw them give him a couple of digs," pipes up Rufus. I hope he is trying to defend me, we always seemed to get on well.

"What you saw and what it meant might be different things, let me do the fucking thinking here." Rick turns that implacable gaze back on me.

"Carry on."

I've decided that nearly the truth is the best way to play it. "They said I was going to get ten years unless I played ball and told them who I worked for, worked with them to put them away. Bigger fish than me, they said they wanted. I said I was working on my own but they didn't believe me. They know fuck all about the scene though, and I think they really believed I was a fan who got lucky as a hanger-on. I told them I was a groupie; they didn't want to go too deep into that I can tell you. I don't think they've got anyone inside here, otherwise they would have known who you were, wouldn't they?"

Rick leans forward and looks into my eyes. I resist the temptation to look down or away, it could be fatal. "I think you turned, gave them what they wanted, gave them me. And now you're in their pocket, grassing on me."

He nearly has me this time, and I'm glad I told the truth, sort of. It helps me look straight back at him and stop my voice having any hint of trembling.

"That's bollocks, I told them nothing about you. I'm more scared of you than them. I'm not going to get ten years at sixteen, first time in trouble, and they know it. They are trying it on, think I'm just a kid."

When he replies I know I've got through it, at least for today.

"But you are a kid, and you will go down for that much stuff and not grassing. I reckon two years in Borstal, that won't be easy for a good-looking boy like you."

"It will be if people know I work for you."

"Maybe, maybe. So, what's the next step with the 'Old Bill' then?"

I produce the fake charge sheet and hand it over. He scrutinises every word while I mentally hold my breath.

"'Possession With Intent'. That's heavy. Ok. What's going to happen is this. They'll be watching you so I don't want you too close, but I'm also keeping you where I can see you. I need to get through the rest of this tour, just another few weeks, without anything frightening the customers. The way things are shaping up with Mr. Bowie I'm going to make millions out of this gig so I need to be his best man. Too much police attention and he'll run a mile. The contacts I'm making are incredible and I'm hoping to get into America if I can persuade him to use me for the next U.S tour, later this year. You'll keep the law guessing whether you'll roll over or not, that buys two weeks, then we'll be back in London for the last two shows. I've got a lot more pull on my own turf, and I might have time to work something out for you from there. In the meantime, we'll set you up just like you said, working it alone, then when you tell them to fuck off they might just believe you, but in the meantime they'll think you are still well in, so worth a shot. That sound like a plan?"

I'm genuinely impressed, and thinking that staying loyal to him and taking the rap might be better than selling out. Either way I'll have time to think it through.

"Yep, sounds good."

He leans back and scrutinises me again. "You're a cool customer for a goody-two-shoes sixteen-year-old. Maybe too cool. Still, you took to the dealing well, so perhaps you're tougher than you look. Rufus here likes you, anyway. But you mark my words, you aren't going anywhere out of my sight until this all works its way through, and if I get the slightest hint you're playing a double game you'll regret it. If you're straight, then I promise I'll look after you."

***

David:

Pandemonium continues. It is no longer about music, or a show. Fans, intoxicated with 'love', repeatedly invade the stage. Boys, and girls, are removed by security, roughly at times. At Liverpool, Bowie decides to call off the security, but the crowd surges forward into the orchestra pit, destroying it. Bowie stops the show at one point, telling a heckler that he is supposed to have come to see an 'artist' and to 'fucking shut up'. Any pretence of playing music is lost under the waves of sexually charged hysteria.

On stage, Bowie is electric. In Salisbury he leaps from atop a speaker and damages an ankle, carrying on from a chair. But the end is coming for 'Ziggy Stardust', a release from the madness for David Jones.

The tour culminates at City Hall, Newcastle, on 30th June, prior to returning to London for the final two shows at Hammersmith Odeon on July 2nd and 3rd. They are to be filmed by DA Pennebaker, who is unknowingly about to record an iconic moment in rock music history.

Chapter Sixteen

'Queen Bitch'
June / July 1973

Danny:

I didn't think it possible, but things have taken a turn for the worse.

There is a party after the Torquay show, in the hotel. Rick has totally blanked me after our meeting, but I have a room in the hotel, booked in my own name, and a new shadow, in the form of Greg, who I don't like, and who has made it plain, doesn't think much of me either.

Greg does a good scowl; in fact, he frowns so much I think he's stuck with it. I've never seen him smile, and his forehead is deeply creased in the centre, I reckon from years of being perplexed about just about anything he can't solve with his fists. He is as thick as pig shit, built like a tank, with a square head, thick jaw and huge hands. If you saw him, you'd think straight away, 'boxer', and you'd be right. But not the stuff in a ring. The fighting that happens on street corners, in back alleys, on waste ground. He's a Gypsy and proud of it, and bare-knuckle fighting was his forte, until he met Rick, who supplied the brainpower to harness that aggression to a more productive, (for Rick), use.

Rick must pay well, because Greg makes no secret of his hatred for 'faggots', and always seems to be suppressing an urge to draw blood from the 'fairies and pooftas' as he calls us, that surround him. It amuses Rick, who treats Greg like a dangerous pet dog., It's worrying that, despite Rick's penchant for boys, Greg clearly respects and fears Rick, is loyal to his core, and that speaks volumes for Rick's importance and capabilities.

It's no surprise then, that Greg has been appointed as Rick's 'eyes' on me. But even that isn't the worst thing, just part of it.

The usual after-show party is in the hotel bar and lounge, with people gradually peeling off as they pair up. Mickey is there, I know a lot of people, and only a few months ago I'd have given everything to be there–in fact I have I suppose, but it feels very different without Rick's unseen arm around me.

And people know, I can sense that the word has got around. There is a hesitance to speak, a guarded aspect to conversation, and my sales are way down, so much so that Mickey finds me in the toilet, and tells me that I am off sales from now on, despite Rick's earlier assertion that I would carry on selling on my own. I am damaged goods, the shadow of the real world, its laws and intolerance, staining my presence in this exotic and gilded company. But even that isn't the worst thing.

I am watching Rick moving in on another kid. This one looks younger than me, about thirteen I'd say. I don't know where he's sprung from, but he wouldn't have got in without Rick's say-so, which is bad news for me. Because the kid has a strange beauty.

He's wearing no make-up – but he doesn't need any. He has an oval face, with eyes of pale blue, like a summer sky, ringed with long white lashes. His skin is pale, almost white, with an inner luminosity that seems to make it shine. He is tall for his age with a sinuous figure, swaying hips unwittingly exuding sex, and he is crowned with a mop of pure white hair.

Rick was fixated from the moment the kid walked in; I know the signs. I watch the full routine being put through its paces, and after an hour or so he and the kid disappear. A chill runs through me. I was banking on my continuing attraction to Rick offering me some sort of protection, a 'Joker' card. It's just been played and found wanting. The joke's on me it seems.

As I watch them walk off, arm in arm, I'm suddenly aware of Mickey sat beside me, taking in the same spectacle.

"Hi Mickey, I think I just got screwed, and not in a nice way."

"That's the way it is, join the club. I was that kid once - about ten before you. He likes them young, told you so. You're already getting too old, and that's not counting your current 'unfortunate' situation, which means he won't touch you with a bargepole. I heard all about you getting nicked, from Rufus. Tell me your side if you want. Not that I can do anything about it."

After a quick debate about whether I can trust him, Rick might have asked him to probe my story, I recount the tale, pretty much as I told Rick. After I finish, he exhales a stream of smoke from his spliff and hands it to me."

"Do you want my advice Danny? Tell me to fuck off if not."

"You might as well. I think I trust you."

"Don't much matter whether you do or not mate, I'm up front. Told you before, he owns me so I'm not gonna tell you anything you wouldn't expect, but I've been around him a long time, seen plenty. And what I've seen means that I'm saying to you, 'do the time'.

You're just a kid, it's a lot of gear, but it's your first time. I reckon you're looking at a couple of years in Borstal, out in 12 months with good behaviour. Don't grass on Rick. You'll be running for the rest of your life, and he'll find you. Your life won't be worth a shit, and if you do go inside, on a reduced sentence for grassing, you won't come out again. There's loads inside with nothing to lose who'd do anything, even murder, for a good bung to their families and to be in Rick's good books.

I told you, he's a main player, right up there with the Krays and all them types. He's got loads of money, and money talks, he comes from the East End, he knows the right people. Don't mess with him. Keep your gob shut, do your time. When you come out he'll owe you, you'll have proved he can trust you, and while you're inside he'll have your back watched. Course, you can just think he's asked me to say this, and of course I'll go down too if you turn, so I'm bound to say this, ain't I?"

"You would, but you've been good to me Mickey."

"Tried to warn you off didn't I? It's a shame how things have worked out for you, but you decided to come, and now you've got to get your head round what's happened and do what's best, for you. And I'm telling you, that ain't getting into bed with the law. They don't give a shit about you, and when they've got what they want, they'll drop you and you'll be on your own. Whatever they promise, they ain't gonna give you a new identity and hide you away and all that shit you see on telly. Anyway, I can see that Greg's finished chatting up that old bird at the bar and he's taking an interest in us, so I'm off. I'll tell him and Rick exactly what I've said, by the way. Got to look after my own back too."

I know he's telling the truth. I think he feels sorry for me, but pity is not what I need. I've got eleven days before my Monday 'court appearance'. Coincidentally, the tour's back in Birmingham on the Friday before my big day. Rick's let me know I'll be staying at the Albany Hotel that weekend. He has something for me to do to prove my loyalty. I don't much like the sound of that, but I'm right up shit creek and another shitload won't make much difference. Still I get to see both shows. I've still got Bowie.

It should have been a triumphant homecoming for me, with Bowie, but now it's all collapsing.

***

Alice:

Friday, my day at the Town Hall concert, arrives quickly. He played yesterday too, two shows a day, 6pm and 8.30pm, it must be incredibly tiring. I can't imagine how he forces that thin body through it, night after night, must be using speed or something. How long can it go on? I suppose while he's making loads of money he'll keep going, but something will give eventually. I've seen him in a couple of interviews recently and he seems increasingly bizarre, like he's in another world. Yes, he's 'arty-farty', but he seems to be in another dimension, and he's dragged Danny into it too. No wonder Danny has made some strange choices and gone weird, if that's the company he's keeping.

I hang around the Town Hall all day, along with hundreds of Bowie freaks, town is jam-packed with them. There is a fever -pitch of excitement, rising and rising as concert time approaches. Security is tight because of the crowds, so I've had no chance to get close to the stage doors. They are besieged, with screaming girls in the main, held back by metal barriers, patrolled by some mean-looking security guards. The roads and spaces outside are jammed with huge lorries which block the view anyway. I've not seen Danny; he could have been in there all day for all I know.

Doors open at Eight. I'm swept through the pillars outside the Town Hall doors in a surge of semi-hysterical kids. I'm up in the circle so I've no need to fight to get to the front. I should get a good view up there. It is absolute pandemonium inside, with waves of screaming, shouting, chants of, 'We Want Bowie', and the underlying buzz of people trying to make themselves heard above the hubbub.

Two hours later, and I haven't caught so much as a glimpse of Danny. To my surprise, I'm totally blown away by Bowie. The concert is a pulsating, energy filled, riot, despite some technical issues and Bowie hurling the microphone stand across the stage in frustration at one point. The sound isn't great, drowned out by screaming girls. but the show more than makes up for it.

The costume changes, Bowie cavorting around as if possessed. I can't believe he has done four shows like this in two days, he must be totally exhausted. Ronson and his superb guitar solos, the whole lot illuminated by a glitter ball and out-of-this-world lighting. Fans are constantly trying to get on stage, hanging onto Bowie's clothes when he's at the front, trying to pull him into the pit when he offers his hands during 'Rock 'n' Roll Suicide'. I have to admit that it's the best concert I've ever seen, and Bowie has won me over. Danny will be so happy - if I can find him!

I leave slightly before the end, and work my way around to the stage door. Security isn't so tight now that the concert is finished, and I guess it's usual to get fans waiting outside afterwards, hoping to catch a glimpse of the man himself. I find a position outside of the mob of die-hard fans, where I have a good line of sight.

The main crowd trickle away, and peace begins to descend on this end of town. About half an hour later, the door opens, and people and equipment begin to leave, under the watchful eyes of some heavies. The remaining fans are disappointed, just technicians and roadies, no sign of Bowie or 'The Spiders'.

A gaggle of figures emerge. One looks to be in charge, directing the others. He is quite striking, with long blonde hair, big moustache and an air of authority. He turns to talk to someone inside, then I see Danny. The blonde guy says something to him and Danny is off at speed, a big black guy making a path through the crowd for him. I faintly register 'blondie' shouting things at the crowd, but I have the excited mob between me and Danny, who has already disappeared down Hill Street.

I frantically fight my way through, luckily the fans are only too happy to help me leave, less competition. By the time I start down the hill towards the 'Golden Eagle' pub, Danny is a distant figure, and motoring as if his life depends on it.

Despite my platform boots I manage to run down the hill and just catch sight of Danny entering the Albany Hotel. He must be doing ok to stay at a posh place like that. By the time I get through the doors I'm gasping for breath, but catch sight of him entering a lift. I dash across the foyer and press the buttons like a maniac, praying that it hasn't gone.

Suddenly the doors open and there he is! His eyes go wide as he recognises me, but I can't read the emotions that flash across his face. Throwing caution to the winds I throw myself at him and hug him. It feels good.

"Caught you, I've been chasing you all the way down Hill Street, I need to talk."

I notice that he is standing stock still, arms by his side, my hug unreciprocated. I step back, suddenly unsure.

"I got the strong impression last time we met that I was the last person you ever wanted to speak to. You're the reason I left Birmingham," he says.

His voice breaks and I notice his eyes well up with tears. But he wipes them and presses the lift door button. After a moment's hesitation the doors open and he steps out into whatever hotel corridor we've reached. I follow him. But he stops dead.

"Let's go to your room so we can talk properly, is it this floor?"

"We can't go to my room. It's...inconvenient."

Ghosts of old suspicions, betrayals, I jump to an obvious conclusion.

"You've got someone else in there, some groupie I suppose – or is it a bloke?" I regret it as soon as the words leave my mouth, but it's too late. His face hardens.

"None of your bloody business, you made it quite plain that you wanted to see the back of me, so I followed your orders like a good boy. Like I always tried to. And now you pop up out of the blue. Expecting me to just be here waiting, on the off-chance you'd turn up, were you? Well I wasn't, I've got other things on my mind."

I'm angry now. "And me, I've got stuff to sort out too, but I've come here because I've got something important to tell you. Thought you might be bothered, but I can see that you're above us ordinary people now that you're hob-nobbing with the rich and famous."

It's like he's stood on hot coals, looking around nervously. I catch him giving a surreptitious glance at his watch and that sends me over the edge.

"Fucking hell Danny, I thought I meant something to you, but you can't wait to go, can you?"

His face has gone a little pale, and I suddenly realise how my words must sound. I'm right. He's not looking at my face, but lower.

"You aren't....up the stick are you?"

"Would you care if I was. No, I'm not – well I don't think so anyway."

The look of relief that crosses his face doesn't improve my mood.

"What did I ever see in you Danny? I thought you were a nice bloke, but you're just like all the rest, a selfish, heartless bastard. It's always been about you hasn't it? Your needs, your problems. God knows why I bothered coming."

I can see he's itching to get away. I'm crying by now. He tries to hold me but I step back. There is only a couple of foot between us, but it's an abyss.

"Alice, I've got to go, perhaps.."

"Perhaps nothing. I'm not staying if I'm not wanted. You can go back to your flash life and forget the little hometown girl. I'm sure I'm just a drag on you now, you must have bigger fish to fry. Well, I'm guessing, hoping in fact, otherwise you're even colder than I thought, that you don't know about your Mom and Dad?"

"I haven't spoken to them, thought about them, don't want to either, to be honest."

"You better go and find some old papers then, they made the headlines a few weeks ago, then you'll see."

"See what?"

I'm cruel too. I just want to get away from here.

"You're Dad's dead. She murdered him Danny. And now you can fuck off up to your room and find someone else's arms to cry in –if you have any tears for them at all. It could have been me you ran to, I'd forgiven you, but I've changed my mind. I never want to see you again."

***

Danny:

A nice room at The Albany, all paid for. A test of loyalty. More of a test than Rick realised.

He needed a favour, a 'bit of business' that I could help with. I soon worked out what sort of help he was after. And I know what it really means. He is finished with me, has a new toy, and plenty more on tap, with Bowie as the bait. Not only doesn't he fancy me anymore, I have become a risk. And Rick doesn't take risks. Not a gambling man. Might play the percentages for a big gain, but even then he tries to have the cards marked before he bets.

There is a man, an important business contact in Birmingham, Councillor or something. He is the key to a new venture, something to do with property development. Rick asked me to be 'nice' to him, to prove myself loyal. I'm not stupid. I saw through it straight away. Whether I do it or not, Rick will wait until he's got all the angles sorted with me and the cops, and I know that he knows cops, especially those who like little boys, so he *will* find out the truth about what I decide.

But Rick isn't one to waste an opportunity, and he has me between a rock and a hard place. I can hardly refuse, can I? I think this was part of his plan for me all along, sort of expected it. That once he tired of me I'd be dealing drugs and doing 'renting' for him. An addition to the stable, with the girls, just another product to be sold for money or favours. Mickey has been warning me from the start, so I can't say I didn't know. And what does it matter really, after what I've done already? If I'm worth something to him, it might just keep me alive.

So, I'm allowed to go to the concerts, got cash in my pocket, my sweeteners. But I'm under strict orders to be back in my room at the hotel by Eleven tonight, ready for the 'customer'.

I'm late getting out of the gig and have to leg it back to the hotel. Five minutes to spare. The last thing I expect after getting into the lift is for the doors to open and Alice to get in!

I'm really pleased to see her, but so stunned that I don't react. Then I realise that I've got no time left. If I don't do what Rick wants, I'm finished, and getting back with Alice won't protect me, in fact it might put her in danger too. While I'm trying to get my head straight, the lift has started rising and she's stepped away. There was a moment there, a split second when things could have changed, but I've missed it.

I can't go up to my corridor in case the customer's there, so I push the buttons in a panic and drag her out at a different level. She's babbling on and the words are flying around my head, but all I can think of are the seconds of my life ticking away - and I can't say a thing to her, can't explain. She'd never understand, and it might put her in danger.

I want so much to go back to Moseley with her, listen to records in her bedroom, be in love again, have that innocent life -

when all that mattered was the latest records and school stuff. It seems a million years ago.

I'm not really concentrating on what she's saying, probably some stuff about us, but I haven't time. Then she suggests we go to my room. In a panic, I blurt out a refusal, and too late, I realise what I've said. She goes ballistic and it all goes downhill from there. I'm so wound up, watching the seconds tick away on my watch, and, I confess, I had a couple of good snorts earlier, which doesn't help.

Before I can think of a way to rescue the situation, it's all gone to rat-shit, and we are all done again, how many times is that?

I can't think, need to get back up to my room.

She mentions Mom and Dad. Not a good moment and I react badly.

She storms off, shouting a stupid comment about my parents, then she's gone. I'm stood in a corridor, my world falling apart, and all I can think about is getting myself upstairs so some old pervert can shag my arse.

He's waiting by the door. He's really old, fat and sweating. He doesn't look too happy at being left in the corridor. I have to put all thoughts of Alice out of my mind and make a big fuss of him. He soon forgets the wait, makes sure he gets what he wants. I zone out, try to get outside of my body. Whilst he's driving into me, I'm singing Bowie songs to myself.

He doesn't hang around, thank God. Bet he can't get it up more than once a week. Once he's finished he seems to despise me, but I think it's himself really. He does sling twenty quid on the bed.

As he dresses, I lay there, trying to forget that this bastard has just screwed me, trying not to look at his repulsive body, the folds of fat. I notice a strange tattoo, like a Greek letter on his shoulder, I've seen it somewhere before, then he's gone, and I'm left, bleeding and full of revulsion for myself. How much lower can I go?

I have a bath, trying to scrub his stink away, and start thinking about Alice.

Before she'd appeared so suddenly, I'd had a fantasy about finding her this weekend, trying to at least be friends again, God knows I need a friend. That dream lies in shreds. What have I done? Fate seems to be against me.

Her final words haunt me. Why would she say such a stupid thing about Mom and Dad, it's not like her at all?

***

Alice:

I spend the weekend in a daze, half-hoping he'll call, but knowing in my heart that last night was the end. How could it all go so wrong?

I'm so stupid, expecting him to be waiting like a pet puppy for me to appear. I should have realised he'd have moved on. And that he'd be in demand, he's still so beautiful, although he's definitely lost weight, and I don't like the haunted look in his eyes. The life he's living is doing him no favours. I worry about drugs, then ask myself why when he's not in my life anymore. I consider trying again, but he'll be gone by now, back into his new life. I briefly consider another concert, there's Oxford on Monday, but it's pointless. He's gone for good. Get on with your own life Alice.

***

Danny:

The next morning I'm woken by Greg shaking me, none too gently. He took the spare key to the room when we checked in. He truly despises me. He knows what I did last night. I've got two days of his company before I go to 'court'. What a treat.

I answer my bail at nine in the morning at Steelhouse Lane Police Station. I'm finally free of Greg by not being free. He won't come near the old red brick police and court building.

Docker is waiting, along with two other blokes. I'm booked in, then stuck in a cell in what they call 'Lock Up'. It's like a little prison, with metal stairs, wire netting, grilled landing floors and old, heavy, metal cell doors. Looks just like 'Slade Prison' in 'Porridge', but I don't think there will be any comedy today.

I'm taken to an interview room. Two men are there, but no Docker. They gesture for me to sit. I wait for the beating to start, but it seems that they just want to talk.

They introduce themselves as DS Fisher and DC Curtis. The DC doesn't say a word, just stares at me and makes notes. He's a big, hard-looking bloke, looks fit. Fisher is a little man with slicked back, jet black hair that reeks of Grecian 2000. He has a nose like a hatchet, a thin mouth that doesn't look like it has known much smiling, and pitiless eyes. He's dressed to kill, real flash. The Cockney accent comes as no surprise.

"Danny, we're from the 'Met'. The big boys, not some second city, second rate outfit. We've taken over your case, seen as you're mixed up with London villains, and live in 'the smoke' now.

We know all about you, and the friends you keep. I don't want you son; I get no kicks from sending kids down. I want the bastard that's in charge, and through him the bent cops that protect him. I've got proper connections, can pull strings for you, can look after you - or make sure your world comes crashing down.

I'm sure my friend Mr. Docker laid it out for you plain, he's a straight- talking man, no beating about the bush. I'm the same, so let's get to the point, you going to play ball or not?"

"Truth is Mr. Fisher, I'm scared, and I don't know what to do for the best. I don't know who to trust, and whether I'll be safe if I help you. What'll happen if I grass? They'll find me."

"Not if I put them away. You deliver him to me and I'll give you a new life."

"He knows I've been asked to grass him up. What use am I going to be? He's frozen me out. Won't go near me, stopped me working. Nobody wants to know me; they all know I was arrested."

"Ah well, that's the beauty of it see. I know he's got cops in his pocket; know he'll be told exactly what happens. But they don't know I know that. He thinks that's his little secret, his insurance, cause some of his friends are high - up. But we've got some better connections of our own. He'll believe his cop snouts, and he'll trust you better than most. You'll have proved yourself, see. Word will get out that you've told us to fuck off, you'll be a double agent, like on the telly."

I take time to answer. That's what I need, time. So that's what I say.

"I need more time to decide."

He shrugs. "I'm playing a long game son. Fisher by name, fisher by nature, and a good angler knows that you need to be patient to catch the big fish. They don't get to be big by being stupid and our mutual friend is no fool. It's taken him a long time to build up his 'business' empire and contacts, it can't be broken up just like that. I reckon at least a year, with you making notes on everything, then standing up in court and swearing to it. We'll get other stuff along the way to support what you see. There are lots of ways we can get your information without meeting up, so you'll be safe."

"But he'll know when I don't go down."

"I hadn't got around to that bit. You'll get six months, first offence. You'll be out in three on parole, model prisoner. While you're inside you'll be looked after, I can promise you that. When it comes to trial time for him, you'll have done your time and you'll walk free, into a new life. That's the clever bit. You don't have to do any acting, you'll have total credibility, he won't think twice about trusting you. The alternative is, you get a good long stretch and you suffer every day, and when come out there'll be nothing for you."

"That's a lot to think about."

There is a silence. He looks at me, assessing. But I'm actually telling the truth, and that must show. He nods.

"I'll give you a week, no more. We'll take you through the tunnel into court in a minute. That charge sheet wasn't fake, although my Brummie mate thought it was. He doesn't know everything, although he thinks he does. In court, in public, we'll ask for a further week for forensics and won't oppose bail, but you'll be transferred to a London court."

A week. Not long. A thought occurs to me.

"Ok. thanks. I promise you Mr. Fisher, you'll have your answer on Monday. Can I ask you a question please?"

It's all big smiles now, we are good mates. "Of course."

"I've been away from home, haven't been in touch at all. Has anything happened I should know about?"

There is a long pause. He seems to be deliberating. Then I know it's all true. Not like Alice to make something like that up, not her style at all. I'm sorrier about what's happened to us, than what's happening to me. Someone up there hates us.

"You've got wind of something then?"

"Yeah, bumped into someone, a mate, over the weekend, who said something I can't believe."

"I said I was straight son, so here it is. Your Dad's gone, dead, although from what I hear that won't cause you no sleepless nights. It was your Mom that did him in, knifed him, quite a lot of times actually. She's inside, waiting for trial."

I'm stunned again. It's becoming a habit. Why can't I have an ordinary life?

"I want to see her. Can you swing that for me before I see you again? It'll show me you've got clout, and that you're bothered about me. I need to speak to her, then I'll know what to do about the mess I'm in."

"As it happens I can, and I will, to show good intent. She's in London, in Holloway. But every word will be monitored. No mention of any of this stuff. Stick to the family business.

We'll concoct a little story for your boss. Close to the truth. You found out in Birmingham. Your brief, who is a friend of ours by the way - you'll see him before court, and in court, arranged it for you. Your mate Rick won't want to be seen providing you with a brief, so will expect a public one to be appointed. He'll weigh up what it means of course, seeing your Mom, just like I am doing, but he won't stop you. Won't show out."

That's pretty much it. I'm taken through a tunnel and put in a holding cell on the court side. The brief appears. He's a Londoner too. A little round jolly man, with a shiny bald head and red braces. He stinks of fags. He goes through the motions, but we both know I'm banged to rights.

I get bail, as promised. I've got a week to decide. Monday 2nd July will be the day. Within minutes of leaving, Greg is by my side. He wasn't in court, but he knows what's happened. That's worrying. How good is Rick's network? Is Fisher underestimating him? A lot of people do, and regret it.

*

Holloway prison doesn't look like I expect, more like blocks of flats. Red brick, but really brutal-looking. And flats don't have a great big wall round them. Mind you, council estates have got walls, you just can't see them. They keep the people in their place just the same.

I've done some research this week at the library, looking through old newspapers. It made the nationals. Mom and Dad on the front page – fame at last for our family. Ha! I could cry, but there aren't any tears left. Not cry for them, but for the life that could have been.

Now it's come to this, I feel sorry for the old girl after all, and a fair bit of admiration that she finally summoned up some guts. Pity she didn't do it years ago. I'd have helped and I'm sure we could have concocted some tale and got away with it. Said he was abusing me or something, which is sort of true, just not in that way. Everybody would have felt sorry for the little kid, and Mom would probably have been praised for protecting me. Too late now though.

I don't really know why I've come. What do I expect? I suppose I owe her a visit, so she knows I'm ok – I'll lie about that so she doesn't worry. I'll try to forgive her too.

There's a load of old bollocks before I'm let in, searches and reading of rules. No bodily contact, no kissing – not much chance of that! I'm expecting it to be like on the telly, with her the other side of a screen and us talking on the phone, but I'm shown into a big open room full of tables.

They direct me to sit at one right in the middle. A bored looking prison warder chewing gum is sat at the next table. She is dog-ugly and reminds me of a cow chewing grass. She's going to listen and make sure we do nothing naughty. Apart from that, the room's empty.

I wait a few minutes and then I hear a door bolt drawn, and two guards bring her in. She looks much smaller, diminished, dressed in nondescript baggy grey clothes. She sits opposite me and the guards go and sit at another table, chatting.

She doesn't look overjoyed to see me; in fact, she doesn't seem to register it's me at all. Same cold fish, even in here, even after what's happened. After a few moments she finally speaks.

"So, you're alive then, nice of you to let me know."

"Yeah, things are ok. Got a job and a flat, made some friends."

"That's very nice for you. Glad you left then?"

This isn't going well. I'd expected her to be pleased to see me.

"You know I had to leave.."

"Not really, you could have stayed at your Nan's, I'd have put it all right with time, you could have come back home."

"Mom, that was never going to happen and you know it. He was just getting worse, the drinking, the violence."

"You know nothing Danny. Nothing. You just drifted your way through your nice little life while I had to cope with his moods. You did whatever you wanted, always have. No thought for me, then you abandoned me when I needed you."

I'm speechless with the injustice of it. She must have been brooding day and night in this place and lost sight of reality, twisting things until they seemed real.

"That's not how it was…"

"Oh yes it is. You were just a kid, still are really. I lived with him, slept with him, skivvied for him, put up with his tempers, the booze, and the other women. Yes, Danny there were other women. Fancied himself, he did. Wasn't nicknamed 'Gorgeous' for nothing.

The women loved him, until they got to know him, then they'd leave him to me, the drudge, to pick up the pieces. I've lost count of how many there were. Why d'ya think he started drinking

241

again, out all the time, losing his temper. He'd got another floozie and this one was much younger, and pretty. She was leading him a right dance. She had him wrapped around her little finger. He was bloody besotted. Getting older, and frightened, see. Losing his looks, thought he'd have to make do with me in the end I suppose."

"Why did you put up with it?" I knew what the answer would be.

"For you Danny, all for you. So that you could have a good home, clothes, food, a family life, be a normal kid. I tried to keep it away from you, but you thought it was all about you. I'll let you into a little secret, now you're all so grown up. The times he hit you, multiply by ten. He left no marks you could see, very clever he was, and I never cried out, so you wouldn't hear. That used to make him angrier, make it worse. His favourite was strapping me with his belt, but there were plenty of punches and pinches. A little speciality was putting his fag out on my chest. My tits look like the surface of the moon, the bloody craters on them. The more he disfigured me, the more he hated me, the more he chased other women. And how could I leave? Where could we go? In the Fifties, even in the 'liberated, love everybody' Sixties, nobody would believe a woman. We were the homemakers, and if home was no good, it was our fault. If we played away we were trash. If we got pregnant before getting married we were sluts. It's still the same, nothing has changed. I'm a murderer, not a victim.

I've got no hope of any sympathy. It's men in charge, and they'll lock me up and throw away the key. Still, at least it's all worth it, losing the chance of my own life, I suppose." Her voice is sarcastic now. "My son's a pervert, a freak, who wears make up, sucks cocks and leaves me."

Her voice is filled with bitterness and anger. Her tears fall. The woman guard has stopped chewing and is looking at us with renewed interest.

How can I answer that? Have I got it all wrong, or has she?

" So, what happened?" I ask, for want of anything better to say.

She looks at me long and hard. The tears are still welling up, but she seems to pull herself together and wipes them away on her sleeve. She spits the words out at me.

"You happened Danny. You wound him up, made him ashamed of you. If you'd been a normal boy, a man, it might just have been enough for him. He might have been content to be with you as you grew up, be mates. As he got older he might have looked more at his family, at us, for his reason to live."

"You can't put this all on me."

"I'm not, not all those years when you were growing up. He was a bastard. Nan saw right through him, told me not to marry him, but I wouldn't listen, I was so much in love. Biggest mistake I ever made. No, it was him, not you, until the last year or two. I hoped that as you grew up, you'd help me, support me, we'd manage him together, because you were the son he always wanted. Yes, he did, really, he was so proud when you were born. I couldn't have any more after you, so you were his only hope. That's why he was so strict with you."

"That's fucking crap. He used to beat me, what sort of love's that?"

"The only sort he knew. That's why he couldn't keep the other women. His head was all messed up. He had a bad time as a kid you know. For him, love was mixed up with what he thought being a man is all about, tough, physical. At the start I felt sorry for him, then I pitied him, then I hated him."

The guard intervenes, telling us to keep it down, then settles back to enjoy the rest of the show. Something to tell her mates about later. But I wonder what she really thinks, she's a woman after all. Surely there must be some sympathy for Mom there?

"You were about to tell me why it's all my fault you're in here."

"Because you ran away, put yourself and your sick life first, above your own mother. It was the final straw for him. He expected you'd come back. I knew that, he was trying to bring you into line. As the days went past, and we heard nothing, he got more and more depressed, drank more. I think he saw there was nothing left for him. Then the other woman told him to get stuffed. I think he must have done something and frightened her off.

That night he came home raving drunk. Told me all about her. He started on me. I was all alone. He just kept on and on, words at first, then slaps and I thought 'this time he's not stopping, he's going to kill me'.

We were in the kitchen. He pushed me off my chair and kicked me. I got up and he punched me, in the face. He'd never done that before, not in a place where a mark would show. That's when I knew he wasn't bothered any more. I fell back against the sink. The knife was in the bowl and as he came for me I stuck it in him, then I stuck it in again.

I don't remember much really, other than that I was terrified that he'd get up, take the knife off me and kill me. But he fell down, so I took my chance and stabbed him again. They say I cut his throat, but I don't remember doing that, I just kept slashing and stabbing until I fell on him, exhausted, and he was dead.

And if you'd been there, it would never have happened. You'd be leaving school or doing A Levels, maybe looking to settle down with that Alice, she was a nice girl. Dad would have had something to stay for. In a year or two he might have finally run off with someone, or I'd have been able to leave him, once I knew you were settled. I could have had a new start, a new life.

But my life's over now Danny. At least you've got one, of sorts. I wish you luck, I think you'll need it. But you won't have me now, you're on your own from here on."

Before I can reply, she stands up and calls the guard.

"I'm finished here, let's go."

The last I see of her is her back. There isn't so much as a backward glance. Then the door slams and she's gone.

Chapter Seventeen

'Rock 'n' Roll Suicide'
June / July 1973

Danny:

Saturday 30th June, 1973. It would have been a day of ill omen in the old days. There is a really long total eclipse forecast, although it can't be seen from here. But somewhere it's pitch black and will seem like the world is ending.

Means bugger all to me. I don't need heavenly signs to know that my world is one step from crumbling.

I always sleep late on a Saturday, all of us in the flats do. Not because we are lazy layabouts, or drugged up, or hungover, but because we don't stop work until really late – or early morning, and Saturday night needs to be approached in an alert state. It's the biggest night of the week.

I fell into my bed last night at 3.30am, thankful of its sanctuary. Seeing Mom yesterday has been preying on my mind, filling it with guilt. I just can't get her accusing face and words out of my head.

Rufus passed me another 'little favour' Rick wants. I'm to go to some hotel in Chelsea and meet another 'business' contact, give him a good time. Rufus said I'll get a hundred from Rick and fifty from the 'customer', so it's a good earner. I'm getting used to the idea, and if I can save up some cash it might help me escape this life when I get out of prison.

I talked it over with the girls during the week, over a spliff or two. They seem to find a way to put the paid sex into a separate box in their lives, like it's a job. I think I might be able to do the same. I suppose that if you can detach yourself, it's bearable.

I've been back in London since court. Greg shepherded me back from Birmingham on the first train, and straight to the 'Sombrero'. Bowie had played Croydon the day before and Rick had stayed in London to see me, rather than go to Oxford with the tour.

There was a second interrogation, in the same office where I'd first seen Rick to talk about the job. In my mind it was years ago, but it's only about six months, or a lifetime. A different Danny sat in this chair then.

This time was easier. I told a fair bit of the truth. About asking for more time. About my Mom. He didn't know about that - first time I've seen a flicker of surprise in his eyes. I could almost hear that brain calculating the angles, but Fisher was right, and Rick agreed that I should go and see her. Perhaps he thought that I'd realise there's no way back – that he's all I've got now. He might be right too. He seemed satisfied that next Monday will be the deadline.

He told me I'm off the tour from now on. Too much of a risk. To stay in London while he looks after the last few nights up North. It's nearly finished anyway. He saw my disappointment.

"I'll make it right with you Danny, you'll be at the big last night at Hammersmith next Tuesday, if you make the right decision on Monday, which I'm sure you will. Then there might be America and further abroad. The way he's going, he'll be worldwide by next year, you'll be out of nick and we'll both be with him. Once I'm sure I can trust you."

So here I am, comatose in bed, when there's a rap on the door. It's Denise. She's got one of the bottom flats, so she always hears the front door. She looks like I feel - shit.

"Cop here for you Danny. I've kept him waiting in the hallway, in case you need to do a bunk?"

My mind races through the possibilities, but I can't work out why Fisher wouldn't just wait. What's changed? As I go down the stairs I'm surprised to see a uniform. Fisher would never send one of those.

It's fair to say we don't hit it off. He's an older cop with a beard starting to turn grey. Seen it all and not impressed. He clearly takes an instant dislike to me, and I'm scared as to why he's here and what it means for me, so I'm not exactly welcoming. I'm conscious that Denise is on the landing above, listening.

"Danny Rogers?"

"Yeah."

"Got some bad news for you, son. Do you want to go and sit down?"

The last thing I want at the moment is a cosy chat in my flat with a cop in full uniform, so I shake my head. "No, it's ok, tell me here."

"Ok, if you're sure. I won't beat about the bush. The thing is, your Mom's passed away. The prison asked us to let you know as they had your details from a visit you made."

I try to process the words.

"That doesn't make sense, I only saw her yesterday – she was fine then. There must be a mistake."

There is a trace of sympathy in his face now.

"No mistake I'm afraid. Found deceased in her cell this morning. Sorry to be the bearer of bad news."

I just can't take it in. It can't be real.

"The prison want you to go and see them, they'll be able to tell you more. Here's a number to ring."

*

Greg wanted to know where I was going. In the end he drove me, and now waits in the car – he won't set foot in the place. I'm ushered into a different part of the complex, no searches this time.

This time it's a lady I see, not a guard. She has an aura of authority.

They found her this morning. Apparently, because she's on remand, *was* on remand, she kept some of her own clothes. She tied some together and hung herself from the top bunk. She was in a cell alone, so she did it herself. She'd said nothing to cause anyone to think she'd do such a thing, so she hadn't been on any sort of special watch. They would say that though, covering their backs, I'll never know the truth.

I know in my heart that she did it, and why. Nothing left for her. She wasn't needed by anyone, Dad gone, me as good as gone, just a life inside to look forward to.

247

She left no note, but she didn't need to. Her parting gift to me is guilt. The prison lady asks me if I'm alright. I don't know how to answer. How do I feel? I don't know. Shocked, confused, guilty, angry, upset. I loved her, I wanted to love Dad, and now they are both gone. I feel totally alone.

I leave the prison with a box of her belongings. That's all that's left of her. I sit in the car with Greg and open it. The first thing I see is a photograph of me.

*

By the time I get back to the flat I've decided to go home and see Nan. I'm in no mood for compromise. I tell Greg what I'm doing and that he can tell Rick what he likes, but I'm not having him shadowing me while I do this thing. I tell him I'll be back in London in time for court and 'decision day'.

Surprisingly he nods, asks me to wait while he phones Rick. He soon returns and tells me ok, but to make sure I'm back to see Rick on Monday after court. Perhaps he's got some notion of decency after all. Some of the East End thugs have a code of some sort and love their Moms. He even gives me a lift to the station.

I phone Nan from Euston. I have to tell her why I'm coming. She cries, and says she'll get my old room ready. No accusation in her voice. I'll have about twenty-four hours in Birmingham before I need to get the train back here.

It's about the most welcome I've felt for ages. Nan hugs me and clings to me for a long time when I first arrive. She's got everything ready, even a meal, after which we talk.

I've not paid her much attention in my life, she's just 'Nan', always has been. What teenager bothers to find out who their Grandparents really are? They just seem like relics of the past, people my age have no interest in looking back, we hurry forward, keen to get to adulthood as quickly as possible. She is the only one of her generation that I've ever known. My Grandad, her husband, died of Tuberculosis before I was born, and Dad was estranged from his parents – never mentioned them, I never met them. I can guess why.

Nan was once young and a Mom. She tells me about her life, I had never thought to ask before. She had it hard, the war and everything, but she loved her husband and he treated her well. Pity he died. If he'd been around he might have sorted Dad out, and the tale of our lives might have been different. She's not stupid either, just a bit slow, and forgetful of names.

She hated my Dad, and to my relief blames him for everything. She surprises me with her view of Mom. Tells me some stories about her as a girl and happy, bubbly, young woman. How she tried to get her to leave Dad, but had to watch powerless as Mom changed, becoming bitter and silent. Nan could do nothing without Mom's help, and that wasn't forthcoming.

She always worried about me, about what was going on inside our house, but Mom would just clam up if she tried to find out, protecting *him* first. She puts all my shyness, then 'rebellion' as she calls it, down to him, and Mom protecting him.

In turn I tell her about what's happened to me. I initially miss out the crime, but I'm honest about the girls - and the boys. Amazingly she doesn't condemn me at all. Says she's not surprised, with a role model like him, and that she knew boys like that, but they had to hide it in her day for fear of prison.

She's so understanding, so kind, I tell her about being arrested. Not about my imminent decision, I can't do that, just about the drug bust. She takes my hand.

"Danny, you've had a bad time, but I know you're not a bad lad. I want you to promise me that, when it's all over, whatever happens, you'll keep in touch and come and see me when you can. There's always a room for you here, if you want to come home."

How could I have ignored this woman? I promise, and then we talk about what happens next about Mom and Dad.

The house was rented. The landlord wants it cleared sharpish, and Nan has arranged for a removal company to put everything in storage until we can decide what we want to do. She's got the keys and has been round, gathering up papers and anything valuable, not that there's much, watches, bits of jewellery – none of it worth much she says. Not much money either, apparently, probably just enough to pay for funerals. She shows me what she gathered up. Mom and Dad in another box. Is that it, is that what it's all about? Nothing left but a box of cheap jewellery and some memories?

I decide to go and take a last look at my old life in the morning. We talk funerals. The Police still have Dad, they said they'd keep him until they knew whether Mom's defence wanted a second opinion, but now she's gone, there'll be no trial.

I haven't the faintest idea what to do, but thankfully Nan does. As far as Nan's concerned, Dad could *'go to the tip with the rest of the rubbish'*, but he *was* my Dad, so she softens and agrees to sort something out. I'll send her some cash, I'm short of parents and friends, but not money. And she'll begin planning Mom's with a local funeral Director. She digs her heels in at any suggestion of joint funerals, but I'm hesitant – what would Mom really want? She stuck by him, in spite of everything he did, must have loved him once, killed him in fear, not anger. Would she want to be with him forever? Does it matter? I can't resolve it right now, we agree to leave it for a few days.

*

Waking up at Nan's, as if London, Rick, Fisher, my flat, belong in some other world, or a dream. Then I realise I'm back there this evening, and tomorrow is a big day. Coming back, speaking with Nan, has been good for me. I'm pretty sure I've made my decision. I'll play back all the angles on the train, sleep on it, and see how it looks in the morning.

On the bus I toss around another idea in my head. Here I am, in Birmingham, on a Sunday, with a few hours spare. No Greg, no Rick. Alice on my mind. It ended badly between us. Could I put it right? Probably not, but worth a try.

First I go home. I open the familiar door, like I've done a thousand times before, but there's no smell of cooking, no sense of occupants. There's a pile of post behind the door. Even though it's nearly July, the house has a coldness, all life has gone from it. Just bricks and a roof.

The furniture is still there, Dad's armchair, Mom's sewing machine. I go up to my room. Mom had taken a lot of my stuff to Nan's, but my hi-fi is still there, the posters on the walls, the photo of Bowie with Rick's number on the back. I didn't take it with me because I have the real thing now. I pocket it. I lay on the bed. Mom must have been the last person to make it.

Eighteen months ago, I lay here on my birthday, kicking myself for not asking Alice out. I was a schoolboy, a virgin, a shy loner with a chip on his shoulder. But it was home. Now it isn't. I cry a few tears for what is lost, then pull myself together. I've got to be a man now, whether I want to or not.

I leave the kitchen until last. I peer tentatively around the door, not knowing what to expect. Blood covered walls? But it's clean, I suppose the Police saw to that. This is where it all ended, Dad's life, our family life, and in the end, Mom's life too.

I've been there less than an hour, it's enough. This is the past. It's over, gone forever, and if I'm to have any sort of a life it's up to me now. I had decided that my future revolved around Rick, but Nan has given me another possibility, and with Nan might come Alice. Because I want her back, want to be with her. I've done wrong by her I know, but it wasn't all my fault. If I can make her understand what's happened, get her support, then I can take my decision tomorrow, and survive, with the hope that she'll be there for me afterwards. It's a big ask, may be a forlorn hope, but these few hours at home have helped straighten my mind.

I spend one last moment on the doorstep, looking down the hallway, before I pull the door shut on my first sixteen years.

***

Alice:

I know it's him when the doorbell rings. I'm in my room playing records, thinking, planning. My thoughts often turn to him, and I feel as if I've magicked him up when Mom announces he is on the doorstep again. She wants to send him away, but I'm filled with anger that he thinks he can just turn up here, click his fingers and I'll be back in his life. I've more self-respect than that. He's broken my heart, and that scene at the hotel, which Mom knows nothing about, was like twisting a knife in my wounds. I don't know if I'll ever love again, how long the damage will last.

I am resolute, and quite proud that I keep it together, even though I really want to hug him, but I'll go mad if I allow him back into my life. I grab the initiative.

"Yes, what do you want?"

"Just to speak. I thought you were being cruel about my parents, but I know the truth now, Wanted to say thank you for bothering to find me and tell me."

"Well you've done that now, is that it?"

He is unsure, hesitant, I see glimpses of the old 'pre-me' shy Danny, he's still in there somewhere.

"A lot's happened to me. I'm in a mess. It's going to get harder too. I want to tell you all about it. I need you…"

"You didn't need me at the hotel, could have had me then, but you had other fish to fry – couldn't wait to get away as I remember."

"It wasn't like that I.."

"It bloody was. You'd got someone else there. I suppose that's finished has it? So, you want old faithful, muggins here, back to listen to your whining, until you find someone else. See if bloody Bowie will be your friend, bet he won't."

"Please Alice, if I told you what's happened, you'd.."

"Doubt it very much. Can't think what you'd say to me that would excuse the lies, cheating, the betrayal of something that to me at least was beautiful. You've destroyed that, and some of me with it. How can I forgive you, or trust you, ever again? No, I'm not standing for it, you had your chance last week."

"I think I love you."

That stops me for a second because it sounds like he means it. But then I remember what he's done, who he is now – a different person to the boy I once loved.

"I don't believe you. I loved you with all my heart once, but you're not that boy anymore, and I don't love what you've become.

You go back to your new life, your new friends in London, and I'll get on with mine. We'll both be happier."

He starts to speak again, but I can't stand it any longer and slam the door. The sound reverberates through the house and brings mom out of the kitchen. She looks at me anxiously.

"It's ok Mom, it's really finished, for good."

I burst into tears and rush upstairs. Don't know if he heard, but the doorbell doesn't ring again, and when I look out of the window, he's gone.

***

Danny:

I wake up the next morning with a clear mind. I didn't expect to, given the weekend's rollercoaster ride. I'm on my own, really on my own, bar Nan, and whilst there is an option there for the future, I can't expect a seventy-odd-year-old woman to offer any more than sympathy and a bed. She might even die before I get out of prison.

When I closed the door at home, I closed it on my family and past. My life starts again today, and it's up to me. No going back.

At least I tried with Alice. It really hurt. She is so beautiful and kind. Perhaps one day she'll understand, and we'll have another chance, when we're older. I've resolved to write to her, tell her everything, then at least she'll know why I did what I did. It will probably put the kibosh on any future for us, but at least, if we meet again, there'll be no secrets and, if there is a chance, we can start with honesty. I need to keep that hope alive, that there is a chance for us, one day.

My faithful shadow, Greg, ensures I get to court on time. Once again I'm taken to a holding area and put in a cell. Fisher and his silent sidekick with the notepad are waiting. I have agonised about this moment for weeks, but now it's here, I'm calm and resigned.

It doesn't take long. He doesn't like it, tries to frighten me, but after what's happened I'm ready. Rick frightens me more. It was Nan that helped, bless her. She gave me some hope that there is a normal life out there for me. I'll take my medicine, and stick with Rick.

Once I've done my time, I'll work out how to get out, go back to Birmingham and get my life back on track. Leaving was a big mistake, I realise that now, and truly I wouldn't have done it without Lowe and his stupid, childish notes, without Dad and his rages. Age is on my side for once. I can move on. By then, Rick will know I'm no risk to him. He won't be bothered as long as he knows I'll keep my mouth shut. He can't really want me around now I've been nicked. There are plenty more where I came from, and he doesn't fancy me anymore. I'm calm. There is hope.

As I stand to leave the cell, to see my brief, Fisher gets handed a note by the court guard. He look at it, screws it up and throws it at the wall.

"Your mate Docker, wants me to ring him. He'll be after using you in some way – you better tell him to fuck off too."

*

The brief is upbeat, and is sporting yellow braces this time. I tell him I'm pleading guilty and he talks about mitigation, which seems to be about inventing excuses by relying on my age. He reckons he can come up with a tale of woe that will pull the heartstrings of the court, that I'm just a courier, that I didn't know what was in the package, that I'm frightened. There is plenty of material. He thinks that I might get as little as six months for a first offence, out in three or four with good behaviour. That doesn't sound so bad, and if Rick's influence is as great as I think it is, serving time will be ok.

The prosecutor asks that I be remanded in custody. That's Fisher's first act of revenge, and one I hadn't thought of. But to my surprise, and my brief's, he successfully argues that I've turned up so far, have a fixed address and it's a first offence. I'm granted bail for a month. Fisher scowls as I leave court and makes a throat-cutting motion. I'm certain I've made the right decision now. I don't trust him. I trust Mickey. And with Rick I know exactly where I stand.

Greg chaperones me back to the 'Sombrero' where Rick is waiting. He says he believes me when I give him the decision, and he's all smiles and promises that I'll be looked after. But I can tell he's not one hundred percent certain until I'm weighed off at court and go inside. Then he'll know. I have a feeling that I'll still be earning my keep doing some work keeping his business friends happy in the meantime. Rick always gets a return on his investments.

One promise he does say he'll keep, is that I'll be at the last concert of the tour, at the side of the stage, best view in the place. It's rumoured that there'll be a big end of tour party afterwards and Rick will do his best to get me in.

As I leave, Greg turns the other way. No longer my shadow. He looks at me for just a second, then nods. I've chosen my 'side'. I'm on a straight path at last – to prison, but what the hell. There'll be an afterwards of some kind to look forward to, an afterwards with Bowie.

*

Rick is already at the Hammersmith Odeon when I arrive. He told me yesterday that he'd decided to take personal charge. It's London, it's the last gig, and he wants nothing to go wrong. This is important to him. Lots of money and influence hang on him getting to stay with Bowie on tour, maybe even America, and of course a supply of willing young meat, moths drawn to the flame of Bowie.

There are crowds outside in full 'Ziggy' and 'Aladdin Sane' mode. Lightning flashes cross faces, some hilariously bad, sequinned space suits, kids tottering around on huge platforms, the haircut, the hair dye, buckets of eyeliner, and that's just the blokes, the whole unearthly mob excitedly milling around under a sign that proclaims,

'From 8pm we're working together with David Bowie'

I'm waved through the barriers and the stage door, soaking up the envy of the queues. I can see them wondering if I'm someone famous, and I admit it's a huge kick to be 'special', it's the reason I'm here in London after all.

Backstage it's the usual chaos. Everyone knows me, and I'm good at keeping a low profile, but I often get little jobs to do, fetching and carrying, running errands for supplies of fags, booze, food.

There's a film crew, the whole concert is being filmed, something to do with RCA. Someone told me they want it for a new type of disc. Who knows? There are always twenty different versions of what's going on, half of them from drug-addled brains, so I take them all with a pinch of salt.

I have to go into the dressing rooms a few times. I think David looks exhausted, and thoughtful, a bit nervous, last night nerves? Angie seems really nervous too, putting on a silly voice and play-acting nonsense chat - for the camera? He's been punishing himself for weeks, often two gigs a day, and it looks like the strain is beginning to show. He's probably looking forward to a few weeks downtime before he does it all again in America.

I go and take a peek around the side of the stage, drinking it all in. This might be the last Bowie show I see from backstage for a while, maybe ever. The Odeon is packed already, the noise level incredible. I can feel the body heat of the fans packed shoulder to shoulder at the front, competing to reach the stage.

As the spotlights play across the excited, expectant, upturned faces, I feel just a hint of what it must be like to be the focus of this adulation and obsession, to be the role model, see yourself cloned a thousand times. Like being hooked up to a permanent drug feed, the best high ever, but it must also feel like they are sucking away his identity.

All they want, all they see, is 'Ziggy Stardust', 'Aladdin Sane', the make-up and costume, not the person hidden behind them. I know, I fell in love with 'Ziggy Stardust', and, even being so close to David for so long, I still feel like I've never really met him, never seen what's inside. I mean, most of the time he dresses like 'Ziggy', and wears the make-up, so even he must be struggling to be himself.

There's a commotion, and Mike Garson walks slowly onto stage, picked out by a single spotlight. That's new, so I stay and watch as he reels off a medley of Bowie songs on the piano, alone.

The crowd, once they realise who it is, sing and clap along. The excitement mounts.

The 'Clockwork Orange' music plays. Then the announcement comes,

'For the last time, David Bowie.'

He's wearing the long gown with the bow-legged pattern. They launch into 'Hang Onto Yourself'. Above the stage are three round white discs with lightning flashes, pulsating to the music. The crowd are instantly electrified, singing every word, shouting, crying out. I can see girls who already look like they are about to pass out, swaying and leaning on each other. Others are crying, their thick eye-liner smearing, panda eyes. Flashes of the lights pick out wet, glistening foreheads. Hands reach out, trying to grab him, the magic imp prancing just out of reach.

Ronson plays a great solo, and then, as the opening riff of 'Ziggy' rings out, Bowie's outer costume is pulled off with a flourish, revealing the white Kimono with the white lace-up boots. It's my favourite costume. It oozes sex and is the one that always makes me want to go to bed with him. I just stare, entranced, at his thighs, as he cavorts around, the short skirt revealing flashes of his bulging crotch, encased in white satin.

Bowie and the band are in top form tonight, Bowie sucking up energy from the crowd as he gets into his stride.

Ronson surpasses himself on 'Moonage Daydream', producing a titanic solo, accompanied by his trademark pain-twisted features as he teases out and prolongs the high notes. The rows of faces in the strobe lights singing every word in perfect time, joined together in what looks like ecstasy.

Bowie scampers off during the guitar solo, returning in red boots, and the green, red and white jumpsuit, open to the navel, revealing every rib on his thin frame. He picks up the acoustic guitar and, with the mirrored globe lights reflecting moving polka-dots across the stage and front rows, renders 'Space Oddity' to perfection. I can see girls at the front actually weeping as 'Major Tom' drifts off into space.

Something new. He sits and performs 'My Death'. Mesmerising. Then he's offstage during a solo, reappearing in the full-length white robe with Japanese writing as the pace picks back up with 'Cracked Actor'. The robe is stripped away to the opening of chords of 'Time', and it's the knitted leotard underneath.

I am rooted to the spot, peering over the speaker stacks. I've seen him so many times, but there is something special tonight. The added songs, the last night of the tour, it feels important, a finale, and here I am. The best day of my life.

Another costume change, to the old 'Woodland Animals' outfit, for 'Width Of A Circle'. He does the wall and door mime sequence during the solo. Ronson is lying on the floor playing, after doing a guitar 'duel' with Bolder. The crowd are frantic, wringing wet with sweat, and, it seems no time before it's 'Suffragette City', the whole place is bouncing and, 'thank you and good night'. Silence of sorts rushes into the auditorium, the stage is empty and ordinary, although the screaming, clapping, and calls for 'more', rise, filling the vacuum.

Cheers and screams, Bowie's back in a see-through dark top. He pays tribute to Lou Reed, does 'White Light, White Heat' and they are off again.

The crowd demand more, more, more. What more can there be? I'm expecting the house lights, but they reappear. Bowie says there is going to be something special as it's the last night, and welcomes Jeff Beck on stage. 'Jean Genie', with Beck and Ronson trying to outdo each other, and Bowie breaking into 'Love Me Do' at one point. Then the old song 'Round and Round', and it's finally over, as Beck leaves. Where is 'Rock 'n' Roll Suicide', that's always the finish?

Bowie is speaking, but the crowd are too wild, and he has to stop a couple of times to make himself heard. He waits a second, indulgent and smiling. He thanks the band and the roadies, I'm just thinking of leaving to find Rick and see about the after-show party, when I realise Bowie is still talking.

'Everybody, this has been one of the greatest tours of our life, of all the shows on this tour, this particular show will remain with us the longest, because not only is it, not only is it the last show of the tour – but it's the last show that we'll ever do. Thank you.'

Cheers turn to cries of, 'no David, no'. Screams of dismay. I can't believe what I've just heard. I can see Woody looking at Bolder in confusion. What does he mean? Ronson is looking away, I can't see his face.

They start playing 'Rock 'n' Roll Suicide', they know it so well I think they can play it blindfold. But I am close to Woody and Bolder and they look stunned and perplexed, mouthing words at each other.

Bowie does the usual reaching out of his hands, but this time there's more desperation than usual from the clutching fans, who seem to be trying to keep him there, forever. He is nearly pulled from the stage, one kid manages to get up and hug him, before being pulled away by security. Then it ends and, with a 'Thank you, bye, bye, we love you', and he's gone, as 'Land Of Hope And Glory' plays.

Our God has left us. What shall we do without him?

*

I can't find Rick. Eventually I locate Rufus holding the stage door line against the seething mass of confused and anguished fans trying to find out what's going on, or get inside the Stage Door. He's shouting over and over again that Bowie has gone, but nobody wants to listen. There are reporters turning up as well, firing questions.

'Is it true Bowie's quit?'

'Why?'

'What about the rest of the band?'

Rufus and the other guards just ignore them. Out of the corner of one eye I see Greg plant one particularly persistent reporter in the face. I manage to get to Rufus' side.

"Fucking hell, it's a riot. Where's Rick?"

"Fucked if I know. He stormed out before Bowie did. Face like thunder. Wouldn't be in a hurry to see him tonight." He pushes some kid with a poorly painted lightning flash away. The kid looks completely lost, devastated. I know how he feels; he's wearing the wrong make-up now – out of date already. But that's all his worry, I've got my whole life hanging by a thread.

"Bowie's gone already?"

"Yeah, raced off to the Daimler without a word, still in costume and make-up, looked in a hurry to get away. What's happened?"

"He said he's quit; this was the last show ever." My voice cracks as I say the words. They mean such a lot.

"Fuck me, no wonder the boss is angry, there was a lot resting on carrying on with this circus, going to America, selling over there, expanding the tour security."

"And the honeypot for his little boys."

Rufus looks at me thoughtfully. "Yeah man, and that might be the worst of it."

I'm in turmoil myself. All I can think of is, *'if this is the end, then I want to be there, at the last ever after-show party'*.

I go out through the front of house. It's nearly empty now. As I walk up the centre aisle of the stalls I take a look back. The roadies are already stripping the equipment down. As I watch, one of the illuminated lightning flashes is lowered. It's like a flag going down when someone has died. But this doesn't stop halfway, it hits the deck and is quickly bundled away. It is beginning to sink in. It won't be used again, ever.

I go straight to Rick's. Stupid, but I'm desperate, filled with recklessness. An era is ending, and I'm within touching distance of being part of the swansong.

There are lights on. I bang on the door. Eventually Mickey answers. His face is ashen. He shakes his head.

"Rick's here. I need to see him."

"You really don't want to do that Danny."

"But he promised. I'm fucking going down the steps for him. He owes me."

I try to walk past him but he puts out an arm and bars the way.

"No, Danny. For your own sake."

It's too late. I can see Rick approaching down the hallway behind him. He yanks Mickey backwards by the collar.

"What the fuck do you want?"

I stammer it out. "I thought we had a deal, you promised I'd be at the party, and it's the last one – ever."

The punch doubles me up. He grabs me by the hair and pulls my face up so I'm an inch from his.

"Fucking party! Fucking party! You little twat. There's no party for you – or me. He's fucked us all off, including his band. Nobody knew. It's going cost me a fucking fortune and its screwed up a load of plans and you wants me to take you to a fucking party! Can you Adam and Eve it, Mickey?"

Mickey is watching and shaking his head slowly. He mouths 'Go' at me, but Rick still has hold of my hair. He begins shaking my head to emphasise every word.

"Think you can come around here, saying I owe you; I fucking owe you nothing you little cunt. You knew the deal, you fucked it up for yourself getting arrested, and now you're a fucking liability. There's loads more where you came from. I thought you might do some good work for me, but all I'm seeing right now is stupidity, and I don't need stupid around me. Tell you what, instead of a party, you go back to the flat I let you live in, and have a good think about your future, cause I'm about this far from kicking your arse out. I've seen enough of that bit of you."

He finally lets go, and with the flat of his hand, pushes me backwards so I sprawl onto the pavement. The door slams. There's nothing for it but to slink home. At least I've got some stuff there, I need something. Bowie's gone. I'm truly alone. It was all for nothing. Alice was right, just an act, and the show has ended. As I trudge along the empty streets I realise that I feel more loss, more emptiness inside, than when I was told about Mom. I must be going crazy.

***

David:

Before the 'retirement' is announced on stage, very few people know, and they are sworn to secrecy. Bowie asks Mick Ronson whether he wants to tell the 'Spiders', but Ronson declines, telling Bowie to do it himself, but after the show.

When the announcement is made, Woody Woodmansey and Trevor Bolder don't know what is going on, or what to believe, but after the final strains of 'Rock 'n' Roll Suicide' they begin to realise that they have just been publicly 'fired'. The disagreements over pay have reached their conclusion.

There is huge confusion amongst fans, the press and even those close to Bowie. It lasts for days, until it is finally understood that it is 'Ziggy' who has retired. Bowie is moving on, talking about making films and saying he's not appearing live anymore.

But as far as the public is concerned, he has finished for good. As 4th July dawns, the headlines are:

'Bowie bows out in pop finale'
'Bowie quits'
'Tears as Bowie bows out'

Across Britain, the glitter, the haircuts, the space suits, the lightning flash and forehead circle make up, the huge platforms, are suddenly redundant. But that is just the surface effect. Those to whom he is a lifestyle icon, who find comfort in his avowed bisexuality, the outrageous dress and make up, suddenly have a nasty little thought enter their minds – was it all just an act, just theatre?

The 'retirement' party, 'The Last Supper', as it is called, takes place at the Café Royal. Bowie and Angie sport outfits designed by Freddie Burretti, the designer they had met at the start of the 'Ziggy' era, at the 'Sombrero'.

It is a star-studded event that finishes at dawn, attended by the likes of Mick Jagger, Ringo Starr, Lou Reed, Lulu, Keith Moon, Tony Curtis, Britt Ekland and Barbra Streisand. Bowie has begun his transition to superstar, leaving Bolder and Woodmansey in his wake.

The next day, Mainman announce that the planned autumn United States arena tour is cancelled. The truth is, that the figures just don't add up.

Bowie wakes, re-visiting what he has done, but decides he has made the right decision. He needs to move on. He is totally drained from touring, fed up with 'Ziggy Stardust', and wanting to pursue different arts, other types of music – including a growing interest in 'soul', and a career as an actor. He has come full circle, from Sixties theatre 'wannabee', via 'rock theatre', 'rock god' and back to his unfulfilled desire to act. Only he knows the mental toll of submerging his real identity beneath that of 'Ziggy Stardust' and 'Aladdin Sane', the rock excesses, the media hype, the drugs.

Whatever the reason, he has killed off his alter-egos, and with them, 'Glam Rock'.

***

Alice:

Another morning. I turn on Radio One, and 'Changes' is playing, followed by, 'Life On Mars'. That's unusual for the cheesy, bubble–pop morning show. As I gradually surface I become aware that Noel Edmonds is talking about Bowie. At first I'm incredulous, why retire with the world at your feet? Then I think of those last few TV interviews, the incredible energy of the stage show, and I begin to understand.

Even though I'm only a late convert to Bowie, it feels as if something special has gone. He was more than his music, a trend-setter, a leader, a flag-bearer, challenging everything. The world will be a lot less colourful and interesting now.

My thoughts swiftly turn to Danny. What is he doing? How is he feeling? What does this mean for him? I know I shouldn't care, but I've got this mental picture of him all alone in some crappy room in London, mourning the loss of his idol, the core of his new life gone. My heart skips a beat, as a fleeting fantasy of him coming home, and it all being all right between us, enters my mind. I suppress it and tell myself off for even daring to entertain the thought.

I'm planning a trip into town later, shopping in 'Oasis' or 'Chelsea Girl'. I'm in no rush though, so I'm still at home when the doorbell rings.

I'm confronted by a police officer, and take an involuntary step backwards. He looks me up and down and seems to come to a decision. His voice is deep but kindly.

"You wouldn't be Alice by any chance, would you?"

I nod my head.

He looks over my shoulder.

"Anyone else at home?"

"Yes, Mom."

"I think you ought to go and get her love. Can I come in?"

Mom has appeared, and we go into the front room. Both of us know trouble when it appears on the doorstep. The officer sits in the same place as Danny did when he came back to me that time – I wish it was him sat there.

The officer takes off his helmet and takes a visible breath before speaking to me.

"Can I just check that you know a lad named Danny, lives in London?"

My heart skips a beat, in fear this time, not the usual love or anger Danny provokes. I am filled with dread. I nod.

"I used to go out with him. We finished when he went to London."

I hope he's going to tell me Danny's in some sort of trouble, or needs something, but I can feel a coldness creeping into my body.

He pauses again, seems to gather himself, and that's when I know.

"There's no easy way to say this. It's bad news I'm afraid. Danny's passed away."

The words go into a loop careering around my head, like a pop tune you can't get rid of. I realise that I've got an arm held out in denial. Mom gently pulls it down and hugs me.

"Do you know what happened officer?" She asks.

"The Metropolitan Police are dealing, they've just asked us to find if there are any relatives we should tell."

"But Alice isn't a relative, and they aren't together now."

There is a finality in the words, 'aren't together now'. My brain fills in the rest of the sentence, 'and never will be'.

As he replies he's talking to Mom, but looking at me.

"We know his parents are both deceased..."

"Wait a minute," I interject, "Only his Dad's dead. His Mom's in prison."

He shakes his head. "You wouldn't know if you haven't seen him. She committed suicide in prison the other day."

I can't believe it. Then I think of Danny on the doorstep on Sunday. His words fill my mind,

'Alice, a lot's happened to me that you don't know about. I'm in a mess. It's going to get harder too. I want to tell you all about it. I need you...'

They were almost the last words he ever spoke to me. He really needed me, and I sent him away. Back to London, on his own, and then he lost Bowie too, lost everybody. Guilt floods me, and finally, the tears come, and I can't stop them. Mom hugs me closer. The policeman just sits there. But what can he do? Even at that moment, the worst in my life, I wonder what it's like to be the bearer of such news, the person nobody wants to see, or see ever again, after the bad tidings have been delivered. An eternal reminder of the worst thing ever.

Eventually I compose myself enough to ask a question that I must ask, but dread the answer. "But I'm not a relative, how did you find me?" I watch his lips forming the words, can see that he is choosing them carefully. He must be a nice man; he knows what they will mean to me.

"He was found in his room. It seems that there was some sort of letter. It had your name and address on it, as if he was going to post it, but didn't......" His voice tails off. Mom knows what it means too.

"Can we see it?" She asks.

"Maybe at some point, but I don't have it. Don't know what's in it. There'll be an inquest - in London, and the note – letter will be presented as evidence to the Coroner."

"I want to know what's in it."

Mom stops me. "Maybe, maybe not. We'll see. They have to do things properly so you're going to have to wait, and we'll have plenty of time to discuss this."

I'm in a state of collapse. In no position to argue, so I just nod meekly. The officer becomes more official in tone.

"Now then, I'm sorry to have brought this news, can see how much it's upset you, but can you help me – do you know if there's any family?"

I tell him about Danny's Nan, but I don't know much and it isn't long before he is leaving, then it's just Mom and me.

She goes to make a cup of tea and I sit staring at the empty seat.

Chapter Eighteen

'Look Back In Anger'
2016

Alice:

The third day of the New Year. My customers are all off work for another week, and then there'll be the usual slow and reluctant emergence back into the world of commerce, so I doubt any paid employment will come my way for a while. Robert has been true to his word. I've heard nothing from him since New Year's Day.

I decide to go for a walk around, soak London up. When you live close to a 'sight', it somehow seems to lose its allure. I remember that first visit with Danny, when I dragged him around until he complained.

There he is in my mind again. I expel him, for a while, but he cannot be banished. He has always been there, at first a presence suffused with love, but since that terrible day in 1973, a source of guilt and torment.

It seems like yesterday. I still remember every detail of the policeman's visit. Mom tried her best to convince me that I wasn't to blame, tried to stop me going to the inquest, but I had to be there. In the end she came with me.

He'd been found in his room by some girl from another flat. I could see straight away what she was, and couldn't stop myself wondering if they'd screwed, even though it didn't matter anymore.

His flat door was unlocked. She said that was normal, that they were always in each other's rooms. She thought he was asleep, until she saw the vomit on the bed, the empty bottle, the pills strewn around. She shook him, but he was cold.

The Police said there were no suspicious circumstances. He died from an overdose. Pills, Cocaine, and Heroin. The syringe he'd used was on the floor by the bed, the spoon and lighter he'd used to cook it, on the bedside table. The detective who gave evidence looked bored to death, just another job, another kid gone off the tracks. A little tragedy, one of many.

What really swung it was the letter to me. It broke me when they read it out. It was Danny speaking, not the detective. It was what I should have let him say, that day on the doorstep. There was only one page. It wasn't finished. It ended abruptly, as if it all got too much for him and he stopped, stopped for good, lost hope.

'Alice. There is so much I want to tell you. So much has happened. I can't seem to see the old me anymore. I've become something else. Something I don't like. I'm so alone. Alone and adrift from everything and everyone I ever knew.. There's nothing left for me here. There was only Bowie, and he's gone now, somewhere I can't follow. I understand why you sent me away. I've been a total shit to you. I deserve everything that's coming. I just want you to know that, now at the end of it, I know for sure that I really love you….'

The officer stopped reading and held up the single sheet of paper. He turned to the Coroner. "It just stops there. We don't know if that was it, or whether he meant to say more. It was on the bed with him when he was found."

He then recounted the death of Danny's parents, and, as he termed it, (Mom looked at him bleakly as he said the words) 'the rejection by his girlfriend'. I can still feel the eyes in the room looking at me, pouring their accusations into me. He also mentioned the arrest and possible prison sentence – another thing I stopped Danny telling me about.

I left, crushed forever. The verdict was 'suicide', but I walked away with all the guilt. I was the only one alive to bear that load, and I've borne it ever since.

That's when cutting myself started, the suicide attempts that they called 'cries for help' the failed relationships, my whole sorry life ever since. I've been punishing myself for that moment when he was on the doorstep. I sent him away, when with a word, I could have saved him. But I sent him off to die, alone.

Nothing Mom or Dad said, nothing counsellors said, has ever touched that pain. The other relationships, the marriage - just attempts to bury the guilt, to prove to myself that there were others for me. But there aren't. Danny has haunted me for nearly forty-three years, and I know in my heart that he will still be there, watching, accusing, on the day I die.

*

Robert contacted me today. He's invited me to his home, his real home. I'm going to go, but I bet this will be just another relationship that will fail in the end. I mean, he's a nice bloke, but it's a bit weird. No attempt at sex, no physicality. It might be that he ends up as my only friend, other than Genie of course. That might be ok. That way, Robert wouldn't run up against the wall I've built within me, the one with me and Danny inside, and everybody else outside.

He wants me there on the seventh, says he has a party the next day. I'm surprised, he seems such a loner, admitted how alone he feels at New Year. But he says it's a tradition, and he invites the locals, likes to see them have a good time.

He picks me up at Axminster station. Immediately I can 'taste' childhood holidays. The station is tiny, like a house, and there are fresh flowers in the toilets. Robert is waiting in the car park. I've never seen him drive, but nobody needs to in London. I spot him straight away. It's the only Porsche in the car park. Bright red. Looks very expensive. He gets out and holds the door, a gentleman as usual. In the bright January sun, I notice his paleness, the thin angles of his face again. Once more, I wonder about his health.

He drives too fast, but it feels safe, and it's thrilling. I need thrills. The road is surrounded by rolling countryside and there are glimpses of a grey sea. Another world. Perhaps I should come somewhere like this to spend my final days. I could be the strange woman in the old cottage that the kids think is a witch. It appeals.

We turn away from the sea, following ever narrower lanes, through tiny hidden hamlets. Once farm labourer homes, now expensive 'little somethings in the country' for Londoners.

Eventually we turn off between stone pillars and make our way through dense trees on a well-maintained single track. After a few minutes we stop. There is a high wall, surmounted by spikes, and imposing gates. There is no name of the premises.

"My little hideaway. Nobody comes up here, the tourists don't even know it exists."

"How do you get post?"

"I have nobody to write to me, and I'm well connected, paid for my own fibre connection. Faster than in London. They keep any post for me at the local shop, but it's mainly junk."

"There's a local shop? Looks like there's nowhere for miles."

"That's because you're a city dweller. There's a village a couple of miles away. This was 'the big house' in the old days."

He presses a button on his phone and the gates swing open. There is a gatehouse, and as we pass I notice an old man stood, watching. He gives a wave of recognition.

"My faithful retainer. He's worked for me forever.. He lives in the gatehouse and looks after this place when I'm not here. There are some other staff, he manages them, keeps the place spick and span, and snoopers out. I like my privacy."

The driveway is wider here, and we suddenly emerge from the trees. "Wow," is all I can say.

Robert grins, "Bought it in the Eighties. One of my best decisions. I was looking for somewhere out of London, somewhere to retreat to when it all got too much, where I wouldn't be bothered. It was half derelict. The locals appreciated the work, renovating it, and a lot of them, and their families, still do stuff for me. Tradition is strong here; I've got tenant farmers who have worked this land for generations. I play the squire; they feel comfortable with that. They earn a living and we all get on famously. Over the years I've done some stuff for them, for the village, protected it, in return they respect my privacy. It works very well. I like to think that I've preserved a chunk of real 'Old England' here."

Gravel crunches as we pull up at a pillared portico. There are steps leading up to double doors. A woman is waiting at the top. She is very tall, with long legs, slim and pretty with a shock of white hair. I admire the fact that she hasn't dyed it, is content with it. She is right, it looks stunning She looks around sixty, but as I get closer I revise my opinion upwards. Once again I wonder if this is 'the one', but Robert puts my fears, (what fears?) at rest.

"Alice, meet Suzie. This is Alice, my guest for the next few days. Suzie has been my housekeeper here forever. She's not a local though, only been here about thirty years. You need at least three generations to qualify."

I clasp her hand and attempt to convey that I'm nothing special, want nothing to do with any servant and guest type malarkey, and she reacts with a friendly smile.

She looks inside the door and a burly man emerges. He looks tough. Robert hands him the car keys and he fetches my cases. Robert doesn't introduce him and he says nothing. 'Not the butler', I decide.

It's not what I expected. In London, Robert is so modern. The minimalist penthouse, the art. This is like stepping into an Agatha Christie novel, with Robert as the mystery. The house is a proper country house, neo-classical, I'm told, dating from the eighteenth century. It has high ceilings, abundant plaster mouldings, huge rooms and perfect period furniture. No modern art here, mainly portraits of, I assume, the previous inhabitants.

I get a grand tour once I've been settled into my room. There are two floors and two wings. Robert has one to himself. It has closed doors and I'm not shown in there. I'm in the other wing. I'd wondered if we would be close, if there might be connecting doors, but it's miles away, and those shut doors seem to indicate that there will be no nocturnal wanderings, no taps upon my door.

Downstairs, there are so many rooms I get disorientated. The tour culminates in a large ballroom. "Where the entertaining used to be done in the old days, and where I have my little parties."

"You never stop surprising me. You just don't seem the party type, especially now I've seen where you live, in the middle of nowhere, behind such high walls."

He laughs, then coughs. That cough that has been with him all the time I've known him. I had put it down to age and winter colds, maybe the aftermath of flu, but I begin to wonder. Is he frailer than he was?

"Yes, it must seem odd. It's one of my traditions, since I got this place up and running. They used to be really wild affairs, but it's calmer these days, my crowd are older, and a few have gone for good. It was originally a useful way of thanking my business associates, maintaining friendships, a contribution to a social circle I moved in. We used to take turns to host get-togethers. It fits nicely with the country house, a good party."

*

The evening is quiet, just the two of us for dinner, served by Suzie, who joins us along with the old man who lives in the gatehouse.

The man introduces himself as Mark. He is painfully thin, bald, with a bushy beard. He is engaging, with an open face and genuine smile. Both Suzie and he have London accents, and Mark keeps the conversation flowing, regaling us with tales of wild doings in his younger days in the capital. He never mentions Robert though, so curiosity compels me to ask.

" You've worked for Robert for a long time then, Mark, and you Sue?"

I catch a slight pause, and a little glance between them, but that great smile returns, lighting up his face. "Yeah, both of have actually. Since the Seventies. We used to live together – but we're just good friends now." There seems to be some sort of private joke going on, as she permits a small smile. I think there is fondness between them, maybe more. I wonder what they get up to when the 'master' is away?

"What did you do before you looked after this place for Robert?" I ask both.

Another slight pause, and this time she answers, filling the vacuum.

'I was in sales, Mark was more logistics, purchasing and moving stuff around. But we both jumped at the chance to come here. We've never regretted it have we Mark?"

"No. Don't miss London one iota. Happy to just fade away here. Mr. Harper has been good to us and we look after him."

Robert finally speaks, "They are both precious to me. I trust them with my life." I think it a strange thing to say, but the conversation returns to small talk.

After dinner we sit chatting for a while, then Robert declares he is tired, he does look exhausted.

"Early night for me. It will be a late one tomorrow and I'll be in full 'mine host' mode, so you might not see me until mid-morning. Alice, feel free to explore,. If you need anything just ask Suzie or Mark. Special day tomorrow, you'll see. Bit of a theme to it."

The three of us watch him leave. I bet we are all thinking the same thing, but I'm an interloper, an unknown, so nothing is said. Robert doesn't look right. Not ill, more stretched thin.

I insist on helping Suzie with the clearing up. Mark remains seated in front of the fire, cuddling a malt whisky. She makes no comment. I try to make conversation when we are alone in the kitchen, but she is reticent, although not unfriendly. In the end I decide to abandon subtlety.

"Can I ask you a question please?"

She stops stacking the dishwasher. "Depends what it is."

"Fair enough. You've been with Robert a long time, clearly care about him. I just wanted you to know that I realise I'm a stranger, an unknown quantity, in the middle of what looks like a very settled arrangement."

She smiles. "You don't need to worry about that. He told us you were coming and how you met."

I stumble over the words. "I mean, I'm not....oh sod it – what I'm trying to say is, I don't know what he wants with me, how he feels about me, and to be honest, the feeling's mutual. We just get on and are taking it a step at a time. We aren't, you know, an 'item'."

She laughs. "I'd be surprised if you were, bit of a loner is the boss. Listen, if it helps, me and Mark, we know that you're friends, and that you're not after his money. Granted, it's unusual for him to strike up a friendship with a random woman, but I've never known him make a mistake about money or people. He says you're ok, and that's good enough for us. He's the boss, always has been. So just enjoy yourself. It might not last long, but if it ends suddenly, don't worry about that either, he doesn't do long relationships." She seems to be speaking from experience.

*

I wake and lie quietly, soaking the room in. If it all ends today it's been worth it, but I would be sad if it did. I realise I'm fond of Robert, and my concerns over his health stem from that. Rich or poor, I think we will be friends at least. I mull over Suzie's words – cryptic or genuine, they imply more than was said. Once again I wonder if he is gay, or so wounded by love that he is a kindred spirit, has decided to renounce it for good. Either might explain the sexual vacuum.

I take a shower and flick on the TV whilst drying my hair. I can barely hear it above the noise, but I switch the dryer off when I see Bowie on the screen. I turn the sound up. Of course, it's the eighth of January, his birthday, but that's not usually cause for a TV slot. Every time Bowie has a birthday it's a little knife to the heart, so I have blocked them out. He lives on, but Danny died.

As I watch, I realise that Bowie has stunned the world yet again. A new album, on his sixty-ninth birthday. A secret that's been perfectly kept from the public and the media. Danny, are you watching? He didn't retire, he's still here, and you could have been too. Would it have made a difference to you, to know that? Could he have given you the support I didn't? You missed so much. Now we know that 'Ziggy' was just the beginning, just another character.

The new album is called 'Blackstar'. I'll download it. I've downloaded them all, play them all. They are all I have left of

Danny. He would find it funny that I'm one of Bowie's oldest fans, but it's not really the music anymore. Bowie is the only person I know is still alive who actually knew him, even if Danny was just another fan. I'd like to meet someone who knew Danny in London. I've tried, but Danny has been wiped from the earth, all trails went cold long ago.

*

Robert isn't up and about. I follow sounds and cooking scents to the kitchen, where Suzie is bustling around. While I'm eating, caterers arrive and she is totally preoccupied with them. I'm in the way so I decide to explore, as Robert suggested.

I spend time in each room, trying to find something of the real Robert. But it is like a museum, like being the other side of the rope in a National Trust house. Everything is perfectly matched. The furniture, the leather-bound books, a piano, the old oil paintings, the wallpaper and curtains. Perfect, and perfectly anonymous. Just like the penthouse in London. Just like he's erased his past and emerged, fully-formed, as the rich man he is.

Eventually, I reach the ballroom. The doors are shut but inside is activity. A stage being erected at one end, people up ladders. I beat another retreat to my room and grab my laptop. I settle down in one of the leather armchairs in a sunny sitting room and download 'Blackstar'.

Social media is full of it, trying to decipher the meaning, amazed at the dramatic surprise Bowie has pulled off. I'm not amazed. He's a showman, a veteran of drama and stage, and he did it before, in 2013 with 'The Next Day' and that haunting, 'Where Are We Now' It still gives me chills when I hear it. A lament for things long past. It resonates, and hurts.

This new album feels very different. There are songs I instantly dislike, there usually are. The faster and more jazz – orientated ones leave me cold. But there are two tracks that immediately clutch at me. They seem to speak of death, of the passing of things, of religious ritual. Not happy songs, but impactive. 'Blackstar' and 'Lazarus'.

I go for a walk around the grounds, with the first line of 'Lazarus' in my head. It could be Danny speaking to me, Bowie his medium. It is one of those beautiful January days, cold and still, with a sky of flawless china blue that promises frost tonight.

When I return, Robert is stood outside, surveying his estate. He is well wrapped up, the dog lying at his feet gratefully soaking up the sun's faint warmth.

"Looks worthy of a walk today. I'm taking the time to take in the view. When I'm away I forget why I bought this place, but on a day like this it seems like the best investment I ever made. I haven't been here nearly often enough. Lunch is ready, then I'll tell you about tonight. I've got a little present for you – although it doesn't matter if you don't like it. I just thought of you when I saw it come up for sale."

We eat with Suzie and Mark again, but they rush off, busy with preparations. Through the window I see a large van pull up, and instruments being unloaded.

"You were going to tell me about tonight."

"Yes. Let's take these coffees over by the fire."

He settles himself. I'm watching for it, and I hear a slight groan as he drops into the chair. 'Has he always done that and I haven't noticed?' I don't think so. I consider him as he sits, bathed in a shaft of sunlight that picks him out in sharp relief. He is thinner, is paler, looks more fragile.

"Robert. Are you ok? You seem really tired and look a bit pale."

"I'm fine, just getting older, that's all. It'll come to you too, the tiredness, the aches and pains, sleepless nights that need catching up on the next morning."

"I've already got most of those, don't worry."

"Right, tonight. I told you I've regularly hosted parties here, for many, many years." He pauses and his gaze becomes faraway, memories filling his head. He brings himself back to the present with an effort. "Anyway, I've decided to retire, so tonight is my last one, my 'retirement do', so to speak. I've had enough."

"That must have been a difficult decision. You've always worked, been driven, been successful, a self-made man."

"I should have done it years ago. Should have stopped and enjoyed this place. I don't need any more money, but it's like an addiction. I always avoided drugs, but got caught by power and greed. Something always gets you. Because I'd always strived, fought for survival, won, won, won, but, as I've told you, at a cost, I've carried on, and on. Knew no other way. But now is the right time to stop. In a way, you helped me decide."

"Me, how, you hardly know me?"

"You befriended me for no other reason than you thought I needed someone. You didn't know I was rich. I was dressed like a tramp when we met. You've shown me something I had lost sight of. That there's good in people too. I had become blind to it. You've got your issues, but you instinctively try to be good. You had time for me. You showed me what I was missing."

"Well, I'm no saint, I can tell you. Be careful before you base any life decisions on me. I've not made any good ones myself."

"It doesn't matter. You are who you are, and I see in you what I've lost, perhaps never had," he laughs, "even though you're a bit battered and scarred by life."

I'm embarrassed, and fall silent. He sees, and changes the subject.

"By coincidence a birthday falls today that means something to me, so it seemed right to make it the theme of my party."

I know the answer to this one. "Bowie?"

"Spot on. In the Seventies I did some work for him and others in the music scene. I've always admired him. Not really for the music, although that's good, but for his sheer survival, his determination, his willingness to change and adapt. A role model in his way."

"That's a bit spooky. He features in my life too, but for a different reason. But I'm not ready to go into that."

"We won't then. Let's just say that, on a whim, I've themed my big party on Bowie and the Seventies. There will be a lot here in fancy dress, but it's not compulsory."

"That's good – although some of my wardrobe is old enough to do it justice."

"Well, I've got you something, had it altered a bit so I think it will fit. I confess I sneaked a look at your clothes size."

He picks up a large box and hands it to me.

"You'll probably hate it, and you don't have to wear it if you don't want to."

I lift the lid, carefully remove tissue paper, and reveal shiny silver fabric. I hold it up. It's an evening dress with a sleeveless jacket.

I stand up and hold it against me.

"It looks like it might fit. It's lovely."

"It's an original, so take care of it. It's yours to keep if you want it. It belonged to Angie Bowie. I bought it at an auction. Don't know why really, I've never worn it. Seriously though, I intended to get it mounted in a case, but never got around to it. I'd like you to have it, and wear it tonight, but no obligation."

*

I do wear it - for Danny. Maybe, just maybe, sometime in the past, he was in the same place as this dress, perhaps even brushed it in passing. I will treasure it. I doubt it looks anything like when Angie Bowie flaunted it, but it makes me feel like a million dollars.

I sit at the window in my room, all made-up, taking in the moment. Expensive cars arrive, disgorging expensive guests. There are villagers too, they've hired a coach. They disembark, a chattering mass, intent on having a good time. It's a nice touch, and it makes me like Robert even more.

The ballroom has been transformed into what looks and feels like a nightclub. Pictures of Bowie adorn the walls, picked out by flashing lights bouncing off glitter balls. I'm surrounded by him, but it is Danny's eyes that look out on me.

A small dancefloor, complete with underfloor lights, has been laid in front of the stage. Instruments await a band, but at the moment a DJ is setting the tone. 'Roxy Music' and 'Virginia Plain'. People are already dancing. It's a real mix, men and women in black tie and cocktail dresses rubbing shoulders with cheaper outfits. There is a lot of fancy dress, Seventies flares and platforms, and plenty of early Bowie style proudly displayed. It's the first time I've seen people with the lightning flash and golden orb face paint for a very long time. None of them look like Bowie though, they are parodies, and none of them come close to Danny in his full 'Ziggy' glory days. The thought of him awakens the usual emotions, the mixture of joy, melancholy and guilt. I wonder what he would look like now? Would he have run to fat, his beauty lost? Instead, he is preserved, frozen in time, forever sixteen. Perhaps that is better.

The double doors to the dining room are wide open, revealing tables overflowing with food and drink, dispensed by uniformed caterers. As I enter, Robert appears, takes my arm, guides me through the rapidly building crowd, to the bar area.

"You look stunning. I'm so pleased you wore it. What do you think of all this?" He indicates with a sweep of his arm.

"Fantastic. You're certainly going out with a bang. So many people. You've got lots of friends."

He gives me a look filled with meaning.

"Not friends Alice. People I know. People I needed to know. People I've done favours for. Some that work or worked for me. The locals, here for a free night out on 'the squire'. Business contacts, people from my London club. Not friends, a lifetime of contacts and acquaintances. Apart from you, I like the locals most. You are the closest to a real friend I've got." He pauses. "That sounds pathetic, and I'm not. I've gone through life with my eyes open. Didn't need friends, didn't want them. I could buy anything and anyone I wanted. It's only the last year or so that I've changed."

"Why suddenly this year?"

He shrugs his shoulders. "Just got older, the days beginning to run out. It makes you think differently. Now, no more misery, this is supposed to be fun, let's go and enjoy ourselves."

For an hour I escort Robert as he works the room. I admire his style; he is good at this. But I'm reminded more of 'The Godfather' than a businessman as we progress. People are actually deferential, a few even bow slightly. I see him in a new light. Behind the smooth businessman, a glimpse of his origins?

He claims fatigue, and we head for a table placed on its own, away from the dancefloor and stage. Mark is there, wearing huge flares, a cheesecloth shirt, ridiculous platforms and some make-up, expertly applied. Suzie, also, her slim figure encased in a silver jumpsuit with knee-high red boots, 'ABBA' style. They both smile greetings. They seem genuinely to like me and we make small-talk. Robert slumps in his seat and shuts his eyes.

"Are you ok boss?" Asks Mark.

"He opens his eyes. His face, etched sharply in the flashing lights, looks weary, the lines brought into sharp relief.

"Yes, thanks, just a bit worn out by all this socialising."

There is a break for hot food, then the DJ calls for Robert, who makes his way to the stage, smatterings of applause and handshakes marking his progress across the room, a royal procession.

It's not a long speech. It's has no depth; I think his heart is not really in it. It's a formality, punctuated with cheers and applause at the appropriate moments. He finishes with a farewell and returns to the table. The lights are on full, everyone claps. I scan their faces. What do they really think of him? From what he has said, some at least are false, maybe glad to see the back of him at last. Perhaps there are scores to be settled, now he has retired, now his hold on power has been relinquished.

The lights dim and there are bands to come, tribute bands. 'T.Rex', 'Roxy Music', and of course, Bowie. People drink, maybe there are other intoxicants. They lose their inhibitions, relax, dance. I drink too much. Can feel myself losing my grip, senses dimming. I dance, with Mark and Suzie, with strangers, as Robert remains seated, the 'Lord of The Manor', surveying his domain. It is a good night. I wonder what my future holds – with Robert, now he has renounced his former life.

I return to the table to take on much needed liquid, in the form of champagne. Robert stands and takes hold of my arm. He bends close so I can hear him above the band.

" It's late. I'm tired. I'm going to excuse myself. You stay and have a good time. But first we dance."

He guides me through the room, to the stage. The Bowie tribute band finish playing 'Heroes' and Robert gets on the stage once more, taking the microphone.

"Thank you all once again for coming. Please carry on enjoying yourselves until dawn. I'm old and tired, and," he looks at his watch, "two am is way past my bedtime these days, so I am leaving you to it. This will be my last farewell. But before I go, a final dance with my lovely friend Alice, who has taught me so much about what really matters, in just a few months."

He steps down and signals the band. It's 'Wild Is The Wind', one of my favourite songs, and perfect for a slow dance. I'm not the smoothest dancer and I'm conscious that nobody else has joined us. They ring the dancefloor. Watching me with curiosity, an exotic specimen they never thought to see. A girlfriend with Robert? The first dance at a wedding. I've done that. A fairy tale that doesn't last. I doubt this dance means anything either.

The music ends. We stop. We kiss. Another chaste kiss, but it draws applause and some laughs, comments I can't catch. Are they laughing at me? Am I deluding myself with this, whatever it is?

"Goodnight Alice. Enjoy yourself. You deserve it."

Then he's gone.

I return to the table. Suzie has gone too. What is she doing here? She is no housekeeper. Mark keeps me company and we both get totally sloshed. I collapse into bed several hours later. There is still music playing, people having fun.

*

I claw my way back to consciousness. I can hear rain beating upon the windows, a discouraging pit-pat. I feel terrible. 'Can't take the pace anymore'. I resolve to never drink so much, or stay up that late again. I need coffee and tablets.

I throw on a gown that is hanging on the door. Another thoughtful touch – no doubt Suzie. I catch sight of the dress draped across a chair. It is inanimate now, sad and dead. More memories impregnated into the fabric.

The house is quiet. The guests are all gone. None stayed, Robert told me that they weren't asked. I pass the ballroom and take a peek inside. The workmen are back. Last night is nearly deconstructed. It will soon be a moment in time, preserved in minds only.

I make strong coffee and throw down tablets. The kitchen clock tells me that it's afternoon already. Suzie appears, fully dressed, made-up, hair perfect, fully functioning.

"You made the right decision, leaving when you did. I stayed too late, drank too much. Can't do it these days without paying for it the next day."

"But did you have a good time?"

"Yes, wonderful. Haven't let my hair down like that since forever."

"Good. Why not. You deserve it."

That's what Robert said to me. Has he been telling her about me? I'm not sure how I feel about that, or what it means.

" No sign of anyone else up yet? Robert?"

"Mark went back to his cottage and I doubt he'll be up until this evening, that's his usual form after a night out. Robert asked me to leave him until about now. I'll go up in a while."

"Suzie, is Robert ill?"

She takes a moment. "Yes, he is."

A chill hand closes on my heart.

"Is it serious?"

"Yes. He has cancer. That's why he's packed it all in. I never thought he would stop, but he's changed."

"How bad is it?"

"Bad. That's all I know. He told me and Mark we would be looked after, afterwards. He takes loads of pills. He refused chemo. I'm watching him fade away day by day. Last night was a huge effort for him, but he has such willpower and determination."

I ponder this news. "How long has he got?"

"He won't say. He's been to the best doctors money can buy. He says we all die sometime, it's how and when that we don't know, and now he does. I'll take him a coffee, he'll have pills to take."

I'm ashamed that my first thoughts are of myself. The usual, self-pitying ones. Poor Alice, poor loveless Alice. Always the loser. I mentally give myself a slap across the face. A man is dying. A kind and generous man that I like. I'm thinking about what to say to him, when I realise that Suzie hasn't returned. What am I doing, sat here, daydreaming, she might need a hand, Robert might. Who knows the toll last night will have taken?

The double doors are shut. I call out her name. No reply. I call again, then press my ear to the door. I'm still unsure of the intimacy of their relationship, after all she knows about the cancer, he's kept it from me, so I'm reluctant to walk in on them.

I hear nothing, so I tentatively open a door, and peer through. She must hear me because she says, "Here, in here." Her voice sounds strange.

I walk along a corridor lined with photographs in frames. Here is the missing personal history. A younger Robert, hair getting longer as the photographs get older. I stop briefly at one of Bowie, in 'Ziggy' get-up, his arm round a denim-clad man I just about recognise.

He is in the end room. Suzie is stood at the foot of the bed, still holding the cup of coffee. I stand beside her and together we contemplate Robert. He is dead. The bottles of pills tell the story. He looks peaceful.

The next day, Bowie joins Robert, cancer as well. He kept it secret too. The whole world is shocked. I take the photograph of them together from the wall when I leave the house. I'm sure Robert won't mind.

They are all gone, and I'm alone with my guilt.

Chapter Nineteen

'Lazarus'
2016

Alice:

My life is back in its old rut, Robert just another tragic memory. I'm still in London, still doing my pathetic little job. Still got Genie, and occasionally I go to the park where I first met him, to contemplate what might have been.

In June I get a letter from a firm of London solicitors. They want to see me, something about Robert. I phone them but they won't give me any details, just that they need an hour of my time.

A week later, I'm ushered into a plush office. A grey–haired man full of false solicitude introduces himself. He is the senior partner, and explains that he is dealing with Robert's estate. He sits me down, and his secretary leaves us alone.

"My apologies for the delay in contacting you. As you may appreciate, Mr. Harper's affairs were very complicated. But, to his credit, he did leave everything in order, with precise instructions. Which is why I've asked you here today."

I murmur surprise, that I hadn't known him long, that I'm unimportant, but he waves my protestations away.

"Clearly not unimportant to my client. Your name features at the very top of the list of his wishes. I'm about to fulfil his last request in respect of yourself."

He opens a file box, and withdraws an iPhone.

"Before I give you this, he requested that you undertake to return it to me immediately after you have used it. Please sign here to that effect." I do so. This is an unexpected development. Who could Robert want me to phone, and why?

"Thank you. There is a sound file on the phone. I have set it to play." He attaches the phone to a speaker. "I am to leave you in here alone for precisely thirty minutes. At the conclusion, you return

the phone to me. And before I leave you in here, you are to temporarily entrust me with your bag, coat and any recording media you have, including paper."

"This is all very cloak and dagger, are you serious?"

"I'm afraid so. It's unusual, but I've done stranger things as last requests, I assure you."

So it is, that, stripped of everything but the clothes I am wearing, I am left alone with Robert's phone. I press the button.

"Alice. If you are listening to this, then I am dead, and probably by my own hand. I've never been one to wait on events.

I'm going to tell you something, something very bad, very evil. There are only four people who know of this, including the victim, and I'm the last one left, so it dies with me. But, to prevent any complications, for other, innocent parties, this phone, and the voice recording, will be destroyed when you have heard it, in order that nobody can use it. This is only for you.

I've known that my time was up for about a year. The pain has been getting worse, so don't feel sorry that I chose to end it. You won't anyway, once you hear what I have to say. I've spent the year sorting things out. I've done a lot of bad things in my life, used and abused a lot of people. I'm not going into detail, you don't need to know, suffice it to say that you wouldn't want to see me ever again, and you won't, so that's ok.

Lately, I've been trying to put things right, using my money to do some good. It will never be enough, I can't undo what's done, but at least I'll have tried. This isn't some big Christian conversion; I don't believe there's anything after we die. I felt the need to right some wrongs, and once I began, I enjoyed it, so I carried on.

And then I met you. A chance meeting. You were sad, hiding something in your past. You gave me a false name to begin with, do you remember? Perhaps you sensed something dark within me, that first day. It intrigued me, you intrigued me. You seemed...so good, despite the melancholy, the broken marriage, and whatever shadowed you, from long ago.

Like most rich men, I'm suspicious first, trusting second. I did 'due diligence' on you. I know people who can find out everything about a person.

I opened the file on you that they provided. I ploughed through the pages, back through time, far, far back, Firstly checking you were genuine, then intrigued. Could I find where it started, your sadness, could it be put right?

I was astonished. I don't believe in fate or destiny, you make your own, but coincidence exists, the chance in a million does happen. I found that our paths had crossed once before. We were different people then, in my case, literally.

I was called Richard; everyone knew me as Rick. I left him behind thirty years ago, when I became, as they say, 'legitimate'.

Rick was a very bad person. A criminal who made it big. I'll make no excuses. I knew exactly what I was doing.

A long time ago, a lad that worked for me got arrested. He was very young. I've never stopped liking teenage boys. I'll leave it at that, other than to say, I never misled you with promises. I told you I was looking for friendship, never led you to expect anything more, so on that subject I've been honest.

He dealt drugs for me. I was running security and logistics for Bowie in those days. It was fantastic. An endless supply of boys, thinking they were in love with Bowie, and some of them were. I controlled access to him, had the lid of the honeypot in my hands. In addition, the crowd around Bowie wanted drugs, girls, boys - you name it, they were into it. It was, as they say, 'Rock 'n' Roll'. They had money to burn. I was happy to take it. I made a lot. That wasn't my only business. I ran doors, prostitutes, protection rackets, and had the foresight to use my dirty money to invest in genuine businesses, property, property development, restaurants, clubs."

I stop the recording. I'm shaking. The past yawns. I compose myself and, with a shaking finger, press the button again.

"The boy that got arrested was called Danny. You were recorded as a witness at the inquest. The note he left was to you.

The sadness in you, thinking it was your fault. It all fitted. This 'confession' is all I can do now to try to put things right. It might help a little. At least you can hate me instead of yourself.

Danny was young, never been in trouble before. To the Police he was a weak link, a chink in my armour. They were ruthless too Alice, in their own way as bad as me. They tried to force him to work for them, to grass me up, put me away for life – that's how bad I was.

But they made a mistake. It was the Metropolitan Police after me. But they came from my home turf. I had lots of police contacts, some very high-up. I'd got stuff on them; they did what I asked. Others just took the money I offered. The Met set up a squeaky – clean team to get me, and it was them who got their claws into Danny.

Their problem was that he wasn't arrested in London. They got a CID man from Birmingham, a man they knew and trusted, to make the first contact, frighten him with prison, soften him up, offer the deal. They picked the wrong man. He was bent. He made contact with me, offering his 'services' for money. I was suspicious at first, checked him out, but soon realised he was a like mind, dressed in blue.

They had to give Danny time to think, and they took him over from the Birmingham cop, but my man kept contact with them. I was desperate to know if Danny was going to grass on me, and he wanted my money. I had all the angles covered. Danny was talking to me, and if he lied, my man on the inside would know, and so would I.

Danny was a huge risk. He knew a lot, and he was clever. He could have put me away right then and there, but neither he, nor the cops realised it.

Danny told me that he'd turned them down, was loyal to me, would do his time. But, I didn't get rich and stay free by trusting without collaboration, so I called my contact. He spoke to the Met cops, and they boasted that they had 'turned' Danny, he was going to work for them. I found out later that Danny was genuine, that it

*was all bullshit between cops, but I didn't know that then. A little lie,
with a big consequence.*

*I honestly didn't know what to do. It's one thing dealing with
London hard men and gangsters, they know the score, another a
lovely young lad, an innocent.*

*But, that very night, Bowie announced his 'retirement' on
stage at Hammersmith. I was effectively sacked, it cost me big. I was
hoping to go to the States with him for the autumn tour, could have
been a big launching pad for me, but it was all over. I was beside
myself with anger. I wanted to kill someone, but I was powerless.
Then Danny turned up on the doorstep, babbling about getting into
the after-show party.*

*I threw him out. I was raging, and afraid. Not only was my
business base fractured, I could go to prison and lose it all. At that
moment I was the most vulnerable I had been since I was a kid in the
East End. So, I sent some people, two men, very nasty, both long
dead. They found Danny drunk out of his head and high on 'Coke'.
It wasn't hard to inject him with enough Heroin to finish him off and
leave the makings lying around. The note was a bonus, It was a love
letter to you, There were several pages. They took all but the first,
because that looked like a suicide note. I read the rest, then burned
them. It was obvious from them that Danny hadn't turned. It was too
late, I'd killed an innocent kid*

*I had someone at the inquest. It was all put to bed. I was free.
They told me that his girl got the blame for rejecting him in his hour
of need, on top of what happened to his parents – and Bowie
retiring. You lived with that for the rest of your life. Now I'm freeing
you from that burden*

*When I found out who you were I tried to make it right, but I
was running out of time.*

I'm sorry, Alice. That's all I can say."

*There is silence. The voice has gone. Forever. Gone to where
I cannot follow.*

*

It is several weeks before my mind settles down enough to process the information, untangle the emotions. Anger, relief, guilt, pity, love, hate. Then, one day it is as if a shadow has been lifted. I have clarity. The burden of guilt that I have borne all these years evaporates. It wasn't my fault after all. Yes, I sent him away, but I was sixteen and rejected, hurt and devastated by my first love. Any girl would have done the same. But I didn't cause him to die. He was writing to me, trying to explain, hoping that I would understand - and I would have. We could have been together after all, could still be. Such a waste.

In September I get another letter from Robert's – Rick's solicitors. I can't imagine what else can be said, but I am drawn back. Ushered into the same room, greet the same man.

"No strange requests this time, you'll be pleased to know. This is standard stuff. We've finally sorted out probate. You have a small bequest from my late client."

"I don't want anything of his."

"Well, you have something, it is yours to keep or dispose of. My advice would be to take the bequest, and do what you will with it. At least learn what it is before you do anything hasty."

I nod. Despite my hatred, I am intrigued. He opens an envelope and flicks through some pages of a document, puts a finger on a page, and begins to read.

'To Alice, who I wronged so much, I leave the paintings she admired, to do with as she wishes.' He continues.

"There are four in all. We have them in storage, for safekeeping. They are very valuable. I have an associate at Sothebys that I can recommend, if you wish to sell them, I can put you in touch with him. There is no rush. The storage fees are paid for twelve months. Take some time and let me know."

For the second time I walk away in a daze.

I never go to see the paintings. I think about destroying them, but that would be a crime in itself. Someone will treasure them, even if I cannot. I hear Danny's voice in my head, and I know he approves.

*

It is almost a year to the day when I return to the house in Dorset. It is the first anniversary of Bowie's death and the day after his.

It is a much shorter journey this time. Along the coast road from Devon. That's where I live now. I've decided to leave London behind, for good. The money from the paintings has made me rich. It is blood money, but I've learnt to live with that. It's payment for a life wasted, freedom for the years I have left.

I have one last thing to do before I can close the door on the past forever, before I can lay Danny to rest.

The driveway is as I recall it. My Range Rover barely registers the rougher surface of the lane.

They must hear the crunch of the gravel, because almost immediately, the double doors open, and Mark and Suzie emerge. They greet me at the top of the steps like a lost relative. Once again I sit in the kitchen whilst Suzie makes the coffee. I sat here a year ago as a different woman, with different hopes and fears.

I observe the easy familiarity between them. They are like a long-married couple and I suspect that they are properly together, that Mark no longer resides in the cottage by the gate. They seem well, and happy, and I hope I'm going to be glad for them in a few minutes, once I know.

Suzie begins. She seems the stronger of the pair.

"You wanted to speak to us?" There is no hostility there.

"Yes. I've got a story to tell you. Rick told it to me. Only to me. From the grave." I see the surprise on their faces when I use that name. "I don't think you've heard it, at least I hope so. And I'm hoping you'll tell me the truth in return, because I need to know a couple of things, or I'll spend the rest of my life wishing I'd asked."

I tell them the whole tale. They sit silently, hanging on every word. I know that they are hearing it for the first time. I finish. "And now the questions." I say.

Suzie answers first. "Ask away. This one time, we'll tell you everything we know, but we won't tell it to anybody else, and you must promise that you'll leave us alone. It's not that we don't like you, but you're a risk to us. If you stir up Rick's past, our past, we *might lose this house," she casts a fond glance at Mark, and he pats her hand, "lose each other. And I won't let that happen. We are owed too, for what he did to us. You lost Danny, but we lost more. Even our real names."*

"I promise. First question. I thought I was the only one left who knew Danny, but the more I thought about you two, the more I wondered. Did you know him?"

Mark answers first, surprising me.

"We both did. In different ways. You might not like what we did for Rick, but we tried to help Danny as much as we could, which wasn't much. He got into such a mess, not really his fault either. He was just a kid, and out of his depth. I thought it from the start."

"The start?"

"I was there, the night Danny first appeared. Can't remember where it was, so many parties, so much booze and drugs. It was Rick's usual game. Spot some pretty boys, get them into the party, or concert, or whatever they were after, then see if he could befriend them. Sometimes it worked, sometimes it didn't. There are always kids who rebel, kids who are confused, kids who are angry, kids without families, kids alone. They think they know it all, and to someone like Rick, they were easy meat. I was one of the first. He corrupted me utterly. I had nowhere else to go, the drugs and booze numbed the pain, so I stuck it out.

Rick couldn't believe his luck. He controlled access to Bowie, who drew in all the boys who were unsure, all the young dudes." He laughs. He still has the nice smile, it dispatches the care lines, although his eyes are filled with dark memories.

"And that's what happened to Danny? I remember him telling me about seeing Bowie, going to the party, I thought he was having me on."

"He was there alright, but he ran away when Rick tried it on. I was sat at the same table, out of my head, but it made me smile. I thought, 'good on you kid', thought he'd got away, but then he turned up in London, that Christmas. I tried my best to persuade him

not to come back, honest I did, but he came all the same. Running away from something, like we all were."

Mark, or whoever he really is, tells me about how he taught Danny to sell drugs, tried to help him look after himself. I guess he is gilding the lily a bit, making himself look better than he was, but it has the feel of truth. After all, he could say nothing if he wanted to.

"And you Suzie, where do you fit in?"

" Mark and I lived with Danny in flats owned by Rick, along with another girl, and a nasty piece of work who was in charge of us. Rick had a lot of business interests. One of them was hookers; boys and girls, young and older. I was a runaway too, ended up as a working girl. We used the flats, sold ourselves for him. In exchange we got money and drugs. I had nowhere else to go, so I stayed too. In the end it becomes your life."

My face asks an obvious question. She picks up on it, a female thing.

"I often stayed with Danny. You won't believe it, but mostly we just shared a bed to comfort each other. He was so young, so alone, that my heart went out to him, and I was pretty unhappy too. We needed each other. But it was never love, for either of us. He used to talk about you all the time. How he was going to make enough money for you to get back together."

Uncomfortable territory, but I asked for it. I feel no jealousy.

"It's ok, it was a long time ago, and it sounds as if you helped him, and liked him. So, it was you he was seeing in his room that night in Birmingham?"

She looks puzzled. "I've never been to Birmingham in my life."

Mark jumps in. "Rick again. He wanted to move Danny away from the drugs because of the arrest, saw an opportunity to use him in another way. Danny had a punter waiting, I remember him telling me that it was a big test from Rick, of his loyalty. Some bloke Rick wanted to buy, or get the black on, that's how he worked."

It all makes sense. I should be feeling guilty again, but my older head knows that the sixteen-year-old me could not have been expected to deal with this. It is comfort of sorts.

They talk some more about Danny. Small memories, he comes back to life in their words. Then it is time to deal with the end.

"You were there, when he died?"

Mark shakes his head. "I was at Rick's house, saw the argument after the concert. I did my best to send Danny away before Rick saw him, but Danny wouldn't hear of it. He was in a strange mood, really angry and upset, didn't seem to care what happened. That's why I wasn't sure later, until today, whether he had done it to himself or not.

I stayed at Rick's that night. I wondered at the time why he asked me to, because he just went straight to his room, didn't want me for anything., But I'm thinking now that I was an alibi, if needed."

Suzie interjects. 'I found him, called the police. I'll never forget it. He looked asleep. He was pale, and beautiful, and so peaceful. First time I'd really seen him look like that, without any cares. I thought he'd topped himself. I knew what had happened with his mom and dad.

I was out working that night, with the other girl who lived there. We had some rich bloke in a hotel up the West End, all night. I often used to knock his door when I came in, look in and check he was ok. Sometimes I'd just get into bed with him. He never locked his door, in case I came by. I was at the inquest. I remember you. I was so sorry for you."

I look at her anew. I had been so upset, but I can just about see a faint image of the blonde girl she once was.

"You both thought he'd killed himself?"

They look at each other. Mark answers.

"We genuinely didn't know. But it seemed the most likely explanation. There was the note, and I knew that Danny had decided to be loyal to Rick and go down for the drugs, so there was no